Up In Flames

Hailey Alcaraz

VIKING

VIKING
An imprint of Penguin Random House LLC, New York

First published in the United States of America by Viking,
an imprint of Penguin Random House LLC, 2023

Copyright © 2023 by Hailey Alcaraz

Visit us online at PenguinRandomHouse.com.

Library of Congress Cataloging-in-Publication Data is available.

ISBN 9780593525548

1st Printing

Printed in the United States of America

LSCH

Design by Kate Renner
Text set in Cotford Text

To my mom,
who believed in my stories
before I even had the words to tell them

Part One

*"In the eyes of love,
we are all sparks
waiting for the flame."*

—Giovannie de Sadeleer

1

Ruby Ortega always got what she wanted.

However, Ruby Ortega also frequently wanted what she couldn't have—which was precisely how she found herself in her current predicament: engulfed by a flock of rowdy boys lavishing her with the attention and adoration she craved on this tedious evening but still feeling just a little bit bored.

Among this crowd were, of course, the Trujillo brothers; they never passed up a chance to brag and boast in front of an audience. Ruby had once found the name of Alex Trujillo, the youngest of that tall brood, doodled in her sister's notebook with hearts and swirls, and suspected an unreciprocated crush. Then there were a handful of other boys she'd grown up with—Mike Thomas, Ian Percy, and Daniel de la Cruz—whose parents either worked with her father, attended spin class with her mother, or operated in some capacity in the high-society circle to which the Ortegas belonged. There were a few others who were less familiar, like Sam Gomez, whose parents sent him off to boarding school last year after a drunken, late-night joy ride in their Beemer that had resulted in several thousand dollars of property damage near Balboa Park. All in all, the boys surrounding Ruby were all fine. No one particularly special, but at least they were better than the girls her age.

As they took turns blustering about achievements they seemed to find impressive—high scores on *Madden* or beer pong tournaments—Ruby feigned interest with a thin smile and a tiger-like scan of the rest of the partygoers clustered around the patio of her family's bed-and-breakfast.

At least two hundred guests had come to Elena's quinceañera. Ruby's father claimed most of them were related to their family, but who could really know with him? He referred to everyone as primo so-and-so or tía what's-her-name. Ruby'd had her own quince three years ago, and he'd introduced her to about twenty people who were "cousins" she'd never met.

Elena had been babbling incessantly about this party for months, and for the past week, no one in her family had been able to talk about anything else. Her sister had gone to everyone but Ruby as she deliberated over the color of her dress (mint green, which no one had the courage to tell her brought out the sickliest undertones in her skin), the party favor (key chains with her face on them—who the hell would want that?), or even the centerpiece flowers (it didn't matter that they were some exotic daisy that her mother had called three different florists to track down—they were still *daisies*). Daddy got to offer his opinions. Mom was integral to every decision. Even Carla, who was eleven, got to make suggestions. But anytime Ruby was proximal to any party planning, Elena would snap, "Oh,

Ruby. I'm sure you're busy getting ready for college. You don't need to worry about my birthday."

It was unrelenting, and Ruby'd had all she could bear.

She let out a bored sigh and locked eyes with Alex across the circle of boys as he shoved a sopaipilla into his face. He glanced around uncertainly before he realized that he was the one who Ruby had zeroed in on. She ran a hand over the shimmery fabric of her dress, acutely aware of the effect that would have on him. The wolfish way he stared at her as he finished off the fried pastry, scattering powdered sugar all over his shirt, was somehow both revolting and satisfying.

Ruby had a slim figure, but it was not offset by the gentle curves most of the other girls had upon exiting puberty. Her skin was fair, but not quite porcelain; it was just light enough for people to comment frequently that she didn't "look Latina"—whatever that meant. She had thick, dark hair that, on her best days, fell in glamorous waves down her back, but on her worst days drew Medusa-like comparisons. While some girls may have listed these qualities as flaws, Ruby in fact knew them to be traits she could use to her advantage with the right amount of confidence and a good deal of batting her eyelashes. There was absolutely no challenge that Ruby wasn't prepared to bend to her will.

Alex barreled toward her, earning more than a few irritated scowls as he did so.

"You look amazing," was all he could muster, a nervous grin playing on his sugarcoated lips.

She smiled back, instantly filled with the familiar satisfaction of having all eyes on her.

He seized her brief silence as his opportunity to interject what he probably thought was his most remarkable trait. "I don't know if you saw the new truck out there." Ruby maintained a blank expression, but he was undeterred. "It's mine. I just bought it. It's got three hundred horsepower. Which is a lot. Most people don't know the difference between horsepower and torque."

How did we go from complimenting me to this *so quickly?* she wondered.

Somehow he had transitioned to towing capacity, which apparently was also different from horsepower, and Ruby resisted the overwhelming urge to point out that all those things were similar in that she did not give two shits about any of them.

She eyed Ian Percy, who stood to the right of Alex's colossal shoulder with a disappointed scowl on his face. She'd always found him kind of skeevy, ever since she heard he had multiple iPhones to text different girlfriends, but perhaps he'd be a more interesting target? "I'm sorry," she cooed to Alex apologetically. "My champagne seems to have disappeared." She held up her empty hands and gave him a helpless shrug.

She flicked her eyes up at him and waited five full seconds for him to realize she was waiting for him to make himself useful.

At last, his eyes brightened with understanding. "I'll go get you one. Bartenders never ask for my ID." He put his own cup to his lips and drained its contents with one cartoonishly loud slurp. "Because I'm so tall," he added unnecessarily.

Ruby rewarded him with an affectionate pat on his arm. "Oh, would you? I'll see you back here in a minute, then." Before the relief of finally shaking the bumbling buffoon (really, *what* did Elena see in that guy?) could sink in, Ruby felt a gentle but firm hand pull her by the arm, away from her gaggle of admirers.

"Ruby. Catherine. Ortega." Instantly, she was spun so her back was to the boys, and she was instead face-to-face with the reproachful glare of her mother—the only person in the world whose whisper could still be heard over the thumping of a DJ. "Are you trying to give your father a heart attack?"

Her father subsisted on a diet that was primarily made of tequila and red meat, so while a heart attack wasn't completely out of the question, Ruby didn't really see how it could be blamed on her.

Before she could answer, her mother snapped, "You know he didn't want you wearing that dress, and I still don't know how you made it out of the house without me seeing it." Her mother's eyes darted furiously over the pale green bodycon dress that clung to her torso, exposing more than a tasteful amount of cleavage. Of course, the dress's fit was only part of her parents' disapproval of her choice. The other part had been Elena's whining that the color was too close to the mint-green gown she'd selected for herself, which Ruby found ludicrous. Everyone knew green was *her* color.

Though it had required borderline espionage to escape her mother's authoritarian watch this afternoon, Ruby personally thought the greater accomplishment had been getting into the dress on her own. She'd had to jump up and down and nearly dislocate her shoulder to get it zipped.

"It wouldn't even have been an issue if Elena had included me in the damas." She dramatically folded her arms across her chest. However, she realized the effect this action had on her breasts—

heaving them upward from her plunging neckline—and uncrossed them, quickly pinning her arms to her sides in faux innocence. Her sister had selected four of her friends to wear matching evening gowns as part of the ceremony and had been very insistent that Ruby was not among them. Ruby preferred her own dress, obviously—but she hated being excluded. She was not one to take being told no in stride.

It was, of course, beside the point that Ruby hadn't chosen Elena to be one of her damas for her quinceañera either.

"It is Elena's birthday, and it was her choice, just like your quinceañera was all your choice." Her mother grabbed the neckline of Ruby's dress roughly and jerked it upward, smashing her exposed cleavage underneath the shimmery fabric. "And that's what this is, Ruby. A quinceañera. A birthday party. Not a nightclub. Now take this sweater and cover yourself up before your grandmother—or worse, your *father*—sees you. *Go*." She'd snatched some hideous gray cardigan off the nearest chair and thrust it into Ruby's arms before marching off.

Ruby briefly thought of mentioning that her grandmother *had* seen her dress before they left the house and had rewarded her with a devilish wink, chuckling that girls her age deserved wild adventures, but she didn't want to get Mama Ortega in trouble, too.

Distracted by her mother's tirade and the faint mildewy smell of her new accessory, she hadn't noticed the towering Trujillo troll returning, sloshing the two beers he held with every step.

She'd listened to him drone on *and on*, and he couldn't even be bothered to remember that she'd asked for champagne? Typical.

"Hey, do you want to go talk out front for a bit?" he offered with a hopeful smile.

She could not think of anything she wanted to do less than retreat to isolation with this boy—even with the mortifying new addition to her ensemble. But before she could say anything, he added, "My brother said Ashton Willis is back from his semester abroad, and he just got here. He's out front with a few friends."

Her words caught in her throat for an instant, in a stunned, ecstatic silence.

This was what she had been waiting for all evening. Maybe even all her life.

She tossed the cardigan back onto the chair where her mother had found it and eagerly latched on to Alex's arm so his gigantic figure would hide her from the judgmental eyes of her family. "That sounds wonderful!"

Ruby had to consciously force herself to breathe, her entire body tingling with excitement and exhilaration. She was anxious for so much these days—to leave for college, to have a life outside her insular community, where she knew everyone and everyone knew her—but there really was nothing like a summer night in Southern California, and she was certain this moment was going to be life changing.

Her pulse quickened as they crossed the crowded patio, bedecked with the twinkling string lights they pulled out for weddings and other special events, and weaved their way between bistro tables and waiters toting gleaming silver trays. The music began to fade, and briefly, they ducked into darkness as they traipsed along the side of the B&B. At last, they reemerged into brightness, making their way to the front of the building, where glowing farmhouse sconces illuminated a small seating area.

Unlike the event space in the back, the front patio was much more intimate, adorned with a few blossoming rosebushes and two shabby-chic benches her mother had found at an antique store and had shipped to Vermont to be restored and refinished. The bed-and-breakfast itself was originally a barn and still maintained some of the rustic charm on the outside, with a peaked archway over the converted doors and distressed whitewashed wood panels. It was a pretty place, almost as much a part of Ruby's family as any person was, and it stirred something in Ruby's heart to have Ashton back here.

He had been studying abroad in Spain since Christmas, and while he had planned to be back in time for Elena's party, a series of flight delays had made his highly anticipated arrival a little hard to predict and utterly excruciating for Ruby. But here he was. He was back.

And he was finally going to be hers.

She was still several yards away from him as she stepped onto the cobblestone walkway, his back to her, but the second her eyes fell on his lanky frame, her insides turned molten. Her heart raced with a dizzying mixture of nostalgia and yearning.

The Willises had lived next door to the Ortegas for as long as Ruby could remember. Ashton was two and a half years older, but they'd grown up side by side, their childhoods intertwined. Hell, there was even a picture of Ashton and Ruby as toddlers in the bathtub together—a relic that used to mortify her, but now one that made her blush excitedly.

Ashton had always been sweet and kind to her, a reliable force of chivalry in a teenage social world that was often dramatic and tumultuous. He'd given her rides in high school so she wouldn't have to debase herself by waiting for the bus. He'd even listen to her complain about her most recent breakups without ever making the snarky comments the girls in her class were prone to about how maybe the problem wasn't them, but her. Sure, there were times she had found him a little dorky, like when he'd go on a tangent about comic books or insist on dipping everything he ate in ranch dressing, but she knew those things weren't a big deal. Ruby saw now that they were meant for each other, that all the time they'd spent growing up alongside each other, they'd also been falling in love without even realizing it. She'd rolled her eyes through way too many romantic comedies for her not to know that the girl next door always got the guy.

It had become clear to her on his first visit home from college almost two years ago. He was tanned from a recent trip to Lake Havasu, which gave his freckled cheeks the most adorable glow, and they'd stayed up all night talking in his backyard, sprawled out on his trampoline underneath the stars like they used to when they were younger. He told her all about college—his dorm, his classes, his fraternity—and she lay beside him in rapture, wondering if his eyelashes had always been so long, if he had always smelled so amazing.

After that, each of his visits was more tantalizing than the last.

He hadn't quite worked up the nerve to kiss her yet, but Ruby felt it in her bones. This would be the night. In her shimmering green dress and peep-toe heels, with her professionally curled hair and just enough alcohol—hopefully—to give her the final dose of confidence she needed to unveil her true feelings. This would be the night.

She inhaled sharply, readjusted her neckline from her mother's tampering so her cleavage resembled the gently heaving bosom of a romance-novel heroine, and released her escort's arm. She couldn't risk sending any mixed signals now that Ashton was here. She quickly tousled her hair, just in time for him to turn and face them. He grinned, and Ruby melted.

Buzzing with a sense of anticipation he could surely feel vibrating off her, she watched Alex and Ashton shake hands before she pulled him into a hug, pressing every inch of her body against his.

"Hi, Ashton," she breathed into his shirt as she nuzzled her face against him.

"Whoa, I had no idea you missed me that much!" He laughed, disentangling himself from her embrace, his cheeks a bright pink even in the half darkness. "I should leave the country more often!"

She batted her eyelashes and smiled in a way that she thought was demure, though in actuality, she had never been demure in her entire life. "Well, maybe next time you run off to Europe for six months, you'll think about taking some of us with you!"

He chuckled, a sweet sparkle in his eyes as his gaze lingered on Ruby. "Believe me, it crossed my mind."

RUBY SPENT THE NEXT HOUR MAKING UNSUCCESSFUL attempts to capture Ashton's attention and lure him away, before resorting to sultry, sidelong gazes and any opportunity to stroke his arm or bump shoulders with him. Finally, the crowd started to thin. Each person made their way back to the party to dance, to get a drink, to find a missing relative—or, in Alex's case, to check for the third time if they were serving dessert yet. The night was nearly halfway over, but at long last, it was just Ruby and Ashton nestled on the bench, awash in the gentle patio lighting as if they were in a world all their own. He was talking in a meandering manner about his semester abroad, describing ancient buildings and unfamiliar foods in a dazzling way Ruby had a hard time following. She felt a warm thrill throughout her entire body as he described the meaty prawns in heaping bowls of paella, which he always set aside because their tails freaked him out, or the mind-boggling, colorful architecture of Barcelona. He had decided to enroll in the arts track rather than Spanish-language immersion, he told her, which Ruby found both impractical and charming. After all, they lived in Southern California, where Spanish was spoken almost as much as English. Though Ashton scarcely knew ten words of Spanish, his love for pretty, intellectual things like museums and classical art trumped the practicality of being bilingual. It was that kind of uncompromising idealism that was so endearing to Ruby. Her brilliant, head-in-the-clouds Ashton.

She felt completely scatterbrained as he spoke, partially because she had never left the country and had nothing to compare this sense of wonderment to, but mostly because of how enchanting she found him in this moment.

She had folded her legs so her feet were tucked beneath her, with her hands resting in her lap, close enough that he could easily hold them if he wanted to. The strap of her dress kept slipping down, and she waited longer and longer each time to return it to where it belonged. But now, she let the sparkly strap linger, revealing her bare shoulder.

A beat of silence passed between them as Ashton appeared to notice for the first time that it was just the two of them. She watched his gaze catch on the exposed skin of her shoulder before settling on her face, and Ruby almost admired his ability to restrain himself from taking in the full effect of her body in the shimmering dress.

"Ruby Ortega." He sighed, his voice warm with adoration. "You look . . . *great*." Ruby could've lived forever inside the contemplative pause that followed his words—if she weren't so eager for him to kiss her already, of course. "Are you excited for college? Can you believe school starts next month?"

She nodded slowly, maintaining eye contact with him. "I can't wait to get out of here." She suppressed thoughts of her irritating sister and her demanding mother. She didn't want to think of them in this moment.

He glanced upward at the stars, strands of his blond hair falling into his eyes that he didn't bother to sweep away. "It is amazing to see what else is out there, but you'll be surprised. You'll miss this place."

Buena Valley was where she and Ashton had found each other, and she would always love her hometown for that. But lately, she'd been feeling like she'd outgrown it. She knew that for her and Ashton to explore their romance, they needed somewhere new, somewhere that wasn't so familiar. That was a large part of why she'd applied to college in Arizona in the first place, though she hadn't actually shared that rationale with anyone. Sure, Arizona State had a robust business program and was far enough from home for her own adventure but close enough to visit often—but it also had *Ashton*. Her Ashton.

"You promise we'll see each other? I mean, I know you have your own life over there. I just want to know that I'll get to see you. I've missed you, Ashton. You'll show me around? Help me out?" Her tone grew softer as she slowly inched her way closer to him, willing him to look at her again. She couldn't take her eyes off him. He had the faintest golden stubble growing along his chin, and she longed to run her neatly manicured fingertips along it.

"Ruby, you won't need my help. You never have," he teased. "But of course I'll show you around. There's actually someone I'm really excited for you to meet." His gaze finally turned away from the sky and fell back on Ruby, glittering eyes and overflowing neckline and all. A brief look of apprehension crossed his face before he added, "My girlfriend, Millie."

Ruby leaned into the word *girlfriend*, tilting her head so it would be easier for his lips to find hers. She personally thought it was too soon to call herself his girlfriend, but she wouldn't protest. Whatever he wanted. She parted her lips just as the word *Millie* hit her like an ice pick to the nerves. She stiffened.

Who the *fuck* was Millie?

She sat upright. *"What did you say?"*

He took a nervous breath, quick and sharp. "Yeah, I've uh . . . met someone. Millie. Millie Hamilton. We met a couple of weeks before I left for Spain, but we've been kind of seeing each other long-distance, and she actually visited me in Barcelona for a few days, and it was great." He was rambling. "She's coming out here this weekend. To meet my family. She gets in tomorrow. She lives in Arizona, but she's coming out here to drive to campus with me, too."

If she hadn't been sitting down, Ruby was sure she would've fallen right over.

Girlfriend? For as long as she had known him, Ashton had never had a girlfriend. She had always thought of him as patiently waiting for her to come around, and now that the stars had finally aligned, he had a girlfriend? *They* were supposed to be together. She was finally eighteen, so if it had been her age that was holding him back all this time, that didn't matter anymore. She was heading off to college at the same school he attended, so they'd have space away from their families while they figured things out. They could be together! They were *supposed* to be together.

Deflated, she slumped against the arm of the bench, and angrily snapped her shoulder strap back into place.

"Girlfriend. Millie. *Wow*," she scoffed.

"It was unexpected, of course," he continued. "These kinds of things always are. But it's really great. I think you'll like her."

These kinds of things? What the hell did Ashton Willis know about "these kinds of things"? The only girl Ruby had ever heard him mention outside of his family and Ruby's family was Wonder Woman, but now he was such a romance expert he was able to make philosophical generalizations about "these kinds of things"? *Please.*

She remained unmoving, her breath slow and furious. "You think I'll *like* her? Why?"

"Because she's a beautiful person, inside and out. She's not like anyone I've ever met. When we're together—"

"She sounds sensational," Ruby interrupted flatly. She'd heard enough.

"She is. I know you're going to like her." He paused, staring at her in his cozy, soulful way. "You know, you're one of my closest friends. I hope you'll like her."

Ruby knew she was going to hate her. She opened her mouth to tell him precisely that, but suddenly the front doors were thrown open and Carla burst through, shouting, "Cake! Hurry. It's time for cake!"

Ashton smiled a half-hearted, thin smile and patted her hand. She couldn't tell if he was oblivious to the fact that he'd just broken her heart or if he pitied her; either way, it pissed her off. "I guess we'd better get back over there."

Ruby nodded. "Yeah. Wouldn't want to miss cake," she said testily.

"The Ruby I know and love would never want to miss cake," he joked over his shoulder as he stood and made his way to the door.

He didn't even notice that she wasn't following him.

She waited until the door shut behind him, until she was sure she was completely alone, to seize the nearest drink—a half-drunk, warm Corona Light—and guzzle it in one enraged swig. She winced at the bitter taste before launching the bottle across the patio. It shattered against the ceramic pot of a bougainvillea.

"*Girlfriend?*" she muttered to herself. "Closest friends? What the hell is he thinking?"

"I certainly have *no* idea."

She sprang to her feet and whirled around to seek out the source of the disembodied voice, teetering precariously in her stilettos. Just as mysteriously as the words had materialized in the dim courtyard, the owner of the voice appeared beside her, a warm hand on her arm to steady her, saving her from topping off her romantic failure with an epic wipeout on the cobblestones.

"Who the hell are you? Where the hell did you come from? And what the hell are you thinking, hiding out in the goddamn shadows like that?" She jerked her arm out of the stranger's grasp and stumbled backward. She braced herself against the bench, trying desperately to catch her breath as she glowered at the olive-skinned stranger who surveyed her with clear bemusement.

He laughed, holding his hands up innocently. "Whoa, whoa. I wasn't hiding. I came out here for some peace and quiet, and before I knew it, you and the white boy were having a moment." She detected the slightest Spanish accent as he spoke, something she might've missed in the chaos if it didn't remind her of the way her grandmother stretched out her vowels and curled her *r*'s when she was distracted. "I didn't want to ruin the mood you were trying to set—I thought he was going to be into what you were putting out there. I don't know what he's thinking." He grinned, his eyes shamelessly flicking up and down her dress.

"Who. Are. You."

"Remy Bustillos. I work with your dad." The smiling stranger held out his hand.

Ruby ignored it. "You work for my dad? How old are you?"

He raised his brows and returned his hand to his side goodnaturedly, as if refusing to shake someone's hand were a normal greeting.

Her irritation and embarrassment subsided enough for her to

feel a twinge of curiosity about this person who had just brazenly inserted himself in what was supposed to be the most romantic moment of her life. He did not seem old enough to be a co-worker of her father's. He didn't look any older than Ruby, after all. He was tall, with dark hair meticulously styled into place. Even in the dim lighting of the courtyard, she was particularly struck by his eyes. She had always found dark eyes to be beady and sharklike, but in his case, the eyes he had fixed on her felt bottomless, infinite. He was kind of . . . handsome—in an over-the-top, flashy, irritating sort of way.

He smirked. "Isn't that kind of a rude question to ask someone you barely know?"

"Isn't it kind of rude to eavesdrop on two people having a private conversation?"

"Oh, it looked like you were hoping it was going to be much more than a conversation."

"And that makes it okay?" She rolled her eyes. "You have no idea what you're talking about."

He shrugged his broad shoulders and tilted his head toward her so he could speak a little more softly. In spite of herself, Ruby found herself unable to resist leaning toward him as well. "Maybe not, but I think he's crazy. Personally, I'd love to have a better idea of what you were talking about." His voice was husky, gentle . . . *flirtatious*?

How *dare* he? Still heated from Ashton's abrupt rejection, Ruby couldn't even begin to imagine what would inspire this guy to think now was the appropriate time to lay on the charm. She didn't care how good-looking he was.

She shuddered. "Absolutely not." She had intended to shout it, but instead her words caught in her throat and escaped as an enraged whisper. She stormed through the front door, marching straight through the empty lobby toward the back patio, eager to pretend she had never met this bizarre witness to her heartbreak.

2

Before rejoining the party, Ruby paused for a minute at the glass-paned double doors that led to the courtyard, the muted sounds of her family singing "Cumpleaños feliz" audible inside the empty bed-and-breakfast. Elena sat perched on a chair in the center of the dance floor, next to a custom ice sculpture of a swan. Engulfed by the bulging, glittering fabric of her gown, she looked like a scoop of pistachio ice cream. Two waiters presented her with a three-tier cake, a sugary monstrosity decked in matching mint frosting and shimmering 1 and 5 candles. The crowd cheered as Elena daintily extinguished both flames, beaming with rosy-cheeked joy.

If Ashton thought she was just going to go lick her wounds and back down, he had another thing coming, she thought as she stepped outside. That was just *not* how Ortegas did things.

"Mija, where have you been?" her father asked, placing a gentle hand on her shoulder.

Ruby's stomach tightened as she remembered her mother's dictum about her dress. She couldn't bear being scolded *again* after everything that had just happened.

But thankfully, he seemed to sense her disappointment and didn't mention her dress. He had a magical way of doing that, of knowing when to drill down and when to let something go—especially when it came to Ruby, who had never let anything go in her whole life.

"You've missed your sister's entire party," he continued.

"Oh, no I didn't. I was just . . . out front for a little bit." She forced a feeble smile. "It's a great party, Daddy."

He nodded, examining the cheerful crowd with pursed lips. "You saw that Ashton is back, I assume?"

Ruby was silent. She had never mentioned her feelings for Ashton to anyone in her family before, but again, she didn't know why she was surprised her father understood.

"His parents told me that he has a special guest visiting him tomorrow. He told you this, yes?" Her father accepted two plates of chocolate cake from a passing waiter and held the bigger one out to Ruby.

She took it and nodded glumly. "Yes, his girlfriend."

"And you're unhappy about this girlfriend?"

She glowered. Could this evening get any worse? Not only had she been publicly spurned by her soulmate, but now she had to rehash it with her father? *God.* She cut off a bite of cake with her fork and shoved it in her mouth. At least the cake was good.

Her father softly clicked his tongue and nodded again, as if she'd responded. "Listen, I know this news might make you feel sad, but you can't force these kinds of things."

She opened her half-full mouth to interject, but he silenced her with a pointed look. Why was everyone suddenly so eager to lecture her on "these kinds of things"? Was she such an emotional dunce that every male in her life felt the need to give her step-by-step instructions on matters of the heart?

"No, not even *you* can force these things. I'm only guessing that's what all *this* is about?" He used his fork to gesture at Ruby's outfit, but his eyes did not leave her face, as if he refused to acknowledge her clothing with anything but his utensil. "It's about Ashton, yes?"

Ruby shrugged. She couldn't *lie* to him, but she also couldn't bring herself to confess her plans of seduction.

"Didn't Mom tell you to stop eating sweets after your last cardiologist appointment?" she countered.

Once more, he nodded, seeming unsurprised. He set his cake down on the nearest table. "Ruby, you are smart and strong and *beautiful*. You do not need to do all of *this* to make someone see that. If they cannot see it on their own, that's their fault. That's their loss."

She felt her eyes tearing up at these words, at the solemn way her father regarded her. She inhaled deeply to keep her composure.

"And you certainly don't need to run around family functions with your chichis hanging out."

She flushed as he issued her one more knowing glance before retrieving his cake and disappearing to talk with someone else— presumably a person who didn't exasperate him with their exposed chichis.

🔥 🔥 🔥

RUBY AWOKE THE NEXT MORNING TO A SHARP CHAMPAGNE headache, as well as a fourteen-point to-do list neatly penned on the monogrammed stationary of Eleanor Robinson Ortega. Her mother was the kind of disciplined woman who successfully balanced an unrelenting schedule of charity functions, exercise classes, therapy, social engagements, and household errands, so it didn't surprise Ruby at all that she had scurried off to her six a.m. spin class the morning after Elena's party. It also shouldn't have surprised her that she expected her daughter to be just as productive.

Sure, Ruby *was* going off to college in two weeks, and sure, she hadn't packed a damn thing. But she didn't see why that had to be resolved just after sunrise—especially after a night like last night.

Despite the daunting length of her mother's list, Ruby's number one priority that morning was to keep her eye on Ashton. She could see the Willises' driveway from the window in her bedroom, where she had been sequestered with a stack of cardboard boxes and a roll of packing tape. Maybe she should've been a little more focused on the tasks her mother had outlined, but she told herself that it was good for her *emotionally* to keep track of Ashton's comings and goings—maybe to move on or maybe to figure out how the hell to knock some sense into that clueless boy she loved.

Around noon, she watched him return from the airport with . . . *her*. She couldn't see much of her at this distance, even after she climbed on top of her dresser and smashed her face against the window. Millie appeared to be blond and a good deal shorter than Ashton. She held his hand as they made their way from his Prius up the walkway that led to the Willises' house. They paused in front of the wrought-iron double doors and shared a prolonged kiss before heading inside. Ruby gaped in horror-struck envy long after they'd disappeared from view.

"Ruby, can I borrow—*what* are you *doing*?" Carla inquired, cocking her head like a curious puppy. Of course, the youngest Ortega sister chose this precise moment to appear in Ruby's doorway.

If it had been anyone else, Ruby would've tried to lie. Unlike Elena, Carla wouldn't rat her out to their parents and, unlike their parents, she was too young to pass much judgment on Ruby. Her age and naturally sweet disposition rendered her neutral territory among the Ortega women.

"Ashton's back with that *girl*," Ruby muttered, dismounting from her dresser and painfully smacking her knee on its beveled edge. She grimaced as she slid to her feet.

"Are you okay?"

"No, I am not okay. He's dating some girl from school after leading me on for months," she grumbled.

"Oh." Carla sat down on the edge of Ruby's bed and began sifting through a pile of bikinis. "I meant your knee. But I'm sorry to hear about that, too. I didn't know you *liked* Ashton. You said he was dorky."

Ruby rolled her eyes and aggressively threw some shoes in the nearest empty box, despite the fact that her mother had clearly labeled it BOOKS. "No. I mean, yes, I used to. But things are different now. Things have changed. He's changed. *I've* changed. I thought we changed together and it was finally time for us to be together, but now here's this girl ruining everything."

Carla's face looked eerily similar to their father's as she weighed Ruby's words. "He brought her here, though, didn't he? So she's not here to ruin things. She's here because he wants her here, right?"

Ruby tossed a single tennis shoe without its mate into the box and glared at Carla. "What is it you came in here for?"

Carla cast her eyes down and timidly picked a bottle of Dior nail polish from a box on Ruby's nightstand. "I'm sorry Ashton hurt your feelings. You know how Mama Ortega says 'what's meant to be will always find a way'? Maybe it's like that." She gave her sister a sympathetic look, her dark eyes sparkling compassionately.

Ruby had spotted her grandmother forcing that irritating stranger Remy Bustillos to cumbia with her at the end of the night, cackling with delight as she criticized his footwork, so Mama Ortega's judgment was dubious at best. Nevertheless, she found her words comforting in this moment.

"Well, I'm sure you could stay home tonight, if you think it'll be too difficult," Carla suggested meekly, unscrewing the top of the nail polish and lightly testing it out on her pinkie nail.

Ruby shot her sister a questioning look. "Stay home? From what?"

Carla examined her finger, blowing it dry. "Dinner." When Ruby's face failed to show any recognition at all, she continued. "At the Willises'?" Ruby's frown only deepened. "They invited all of us over tonight to meet Ashton's new girlfriend. Mom told us this morning in the kitchen."

Ruby did recall being in the kitchen this morning. Granted, her mother had been simultaneously making a protein shake and disputing a credit card charge over the phone as she spoke to Ruby and her sisters—and Ruby had, of course, been preoccupied with selecting the perfect Instagram filter for last night's photos. But now that

Carla mentioned it, Ruby did sort of remember dinner being one of the many things their mother had talked about.

She mulled it over, rolling the idea around in her mind until it became much more than a neighborly outing—it was an opportunity. Exactly the one she needed.

"Dinner. At the Willises'. Right. Of course," Ruby mumbled, her thoughts racing. With any luck, Ashton would take one look at the two of them side by side and send that girl packing so they could put this whole messy affair behind them before the first day of school.

3

Over the years, Ruby had eaten dinner at the Willis household nearly as often as she had eaten at her own house. While her parents usually insisted on a certain amount of decorum at their dinner table, Mrs. Willis was much more laid-back. Ruby could think of several times when she had eaten dinner in just her swimsuit following an afternoon in their pool, and many more when they had eaten their food in the living room while watching cartoons—conduct that never would have been acceptable in her own home. Ashton said it was because his parents were white; that's just how they did dinner. But Ruby's mother was white, too, so she didn't see how that could be the only explanation. In fact, she'd spent much of her adolescence wondering if her family's peculiarities were typical, weird family things that everyone experienced, or the result of subtle cultural differences. It was impossible to know sometimes.

Despite the lax dress code, Ruby found herself intensely scrutinizing her outfit that evening. She had decided on a new pair of jeans and a crop top. Her competitive edge told her to throw on a pair of Prada platform sandals that made her legs look incredible, but she knew her mother would suspect something if she showed up at a midweek barbecue in heels.

With one final glance, she slipped her favorite Tory Burch sandals on and grabbed her cell phone off her nightstand.

No text messages.

Her contact with Ashton had been intermittent while he was in Spain, but they'd caught up every couple of days. He'd tell her about his favorite tapas bars or weekends traveling in Seville or Lisbon; she'd find discreet ways to send him flattering faux-candid selfies. He'd been radio silent since the quinceañera and Millie's arrival, though. It wasn't hard to figure out why, but it still stung.

She did have another notification, however: a new follower on Instagram. She didn't know the username, but when she clicked on it, she immediately recognized the smirking face of Remy Bustillos. As if their initial encounter hadn't been disconcerting enough, now he'd found her on social media.

Ruby's lip curled, and as she toyed with the idea of blocking this peculiar and persistent person, her attention was diverted by her mother's figure in her doorway. Eleanor wore a sunny Lilly Pulitzer shift dress, her wheat-colored hair pulled back into a loose bun. A discerning furrow marred her immaculately sculpted eyebrows.

"Are you . . . *ready*?"

Ruby knew instantly she was asking much more than whether Ruby was dressed. A classic Eleanor Ortega veiled warning. "I don't know, *am* I?" she shot back, cringing at her petulance even as the words flew out of her mouth.

Her mother's lips pursed into the subtlest expression of displeasure, so discreet that Ruby was sure anyone else would've missed it. Eleanor Ortega was the essence of poise and patience, while Ruby tended toward what she thought of as passionate on her best days and pigheadedness on her worst days—traits she had inherited from her father. She knew she could probably work her whole life to be half as calm and restrained as her mother, and still never achieve it.

"I realize your feelings are hurt by Ashton's new relationship, and I'm sorry about that. I wish that wasn't the case, but it is, and you must deal with it—hopefully in a mature way. And if not in a mature way, then in a *private* way. Ashton has known you your whole life, and he cares for you, even if it's not in the way that you hoped. He's not trying to hurt you, and I don't want you to jeopardize a lifelong friendship simply because your ego has been bruised."

Ruby's pulse quickened, thumping in her forehead. *A bruised ego? Is that all she thinks this is?* "Mom," she said through gritted teeth. "I'm not pouting because he bruised my ego. It's more than that. It's . . ."

Her mother held up her hand, the diamonds in her tennis bracelet gleaming in the afternoon sun. "Okay, perhaps I misunderstood. If this really is about more than that, if this is about deeper feelings, then my hope for you is still the same. You won't convince him of your affections by attempting to destroy his relationship."

Ruby nodded reluctantly. Though she didn't particularly like the comparison between her romantic pursuits and a force of destruction, she could at least understand the logic in her mother's argument.

Eleanor turned to leave before pausing and casting her daughter one last, thoughtful look. "So you do think you have real, serious feelings for him?"

"Yes, Mom."

"It's not just you wanting something you can't have?"

"Mom." It was a valid inquiry, but it rankled regardless. She wasn't just a boy-crazy kid anymore. She was capable of real emotions. She was capable of falling in love. Why did her parents have such a hard time believing that?

"Okay, I'm sorry. I just had to ask." Her mother sighed. "And you think you're right for each other? You think you could make each other happy?"

Ruby didn't hesitate for a second this time. "Yes."

"All right," she conceded. "Well, please think about why you feel this way. You don't have to tell me, but you should know for yourself. Understanding why you feel what you do is part of being an adult." She turned down the hallway and issued one last demand. "And behave yourself at dinner tonight."

With a frustrated sigh, Ruby tucked her phone in her pocket and followed, only to discover Elena lurking just outside her bedroom door, clearly eavesdropping.

"I'm surprised you're willing to show your face after what happened at my party," Elena hissed, a cruel bite to her words. "*Everyone* saw you throwing yourself at him all night."

Ruby flushed but refused to dignify the snide remarks with a response. She pushed past her sister to join her parents downstairs, telling herself there was no way everyone knew what had happened, and even if they did, she didn't care what her sister's little friends thought of her. The only people who truly knew of the conversation were her, Ashton, and her newest Instagram follower, Remy.

Even so, her cheeks remained hot as she walked across the street with her family.

WHILE RUBY'S PARENTS TENDED TO OVERLOOK UNDERAGE drinking on special occasions, surrounded by the watchful eyes of loved ones, they certainly did not make a habit of condoning it. Watching Millie sip a second glass of wine just solidified the feeling of being robbed of the privileges she desired. Ruby could scarcely even stand to look at her. Ashton found her gaze as he selected a Coors Light from the cooler and offered her a sympathetic smile before making his way toward her with Millie at his side.

A clamminess seized hold of Ruby as they approached. It wasn't embarrassment, though; she knew how she felt for Ashton, and she knew she had every right to feel this way. The prickling in her temples was the fury of being denied something—someone, rather—she was positive was already hers, even if she was the only one who recognized it right now.

"This is Ruby, the neighbor I've been telling you about," Ashton said blandly, a hand outstretched toward Ruby. "Ruby, this is Millie."

Ruby forced a stiff smile. Sure, he had referred to her as a *neighbor* when she thought there were about a dozen other titles he could have applied—though she conceded that referring to her as his soulmate might have been a little awkward. But, *neighbor*? As if she were just a girl he waved at occasionally when he was unloading groceries from his car.

But he did say that he had told her about me, she reminded herself. *That means he's been talking about me, which means he's been thinking about me.*

"It's good to meet you, Millie," Ruby said tepidly.

Millie absolutely beamed. If Ruby had been willing to give her any credit at all, she might've said she had the kind of smile that lit up a room. But she wasn't, so she didn't. "All I've heard about for *weeks* is the famous Ruby Ortega, so I told Ash I absolutely had to meet you! I'm so happy we finally get a chance to connect!"

"Ash?" Ruby repeated the cutesy nickname with a raised eyebrow.

Ashton's cheeks turned pink, but he didn't say anything. He'd always hated that nickname ever since a group of third-grade bullies realized how similar it sounded to *ass. I guess he's okay with it now*, Ruby thought sourly.

Dinner itself was comparable to a national parade in the happy couple's honor. Her own mother spent nearly forty-five minutes gushing over Millie's bobbed haircut, treating the girl like she was a guest on a late-night talk show. What was she studying? Where was she from? How did she and Ashton meet? What did her parents do?

Blah, blah, blah.

The questions were bad enough on their own, but her mom's reactions to Millie's responses were what really pushed Ruby over the edge. She briefly contemplated feigning an illness just so she could stop listening to her mom rave enthusiastically about how smart it was of Millie to choose communications as her major, how proud

Millie must be that her father was a firefighter, how sweet it was that Millie met Ashton through mutual friends at the library.

Blah, blah, barf.

She shoved a french fry into her mouth and offered to help Mrs. Willis clear the table while Ashton and Millie regaled her family with anecdotes and cozy selfies from Millie's visit to Spain.

When she finally returned to the living room, she found Elena was now the focus of the conversation. Her sister scowled sullenly with her arms across her chest, pleading with her parents.

"It's not *fair*," Elena whined. "I'm *fifteen* now!"

"Sí, you are only fifteen," Daddy said firmly. "You still have a curfew, and there's no way you'll be back by then."

Elena rolled her eyes. "But I'm sure *Ruby* gets to go because Ruby gets whatever she wants!"

"If only," Ruby muttered to herself, despite the fact that she had absolutely no idea what had inspired her sister's meltdown.

Ashton turned to her from the love seat, where he and Millie were nestled. "I was just telling your family that Millie and I are going to a bonfire on the beach tonight to meet up with some friends. I invited you and your sister, but your parents said no. To Elena. You're still welcome to come." He glanced at Ruby's father with the anxious deference that he always showed her father, who not so secretly scared him a little. "Right?"

Her father shot her a warning glare. "Ruby is eighteen. She's an adult. She is, of course, *allowed* to go." The emphasis on the word *allowed* told Ruby her permission was conditional. She was allowed to go only if she did not use this as another opportunity to hurl herself at Ashton.

The room was silent except for Elena's loud, disappointed groan.

If Ruby didn't go—well, that would feel like cowardice, like giving up. But if she did go, she'd have to continue to watch Ashton dote on this girl.

It ultimately came down to the fact that she'd *missed* Ashton after so many months apart. All her life, he'd been there for her, ready to hang out or talk, and it had been hard adjusting to his absence. Even when he'd left for college, he texted and visited home often enough that the longing wasn't so bad. She'd give anything to be transported back in time to the days she'd flop down next to him on the couch in his family's rec room while he explained for the millionth time the difference between the DC and Marvel universes. She missed him. She missed him, and even now that he was back, she was *still* missing him. He was home, sure, but he was no longer hers. He was Millie's now.

So, despite her reservations, she heard herself saying yes.

4

As Ruby settled herself in the back seat of Ashton's Prius, it occurred to her how phony this whole excursion felt.

Their hometown, Buena Valley, was a small ranch community in the foothills of San Diego. For them, going to the beach was a full-day activity. In the best conditions, their houses were still a forty-five-minute drive from the nearest oceanfront; with any traffic at all, which was usually the case, it was over an hour. Spontaneously attending a bonfire was an inconvenience and not something they'd ever done before. It was clearly all for Millie's benefit, to glamorize the California lifestyle for her. If Millie was too oblivious to notice that the horse properties and farmhouses in their area were a far cry from the surfer towns and sandy beaches of TV's California, all Ruby could do was hope that Ashton would realize that.

She did notice, with revulsion, that Ashton was driving with one hand on the wheel and the other resting intimately on Millie's upper thigh, his fingers absently drumming on the polka-dot fabric of her sundress. Millie blathered on about the scenery, evidently so accustomed to Ashton's touch that she didn't even notice his hand—or the envy radiating from Ruby in the back seat.

Ruby distracted herself by pulling out her phone. Remy's Instagram page, the last thing she'd looked at this afternoon, was still open, and the bemused smirk on his profile picture made her feel like he'd been watching (and laughing at) her all evening.

She idly scrolled through his pictures: tropical beaches and luxurious resorts, fancy meals and decadent cocktails, and snapshots of Remy, usually in some sort of unusual outfit, sporting a beautiful girl on his arm. She tapped a recent one of him in a tuxedo with a tan blonde in a navy evening gown grinning by his side. The picture was tagged in a fancy New York City hotel, and the caption read, Honored to have our app recognized at tonight's awards ceremony!

An app, huh? She zoomed in on his face, assessing his smile and gleaming black eyes. He didn't look like the nerdy tech types that sometimes came down from Silicon Valley. But then again, he didn't look like any of the people who worked for her father either. It was more than his young age that stood out to her, though. She just couldn't put her finger on it.

Regardless, she didn't think Ortega Properties even had an app.

Who was this guy?

She scrolled through a few more pictures. Remy vacationing in Bali, Remy running a marathon, Remy enjoying a beer at a rooftop bar. The comments on these idyllic snapshots were almost more intriguing than the images themselves. On a picture of Remy sporting a pair of very tight swim trunks on a white sand beach, a user named "ashleyyyyyyy" had commented with a series of heart emojis, pointing out that the beach was nothing compared to the ones they'd visited together on their Mediterranean yacht tour last spring. Other girls left notes alluding to innuendo-filled DMs, late-night skinny dipping, and a myriad of other provocative activities that made Ruby's eyes widen to see on a public platform like this.

Who *was* this guy?

She tapped his most recent picture, posted this morning, an artsy shot of a coffee mug on a beachfront balcony, with a back-drop of cloudless sky and sandy terrain. He'd captioned it, Enjoying a wonderful business trip in beautiful California. The location he'd tagged was a ritzy resort where politicians and celebrities were known to vacation.

Ortega Properties was growing, sure, but right now it only con-sisted of the luxury bed-and-breakfast on their ranch. They'd recently begun construction on a reception hall to be built next door to the B&B, and there were talks of a vineyard or farm-to-table restaurant in the future, but it was all very local. What would they even need an app for?

She frowned and was about to google his name when she noticed Millie's face peering back at her from the front seat.

"So, do you?" Millie chirped, clearly continuing a conversation that she'd been having with Ruby, unbeknownst to Ruby.

"Um, I'm sorry. Do I what?" She clicked the screen of her phone off, hiding Remy's mischievous face yet again.

"Do you have a boyfriend? Are you seeing anyone?" Millie asked with a giggle.

Ashton's eyes darted up from the road to watch Ruby in the rear-view mirror, lingering on her until she spoke. "No, not exactly," she said slowly, directing her response more to Ashton than to Millie.

Millie grinned encouragingly. "Not exactly? So there is someone?"

"You could say that. It's . . . complicated."

Ashton's brows furrowed in the rearview mirror. The rest of his face was hidden from her view, so she couldn't decide if he was worried or confused by her response.

"Well, I'm only asking because one of our friends from school—Ashton's roommate from last year—is in town with his family and he's meeting us at this bonfire tonight," Millie explained, almost reading Ruby's mind. "I don't know your type or anything, but he's really cute and so sweet, and I thought at the very least it might be nice for you to meet some people who will be on campus this year. But who knows? Maybe you'll hit it off, and you can move on from whatever complicated situation you're in. You don't want to start college off with a mess like that! And Charlie's so *nice*. But obviously, you don't have to date him if you—"

"What?" Ashton interjected suddenly, in a garbled noise that was half cough, half bark of laughter. "Charlie and Ruby? What? No." He laughed again, and the shrill, flabbergasted sound stunned Ruby for a moment.

She eyed the back of his head curiously, studying the tops of his ears and the freckled nape of his neck.

Was he . . . *jealous*?

His hazel eyes flicked up to the rearview mirror once more, a flash of unguarded distress in them that delighted Ruby beyond words.

Millie shook her head at Ashton in a good-natured but baffled way. "I don't know. It's worth a shot, isn't it? He's just a wonderful guy and a really good friend."

Ruby grinned, keeping her eyes locked on the rearview mirror, but Ashton refused to meet her gaze again, so instead she fixated on the splays of tawny hair that fell across his forehead. He *was* jealous!

"Definitely worth seeing how it plays out, then," Ruby responded coolly, a fiery sense of anticipation flickering in her chest.

RUBY KNEW THAT AS LONG AS ASHTON WILLIS WALKED THE earth, no other boy would measure up in her eyes. That being said, she still couldn't imagine a more incompatible, inadequate romantic prospect than the soft-spoken, quivering Charlie Hampton.

She could endure the dopiest of dopes if it meant a chance to get Ashton's attention, but *come on*. It was hard to believe *anyone* would feel even the slightest bit intimidated by Charlie of all people.

She had also been a little put off by Millie's gall, the fact that she felt inclined to set Ruby up on what was basically a blind date even though they were practically strangers. But when Millie and Ashton deposited Ruby with Charlie mere minutes after joining their friends? That was just plain ballsy. Maybe Ruby had underestimated her. Maybe she knew exactly what was going on here and this was all part of her evil plan. Maybe listening to Charlie sputter through his bland list of hobbies was the punishment Millie had been plotting for Ruby all along.

Ruby almost hoped that was the case. That was at least something she could understand.

"D-do you know what d-dorm you're living in?" Charlie inquired with a visible tremble.

"Yes," she said in a clipped tone that did not inspire a follow-up question.

"I remember feeling overwhelmed as a freshman. It's a lot to take in. But don't worry, you'll know your way around in n-no time." He flashed her a nervous smile, his lips twitching as if they couldn't decide what expression to make.

Actually, Ruby couldn't have been less worried about college. She knew it was silly, but many of her expectations were tied to her hopes for a romance with Ashton. Her daydreams about studying in her dorm room or attending football games or walking to class had always featured him in a prominent and essential role. Even after the incident at Elena's party, Ruby hadn't considered that those fantasies might not come to fruition—and she certainly hadn't given much thought as to what college might be like if she weren't with him. But even if she wasn't going to give up on him, she knew she should be working out all the other logistical things about school.

I still have time, she told herself. *I'll figure it all out soon.*

"So you're from San Diego?" Charlie ventured shakily. Though his nervous stammering had subsided, his soft tone was barely audible above the sound of waves crashing against the shore in the distance.

Normally she would've pointed out the distinction between rural Buena Valley and San Diego proper, but instead she just nodded and pulled out her phone for the dozenth time. She knew it was rude, but she also didn't want to give this guy any illusions that this exchange was going well.

She spotted a new notification on her phone as Charlie squeaked, "What are you majoring in?"

"Business." She opened the new message.

REMY

You sure move quickly 😊

The back of her neck prickled. Was Remy *here*? Was he watching her? A strange, curious thrill tingled inside her as she quickly scanned the dark beachfront. Aside from the ten people clustered around their bonfire, there weren't many others nearby. A few dim shapes along the beach between their gathering and the next fire pit—but then she spotted him, leaning against the retaining wall that separated the beach from the sidewalk. She recognized his broad-shouldered silhouette as soon as she laid eyes on him.

"Will you excuse me for a minute? I think I see someone I know," Ruby interrupted, returning Remy's fierce gaze.

Charlie's eyes flitted nervously between the two of them. "That guy standing alone in the dark staring at us?"

She shrugged. Between Charlie and Remy, she'd rather take her chances with the lurking stranger at this point. "I'll be right back," she called over her shoulder.

She approached Remy, instinctively smoothing any stray hairs caught in the sea breeze. "What—you're stalking me now?" she shouted. His smile widened with every step she took in his direction, but she fought the urge to return it, forcing her lips into a playful smirk instead. No amount of handsome could make up for how weird it was that he'd just shown up here, she told herself unconvincingly.

"Well, if I was stalking you, I'd have a pretty easy job." He uncrossed his arms and put his hands in his pockets. "You've posted your location three times since you've been here. Anyone could find you. Besides, my hotel's right down the street." He tilted his head toward the right, and Ruby recognized the palm-lined terrace of the resort he'd tagged this morning. "It's good to see you're moving forward with your life after what happened at the party, but I've got to say, I'm surprised by your choice." They both glanced toward the bonfire, where Ruby could still make out Charlie's scrawny figure standing on the periphery of the crowd, watching them.

She rolled her eyes and ignored his comment. "If you work for my father, why don't you live here?"

Remy clicked his tongue and chuckled. "I don't work *for* your dad. I work with him. I have my own company."

Ruby still had not seen him in full light, and again she found herself wondering how old he was. All his pictures showed a fit, brown-skinned guy with thick, glossy hair and a grin that easily could've belonged to the debonair hero—or perhaps, in Remy's case, the slick evil twin—of a telenovela. He couldn't have been more than a couple of years older than her, but there was still something about him—in his smile, in his clothing maybe, in the way he carried himself—that seemed older. More mature.

"An app, right?" she pressed further, still scrutinizing his appearance. Tonight he was wearing a pair of shorts and a gray T-shirt that was pulled tight across his muscled chest.

His eyes glittered as he nodded smugly. "Looked me up, did you?"

She pushed past the embarrassment she felt creeping up on her. "I didn't even realize my father knew what an app was," she said. She pictured her father puttering around on their ranch—pruning flowers, petting horses, and pausing to send a tweet? She couldn't think of anything less likely.

"Well," Remy acquiesced, "he doesn't, really. But he's learning. He's a smart guy, and he's just interested in what it's going to take for local establishments to get on the cutting edge of the hospitality industry. He's looking for creative ideas to keep up with the next big thing."

That did sound like her dad. He was not a fan of technology, that was for sure, but he was cutthroat when it came to the business he'd built from scratch, and she knew he'd do just about anything to keep it successful—even taking meetings with smarmy kids who would lecture him about hashtags and influencers and algorithms.

"And that's what you do?" There was something about this smooth-talking mystery man that both intrigued her and put her on edge.

He nodded again. "Yeah, for the last year or so. I travel around and help businesses—mostly hotels, but a couple event venues and tour companies—develop some more personalized features that focus on consumer experiences. This week San Diego, next week Miami."

Though she didn't really understand what he meant by *personalized features* or *consumer experiences*, she didn't let on. "Where do you live?" She perched herself on the wall that Remy leaned against so they no longer faced each other but looked out at the beach together. He remained standing, but their bodies were now close enough that Ruby could feel the faint tickle of his arm hairs against her skin.

"Funny you should ask, not that far from where you'll be living," he laughed, playfully bumping his shoulder against her. Her skin immediately erupted in goose bumps as soon as his warm skin touched hers. She quickly rubbed her hand along her forearm to dissolve them before he could notice. "Relax," he teased. "Your dad told me you're going to Arizona State this fall. I have a condo in Scottsdale, though I'm not there too much these days."

Just then, Ruby noticed three figures making their way from the bonfire toward them: Millie and Ashton, with a clumsy Charlie bobbing along behind them. Apparently what it took to get Ashton's attention was Charlie tattling on her for disappearing into the night with a tall, dark stranger.

"Hey, man. Ashton Willis." Ashton thrust his hand out to Remy as he approached, his tone brusque and strangely assertive. "This is my girlfriend, Millie, and our friend Charlie. You were at Elena's party, right?"

Remy shook Ashton's hand, and Ruby wondered if Remy was flexing his forearm intentionally as some sort of display of dominance or if his muscles always had those distinct edges. "Yeah, I remember you." A brief, almost undetectable smirk flashed across his face, and Ruby prayed Ashton hadn't noticed. "Remy Bustillos."

Ashton's posture remained stiff, and he gave a quick nod. "Oh, right. How do you know the Ortegas?"

There was that delicious bite of wariness in Ashton's voice. Ruby fought to choke down a self-satisfied cackle as she watched them.

Remy's devious smirk reemerged. "I'm a colleague of Ruby's father. I just happened to be in town for a couple meetings, so he invited me. It was a good party." His gaze slid over to Ruby, and this time he dared to wink at her. "I had a great time."

Her body instantly filled with hot mortification. Ashton's eyes widened; his furrowed brows told her that he had not missed the exchange.

"Cool." Ashton's voice was flat as he attempted to feign disinterest. "Well, we just came over to grab Ruby. We're about ready to head home."

Ruby couldn't help but notice he wasn't asking if she was ready, but his blatant jealousy sent her over the moon regardless. She dismounted from the wall with a gleeful bounce in her step. "See you around, Remy!"

Remy surveyed them, his perpetually laughing eyes lingering on each of them, and she wondered what was going through his mind. Had he detected Ashton's jealousy, too?

Not that she cared. It didn't matter what Remy thought about them. She had no interest in what Remy thought about her or her life.

"Drive safe!" This time, Ruby was sure he waited for Ashton to look at him before he winked at her one more time. "Maybe I'll see you in Arizona."

5

In the days that followed, Ruby replayed the tense car ride home from the beach over and over in her head. Ashton's terse interrogation about Remy and his disapproving grunts were like music to Ruby's ears, and it was a welcome soundtrack to her chaotic last days at home. She was so thrilled by his sulkiness that she hadn't even been *that* annoyed to discover that Millie had given Ruby's phone number to Charlie without her permission. Ashton's thinly veiled jealousy was all she needed to glide through any challenges that awaited her, whether that might be timid texts from Charlie or the last-minute preparations for her move. For the first time since Millie's arrival, she felt genuine excitement.

Her final night at home found Ruby sitting on her back porch, gazing at her family's sprawling hillside ranch. When she was little, it had been home to three horses, a small grove of avocado and orange trees, and an ever-expanding garden where a new type of vegetable or herb would pop up every season. As she grew up, the ranch had grown, too, and now the property stretched for just about as far as Ruby could see. The bed-and-breakfast, aptly named Rancho Ortega B&B, sat at the foot of a hill that formed the boundary of what Ruby thought of as their backyard, though technically "yard" was a quaint way to think of the verdant compound. Her parents had acquired the land and building from a neighboring ranch about ten years ago and converted it into a charming twelve-room bed-and-breakfast. The first full-time employees they'd hired were a married couple named Jorge and Paola, who had looked after the land and hotel with such love and care that Ruby often thought of them as extensions of her family. The staff had grown as they expanded; her father and Jorge could be found debating the logistics of her father's next big goal for the business on an almost daily basis.

She heard the back door swing open behind her, and her father stepped outside carrying a glass of amber liquid. He didn't drink most nights, but he reserved his special sipping tequila both for hard days and for good days. Ruby wondered which type this was for him as he settled into the patio chair beside her.

He sighed. "I love the way this place looks at sunset."

The entire property had taken on a pinkish hue as the sun hovered slightly above the surrounding hills. A cool breeze rustled the avocado trees, and she could hear the faint sound of the horses bustling around in their stalls, snorting and whinnying to each other.

She smiled at him tenderly, savoring the wistful nostalgia in his voice. Both her parents loved this place, of course—but her father especially. For him, it was the embodiment of the American Dream.

It was *everything*. And while Ruby didn't quite feel the same deep gratitude or amazement toward each flower bud or bale of hay on the property, she did love how much her father loved it. And, of course, it was home. A beautiful home.

"I started saving to buy this land when I was in high school, you know," he said, beginning a story Ruby had heard countless times throughout her life. Normally this kind of repetition would strike her as boring, but not from her father. Things were always different with him; she could condone all sorts of stuff she'd never put up with from anyone else.

Besides, she loved this story.

"Of course, this neighborhood was nothing like it is now. Not a Starbucks or Pilates studio in sight—much more rural," he continued with a familiar snort. "Back then, people assumed I was the gardener when I showed up to this plot of land." Ruby joined him in an exasperated roll of their eyes. "We lived in a trailer while we were building this house, your mom and me. Can you imagine? Your mother living in a trailer!" He chuckled.

No matter how many times Ruby heard it, that part of the story was always hard for her to picture.

"We worked hard," he told her reverently. "We both worked full-time and spent every weekend at the farmers market with whatever crops we could get."

The way her father always described it, they were sustained by his ambitions—living frugally but fueled by the knowledge that his dreams would change all that. Her mother was usually a little blunter about the challenges, the realities of how taxing those years were, but she always reminded them that true partnership meant supporting one another through life's quandaries.

It was all very romantic to Ruby.

"And just look how far we've come," her father said with a sigh. "Look how far you can go with hard work, Ruby. Never forget that." His eyes swept over the scene before them, then settled back on her meaningfully.

Ruby nodded at him, this well-known family motto suddenly hitting her with new gravity now that she was facing so many imminent changes—changes she'd looked forward to, but changes that held unknown adventures, nevertheless.

She turned her gaze to the most recent addition to the ranch, at the east end of the property, what would soon be a full-fledged reception hall. Ortega Properties' gateway into the wedding-and-event industry. They'd held birthday parties and small functions on the B&B patio, but this expansion would allow for a whole new level of large-scale events. It was still in the preliminary phases, with just a concrete foundation and skeletal framework, but Ruby's father had already booked the inaugural event next summer. Just a few weeks ago, they'd celebrated the fact that California's first female governor, Claudia Cortez, whom her father had met at a chamber of commerce meeting years ago, wanted the space for a three-hundred-person event in July. She hadn't been super specific about what the event was, but she'd been adamant that she wanted to be the first to use it. Her father thought the governor was gearing up for a senatorial race, and even though Ruby wasn't particularly interested in politics, she was excited about this mystery soiree. For the most part, the day-to-day operations of the family business were incredibly boring to Ruby. But a big, fancy party full of important people? Well, that piqued her interest.

She sighed, letting out a breath of air that felt tight with emotion as it left her chest.

For the most part, the time she'd spent outside on the ranch had decreased as she got older, as her chores were handed over to full-time groundskeepers, but over the past few months, especially, she'd taken solace in this land that was her home. Sitting on the porch or taking a stroll through the property, patting the speckled muzzles of the horses or plucking a strawberry straight from the vine and sinking her teeth into it right there in the garden. She mostly spent this time mulling over her lovesick agony in Ashton's absence, an excuse for her to set her phone aside instead of anxiously willing it to summon a text from him. Now, on her final evening, she realized how much peace this place had brought her and how much she'd miss walking the land in times of turmoil. How weird that she'd have to find her footing without tromping over the familiar soil, without smelling the orange blossoms in the air, without the comfort of a world created by her parents precisely to give her a sense of belonging.

"Ruby Catherine, we are just so proud of you," her father continued, his voice barely concealing its emotional warble.

She folded her legs close to her chest so her cheek rested on her knees and smiled tenderly at him. In the fading light, she could see his eyes were glassy.

"When your grandmother came to this country, I was just a baby, you know." He spoke slowly and softly. He wasn't prone to tearful outbursts, and she could hear the restraint he exercised as he spoke. "After my dad left, she knew there was nothing in

Mexico for us, so she came here. Just me and her. She knew *yes*, *please*, and *thank you*, but beyond that, she spoke no English." He brushed away the tears brimming up in his eyes before taking a hearty swig of his drink. "She wanted two things. She wanted a ranch." Holding his glass, he gestured toward the sprawling yard. In the distance, Bonnie, the most vocal of the horses, whinnied, almost in response. "A ranch to keep us connected to her life back in Mexico, to our heritage and way of life. But she also wanted a step forward, more opportunities." He sipped his drink, sucking the tequila through his teeth noisily. "She wanted me to go to college. She talked about it all the time." He cast Ruby a meaningful glance and inhaled deeply. "As you know, that didn't happen for me. I'm proud of what I've accomplished, of course, but college just wasn't in the cards. It still breaks my heart I couldn't do that for my mom, who did *everything* for me, but I made all this happen; I gave us a home, roots here. And I made you and your sisters, and you will go to college. She'll get to see you accomplish that dream. You will be the first Ortega to graduate college. That's an amazing thing, Ruby."

At this point, he'd stopped trying to contain his emotions; two silent tears raced down his cheeks as he spoke. Ruby felt a sharp sting in the back of her throat as tears of her own threatened to escape. She nodded, her bottom lip quivering ever so slightly. This was a birthright that had been discussed regularly throughout Ruby's childhood. It was something she'd never questioned, but the imminence of finally fulfilling this generations-long family destiny hit her with unexpected weight.

"You are going to do amazing things, mija." It was a statement of fact, not a compliment, delivered with unwavering certainty. "But don't forget about home. Don't forget where you came from."

"*Daddy.*" She laughed, her voice catching in her throat as a half sob, half giggle. "I'll be a one-hour flight away. It's not as if I'm going away *forever*. I'll be back all the time."

A smile broke out across his face. His brown cheeks were rosy— from tears or tequila, or both. "I hope so. We'll miss you."

She smiled. "What time is Mama Ortega getting here tomorrow?"

A few weeks ago, when Ruby had daydreamed about moving day, she'd pictured herself driving across the desert to her new life in the passenger seat of Ashton's car. She hadn't spent much time or energy on how impractical or unlikely this scenario was. First of all, less than a tenth of her wardrobe would fit in the trunk space of Ashton's Prius, so the logistics of moving all her boxes were flat-out absurd. Plus, her acceptance into college was a ceremonious, collective Ortega accomplishment, like her father had said. There was *no* way they were missing any crucial moment of her experience— which included the road trip to Tempe and getting Ruby settled into her dorm room. She honestly wouldn't be surprised if they were planning on attending her first class with her. Her grandmother, who hadn't left California since she'd arrived in the United States fifty years ago, was driving up from Chula Vista in the morning to accompany them on the journey.

"You know your grandmother. We told her to be here by eight, so she'll probably arrive just before sunrise." He chuckled affectionately. "She's very excited, Ruby." He tilted his glass backward and loudly swallowed the final gulp of his drink. The last drops of tequila settled his tearfulness, and when he spoke again, his eyes were clear and his tone businesslike. "I'm glad we can get on the road early, though. I don't think they've put out that fire near Imperial, so traffic might be difficult—road closures, evacuations, you know."

Ruby nodded. They'd had a particularly dry summer, and the ever-present threat of the entire state burning to the ground was unavoidable—blackened hillsides and smoky horizons as common-place as street signs and stoplights.

"You're unusually quiet this evening," her father noted with a frown. "Are *you* excited?"

She was not the type of person who was easily excitable, due to her unerring expectation that what she desired would inevitably come to be, so it was an unusual feeling. For one of the first times in her life, she faced a future filled with new experiences and unknown possibilities—even if Millie was among those.

She grinned. "I am excited, Daddy."

"Well, I think we've both earned a *small* sip of tequila, then!" he announced, rising to his feet. "A toast to our first college-educated Ortega!"

Part Two

"And I shall seek you endlessly,
for I am a moth, and you're my flame.
Knowing that I'll burn
at your touch I return,
for you're a fire; untamed."

—Zubair Ahsan

6

Ruby emerged from the stuffy library building into the bustling, blaringly bright campus courtyard, muttering to herself irritably as she shoved her MacBook into the Louis Vuitton bag her parents had given her as a graduation gift. The four boys in her economics study group hurtled past her toward the stairs, laughing.

One of them, a guy named Parker, paused on the final step and turned to Ruby. "Did I tell you how cute you look today?"

Ruby's scowl did not falter. "No, that's about the only thing that didn't fly out of your big mouth. Don't you ever let anyone else talk?"

Parker grinned, clearly misreading Ruby's aggravation as flirty banter. "You're so funny. Let's hang out soon. I'll text you." He turned to race up the stairs too quick to catch the middle finger Ruby thrust up in the air at him.

She was the only girl in her economics study group, and every single time they met, she spent half the time being talked over or just being flat-out ignored—even though they certainly had no trouble paying attention to her at parties. The whole herd of those boys' club bozos had practically tripped over themselves trying to track down a mango hard seltzer for her at a tailgate last weekend after they got a good look at her in a crop top.

She should remind them that she'd gotten As on the past three tests even though she'd been hungover for two of them. Her father had always told her to let her work speak for itself, but if she had to listen to them mansplain capacity utilization again, she was going to scream.

She needed a cup of coffee.

She and Ashton had planned to meet up five minutes ago, but as she scanned the thinning crowd of ambling students, his distinct, lanky figure was nowhere to be found.

Gritting her teeth, she pulled out her cell to call him but discovered a text message from Charlie awaiting her instead.

CHARLIE

We on for dinner this weekend? 😀 😀 😀

She had to hand it to him: for as mild-mannered and timid as Charlie Hampton was, he sure was persistent. She hadn't been able to shake him since that night at the beach—though she suspected Millie's meddling was also a contributing factor.

Either way, she had accepted his offer to see a movie shortly after she'd moved, a few nights after her family had bid her farewell and returned to California. Earlier that day, she'd learned that Millie and Ashton were moving in together, and blinded by this distressing news, she probably would've agreed to medieval torture if the opportunity had presented itself.

He was hardly the only boy Ruby was using to distract herself from Millie and Ashton's love affair, although he was perhaps the most unlikely. But since he was among Ashton's circle of friends, she figured he was worth keeping around for the time being.

She quickly liked his message, the kind of noncommittal gesture that kept boys like him on the line, when she heard her name called in a voice that had recently begun haunting her nightmares. She forced a grim smile and turned to face Millie and Ashton.

Whenever she and Ashton made plans, he never mentioned including Millie, but still Ruby couldn't remember the last time she'd seen him alone. *Do they go to the bathroom together, too?*

"Hey, Ruby, how was class?" Before Ruby could remind Ashton that she hadn't been in class, he continued, "Have you called your parents recently?" Again, she opened her mouth to answer, but he cut her off. "I just got off the phone with my mom. She said they can see the smoke from the fire from their backyard. It's . . . really close."

"That's scary," she mumbled blandly. Ruby realized she wasn't exactly sure when she had last called home. A week ago? Maybe a little longer. "I'm sure it'll be fine, though. The fires get close sometimes, but they never make it across the highway."

Millie and Ashton nodded in unison, as if synchronized by shared thoughts.

For the first few weeks of school, Ruby had been really good about calling her mom each afternoon, walking back to her dorm after class. Her mom was so eager for details about her new life: what she was learning, who she was spending time with, what she was wearing, how she was feeling. She had always maintained a healthy—sometimes teetering on overzealous—interest in Ruby's comings and goings, but this information had been so readily accessible to her, she often didn't even need to speak to Ruby to find out about her day. A glance at her calendar, a quick chat with Elena or Carla, or a scan of her Instagram Story could provide all the facts her mother needed. But now, a state away, the flow of information had changed, and Ruby found herself in control of her own narrative for the first time. They'd talked for nearly two hours the first week; it had almost been like catching up with an old friend she hadn't seen in years, even though they'd actually been apart only a matter of days. It was the first time in their relationship that Ruby felt as if she weren't recounting the events of her day for her mother's approval but just having a two-way conversation with someone who was genuinely interested in her life.

Recently, though, Ruby was often busy. Whether it was texting Ashton, going out with classmates, or that one time last week when she ended up making out in the common room with the tall guy who lived three doors down—her daily phone calls had sort of fallen by the wayside.

Later, she told herself. *I'll call her later.*

She crossed the plaza and nabbed a vacant patio table with Ashton and Millie, just outside the student union. She recalled passing these tables, shaded by sail-like awnings, on the first few days of school and wondering who would possibly sit outside in this heat. It was so hot that the metal chairs literally burned grid lines into people's legs when they tried to sit down. More than once, Ruby had questioned her decision to abandon the moderate climate of San Diego as the relentless sun of her new home induced waves of sweat and homesickness. But finally, October arrived and the triple-digit temperatures eased into a gentle breeziness that wasn't exactly autumnal but at least tolerable.

Ashton scurried inside to get coffees as the girls settled themselves at the table. Across the courtyard, a small demonstration about immigration was going on. These kinds of rallies had initially shocked and intrigued Ruby; on several occasions, she'd endured an extra moment in the sweltering sun to read the signs of protestors and listen to their demands, but now she'd come to understand how commonplace they were on college campuses.

"Hmm, they're noisy today," Ruby murmured, trying to sound casual despite the curiosity she still felt when she saw groups like this.

Before arriving at school, she'd never really seen a protest like this up close, firsthand—certainly not in the close-knit, harmonious community in which she'd been raised. She wasn't naive; she knew they happened all the time. She'd seen the news, and she had TikTok, of course. It was just that Buena Valley never had any need for such discord as a protest—at least, none that Ruby knew of.

At school, though, it seemed there was a different demonstration every day, a new cause that needed their attention. Equal pay, climate change, human trafficking—there was no end to it. Though she had stopped lingering in front of every group of activists— honestly, who had the time for that?—Ruby's mind nevertheless boggled at all the ways in which the world was in crisis.

Millie nodded, her eyes lingering on the group thoughtfully. "Oh yes. In this human rights course I'm taking, we just had a panel on growing anti-immigration sentiment in the US. One of the girls in the class shared about having her car vandalized because she wore her hijab to school. They spray-painted the word *terrorist* on it. I just . . . I can't believe people act like that, you know? I can't even imagine what that's like."

Ruby's eyes narrowed in scrutiny, studying Millie while she was still distracted. Was she really this openly distressed, or was it all some sort of doe-eyed act?

She just couldn't figure this girl out.

"Charlie says he's seeing you this weekend?" Millie said brightly, her focus shifting back to Ruby.

Ruby shrugged. She could see Ashton inside the union, waiting patiently for their coffees to be made. His constant efforts to do kind things for her were a large part of her love for him—even if these thoughtful deeds were now lumped in with Millie.

"You two sure have been seeing a lot of each other," Millie continued, an expectant smile plastered on her freckled face.

"I don't know if I'd say 'a lot,'" Ruby responded dryly, hoping her nonchalance would quell some of Millie's eagerness.

Before Millie could inquire further, thankfully, Ashton approached with three hot coffees balanced in his hands. He stooped to place the paper cups on the table and bestowed a kiss on Millie's cheek before taking a seat.

Millie beamed. "Well, all I know is, he talks about you all the time. I think he's really head over heels for you."

Ruby had no reaction to this piece of information. Instead, she took a small sip from her cup, trying to suppress her mild irritation that Ashton had forgotten she liked cream in her coffee.

Ashton cocked an eyebrow at Millie. "Are you talking about Charlie? Oh yeah, Ruby, he's got it bad." He laughed, a strange nervous sound that puzzled and pleased Ruby. "But I guess that's nothing new for you. Guys have lost it over you for years."

Ruby smiled and quickly searched Millie's expression for a hint of jealousy. Did it bother her that her boyfriend thought of Ruby as someone who was known for capturing the attention of any male who crossed her path? *Well, almost any male*, Ruby thought with a sideways glance at Ashton. But, if it did bother her, Millie didn't show it.

"Oh, you know what? The four of us should do something together!" Millie suggested happily, patting Ashton's arm. "What about this weekend?"

"Um." Ruby shifted her weight on her chair.

"Oh, it'll be so fun! How's Saturday? Maybe at our place?" Millie tittered, practically luminous with excitement.

Ugh. An evening with both Millie and Charlie was hardly what she'd call a good time, but she rarely passed up an opportunity to hang out with Ashton. It would be an unpleasant challenge, but nothing she couldn't handle.

"Ashton, don't you have class?" She scrambled for a subject change as, all around them, students began to clear the courtyard, closing laptops and slinging backpacks over their shoulders before wandering toward the surrounding buildings.

Ashton's eyes flitted to Millie's for a brief private moment before he responded. Ruby couldn't decide if they'd just silently communicated something important between the two of them or if this was just one more nauseatingly intimate display of affection she was subjected to. He shook his head. "No, not today. It's canceled."

"Weird. You seem to have had a lot of those lately." They were in the midst of midterms, and Ruby felt like all her work had doubled, while Ashton's appeared to have been cut in half. He didn't look at her as she rose and collected her things. "Well, thanks for the coffee. I guess I'll see you this weekend."

"Oh!" Millie sounded surprised. "That was so quick. You're so busy, though. Okay, well, yes, we'll see you soon! I'll text you!" she called as Ruby walked away, waving dismissively over her shoulder at the annoyingly happy couple.

RUBY'S ROOMMATE, A SHY BUT SWEET GIRL NAMED PATTY, had been randomly assigned by the powers of the residential-life department. The nameplate on their door the first day of school had read PATRICIA PETERS, but Patty had insisted that Patricia was too old-fashioned and that she always went by Patty. She was nothing like the girls Ruby had hung out with in high school, but Ruby hadn't ever liked any of those girls anyway. She didn't have much experience with sharing such a small living space—or sharing anything, really—but she figured, as far as roommates went, quiet, clean, and kind Patty Peters was a pretty good one.

Patty's round-faced, curly-haired presence was more or less a constant in their small dorm room. She occasionally popped out for midafternoon chai lattes at the Dutch Bros around the corner, where her girlfriend, Hannah, worked, but other than for her classes, she rarely ventured farther than their dorm building. Whether Ruby was stumbling home after a night out or returning from class, Patty was almost always sure to be snuggled in bed, cheerily tapping away on her laptop.

It was barely five o'clock as Ruby returned from her overcrowded coffee date, and as expected, Patty was already in her donut-patterned pajamas and puttering around her side of the room, humming along to a Taylor Swift song playing softly in the background.

"Oh, hi, Ruby!" They'd been living together for nearly three months, and still Patty always sounded pleasantly surprised to see her. "Look what arrived!" She gestured toward Ruby's desk, where there sat a crystal vase full of bright, beautiful flowers.

Ruby indulged in a self-satisfied smile and—despite the fact that she had just witnessed him fawning all over Millie—felt a pinch of hope that they were from Ashton, a covert gesture of his true feelings.

Patty hovered giddily as Ruby retrieved the card. "Do you know who could have sent them?"

She gave a quick shake of her head as her eyes scanned the card. When her gaze finally fell on the signature, her stomach tightened.

Whatever she'd expected, it certainly wasn't this.

7

"You *are the* most intrusive, self-assured—"

"Thoughtful, generous, *charming* man you've ever met." Despite the fact that she'd immediately launched into her tirade as soon as Remy had answered the phone, he did not miss a beat in finishing her sentence for her.

She couldn't resist the urge to roll her eyes and, as if sensing it, he added, "I reserve the right to buy you pretty things whenever I feel like it, Ruby Ortega."

"How did you even know my address?" she demanded, determined to ignore what Remy surely thought was endearing banter.

"I'm very resourceful."

She figured asking how he'd known peonies were her favorite flower would only further validate this bizarre breach of boundaries and his obviously high opinion of himself, so she let that one go. She sighed. "So this is just a random, out-of-the-blue, no-strings-attached, enormous floral arrangement?"

"I didn't say that," he said warmly. "I always have a reason for the things I do."

"Which is?"

"I'd like you to accompany me to a fundraising gala this weekend."

The words suddenly caught in her throat. Though she found him to be arrogant and flamboyant, it was difficult to cling to her annoyance as he spoke. She couldn't deny the appeal of donning a pretty dress for a fancy party—even if her date wasn't exactly the target of her affections.

"Well, what's the fundraiser for?" She was stalling, pacing back and forth in front of their doorway with her phone pressed to her ear.

"Does it matter?" he retorted smoothly. "Don't make me beg, Ruby. Say yes."

She almost laughed. *Remy? Beg? Fat chance of that.*

"It's at La Princesa Resort downtown," he continued. "There will be good food, good drinks. You can't tell me you aren't sick of dining hall food by now. Just say yes, okay? I don't want to go to this thing alone."

"What if I already have a date?" She was glad he wasn't there to see the smug smile that had found its way to her face.

"Cancel it," he countered without hesitation, as if it were well within his rights to impose upon her schedule like this.

She had a difficult time believing Remy didn't have other options, but she was nonetheless flattered by his persistence. "Fine. I'll go."

"Great. I'll pick you up at six thirty." She could hear him grinning.

"You should wear green again, like the dress at the quinceañera. You look good in green."

Again, her stomach fluttered, but she didn't let on as she shot back, "I'll look good in anything. See you Saturday."

He was laughing when she hung up.

AS RUBY WAITED FOR REMY TO ARRIVE SATURDAY NIGHT, SHE admired her reflection in the mirror mounted on the back of their bathroom door. She'd borrowed a dress from Patty's girlfriend, Hannah, who, fortunately for Ruby, was both the same size as Ruby and very generous. Of course, Ruby would've preferred to buy a new dress; it had been forever since she'd been shopping. However, that would've meant calling home to ask for extra money on top of her modest monthly allowance, and since she still hadn't called to ask about her family's safety and proximity to the fire, she felt guilty about finally reaching out only to beg for more money. Besides, that would've probably invited a whole other line of questioning, which she didn't really feel like including her parents in. She knew her father liked Remy. But respecting him as a colleague and wanting him to date his daughter were two completely different things.

Either way, Hannah's collection of formal wear had been a perfectly fine plan B. She had picked a floor-length gossamer gown with a high neck and open back, featuring a delicate pattern of light green and pink flowers. She felt pleased that it still included the color Remy had wanted without being obvious that she'd cared about his preferences when choosing her outfit.

After all, he wasn't wrong. I do look good in green, she thought, smoothing her hand down the skirt.

Her hair wasn't being cooperative today, and it was making several wiry attempts to spring from the bobby pins and hair spray securing it in a low bun at the nape of her neck. Even with a few fly-aways, she still looked pretty—a sentiment that had been affirmed by Patty as she had bustled to the laundry room with a hamper perched against her hip.

Earlier she'd received a text from Charlie telling her to have fun tonight and asking when he could see her next. He'd been fishing for details ever since she'd canceled their double date with Millie and Ashton. If Ashton had been the one to ask, she would've eagerly disclosed more information in hopes of sparking some jealousy, but she didn't really feel the need to boast about her evening with a guy who was essentially the physical embodiment of tall, dark, and handsome to poor, average Charlie.

She ignored his message. She'd wait until Ashton was around to drop hints about Remy's wealth and maturity. She'd omit his obnoxiousness, of course.

No sooner had she set her phone down than she heard a curt knock at her door. The entrances to her dorm building all required a swipe of an ID card to unlock, so she'd expected to receive a phone call from Remy waiting to be admitted. But there he was, in a charcoal suit and crisp white shirt, the black leather of his shoes and belt gleaming almost as distinctly as his eyes. He was six minutes early, and she was begrudgingly pleased with his punctuality, a value her father had always emphasized as important. When Charlie picked her up for their dates, he was usually a few minutes late, flustered and sputtering about some mishap or another.

"You look surprised to see me," Remy said with a cocked eyebrow, bypassing a formal greeting altogether. "You weren't expecting someone else, were you?" The smile that played on his lips was more teasing than friendly.

Ruby flushed. Maybe this had been a mistake, after all. There was no doubt that Remy looked refined, but each time they met, she was struck with the impression that there was something a little dangerous about him.

"I just figured I'd need to meet you downstairs," she said brusquely, stepping aside so he could enter the room. "I forgot your pushiness knows no bounds."

"Resourceful, remember?" he said with a wink. "I was walking in as someone was walking out. They pointed me in the right direction." He looked around the room curiously, lingering by Ruby's desk. At first, she thought he was admiring the flowers he'd sent her, which occupied a large portion of the cluttered desktop. But before she could even worry that he'd realized the flowers were so close to her pillow because she enjoyed smelling them before bed— which surely would've inflated his already enormous ego—she saw that something else had caught his attention.

Mounted on the wall above her desk was a small bulletin board, which was what Remy appeared to be examining. She was familiar enough with the photos to know what he saw: a few snapshots of her family at her own quince; at Elena's quince; a trip to Disneyland with some friends at the end of senior year; her in her graduation gown, hugging Mama Ortega; and in the top right corner, two pictures of her with Ashton. She could tell by Remy's craning neck that those were the target of his focus.

One was from Ashton's senior prom, about three years ago. They hadn't gone together; this had been about a year before Ruby's romantic epiphany that he was more than her dorky compatriot. Ashton had taken his chemistry lab partner, and Ruby had gone with a guy on the basketball team. But before they'd met up with their respective dates, they'd gathered in Ashton's backyard to take a few pictures just the two of them. In this picture, they were scrawnier, ganglier versions of themselves, faces shiny with excitement and the last remaining vestiges of puberty. They stood side by side, not even touching, and Ruby was often awed by how these goofy kids had no idea what kind of emotion was in store for them.

Pinned next to this picture was the infamous shot of Ruby and Ashton as toddlers, naked in a bathtub together. He was handing her a toy boat, and Ruby's chubby face was scrunched up in laughter.

Remy glanced over his shoulder at her. He didn't have to say anything. The ridicule in his eyes spoke for itself, and for the second time in three minutes, Ruby felt her cheeks turn scarlet.

"It's a nice room you have here," he noted, finally turning away from the bulletin board and letting his eyes sweep over the rest of the room. She and Patty had spent a good portion of the morning cleaning: making their beds, vacuuming, throwing out the expired string cheese from the minifridge—most of which was Ruby's mess. "How are classes going? How's school?"

"Classes are going well," she replied flatly. She approached school as she did most things in life: with an unrelenting deter-mination, as if it were impossible to be anything but successful, so to her, this question seemed a little obvious. "School's good. I like it here. I've met some nice people. I like my roommate. I stay busy."

His eyes settled on her in a searching way as he nodded. Whenever he looked at her, she couldn't shake the feeling that something else stirred beneath the inky surface of his irises, as if he weren't just looking at her but scanning her insides to fulfill some secret objective.

It made her heart go haywire every time.

At last, his wry expression dissolved into a grin. "Well, you look good, Ruby. Those green eyes of yours in that dress?" He let out a soft appreciative whistle as he gestured toward her. "It's really good to see you."

She'd been on high alert since he'd gotten here, his inquisitive presence inspiring a quick-pulsed defensiveness almost instantly. But to her relief, it seemed he was ready to behave himself.

"It's nice to see you, too. I was a little surprised to hear from you," she said motioning toward the bouquet of flowers. They'd ex-changed a few text messages since she'd moved, but nothing more than restaurant recommendations or casual joking. Though he always initiated the conversation, he was also the one who contin-ually failed to respond to the last message. Ruby told herself he was a busy person and probably just forgot from time to time, but the consistency of this pattern made a small part of her wonder if it was some sort of weird power move—mostly because it was a tactic she had employed on a handful of occasions. Also, considering he apparently only lived a few miles from campus, she was a little perplexed that almost four months had elapsed since that night at the beach without him making an effort to see her.

Remy's mouth twitched almost imperceptibly, like something had occurred to him, but he caught himself before he uttered whatever it was out loud. "¡Vámonos! Are you ready?"

Ruby retrieved her handbag from where it rested on her bed and nodded. "I'm ready when you are."

8

"I can't believe you drive a pickup," she said with a wrinkled nose as they approached the glossy black truck parked outside her dorm building.

Remy cocked a dark eyebrow as he opened the passenger door for her.

"I just assumed you'd drive something ridiculous and over-the-top, like a Ferrari," she said as she collected the skirt of her dress in one hand and climbed inside.

He let out an amused cackle before firmly shutting the door. Though she could no longer hear him as he crossed in front and made his way to the driver's side, he appeared to still be chuckling to himself.

As he settled into his seat, Ruby asked again what kind of fundraiser they were attending. He still hadn't provided any details since his initial invitation.

"It's a gala to raise money for the evacuation centers helping people affected by the fires," he explained as they merged onto the freeway.

Again, a squeeze of guilt struck her. She was sure her family was fine, but she really did need to call home.

"How did *you* get involved? Are charity functions a regular thing for you?" she asked. His eyes were focused on the road, and she took this opportunity to study his profile, framed against the whirring desert outside his window. She watched his full lips curl up into a smile.

"Yes and no. Because of my business, lots of organizations reach out to me to see if I can support their cause in any way—donating, promoting, whatever. I obviously can't say yes to all of them—but this one was kind of mutually beneficial." He tapped his fingers along his steering wheel.

"What does that mean?"

"Well." He tilted his head to the side, as if trying to decide on the correct words. "They asked me to donate some services to their silent auction." He glanced at her out of the corner of his eye. "Do you know what my app does?" Ruby shook her head. "Okay, well, long story short, it basically lets hotel guests have more personalized, special experiences wherever they go—creature comforts or things that reflect their interests."

Ruby frowned. "What does that mean?" she repeated, a little more impatiently.

"Well, at first it started as a way for small places, kind of like your B&B, to stay relevant, especially in areas that aren't served by Grubhub or Uber Eats or anything that can provide those on-demand services. But now it's also grown into much more extravagant, niche things, too. Users can request special decorations or specific food and drink or activities; it's pretty broad. It allows consumers to design their own vacations down to the littlest detail."

"People are willing to pay extra for that kind of thing?" she asked, incredulous that someone would bother downloading an app and paying to make sure their hotel had the correct birthday banner or right brand of soda in the minibar. Though she supposed she didn't spend enough time at the B&B's front desk to know if that was something guests really wanted.

Remy nodded, an expression of amusement on his face that said he fully recognized how silly it was. "It's especially big with the bachelorette crowd, but we are seeing lots of growth with birthdays and anniversaries. I think it's about the VIP experience, more than anything else. Like it doesn't really matter if what they're requesting is a big deal, as long as they feel like it is, you know?"

Ruby wasn't sure she understood completely, but she definitely recognized the importance of status and exclusivity, so she was willing to grant the concept some credit. "If you say so. What did you donate?"

"Two things, sort of. I have some connections and resources in the hospitality industry, which is obviously tapped right now with people being forced out of their homes." He glanced at her, as if gauging her reaction. "I've donated a couple nights at this cool property I work with in Austin that includes a customizable pub crawl; people can select different themes and bars and all sorts of specialized components. One group did a karaoke crawl in wigs and roller skates. Anyway, all of the proceeds from the winning bidder will go toward food and water for people being lodged at Buena Valley Community College. They've converted their basketball stadium into temporary housing for people displaced by the fires."

Ruby nodded. "What's the other thing you donated?" she asked, trying to temper her interest. She was struck with her need to manipulate her feelings around him—to tone down her curiosity—like they were playing a game of emotional poker. It wasn't a new feeling for her; she often found herself playing coy with guys, but Remy seemed to be in on the game as well. And *that* was certainly new.

"Well, this is where it gets into the mutually beneficial part. I can't just hand out free things whenever people ask. I've got a business to maintain and grow." He eyed her again. "I created a promo code for people who have been displaced by the fires to have discounted stays at our affiliate properties. The evacuation centers and aid agencies are helping me advertise."

She frowned. "I'm assuming you charge some sort of fee when people stay at these 'affiliate properties'?" At this, he nodded. "So, you're basically profiting off people who lost their homes? How much is the discount?"

"I'm a business—a *small* business. I'm not the Red Cross!"

"How much is the discount?" she pressed.

"Fifteen percent."

"Fifteen percent!" she guffawed, a shocked cackle bursting through her words. "That's not a donation—that's a marketing campaign!" Her voice had risen, but she wasn't angry. She couldn't believe his shamelessness, his audacity to pass this scheme off as charity when it barely scratched the surface of helping others. It was so . . . bold. So brazen. It was astounding that he could not only get away with something like that but be praised for it. She was fascinated.

He tsked. "Listen, Ruby. Someone's going to profit off this whole mess. People are going to need new homes, new things. Why shouldn't it be me?" As she shook her head in mild disbelief, she could see the approaching silhouette of the resort, castle-like in its adobe-style angles, framed by a pink sunset as Remy exited the freeway. "This hotel uses our app. You can choose different air fresheners for your room or have a personal sushi chef cater for you." The truck slowed as they approached the valet stand, and Ruby began to unbuckle her seat belt. "You can even have the beach towels monogrammed to take down to the pool with you."

Ruby rolled her eyes at him. "Well, fiddledeedee. Isn't that fancy!"

FROM THE MOMENT THE VALET APPEARED IN A TUXEDO complete with pristine white gloves to open the passenger door of Remy's truck and guide her to the curb, Ruby was transported to a scene of pure extravagance and wonder unlike anything she had ever experienced.

A kind of Christmas-morning glee overtook her as Remy appeared by her side, placing his hand on the small of her exposed back and sending fireworks of delight throughout her entire body. He handed the valet a folded twenty-dollar bill with an unthinking naturalness and led her through the tall glass doors of the hotel lobby.

They floated across the marble floors toward a welcome table, where a woman in a plunging Versace gown with a volunteer badge pinned on one of the beaded straps checked them in with a squeal and a warm full-body hug for Remy. Ruby couldn't help but notice the familiar way she patted Remy's bicep as she asked how he was.

"Ruby, this is Isabelle Wyatt. Her father owns a chain of steak houses I've worked with, and Isabelle's generously starred in a couple of the promotional videos for Capitán's social media."

"Capitán?" Ruby repeated.

Isabelle shot Ruby a withering stare underneath winglike false eyelashes. "His *app*."

"*Be the capitán of your own adventure*," Remy quipped, with the practiced cadence of a market-tested slogan. He winked at Ruby.

"Well, as long as you promise to find me later so we can catch up, I'll get you your name tags and you two can be on your way," Isabelle purred, bending over a box of paper badges in such a pro-vocative way, Ruby half wondered if she'd get paper cuts along her cleavage.

She handed Remy two sets of name tags and a small white gift bag, which Remy immediately passed to Ruby. A discreet peek inside the tufts of tissue paper revealed a box of Godiva chocolates and a travel-size bottle of La Mer body crème.

Not too shabby.

Isabelle flitted off to try her hand at seducing someone else, and Remy pinned his name tag to the lapel of his suit before handing Ruby her own. REMY BUSTILLOS—CAPITÁN was now emblazoned across his chest on thick card stock.

Ruby peered down at the flowing folds of fabric of her dress, trying to decide the least obtrusive place for her guest badge.

"Need any help?" he asked with a wily wiggle of his eyebrows.

Ruby rolled her eyes, clipped the name tag to the strap of her purse, and marched forward into the open ballroom, following the sounds of polite laughter, the tinkle of cocktail glasses, and the soft melody of a live string quartet.

She had grown up with parties literally in her backyard, in an elite world marked by private school polos, nannies, and yacht club memberships—but this? This was something else.

She was still gaping when Remy stepped beside her, swiftly snagging two gold-rimmed champagne flutes off the tray of a passing waiter and extending one to her. He smiled as she tried to compose herself.

"This is a *fundraiser*? Maybe one less chocolate fountain and they'd be able to buy more blankets for the poor, homeless children," she scoffed in bewilderment. Though the ambiance thrilled her, it did not escape her how strange it was to be surrounded by luxury to benefit people who had lost everything.

Immediately, Ruby plucked an oyster off the tray of another passing waiter, where the half shells rested in a spiral arrangement on a bed of ice. Her eyes sparkled greedily as she pressed the chilly shell to her lips and tilted her head back. As she slurped the oyster into her mouth, cool and salty and delicious, Remy stepped toward her and whispered into her ear, "You know, oysters are aphrodisiacs."

She coughed in surprise at this crass remark, puckering her lips to make sure she didn't spit the oyster out across the room. She wound up with the uncomfortable feeling that it was about to pop out her nose. She clasped her hand over her mouth, inhaled deeply, and managed to swallow it, all the while glowering fiercely at Remy.

He took a sip of his champagne. "*That*, however," he said, gesturing toward her with a grin, "was not an aphrodisiac."

She rolled her eyes yet again but couldn't bite back her own laughter. "You're disgusting."

"Yes, well. I contain multitudes. All the best people do, don't they?" A moment passed between them while he gazed at her with undeniable fondness, the corners of his eyes crinkling in a warm smile. He cleared his throat. "Mind if I introduce you to a few people? This is one of those schmoozing and networking kinds of things."

Though the instinct to fire back another teasing quip certainly rose, instead she just nodded. She may not have had romantic feelings for Remy, nothing that even compared to how she felt about Ashton, but she could not deny that she found everything about this evening deeply exhilarating. The fineries. The elegance. The other-worldly adultness of it all. It was unbelievable.

And she had to admit, so was Remy. He had his rough moments when he was a bit too much in all the wrong ways, but he was still . . . fascinating. Something inside Ruby sparkled and fizzled watching him. The hearty boom of his laughter, the brilliance of his smile, the cavalier way he retrieved his business card from the silk-lined pocket of his jacket. Ruby found it mesmerizing.

Found *him* mesmerizing.

And she suspected those feelings were not one-way. As they moved throughout the evening, she kept looking up to find those dark, bottomless eyes fixed on her, no matter what was going on around them. And each time she met them, the flicker of excitement inside her chest burned hotter.

Ruby accepted a second glass of champagne as they perused the silent auction prizes. Remy's hotel package in Austin had sold for eight thousand dollars, and he was so pleased, he bid on an Hermès clutch for Ruby. He didn't win, but Ruby was impressed he'd stayed in the running until the price surpassed five thousand dollars.

After dinner, the organizing committee of the gala gave a toast to the supporters and encouraged further donations. They asked Remy to stand and thanked him for the discount program he was offering victims of the fire. Ruby had found herself delighted to see his bronze cheeks take on a rosy tinge; she wasn't sure if he was embarrassed by the unmerited gratitude or the fact that she had burst into an insuppressible fit of giggles at the whole facade.

He settled into his chair and leaned toward her. The smell of alcohol mixed with the sharp scent of his cologne was a heady combination. "Let's go get some fresh air," he murmured silkily. She was distinctly aware of how many people were still watching him—*them*—and she turned to look him in the eye.

Ruby agreed to wait for him on the patio while he grabbed a bottle of champagne for the two of them. Rising from the table, she swore she could feel his eyes following her as she walked away.

Outside, she strolled to the edge of the patio. Standing with her arms on the stone railing, she gazed out at the glittering desert sprawled before her. The early autumn heat had given way to something arid but pleasant now that the sun had set. The silhouettes of the mountains were dark and sharp against the twinkling lights of the city.

Not far from her, a group of girls about her age were gathered around the patio furniture, sipping brightly colored drinks and gossiping in slurred, snickering tones.

"You saw he's here, right? I *told* you he would be," one laughed.

"I've never actually seen him out, just pictures. He's even hotter in person." Her friend snorted. "My brother showed me some article about him. It said he's one of twenty-five under twenty-five tech leaders to watch, or something. He was the youngest one on there! It called Capitán . . . what was it? Delightfully frivolous or frivolously delightful? Whatever it was, my brother says the idea wasn't even his. That he stole it from his frat brother or something before he got expelled his freshman year."

Ruby turned her head slightly. Her back was still toward them, but she could see their outlines, hunched together as if sharing secrets. Unaware, in their drunken state, how loud they were actually speaking.

"I saw a TikTok about him, too," the first girl said. Wisps of her dark hair bobbed as she spoke. "It said he was practically begged by producers to join one of those sex-island reality shows, you know, where people go to some weird location and just hook up nonstop. He apparently declined for business reasons, but I bet it was because he'd already slept with most of the girls on the show." She hooted, tilting her head back wildly.

A third girl shoved her friend's shoulder playfully. "I heard he hooks up with someone at every hotel he works with."

These rumors should've appalled Ruby, she realized; her parents certainly would not have approved—especially her mother. From his Instagram alone, she'd suspected he led a colorful life. But mostly, listening to these girls gossip and fawn over Remy, she felt a perverse pride to have won the attention of someone who was at the heart of such salacious scandal.

Even before he swept a tendril of her hair off the back of her neck with his fingertips, Ruby sensed Remy was near because the girls had suddenly fallen into a stifled silence that filled Ruby with an inimitable sense of superiority. She turned to face them, relishing their wide-eyed awe, before smiling at the handsome young man holding a bottle of Veuve Clicquot in one hand and a plate of ahi tuna crostini in the other. The languid way his eyes swept over the cluster of girls suggested he knew what they were talking about but didn't care. He smirked at Ruby as he balanced the plate along the railing and muscled the cork out of the bottle with a satisfying pop.

"Are you trying to get me drunk?" She laughed, watching him.

He paused, his expression suddenly serious. "Are you drunk?" His gaze flicked to her half-empty glass of champagne before returning to her face.

She laughed again, this time a little louder, a little more forced. She had only been joking—flirting, if she was completely honest. She hadn't expected him to respond so somberly. She shook her head. "No. This is only my second glass."

He nodded but did not make any move to pour the opened champagne.

"Really," she said, yanking it out of his hands and taking a hearty swig straight from the bottle. She flashed him a playful grin as the cool bubbles dissolved on her tongue. "So you're kind of famous at this party." She was just as eager for a subject change as she was to get more information about what she'd overheard from those girls. She held the bottle back out to him.

"Oh?" He took a quick sip and cocked an eyebrow at her.

"People seem to know a lot about you."

"Ah," he said with a bark of laughter that shook him so much, champagne sloshed out of the bottle. "I think you mean *notorious*, not *famous*." He took another drink, a longer one, maintaining eye contact. "Is that a problem?"

"I haven't decided yet." Ruby fought her own smile, determined to keep her expression as even as possible, but from the way Remy's eyes glimmered, she doubted she was successful.

He extended the bottle back out to her. "You know, I made reservations for us here tonight," he said breezily, tipping his chin toward the hotel.

Ruby froze, arm outstretched. "I—you . . . *what*?"

Another roar of laughter rolled through him. "Relax. I got you your own room—though I certainly wouldn't turn you away from mine, if that's what you wanted," he said, his voice so deep and smooth it almost sounded like a purr.

She tugged the bottle out of his hand and again raised it to her own mouth. The thrill of having her lips against something that had just touched his made the bubbles even more delicious.

"I was just trying to be a responsible adult and avoid drinking and driving," he added, his eyes flashing as he watched her. "People do reckless things after a few drinks, you know."

RUBY AWOKE SLOWLY THE NEXT MORNING, SAVORING THE buttery softness of the sheets on her skin as her eyes fluttered open. As she sat up, gazing around the immaculately decorated hotel suite, with its plush cream furniture and modern artwork, she caught herself smiling.

Last night was . . .

She sighed.

It was something. She couldn't deny it.

She looked down to note she was wearing a cozy fleece robe. A cursive *R* enclosed in a red heart was embroidered on the left-hand side right over her own heart, undoubtedly the work of Capitán. She wasn't sure if the *R* stood for Ruby or Remy.

Memories of last night drifted in and out in fuzzy snippets as she rubbed her eyes sleepily. The champagne, the food, the *flirting*.

She could see Remy standing in the doorway of her room, framed by the fluorescent hallway lighting. It was late, and his eyes were glassy, but their intensity was relentless as he spoke to her in soft, deep tones that sent shivers down her spine. He was leaning against the doorframe, his head bent down toward her, his finger-tips tracing the length of her arm lightly in a way that was so gentle it rendered her immobile.

"I want to come in," he'd said. For a fleeting instant, his words had sounded a bit strained. "But not like this."

Whether "this" referred to the drinks they'd had or the romantic gray territory they inhabited where the omnipresent figure of Ashton loomed in the distance, she wasn't sure. Her feelings for Ashton, after all, were the secret that had brought them together, and they were the secret that held them apart. His clear desire had made her feel powerful, and he looked *striking*. But that didn't remove her love for Ashton from the equation. She had savored the tension for a moment more before whispering good night and closing her hotel door.

9

Once she had finally managed to peel herself from bed, Ruby was slightly relieved to discover a succinct text from Remy, saying he had an early flight but had arranged for a car to take her back to campus. She wasn't sure what to make of the confusing emotions last night had stirred up inside her, but she was certain she was not ready to face him again quite yet.

She was not relieved, however, to find Charlie waiting in the courtyard of her dorm building, pacing and muttering to himself as she climbed out of the town car. His expression changed from confusion to shock as he took in the sight of her: evening gown, bare feet, and mussed hair.

"Ruby." He gasped. His anxious eyes blinked furiously, as if her morning-after look was merely a result of poor eyesight.

"What are you doing here?"

He thrust two paper coffee cups in the air as if that were explanation enough.

"Okay," she began, but he cut her off.

"You—you cheated on me!" he yelped.

Ruby reddened as his volume drew the attention of a few snickering passersby exiting the dining hall. "Charlie, I—"

Eyes widened, he gestured toward Ruby's dress. "Look at you! You were out—*all night!*"

She rolled her eyes and folded her arms across her chest. "If you would just listen—"

"How could you do this to me?" he pleaded, his voice thick with tears, spittle flying from his mouth.

"I didn't—"

"Ruby, don't *lie* to me!"

There was clearly no point in explaining to a hysterical person— a person who wasn't even her boyfriend, a person she'd known for only a few months.

It didn't even matter that nothing had happened with Remy last night. *Well, maybe not* nothing, she thought as she recalled the electric jolt she felt every time he'd touched her. Either way, it was not worthy of this type of meltdown, especially from someone she saw as nothing more than a temporary plaything.

It was also seriously not worth being shamed in public. Charlie's bawling and squawking had attracted the attention of a small group of people who were peering at them from the nearest bike rack.

"I think you'd better go," she suggested as calmly as she could.

His pale blue, bloodshot eyes widened. He was obviously wondering how she could be so heartless as to dismiss him in this state, but Ruby saw this was going nowhere. He wouldn't let her get more than a few words out. He was not interested in an explanation. He wanted her to be in as much anguish as he was. He wanted an apology.

And that just wasn't going to happen.

He blinked, mouth agape, but did not move. So Ruby took her own advice and bolted upstairs to her room.

SHE WAS BACK OUT THE DOOR AGAIN MOMENTS LATER, ORdering an Uber and far too distracted to even notice whether Charlie had left yet.

She needed to see Ashton—*immediately.*

Her phone had started buzzing with incoming messages almost as soon as she'd changed out of her dress. A few from Charlie—*what more could he possibly have to say?*—a couple from Millie, and one cryptic, alarming one from Ashton: Ruby, I'm not sure what's happened exactly, but I think it's best you lay low for a while.

She couldn't decide what she found more infuriating: the fact that Charlie must've called Ashton and Millie the moment she walked away, or that Ashton was making this completely asinine request as a result.

Lay low? What the hell did that mean? Was Ashton seriously this pissed about this ridiculous misunderstanding?

There was only one way to find out, and it certainly did not involve "laying low"—a phrase that was hardly in Ruby's vocabulary.

Breathlessly, she hurled herself into the back seat of the Uber and tried to sort out what to say. *How can I make Ashton understand that even though I don't care about Charlie, I didn't try to hurt him? How can I say that the only reason I'd agreed to see Charlie or Remy was to distract myself from my feelings for him? How can I make any of that clear without sounding like a selfish bitch?*

She burst out of the car as it was rolling to a stop in the parking lot of Ashton and Millie's apartment complex, calling out a brief thank-you to the driver as she rushed toward the stairs. She bounded up to the second floor, taking the steps two at a time in sandals that, in her haste, she hadn't noticed were mismatched. Her phone began ringing as she spotted Ashton and Millie's door, and reflexively, she smashed it to her face. "What?" she barked.

She stumbled to a stop on their doorstep as her youngest sister, Carla, burst into tears.

10

"**Ruby!**" **Carla's voice** cried. "The fires—they're up to Vista Lane. They canceled school. Elena even said she heard the Trujillos lost their house. Their neighborhood was evacuated a few days ago, but Ruby, they don't live that far from us! The smoke is everywhere, and the police came to our door and said it's time for us to go. *Ruby,* what if the fires burn our house down?"

Ruby took a seat at the top of the stairs, her breath caught in her throat as her sister's frantic, hurried words sank in. Finally, she managed to cut in, "Carla, it's going to be okay. Everything will be okay. Can I please speak to Mom or Daddy?"

"They don't know I called. They didn't want to worry you at school. You've seemed so busy."

Ruby's stomach twisted. *What kind of daughter is too busy for this?*

"The news is saying people should evacuate," Carla said, her voice breaking. "But Daddy says they're overreacting. We're staying, but Ruby, it's just . . . it's so scary."

What an understatement, Ruby thought. "I know, Carla. I'm so sorry you have to go through this. Daddy knows what he's doing, though. If he doesn't think you need to evacuate, then I'm sure he's right."

"I wish you were here." Her voice was barely above a whisper. "Elena's a monster without you." She sniffled softly.

Elena was a monster with or without Ruby, but at least she was cowed into behaving tolerably from time to time as the middle sister. Ruby could imagine she was wildly exploiting the role of oldest child in Ruby's absence. Poor Carla.

"I know. I wish I was there, too. But everything's going to be okay. I love you, and Daddy loves you. He would never put you in danger. You know that, right?"

"Yeah, you're right," Carla said. "I love you, Ruby."

"I'll call you tomorrow. Chin up." She hung up but sat perched on the top step with her phone clutched between her hands for several minutes after the call had ended.

There had been no need for her to storm over here like this. She saw that now. Ashton would come around; they'd get through this. She should return to her dorm, call her parents, maybe.

She rose to leave but paused before she even took a step.

If the fires were this close to her house, surely Ashton's parents were freaking out, too.

She turned and lightly knocked on their front door. Millie swung it open, her golden eyes gleaming with sympathy and affection. "Oh, hi, Ruby. Are you okay?" Her voice was tender and sweet, as if she were speaking to a child who had just fallen off their bike.

"Yes. I mean, not really." She tried to peer around Millie. "Is Ashton home?"

Millie glanced apprehensively over her shoulder before inching the door closed ever so slightly; her thin frame occupied most of the narrow opening. "Oh, I'm not sure now is the best time."

Good lord, is everyone really this upset about my stupid fling with Charlie? It's not like I murdered him. With a quick flicker of thought, she wondered if Ashton was jealous that she'd been out all night with someone. How would he react if he knew it was Remy, of all people, that she'd been with? With great effort, she pushed that idea aside for the time being.

"Listen, I'm not here to talk about Charlie or whatever. I need to talk to Ashton. It's about his parents. Both of our parents."

Millie's protectiveness over Ashton as she mulled this over infuriated Ruby. Who was she to be the guardian of Ashton's well-being? Ruby had known him and his family her entire life; didn't that count for anything?

Finally, the trace of wariness disappeared from Millie's face and she stepped aside to allow Ruby in. "I'll go get him," she said, gesturing for Ruby to take a seat on the barstool in their small kitchen.

Millie crossed their living room and opened the sliding glass door to their patio space, where Ashton was doing . . . *sit-ups*? Maybe he was just sitting on the ground reading? But, with a second glance, Ruby realized she had been right the first time. He was dressed in gym shorts and a tank top, curling his lean body up toward bent knees. Millie knelt to talk to him, gently pulling one of his earbuds out of his ear. She had left the door ajar, and from across the room, Ruby could hear his labored breathing as she waited impatiently.

Since when does Ashton work out? Ruby wondered, staring at the peculiar sight in disbelief. She had vivid memories of Ashton bawling when his dad forced him to try Pop Warner football in third grade, and he'd sworn off anything more strenuous than a nature walk ever since.

After a couple of minutes, Millie uttered whatever magic words Ashton needed to hear. She helped him to his feet, and they both re-entered the apartment. Ashton's shaggy, golden hair was matted to his head, and his gray tank top bore rings of sweat under his arms and in the center of his chest. His slim frame looked strikingly different, the sinewy, taut muscles gleaming with sweat catching Ruby by surprise.

"Hey," he said coolly. "What's up?" He barely glanced at her as he walked straight to the fridge, retrieving a bottle of water without offering her one.

"I just talked to Carla. The fires are . . . really close. Our parents were told to evacuate." She was stunned at how weird it was to say this out loud, to refer to her own life in this way. She'd heard about people being evacuated on the news countless times, but to say these words about her own home and her own family felt incredibly unreal, like she was speaking in a language she never knew she could speak. "I just wanted to make sure you knew."

His flushed, moist cheeks turned pale before her eyes. "I—I knew it was a possibility, but . . ." He placed his hands on the counter to steady himself, and Ruby watched a bead of sweat trickle from his nose to the countertop.

"My family's not leaving," Ruby added. "So maybe it isn't as serious as it seems. Maybe that's why your parents haven't told you."

"Oh," he said with a frown, like he wanted to ask her a follow-up question but couldn't decide on the words. He sighed heavily. "Thank you for telling me. I'll call them right now."

Ruby nodded and stood, thinking about hugging him, telling him how thankful she was they had each other. He'd pull her to him, against his damp shirt, with his warm, wiry arms clasped around her, and they'd face this challenge together. They'd figure out how to cope with the anxiety of waiting to find out if their homes would survive this natural disaster.

But, to Ruby's dismay, Ashton was not the one to embrace her. As soon as Ruby was on her feet, Millie had seized her. "Oh, I can't even imagine how you must feel. But I'm sure everything will be fine. I know we will all get through this together!"

RUBY CALLED HER FATHER AS SOON AS SHE MADE IT BACK TO her dorm.

"Really, mija, the news is making it out to be worse than it is," her father said with audible weariness in his voice. "We are fine. It's just a little smoke."

Ruby sat in front of her laptop, studying a map of the fire activity and trying desperately to connect it to her father's nonchalance. Patches of dark red covered Buena Valley and the surrounding areas, and she couldn't shake the image of him standing at the window, watching flames lick the walls of the house as they spoke.

He loved their home, but surely he wouldn't jeopardize their family's safety for it.

Right?

"We're not even in a mandatory evacuation zone," he added, as if sensing her skepticism. "It's voluntary."

That didn't comfort her the way he'd likely expected it to. "Okay," she said slowly. "But you will leave if they tell you to, right, Daddy?"

"Claro que sí," he replied without hesitation.

"Okay," she said again. "And you'll let me know if you need anything? If there's anything I can do?"

"All you need to do is focus on your schoolwork and don't worry about us. We'll see you soon for Thanksgiving, when all of this mayhem has settled back down and we can laugh about what a strange adventure it's been. Really, mija, you'll be home before you know it."

She shut her laptop, unable to look at the map any longer. With a sigh, she willed herself to believe her father.

Everything would be exactly as it should be soon enough.

11

November brought the first chill in the air, but despite the pervasive cool breeze of autumn, Ruby felt trapped in a constant fever dream. From the moment she'd found out how close the wildfires were to Buena Valley, she'd felt the heat of anxiety creeping up on her at every turn. She tossed and turned at night in fits of sweaty wakefulness, and each morning she arose with aching eyes and throbbing temples. She trudged through her classes and schoolwork with the staggering, stumbling fatigue of a person lost in the desert, checking her phone constantly for updates.

The day after she'd spoken to her family, Ashton told her that his parents had evacuated. When she mentioned that to Carla, she learned that the Ortegas were, in fact, the only ones on their street who had chosen to stay—a detail that sent sharp pangs of panic throughout her entire body.

She trusted her father. He was smart and loving and responsible.

But he could also be stubborn, which she knew perhaps better than anyone because she was exactly the same way.

She was haunted by the sickening possibility that, at any moment, her family could be trapped inside the fiery inferno of their beloved home—and there was nothing she could do about it.

Charlie had reached out a few times following their fight, seeking amends and explanations. Even if she hadn't been completely preoccupied, she doubted she would've responded. His jealous and insecure overreaction had destroyed any fond, or even tolerant, feelings she'd once had toward him.

Remy had also been in touch, a couple days after the gala, with a picture of himself sipping a large neon-colored cocktail on a balcony overlooking Bourbon Street. He was in New Orleans for work, though the rowdy crowd behind him and the cheeky grin he wore hardly seemed fitting for a business function.

Salud was all he'd written, and though a tiny part of Ruby searched for some hidden meaning in a text that said nothing more than *cheers*, she ultimately found it just as hard to make sense of as those dark eyes that gleamed back at her in his picture. Anyway, the physical distance and his blissful ignorance of the chaos Ruby found herself immersed in made the night of flirting they'd shared feel as if it had taken place years ago. In another life. To another person.

It was easier just not to think about it.

She liked his picture and left it at that, deciding it was best not to share what was going on. Every news source imaginable, from CNN to BuzzFeed, had some sort of coverage of the fires, so she was sure Remy knew they'd made it farther south, even if he hadn't made the connection to her home quite yet. There was no need to burden him with the details of her own personal struggles. His only concern regarding the fires was how to use them to his benefit, and while that did annoy Ruby a little, she was mostly jealous of his detachment from the situation.

She desperately craved Ashton's empathy, longed to bear the weight of their worries together almost as much as she longed to return to a home that was as picturesque and unscathed as it was in her memories.

But he was as remote as ever.

She told herself he must've been as lost in his family's troubles as she was, and that explained why she never saw him on campus or heard from him anymore. She was drifting through her days, bobbing on the surface of her former life; Ashton must've been, too.

However, among all these mismatched figures ill-equipped to accompany her through these draining days, Millie emerged as a stolid and responsive force.

Well, "emerged" was putting it lightly. For such a courteous and unassuming girl, Millie barged her way into Ruby's life with shocking forcefulness. She was never rude, exactly, but she was absolutely insistent that she and Ruby needed each other.

Just a week ago, Ruby might have regarded spending her days alone with Millie as more painful than walking through the wildfire itself. But her defenses were down; she was stressed and exhausted. And she succumbed to Millie's assertive affection.

"You'd be surprised what you can get used to," Millie had told her. "It's always just been me and my dad, and when he used to leave for a shift, I remember feeling *so anxious*. I wouldn't calm down until he got home the next day, and then it would just start all over the next time he left. And then when he signed up for Phoenix Fire's wildland crew to help with fires across the country? He'd be gone for weeks at a time. Did I tell you he was sent out to Buena Valley with his crew a couple days ago? Well, anyway, I wish I could tell you it gets easier, but I think you just get better at living alongside the worry by staying busy and hopeful."

Everywhere she turned, Millie would be there, waiting outside her class with a cup of coffee and friendly smile, settling down at the library with a stack of books across from her, or insisting she come over to relax and watch a movie. Ruby had come to expect this kind of over-the-top compassion from Millie, but what surprised her most of all was Ashton's continued absence. Every time Ruby accepted one of Millie's various invitations, she clung to a thin hope that Ashton would show up, too, but he rarely did.

Where was he through all this? Was he avoiding her?

And why?

ONE EVENING, THREE DAYS INTO THE VOLUNTARY EVACUA-tion, Ruby was cleaning up the kitchen after Millie had insisted they treat themselves to midweek ice-cream sundaes and Ruby, never one to refuse a decadent dessert, had agreed. She'd asked about Ashton, like she did almost every time she saw Millie, and she'd gotten the same vague answer about errands or the gym, but tonight she was officially feeling alarmed by his absence.

Was it still because of the thing with Charlie? Because that felt like ages ago at this point. Or was there some other reason he didn't want to—couldn't bear to—see her? What the hell was going on? She missed him, but that feeling wasn't unique to him. Her days were ruled by the things and people she missed. She *needed* him.

Suddenly, the front door popped open, and Ashton crossed the threshold. Ruby caught what she thought was a brief flash of dismay on his face before he gave her a perfunctory smile and moved toward Millie.

He kissed Millie's cheek, asking distractedly about their day, and Ruby became immediately aware of an uneasiness in him. He was tense, nervous almost.

Her heart sank. "Oh, no, Ashton. What's wrong? Did you hear from your parents? What's happened?" Maybe the reason he'd been so distant was because he was shielding her from some awful news of their home. Immediately, she was equally irate with him for keeping anything from her and touched by his protectiveness.

He seemed surprised by this sudden line of inquiry, shaking his head. "What are you talking about? Nothing's wrong. I spoke to them, but they're fine. They're still at my aunt's house."

She nodded as he spoke. Surely if there were something wrong at home, she would've heard it from her family anyway. She should've felt relieved, but Ashton still appeared to be on edge.

Millie patted his shoulder and smiled at him lovingly. "I think you should get it over with, Ash. Just tell her. Don't drag it out."

Ruby's eyes darted between the two of them, equal parts curious and furious. Tell her what? What were they keeping from her? She folded her arms across her chest and glared.

Ashton inhaled, his apprehension palpable. Millie nodded at him, as if nudging him toward summoning the courage to speak.

"I know you've noticed I haven't been on campus much," he began, his eyes fixed on the countertop. "Well, that's actually because . . . I never enrolled in classes this semester." At last, he lifted his eyes, first looking at Millie, who smiled approvingly, and then finally landing on Ruby.

"What? What are you talking about?"

"All my life, I thought I'd be a lawyer like my dad, but when it came to the classes I was taking—all the philosophy and political science, it just wasn't for me. I wasn't happy, Ruby. I started to feel . . . I don't know. I mean, I'd be graduating next year, and it all just felt *wrong*. I couldn't go through with it. So I started talking to Millie and her dad about it."

Ruby's skin prickled. She shook her head unknowingly, willing whatever Ashton was about to tell her not to be said, not to be.

"I started working out with him, hanging out around the fire station."

Her heartbeat thumped in her ears. "No, Ashton."

"With all the fires going on, there's a big need. He helped me get a spot on one of the wildland crews."

"*No.*"

"We just finished our academy. I'm leaving . . . the day after tomorrow," he finished quickly.

Her heart was beating so fast and so loud, she didn't so much hear his last words as feel them. He couldn't be *serious*. Not her kind, sensitive, bookish Ashton!

She felt her fury rising, hot and full in her chest, burning in her throat, and when it finally exploded out of her body, the target was Millie. "*You!*" she snapped. "This is all *your* fault! You're going to let him do this?" *Let him throw his life away like this*, she thought, but couldn't bring herself to utter those words out loud.

Millie's lip quivered, but she returned Ruby's fierce, unwavering stare. "I think it's very brave of him, and I think we need anyone who is willing and able to help stop these fires. They're ruining people's lives."

Of course Ruby knew this. Her own family was the people Millie was referring to, for God's sake. But that didn't mean it had to be Ashton running to the rescue! How could she let him do something so foolish, so dangerous?

She couldn't stand to look at the two of them, Millie quietly bolstering Ashton up to do this reckless thing.

With an exasperated groan, she stormed out of the apartment, slamming the door so ferociously she could hear the rattling of the dishes in the cupboards from the hallway. She paused on their doorstep, willing her shaking hands to put her sweater on, but she was so consumed with anger and hurt and fear, her body just wouldn't cooperate. She'd put it on inside out twice already when she heard their door open behind her, and Ashton slunk out, looking like a remorseful puppy seeking consolation. It was both irritating and heartwarming to Ruby.

"You can't do this!" The words barely escaped in a whisper before catching in her throat in an unfamiliar squeak.

"I have to," he insisted softly. "It's our home."

Again, she shook her head. He misunderstood. She hadn't meant that he couldn't do this to her, though she certainly felt that somewhere inside herself. She had meant that *he*, Ashton Willis, couldn't do this. He wasn't capable. He was sweet and smart and goofy—but those were not the skills needed to survive in a fire. If he left, Ruby feared she'd never see him again. How could he be so stupid?

How could he expect her to accept this?

"I know that," she said. "But this can't be—there's got to be something else *you* could do. Why does it have to be this? Why does it have to be firefighting?" *Why does it have to be losing you?*

Still framed by the doorway, he tucked his hands into the pockets of his sweatpants and looked away. She wanted so desperately to believe that Ashton was a man blazing his own trail, rising to the occasion in the most unexpected way. But the more she gazed at this familiar boy, with his sandy-blond hair and long eyelashes, she couldn't help but worry he was fumbling his way through a disaster, unsure of what to do next. It terrified her.

"I know you're upset, Ruby, but I just came out here to ask if you'll look after Millie while I'm away?"

Every muscle in Ruby's body went rigid. First he'd asked her to support this absurd and suicidal plan that Millie had undoubtedly concocted, and now he wanted her to protect Millie from the big bad consequences as well?

"Look after her? Like she's a cat?"

He smiled, but it didn't reach his eyes. He met her gaze briefly before looking down again, but she could still sense his worry, his trepidation. "No. I just mean . . . With both me and her dad at the fires, I just don't want her to worry herself sick. I want to know someone will be here for her, to check in on her, to make sure she's taking care of herself."

Ruby felt like she was going to vomit. The audacity! He *knew* how she felt, and yet he laid all this on her: to risk losing him to a fool-ish notion and then console his heartbroken girlfriend. What about Ruby's feelings? Who was supposed to take care of *her*? "Why don't you ask one of her friends to do that?" She knew Charlie was too weak for such a task; he'd probably get her more worked up, but there had to be someone else. Someone other than Ruby.

Ashton finally stepped toward Ruby, who was herself gather-ing the willpower to leave, to walk out on all this needlessly painful nonsense he was trying to bring crashing down on her. There was something false in the way he moved, something that reminded her of make-believe or playing house. It was like his gravity in this mo-ment was a facade, a mask, though whether he was wearing it for his own benefit or Ruby's, she wasn't sure. He placed his hand on top of hers along the railing, and she felt goose bumps course down her body, quelling the smoldering rage in her stomach.

"You're the one I trust," he said soberly, tenderly. "You're the strongest person I know." It was so sweet, so genuine, Ruby desper-ately wanted to believe it was a romantic proclamation, wanted to ignore the underlying commitment to Millie that he was forcing on both of them. "It'll make me feel so much better knowing she has you to count on while I'm away."

She clenched her jaw. "You know I'll do it. We'll be fine. If anyone needs someone to look out for them, it's *you*." *It's you who needs me, you dummy.*

They stood for a moment in silence, holding each other's hands. For the first time since this nightmarish conversation had begun, he met her eyes for longer than a heartbeat. She searched his face for something changed, something that told her that beneath the surface of this sensitive and quiet young man was something tough and resilient, something strong and ruthless.

The sensation that this might be the last moment they had together—that this was her last chance to make him see things clearly—struck her, and she moved her hand upward to his face, cupping his rosy cheek in her palm. This was her opportunity. He was Sleeping Beauty or Snow White or whichever helpless princess who needed to be woken the hell up. She was going to save him. This was it.

She tilted her head up toward him. He didn't move any closer, but he also didn't pull away. He was frozen, barely even breathing, as she willed his mouth to close the last inch between them.

She heard him swallow, saw his lips part, and for an instant, he finally did lean toward her, before seeming to catch himself and pulling back, running a hand along his jaw.

"Ruby," he started in an unsteady voice.

"Yes?" she croaked, her entire body taut with anticipation.

"I . . . I'll drive you home."

At last, he stepped backward. As he put physical distance between them, his expression hardened, like he'd suddenly splashed cold water on his face. He stuck his hand into the pocket of his pants, retrieving his keys with a soft jingle, the only noise between them. Wordlessly, she followed him down the stairs to where his silver Prius gleamed under a streetlight. She chanced sidelong glances at him as they walked, a thousand thoughts racing through her mind, but he kept his gaze downward until they settled into the car.

She wondered feverishly what was going through his head. About the firefighting bullshit, of course. That was a whole mind-boggling ordeal. Maybe she could call Ashton's parents? The Willises would never stand for something so foolish and reckless, something so different from the plan they'd always had for Ashton. He only had a year and a half to go, for God's sake!

But also, what had just happened? It may have been just a moment, but there was something intense in that moment. Something important.

She was openly staring at him now as he drove, hoping her unabashed focus would draw him out of his head.

He was so stiff, so serious. His jaw clenched, both arms outstretched to the steering wheel. A slight dip in his eyebrows beneath the wispy, tawny feathers of his bangs.

What is he thinking? She couldn't stand not knowing.

She heard him move almost imperceptibly to flick on the blinker, and she noticed with horror that he was pulling into one of the empty metered slots outside her dorm building. Her mouth went dry as he shifted into park.

"Ashton," she said, trying to summon enough firmness in her voice to command his attention, but it still came out sounding breathy and weird.

Finally, he turned to her, his expression strangely dark. "I just . . . want to do something brave, you know? Meaningful." The sentiment sat between them for a beat, thick and mysterious to Ruby, before he suddenly propelled himself toward her and kissed her. His mouth was quick and pushy, almost like he was afraid he'd lose his nerve.

He was already pulling away by the time she even realized what was happening. Before she'd even parted her lips to meet his or reached to touch his soft, mussed hair, he was gone, sitting back into his own seat, his seat belt retracting back into its anchor.

To his credit, he looked almost as surprised as she did, but there was an edge of disappointment to his mood that was not lost on her. "I'm sorry," he said gruffly. "I don't know what I'm doing. Can we . . . can we keep this between the two of us, please?"

"You don't have to be sorry," she said, touching her fingertips to her mouth in disbelief. Had his lips really been on hers just a few seconds ago? Had he really kissed her?

It wasn't the first kiss she'd dreamed of, of course, but it happened, right? They had kissed!

"No," he insisted. "I don't know what I was thinking. Really." He shook his head. In the darkness she couldn't be sure, but she thought she might have seen his lower lip quiver just the slightest bit. "I should get home. Good night, Ruby."

She nodded, more to herself than anything because he was no longer looking at her. She unfastened her seat belt, slowly. He didn't say anything more as she swung her door open and stepped out. The door hadn't even fully snapped shut before the car was back in motion, and Ashton was on his way back to Millie.

In a stupor, she stepped onto the curb, an unsettled, almost seasick feeling in her stomach. She was fumbling in the pocket of her sweater for her keys as she approached the gate when she heard a familiar husky voice over her shoulder.

"Good evening, Ruby Ortega."

12

Ruby groaned, turning to find Remy leaning against his truck and smiling. "Oh my *God*. You know I have a phone, right? You could just call."

"Where's the fun in that?" He straightened and crossed the sidewalk toward her. A grocery bag hung from his hands.

She shifted on her feet cautiously, unable to read the mischief flickering in his eyes. Had he seen Ashton kiss her? And if he had . . . well, what would he make of that?

This was the first time she'd seen him since the gala, and his sudden reappearance put her instantly on edge.

"And, of course, I would've missed the romantic spectacle of a lifetime if I hadn't shown up in person," he added, a gravelly dryness to his voice that reverberated throughout Ruby's entire body.

She rolled her eyes, the queasiness in her gut rippling into something sharper. "You know, Remy, I'm not really in the mood for all your taunting and teasing bullshit tonight."

He cocked an eyebrow, seeming not exactly surprised, but intrigued by her curtness. "Really? Why the long face? It sure looked like everything was falling into place exactly like you've always wanted."

"You have no idea what you're talking about," she spat. "I'm going inside. I don't need to stand out here in the cold listening to you make fun of me for something you know next to nothing about."

She turned away from him, clutching her keys, but he placed his hand on her shoulder to stop her.

"Listen, I've been following the wildfires on the news, and that's why I wanted to come see you," he said with an evenness that sounded very deliberate. "I didn't realize I'd be interrupting ... *that*." His lips twisted into what Ruby suspected was an involuntary grimace. He sighed. "Any word from your family?"

She nodded skeptically. How was he able to switch between malicious and compassionate so quickly? And why would he bother? "Yeah. They're still there. They're fine. But it's scary."

"At least they're safe. No matter what, things can be replaced."

She had no response to that. It was precisely the type of thing someone felt compelled to say when they were not in the crux of the crisis. Remy was profiting from this whole ordeal; of course he could wax poetic about how it could be worse.

"I know that's probably not what you want to hear," he admitted. His icy demeanor seemed to thaw, and he spoke a little more easily. "Especially after that night at the gala. All that money and extra stuff—it really does seem weird when it comes down to it. Or . . . tacky, maybe? I don't know, but I've been thinking about it a little, wondering if that was the right thing to do, or if it was even helpful. It's hard to know, I suppose."

Ruby was too stunned by this thoughtful reflection to manage more than another nod. What exactly was he doing here? What did he want?

"I know I'm probably not who you were hoping would comfort you through all this, but hey, I'm the one who stuck around," Remy crooned in a self-deprecating tone that oozed faux sincerity.

She rolled her eyes, refusing to dignify that jab with a response. The abruptness of Ashton's affection was still raw and tender inside her, and she certainly did not need Remy poking around it. She swiped her ID card at the key reader with an angry flourish and jerked the gate open.

"Whoa, whoa. Come on! Where's the badass Ruby Ortega I met this summer? Where's that gutsy girl who says everything she's feeling?" Remy jumped in front of her, blocking her entrance with his wide frame, a challenging light in his bottomless eyes. He waited with bated breath for her to respond before he inched close enough that she was forced to look at him. "Come on. I didn't mean to upset you." Though she still didn't like the words coming out of his mouth, she could hear there was something gentler to the way he said them, almost beseeching.

"Oh, right. You came here to sweep me off my feet by making fun of me for my . . . Because I . . ." She couldn't bring herself to say Ashton's name to him, to acknowledge the secret Remy harbored. "*Move*, please."

He chuckled again. How was it that the angrier she was, the more entertained he seemed to be?

"I knew the fires were close to your house, and you hadn't answered my last few texts. That's why I'm here. That's it. I brought wine." He lifted the grocery bag, and Ruby could hear the distinct, soft clanging of two bottles bumping into each other. She noticed he didn't mention anything about the gala and wondered distantly if it hadn't been anything noteworthy for him after all. But he also didn't mention Ashton again, to her relief. "You look like you could use a drink—especially after dealing with the likes of me." He winked.

She hesitated. "Only because you have wine," she muttered before forcing her way past him and subtly nodding her head for him to follow her.

RUBY FELT A PANG OF APPREHENSION WHEN THEY ENTERED her room to find it empty. It was past nine o'clock, and she'd fully expected to find Patty curled up on her bed with a book and a cup of tea.

She tried to gauge Remy's reaction as she shut the door behind them. She didn't want him getting the idea that she'd purposefully invited him upstairs to an empty room. But he said nothing about her roommate's absence as he withdrew a bottle of red wine and asked for a wine key. Silently, she retrieved one from the box of miscellaneous kitchen supplies she and Patty kept on top of the minifridge. She held out two red Solo cups as he wrenched the cork out, and he emptied the entire bottle between the two of them.

He gently tapped his cup against hers. "To Ruby Ortega, a girl with rare spirit." His lips twisted into a mysterious, contemplative smile before he brought his cup to his lips.

Ruby had absolutely no idea what he meant by that but refused to humor him by asking. She took a sip of her wine and perched herself on her bed, her usual sitting spot. A brief moment of panic washed over her, realizing what she'd just done. Would he try to join her on the bed? Would he take that as a signal, with the two of them alone like this?

But he just pulled out her desk chair and eased himself into it, facing her.

"You know, when I first saw you, I thought you were very beautiful," he said in a surprisingly serious tone, as if continuing a conversation they'd been having all along. "Obviously, I was not alone in thinking that. And while I certainly appreciated how you looked in that green dress, there was something else that stuck with me. Something else that keeps drawing me to you." He took a slow drink from his cup, keeping his eyes on her as he did so. He appeared to be waiting for her to ask what it was, but Ruby bit her tongue. Though she desperately wanted to know, she even more desperately didn't want to feed into whatever game he was playing. "I thought, there's someone *unstoppable*, someone who won't let anything get in her way or keep her down. Someone so intense, she'll break a few beer bottles at a moment's notice."

She flushed and brought her cup to her mouth to hide her reddening face. He clearly meant this as a compliment, but it unnerved her that this was the mental image he had of her.

"She doesn't play hard to get. She knows she's one in a million, and she goes after what she wants." He surveyed her pensively. She couldn't help but think how out of place he looked, this hulking young man, dressed in a crisp flannel shirt, drinking what was assuredly an expensive wine in her tiny dorm room, surrounded by her colorful pens and notebooks, girlish trinkets that reminded her of the different stages of life they were in. "I think I was wrong, though."

An instinctive jolt of disappointment hit her. "Why is that?" she inquired flatly, in spite of herself.

"You're still falling all over yourself for that guy in the hopes that he'll pull his head out of his ass and notice." The words came out so quickly, Ruby had the impression that it wasn't the first time he'd thought them.

"So? What does that have to do with anything? *He's* who I want!"

He began fidgeting with a pad of hot pink Post-it notes on her desk. "What do *you* know about what you want?" he said so softly, it seemed he was thinking out loud to himself more than anything. "You're . . . eighteen?"

She nodded reluctantly, a flush of something between irritation and embarrassment rising up in her.

"There's a whole world out there, Ruby. You don't have to tie yourself to what you've always known just because it's familiar and easy. There's—"

She held up her hand to cut him off. "Please. You're what—a year older? Two? I don't need to sit here and be lectured by you when you have absolutely no clue what you are talking about," she snapped. "I might be young, but I'm not an idiot. I know enough. I know that you're *horrible*."

"You know, sometimes I think the same thing about myself," he admitted with a quiet chuckle. "Ruby, there's so much more out there than Ashton. Like it or not, I know about your secret feelings. And while I have no intention of exposing you to Millie or anyone else, I'm not exactly the type to sit idly by. So what do you want? Do you want me to coddle and console you, tell you it's only a matter of time before he realizes that your green eyes are like two sparkling jewels and that he'll fall deeply in love with you forever?" He said that last bit with a whiny tone in his voice that Ruby suspected was his impression of Ashton. "Is that what you want to hear?"

"Why do you have to say anything at all? It's none of your business!" she countered, her body roiling with white-hot hate.

Suddenly, he stood. "I believe in speaking out when it's something I care about, something that matters."

He placed his hand on the edge of the bed, and she felt her mattress sink a little lower with his added weight. He loomed over her, so near she could see her own reflection in his shining black eyes. She opened her mouth to tell him what she really wanted was for him to leave, to never have to see his jeering face ever again. But no words came out.

"Or do you want me to tell you how irresistible I find you when you're all worked up like this?" he asked, his voice a jarring mix of tenderness and brutal honesty. He was almost whispering he was speaking so softly, and Ruby caught herself watching his full lips move as he spoke. She could feel the warm breath of these words on her cheek. "I know I'm not the one you've been pining for, but I can't stop thinking about you. I think we could make each other happy."

She didn't dare move. It wasn't as if she could turn off her love for Ashton, even if she wanted to. But there was something she couldn't ignore about Remy. Something annoying and infuriating, sure, but also electric and exciting. Something that piqued her interest, though she couldn't quite explain it. She didn't know if she wanted to explain it.

He remained like that, mere inches away from her. Her mind raced with questions she could not bring herself to utter out loud. *Is he going to kiss me? Do I want him to? What makes him think he knows what it takes to make me happy?*

She would've thought a night when two handsome men unexpectedly kissed her would be a lot more fun, but she was so mixed up at this point, it was practically painful.

But he didn't kiss her; instead, he just lifted his hand from her bed, putting some space between the two of them. Her mattress softly squeaked back into place. He drained the last contents of his cup before saying, "You can save the other bottle for the next time you're having a hard day."

And then, as unexpectedly as he'd arrived, he was gone.

13

The day after Ashton left for Buena Valley, Ruby was distractedly editing her marketing essay when she was interrupted by a ringing cell phone. Millie had begged her to stay over at their apartment while Ashton was away, and haunted by the promise she'd made him, Ruby reluctantly agreed; it wasn't like she was able to focus on anything but the disaster at home anyway. As she reached across the couch for her phone, she realized it wasn't even her ringtone she heard. Over the past few days, she'd been fielding nonstop calls from her family. Her sisters were understandably frightened, both by the fires and by their parents' recent fighting. And her mother? Ruby couldn't quite put her finger on what her stoic mother was feeling, but from the handful of stilted phone calls they'd had recently, she knew it wasn't good.

"Oh, you know your father," she'd said, after several attempts to engage Ruby in half-hearted small talk about her classes. She sighed. "I do wish he'd be just a bit less stubborn and let us take the girls to Mama Ortega's for a few days." Ruby scrambled for the words to console her mother—something she'd never had to do before—in the melancholy silence that followed, but Eleanor Ortega beat her to it, with a tone that was determinedly brighter. "At least there's no traffic right now, what with half the town gone."

Ruby had joined her mother in a cheerless chuckle, out of pity and discomfort more than anything else. Nevertheless, her comments continued to trouble her even now, days after that phone call had ended.

Millie's voice, answering her phone in the next room over, pulled Ruby out of her thoughts as she stared at her own darkened screen. Now that she actually thought about it, her phone had been eerily silent all day. The only thing more distressing than incessant calls from her family was not hearing from them at all, she realized. She fired off another round of How are things going? to Carla and Elena. She was sure they were fine, but it was unlike Carla to be out of touch these days, and it was especially unlike Elena to not have her phone with her at all times.

She strained to hear what Millie was saying, hoping it was Ashton on the other end. He'd texted Millie last night, telling her he'd arrived safely, accompanied by a picture of him in his turnouts that had been so gut-wrenchingly handsome Ruby had to keep reminding herself about their secret kiss to keep her from throttling Millie out of pure envy. Though she was glad Millie had shared the message with her, Ruby still wondered why he hadn't called; she was aching to hear his voice. Sure, it had only been a day, but when a loved one was somewhere so remote and dangerous, a day could feel like weeks. She nudged her laptop and phone aside before marching over to Millie's closed bedroom door. Her fist was just about to knock when she heard—what was it?

Ruby leaned closer, her ear almost pressed against the door.

Sobbing.

Millie was crying!

Ruby thrust the door open to find Millie hunched over on her bed, her back to Ruby. Her shoulders were visibly shaking, and between tearful gasps she heard her croak, "But are you okay?"

Icy dread gnawed at Ruby's stomach as she crossed the room and sat down next to Millie, who hadn't even taken notice of Ruby's presence yet. *What happened to Ashton?* She'd known he wasn't cut out for this. He'd been there a *day*, for God's sake!

She could hear the muted mumblings of a male voice coming from Millie's phone but couldn't make out any words. The tone sounded awfully deep to be Ashton's voice, and a jolt of panic struck as she wondered if maybe he was too hurt to even make this phone call himself.

"Don't be silly, I'll figure it out." Millie sniffled, her eyes, red-rimmed and puffy, flicking up to meet Ruby's.

The last few minutes of her phone call felt infinite to Ruby as she sat in tense silence listening to Millie cry and whimper, "Are you sure?" At last, Millie put down her phone with a solemn sigh.

"So? Is he okay?" Ruby instantly snapped.

Lip quivering, Millie nodded. "He broke his legs. I mean, he's fine. But he's in the hospital."

Ruby's eyes bulged. "Legs? As in *both* of them? How? What happened? When?"

"He says he tripped and took a nasty spill. You know, that's actually one of the most common ways firefighters get hurt in wild-fires," she said, a tearful catch in her voice. A flicker of impatience lit up inside Ruby as she listened. Leave it to Millie to try to teach her lessons about safety protocols when there was much more important information to be shared. "It happened yesterday, but he was so drugged up that he didn't have a chance to call until today." She wiped away two large tears that had begun trickling down her cheek, as if provoked by her recalling the upsetting details. "He sounds okay, though. He'll be out of work for a while, of course, but he sounded okay."

Ruby's jaw clenched and she nodded. She couldn't think of any-thing to say as the overwhelming dread of Ashton's death slowly faded. He was all right. He was alive.

Millie gently leaned her head against Ruby's shoulder. "Oh, I'm so glad you're here. Thank you! You're so sweet to be so concerned about my dad. I don't know how I would've dealt with this on my own."

Wait. Her *dad*?

Ruby stiffened, shifting her arm to force Millie's head off her. "You weren't talking about Ashton?"

Millie's eyebrows were furrowed in puzzlement. "No. That was my dad who called. I haven't heard from Ashton quite yet." Her straw-berry blond hair was pulled back in a loose braid, and Ruby couldn't help but think she looked like a small child, especially with the con-fused, sad way she searched Ruby's face.

Ruby was immediately overcome with a mixture of relief and annoyance. She obviously didn't harbor any ill will toward Millie's dad; she'd never even met the guy. But how could Millie be so dense to believe that Ruby would be this distraught over a complete stranger? Of course she had assumed it was Ashton! Only a bone-head wouldn't have realized that.

Ruby rose to her feet, pacing back and forth across Millie's room. Ashton wasn't hurt, that was all that mattered, really. Millie was understandably upset, and Ruby knew she couldn't—*shouldn't*—hold the miscommunication against her. She just didn't have the energy to conjure any deeper compassion for her right now. She took a deep breath.

Millie's glassy eyes followed her. "I'm ... I'm sorry? I didn't mean to worry you ..."

Ruby nodded dismissively. "It's fine. Will you be going to see him?"

"Yes. I need to look up flights," she said, her voice trailing off. "Although, I know they've been limited with all the smoke. Maybe I could rent a car? How old do you have to be to do that? I guess there's always a bus, but I think those take a lot more time ..." Millie's shoulders sagged, as if physically burdened by the choices she faced.

Ruby surveyed her critically. Again, as she watched this frail, lost girl, she was reminded that this was what Ashton had had in mind when he'd asked Ruby to take care of her. She was all smiles and optimism as the disaster closed in on them, but when things finally became real, Millie was helpless. Ruby rolled her eyes. "Hold on. Let me go grab my phone, and I'll help you look up your options. When would you like to leave? Tomorrow morning?" she called over her shoulder.

As she picked up the phone, she saw the text she'd sent to her sisters right before she'd gone into Millie's room still open on her screen.

Her heart lurched.

Next to the message she'd sent was a small red exclamation point. Not Delivered.

Her family wasn't just out of touch. They were out of service.

She tried to resend the message, her fingers fumbling nervously against the screen. But no matter how many times she clicked Try Again, the result was the same.

After three rapid-fire attempts, she tried calling, pressing down on each of their numbers and jamming the phone to her face, as if the harder she pressed, the more likely her call would be to break through whatever cellular barrier was separating them.

She called her father, her mother, and both of her sisters. Each time it rang once before sending her straight to voicemail.

She stared at her stupid, useless phone, every muscle in her body drawn tight as she tried to gather her thoughts, when she noticed another unusual notification on her screen. A voicemail. As quickly as humanly possible, without even looking to see who it was from, she clicked on it and returned her phone to her ear.

"Ruby, mija, I'm calling about your parents." Mama Ortega's voice sounded out of breath amid a din of unfamiliar background noise. "Cell service is bad, even here. Something about the towers, yo no sé. Have you heard from your parents or sisters? I tried to call after I saw the news about high winds, pero—"

And then, silence.

Ruby ripped the phone away from her face and discovered that was the end of the voicemail. It just stopped midsentence like that. Cut off.

Shit.

The knot of dread in her chest swelling with every heartbeat, Ruby called her grandmother back, but she was abysmally unsurprised when this call, too, was unable to go through—perhaps why her phone hadn't rung in the first place.

"Ruby?" Millie appeared in the doorway. "Did you hear me?"

She glanced up at Millie with wide-eyed alarm but was unable to formulate any words.

When was the last time she'd heard from her family? Last night? Or was it even longer? How could she have been so thoughtless? Why hadn't she reached out earlier?

Oh God. What if they were trapped in their house? Or what if the fires had already reached them and they were—?

No. She couldn't think like that. It was probably just the cell towers, like Mama Ortega said. They were fine. They just couldn't call her.

But what if something *was* wrong?

Mama Ortega's intuition was usually spot-on, and if she was worried...

Ruby had to get to them.

She stared at Millie with grim resolution. She couldn't bear to utter her fears out loud. She needed to push it all aside to focus on what she needed to do next.

She couldn't think about where her family might be or what could've happened to them.

She needed to do something.

"I need to get back home."

Millie's eyes widened in surprised. "Oh?" She was clearly waiting for more, but Ruby had no time to explain herself.

"I need to go home," Ruby said, this time a little louder. "I'll go with you. We leave first thing tomorrow."

14

As Ruby's mind raced to formulate a way to approach these obstacles, Millie's mouth raced to fill every second of silence with incessant questioning. Ruby was devoting every bit of energy toward channeling her fear into focus and scheming, so she could not summon the words to tell Millie to shut the hell up, let alone answer any of her concerned musings. Instead, she responded only with seething silence. She tried twice to leave the room, ducking first onto the balcony and second into the bathroom, but Millie trailed after her both times, oblivious.

It wasn't until Ruby ordered her to start packing that Millie stopped following her—though, to be fair, she'd asked what to bring and hadn't actually started until Ruby had pulled her suitcase out of her closet, thrown it on the bed, and began hurling in whatever items she could find. Millie snatched up a pair of furry slippers that Ruby had just launched across the room, and finally stammered, "Oh, okay, I think I've got it from here."

As Ruby began packing her own bag, she tried one more time to call her father, just like she had done every twenty minutes since she'd realized they were out of service, but she hung up at the familiar sound of his voicemail greeting. Frustrated, she tossed her phone down on the coffee table and tried to think of a plan.

Thanks to her mother's insistence that she learn about independence and the "value of a dollar," she didn't have her Jeep or more than thirty-seven dollars in her bank account. Even if she could afford it, it was unlikely that she'd be able to convince an Uber to drive her the six hours back to Buena Valley under any circumstances—let alone in the midst of a natural disaster. But none of that mattered. She was going to figure out a way to get home. There was no doubt about it.

After she'd racked her brains trying to come up with another way, the unpleasant solution hit her like a slap to the face.

She hadn't spoken to him, not even a text or a like on social media, since that strange, awkward night after Ashton kissed her, but she knew if anyone was able to get her—a penniless, carless college student with a tight time frame—out of Arizona and into the epicenter of fiery danger, it was him.

So with a sense of bitter determination, Ruby called Remy Bustillos.

IT WAS WELL PAST MIDNIGHT WHEN RUBY COLLAPSED IN A fitful heap of exhaustion on Millie's couch. She tossed and turned all night, spending most of the time watching the news in open-mouthed horror as they panned over charred images of her hometown. Beloved landmarks jutted out to her, scarred almost beyond recognition. The entire north wing of her high school was half collapsed into blackened shards. A dark-haired reporter shared financial estimates of damages, numbers large and unfathomable to Ruby, while he stood near the bench where Ashton used to wait for Ruby to drive her home each afternoon. The bench itself was nothing more than a twisted knot of melted metal, but Ruby could still see Ashton's shy smile as she'd cross a crowded courtyard toward him on a sunny afternoon.

All the while, numbers flashed across the bottom of the screen in a bright red banner. A dozen known casualties. Estimates of missing people were somewhere around 150. Each time Ruby's eyes flicked down to those scrolling numbers, her stomach turned as she wondered which category her family fell in.

SHE WAS ALREADY AWAKE WHEN HER ALARM WENT OFF, AND she dragged herself to the bathroom to try to address her rumpled, pallid appearance before Remy arrived. The burning disappointment of their last sloppy encounter still irritated her. She much preferred that he think of her as the dazzling versions of herself she'd been at Elena's party and at the gala. However, all the concealer and dry shampoo in the world couldn't undo the dark circles under her eyes and the greasy, matted texture of her hair that the sweaty wakefulness last night had produced. She knew the way she looked shouldn't bother her at a time like this, but with everything in her life spiraling out of control, she yearned for just one thing she could fix.

It annoyed her even more when she opened the front door—five minutes before their agreed-upon time—to find Remy looking as if he were headed off to brunch, in neatly pressed jeans, a collared shirt, and a shave so fresh that Ruby could smell the clean scent of aftershave as she greeted him numbly. In his hands he held a carrier with three coffees and a pink cardboard box, the logo of a Mexican bakery stamped on the top of its lid. Though it was infuriating that he seemed to think they were going on vacation, Ruby's stomach growled at the mere possibility of a real breakfast. Lately, she'd been too torn up with anxiety to feed herself anything that required more effort than energy drinks and granola bars.

"Good morning," he said. How was it possible for him to make a casual greeting sound like a snide remark?

"Thank you for doing this, Remy," she mumbled as she stepped aside so his large figure could pass through the doorframe. "I think Millie is almost ready."

He nodded, setting the drink carrier down to check the side of one of the coffee cups. He extended the one marked WITH CREAM toward her. "I'm very much looking forward to getting to know the famous Millie, even if it is under such unfortunate circumstances," he said, a flash of something indiscernible in his gaze as he pressed his own cup to his lips.

Ruby couldn't keep herself from frowning at him. They didn't have many other options, but it was disturbing how much Remy seemed to delight in having to come to her rescue. What was wrong with this guy that he found such pleasure in a predicament like this?

He opened his mouth to say something more, but Millie appeared from her bedroom lugging a large tote bag behind her, and he turned his unspoken words into a cough, angling away from Ruby and toward Millie in the process.

"Oh! Our hero is here! Hi, Remy! It's *so* nice to see you again!" She slung her bag onto the couch and threw herself at Remy in a surprisingly warm embrace, in Ruby's opinion, considering they'd only met the one time on the beach months ago.

Remy's eyes lit up deviously. "I'm happy to help out. Here, have some breakfast. Have you ever had pan dulce?" He popped open the lid of the bakery box with a flourish, revealing an assortment of brightly colored pastries in a variety of shapes.

Ruby cocked a curious eyebrow at him as he pointed out the different flavors. Pan dulce was a special treat her father always saved for when they visited Mama Ortega in Chula Vista; they'd pop into a panadería and select different pastries from the tall glass cabinets that lined the walls. She hadn't seen any Mexican bakeries near campus, and she definitely had never seen them in Buena Valley. She felt an odd pinch of intrigue trying to imagine Remy, in his expensive clothing, choosing the pig-shaped gingerbreads and pink conchas specifically for them.

"These are my personal favorite." Remy pointed to a couple of triangle-shaped cookies, with pink-, brown-, and white-colored corners. Those were also Ruby's favorite, but she kept that to herself.

"That's *so* nice!" Millie cooed, selecting one of the seashell-shaped pastries, a glowing smile on her lips. "Ruby, you never mentioned how nice he is!"

Ruby's eyes locked on Remy's, who was sinking his teeth into the chocolate corner of his sweet bread. "Yes, well. I guess I didn't real-ize just how 'nice' he is," she muttered. "Anyway, I read online there are a few parts of the highway closed, so it may take a little longer than usual. I'm going to start loading up the truck while you two enjoy your breakfast. I'd like to get on the road as soon as possible." She dramatically hoisted Millie's enormous bag over her shoulder and dragged her own duffel to the door under Remy's amused gaze.

She paused near the doorway, waiting for his chivalry to kick in, but instead she heard him call out to her, "Sounds good. We'll see you down there in a few minutes!"

15

Remy insisted Millie sit in the front seat, twirling his keys for a moment before clicking the fob and unlocking his truck. "Don't worry. The back seat is *very* comfortable, too," he assured Ruby with an irritating wink.

He snapped his seat belt into place and craned his neck backward so he was facing Ruby. "You ready to go back there?"

She smiled icily. "*Yep.* Let's go."

"I'll let Ashton know we're getting on the road," Millie peeped as Remy backed out of his parking spot. "They get out there pretty early, so he's probably on the fire line already, but at least he'll know when he checks his phone later today."

"Smart. He's got enough to worry about without wondering where you are," Remy agreed with a quick flick of his eyes to meet Ruby's in the rearview mirror. "Let him know you two are in good hands!"

Ruby hoped with everything else going on that he didn't plan on bringing up their last encounter or, more importantly, the clandestine kiss he'd witnessed. But there was a malicious gleam in his eyes at the mention of Ashton's name that told her just because he hadn't said anything, it didn't mean he'd forgotten it.

Or that he'd let it go.

RUBY HAD EXPECTED THE SIGNS OF THE FIRE TO APPEAR gradually, hints of the devastation along the way as they got closer. Aside from a few more cars on the road than usually found on the long stretches of desert highway, she noticed nothing out of the ordinary for most of the way. But after they crossed over into California, she was shocked at how abruptly the world transformed from the sandy hills of the desert to a hazy, charred disaster zone. She could've drawn a line in the sky, the distinction between clear blue and blackened smokiness was so drastic.

As they drew closer to Buena Valley, the blackened roadside was increasingly peppered with police officers wearily directing traffic and flashing road signs warning of the hazards associated with traveling through an ongoing natural disaster.

What stung Ruby's heart more than the sight of homes reduced to ash was the randomness with which the fires had struck, decimating some houses and leaving others virtually unscathed. They drove past entire neighborhoods of scorched lots, where the only remaining signs of human existence were some strange blackened artifacts that had withstood the flames—a bike frame or chimney. Sometimes, after rows and rows of completely destroyed houses, one would emerge almost completely untouched. What determined that while all their neighbors lost everything, these people would be just fine? She couldn't help but wonder who had borne the brunt of the damages in her own neighborhood. Who had been spared?

Every few minutes, Millie would inhale sharply and mutter something like, "Oh, these poor people" or "I can't even imagine."

Perhaps she thought she was being sympathetic, but these comments spiked pangs of rage as Ruby anxiously surveyed the destruction, hoping to detect some sort of pattern that would prove that her house, her community, her family would be just fine. She was annoyed that Millie's home back in Arizona was undeniably among the ones still standing, hundreds of miles away, and that she insisted on reminding Ruby of it every time she softly tsked or whispered, "Oh my goodness."

Dejectedly, Ruby let her head *thunk* against the window. Remy's eyes darted up in the rearview mirror to meet hers for a brief moment, but no one said anything.

SHE DIDN'T PERK UP UNTIL ABOUT AN HOUR LATER, AS SHE began to vaguely make out a few of the landmarks around her and realized they had entered Buena Valley without her even noticing. Many of the blackened storefronts were unfamiliar in their damage—which she had foolishly thought last night's news coverage had prepared her for—but every block or so a donut shop or gas station would remind her that she really was home. As they passed the misshapen tree stumps and debris that lined the sidewalks, she kept reminding herself this was in fact the place where she had grown up.

Ruby had to show her driver's license at one police checkpoint to prove they were residents, which the officer said was to cut down on potential looting. And while the scenery indicated desolation and abandonment, Ruby wasn't alone in making the journey home to assess the damage. Everywhere she looked were clumps of people sadly sifting through the remains of their home, store, or school.

"What's going on over there?"

It was the first time in hours Millie had said something besides her pitying murmurs. Despite her apathy for anything except getting home as soon as possible, Ruby craned her neck to see a large group of people in the midst of a commotion.

Clustered in a parking lot were several police cruisers, lights flashing brightly, surrounding a crowd of people. Even from a distance, Ruby could hear the din of frenzied cries, sharp tones, and the mix of Spanish and English. Parked just on the other side of the crowd was a dark van and two white buses. Though the letters on the van were concealed by the mass of bobbing heads, she spotted several uniformed officers wearing bulletproof vests labeled POLICE ICE.

Immigration and customs? What were they doing here?

"Oh my God, as if things aren't scary enough!" Millie gasped. "Those people probably lost just as much as everyone else, and now they have to deal with all that?"

Buena Valley was only about an hour from the Mexican border, and Ruby had lived among people with varying degrees of immigration status all her life, though it was rarely mentioned explicitly. Her father was one of the only people she knew who spoke about it; he'd gotten in a heated argument at one Fourth of July barbecue with Ashton's father about undocumented workers. Mr. Willis had made some sort of loaded comment about the burden of "illegals," and her father pointed out that he didn't seem too burdened when he hired them at cheap rates to mow his lawn or clean his toilets. Ruby knew their own family history wasn't too far removed from the hardships of people seeking citizenship. A generation ago, it could've been Mama Ortega and Daddy in that crowd of people being interrogated by a group of officers.

She flinched as she watched an officer grimly shove a woman against the side of a bus and handcuff her. The crowd erupted in panicked screams, and she could see other officers beginning to react similarly to the first, restraining some of the outraged bystanders with a level of forcefulness that made Ruby's stomach sink. Chaos roiled the crowd as the ICE officers swarmed through. People were slammed to the ground, others struggled to free themselves from choke holds, and children were torn from their parents' arms despite their pitiful cries.

"What is happening?" Ruby cried, unable to contain her horror a moment longer. "How could they do that, especially at a time like this?" She shook her head vigorously, clenching her eyes shut, though the desperate sounds of fear were still loud enough to reach her. It was too awful to take in.

"They're loading up all the people into those vans and buses," Millie whispered, her voice fragile with disbelief. "And look. They're . . . they're separating the children. They're putting kids on different buses than their parents."

Against every instinct in her body, every primal urge to hide from the atrocities Millie was describing, Ruby eased her eyes open. She forced herself to seek out the line of trembling children along the far edge of the parking lot, separated by several squad cars and armed officers from the adult line and vehicles.

"Where do you think they're taking them?" It seemed Millie knew the answer already; the flat dejected tone of her voice made that clear enough.

"They're deporting them," Remy said automatically.

"But w—?"

Remy cut her off before Millie could even finish the question. "Because children and adults go to different facilities."

The three of them sat wordlessly inside the truck, so transfixed by what was happening, they didn't notice the light had turned green at the intersection until a Tesla whizzed by with its horn blaring. Remy rubbed at his chin roughly, as if trying to wake himself up, and pressed the gas.

"Remy, I'm so glad you're here with us," Ruby rasped as the truck lurched into motion. "I don't know how I could've handled all of this without you, what's happening here. In Buena Valley, of all places. I can't believe it. I don't even recognize it. I'm just . . . I'm so thankful you were free to help me." She could feel her sadness lodged in her chest like an iron ball. She touched his shoulder, letting her hand linger like he was a lifeline keeping her afloat.

He stiffened beneath her touch.

When he turned to look at her, the expression in his dark eyes was hard for her to decipher, but a chill coursed through her body nevertheless. She felt the truck's speed begin to slow.

Silently, he turned into the parking lot where the crowd was being detained.

"What are you doing?" Ruby's eyes quickly flitted from the mass of people to Remy.

He parked about thirty feet away from the nearest bus. Now that they were closer, they could hear officers shouting, "Back away! Form an orderly line!" to responses of, "¡No entendemos! ¡Ayúdanos! ¡No dispares!" Ruby's limited Spanish was able to pick up these frantic phrases as they were repeated in an agonizing loop.

We don't understand.

Help us.

Don't shoot.

"Remy, what are you doing?" Ruby repeated, her voice peaking in alarm.

He swung open his door and stepped out of the truck, his movements rough and purposeful.

She burst out of the back seat and met him with wild eyes. *"What are you doing?"*

The muscles in Remy's jaw tightened as he squared up to face her. "What you said was right. We are very lucky that I was 'free' to help you. We're lucky that all of us are free. But I'm also free to help them." He pointed to the mass of people, now collectively wailing in between police instructions. "Or at least try." To her disbelief, he started walking right past her, toward the crowd.

"I don't understand. What are you going to do? What are *we* going to do?" Ruby cried.

He turned. "You're going to take my truck and go home. You're going to be fine."

She felt anger swelling at his condescending words. "And you? What the hell are *you* going to do?" she spat.

"Something," he said ominously. "I can't just do nothing."

She grimaced. "You're unbelievable."

A wry, dark smile crept onto his face. She had meant it as the lowest insult she could think of, a complete condemnation of his character, but the glimmer in his eyes told her he'd heard something else entirely. He nodded. "You are way more formidable than any natural disaster. Even a raging wildfire. You, Ruby Ortega, are a force of nature. You don't need me. *They* need me—or someone, at least. I can't just drive by and pretend this isn't happening. I don't expect you to understand, but it's something I need to do."

He took her hand in his, his skin silky and warm, and pressed his keys into her palm. Despite her fear and anxiety, her pulse quickened at his touch. There was a brief, sudden moment when he bowed his head toward her in a way that almost made her wonder if they were about to embrace, but she tore her hand out of his reach before she could decide what he was doing.

A dark-haired woman ran to them, breathing heavily and clutching the hand of a small child. Though Ruby had never seen the woman before in her life, in a heart-wrenching instant she saw Mama Ortega's face before her, the young boy transforming into the photographs Ruby had seen of her father at a young age. The illusion lasted only a heartbeat, shattered by the sounds of nearby wailing, but it was enough to turn Ruby's insides leaden as the woman searched each of their faces—feverish eyes darting from Ruby to Remy to Millie, who had wordlessly exited the truck and was watching all of them with a somber expression. The woman seized Remy's hand and launched into rapid-fire Spanish.

Remy nodded as the woman spoke in pleading tones, holding her child close to her as she gestured toward the buses despairingly. Ruby could catch only snippets. Something about the police, maybe someone she knew had been arrested. Something about her son. She wanted Remy's help, but to do what exactly, Ruby couldn't be sure.

"Entiendo, señora. Nos vamos," Remy told her as he turned to walk with her toward the crowd of people without another glance back at Ruby. She saw him pull out his phone and open up the camera app as he walked.

"Maybe we could wait for him?" Millie said softly, the end of her suggestion drowned out by more shrieks, rising in an urgent wave. Both the girls' eyes automatically sought out the source of the cries, only to spot the electric crackle of a Taser and the twitching body of a young man facedown on the sidewalk not far from where they'd watched Remy's figure disappear into the crowd.

Millie gasped, and Ruby felt herself begin to tremble as she fought the urge to squeeze her eyes shut again. She tried to take a steadying breath, but the air entered her body sharp and noxious, somehow amplifying the sounds of pain and distress pulsating throughout the parking lot.

It took considerable effort to keep herself from thinking about the kind of violence and discrimination and *inhumanity* that was unfolding in front of them, but she forced herself to focus on her goal. She had to. She needed to get home to her own crisis. She couldn't let herself be deterred when her own family needed her.

"Wait for him to do what? Get himself arrested?" Ruby barked, the words sounding hostile and insincere even to her own ears, but she let herself dwell in her anger toward Remy. It was easier than processing what was happening all around them. "Millie, I need to get home. That's why we came all this way. My family could be . . ." She trailed off, unable to finish that sentence.

There was so much that was so hard to bear right now.

She needed to get a grip. Having a meltdown would not do anyone any good.

She turned, jerking the driver's door open. "I am going *home*, Millie," she said. "Remy can and will do whatever he wants, apparently." She hoisted herself into the truck, settling herself into the seat, still warm from Remy's body. "He'll be *fine*," she muttered, echoing the same infuriating proclamation he had made about her moments ago.

She didn't look up—couldn't bring herself to chance even one more glimpse of what they had stumbled upon—as she began adjusting the seat. She could feel Millie eyeing her as she climbed in, but Ruby refused to meet her gaze.

She backed out of the parking lot and turned onto the empty road, relieved to have some physical distance between herself and that godforsaken parking lot. As she drove, she couldn't stave off her bewilderment at Remy's sudden act of charity. Of course it was heartbreaking, but . . . well, it wasn't his battle, was it? The world had clearly gone to shit. What the hell was Remy of all people going to do about it? They had enough to contend with, and he'd already agreed to help her. And yet he had abandoned them without a moment's hesitation.

16

Millie was unusually quiet as they drove, not that Ruby was complaining. At this point, she didn't have the energy to deal with any more of her babbling nonsense. However, a few sideways glances at her troubled face hinted that her silence probably wasn't just her being sensitive to Ruby's foul mood. She was clearly despairing about Remy. Though they scarcely knew each other, it was just like Millie to worry about him in a predicament that was entirely of his own making.

What were we supposed to do in that situation? Yes, of course what was happening was horrible, but did she really think they should've hung around to get themselves thrown in jail, too? Was she forgetting the whole purpose of this trip, just like Remy clearly had?

Besides, if Millie was feeling guilty about not joining Remy in his act of heroism, she was clearly overlooking just how fickle his sense of duty was. He felt he had to help those people, but he hadn't finished helping the people he'd already committed to! He had no qualms about abandoning them in their time of need. And maybe he had been a little bit right; she didn't "need" him in the true sense of the word, but it had been a small comfort to her to think of facing the upcoming challenges with someone as strong and levelheaded as Remy by her side, though she'd rather throw herself into the wildfires than admit that to him.

It was probably only a matter of time before this call of duty no longer appealed to him and he left the immigrants they'd encountered in the lurch for a more glamorous act of charity.

I can't think of him right now, she reminded herself. *I'll think of all that later.*

Ruby turned right with a swift jerk of the steering wheel, and before her brain could catch up with her body and realize that this was *the* corner, *her* corner, *her* street, she heard Millie croak, "Is . . . is that Ashton's house?"

Ruby's eyes instinctively followed the familiar path where she knew Ashton's house to be, but calling what remained a "house" was cruel and misleading. Two walls of what appeared to be their garage remained, surrounded by piles of blackened debris—but there was nothing recognizable, nothing memorable left of the house she'd spent her childhood dashing across the street to.

"Oh no," she breathed in anguish.

She couldn't take it in. She couldn't dwell on it. Not now, not when they were so close.

She took a deep breath as she turned to face what she'd come all this way to find.

Her home.

It's . . . still here.

It's still here!

Ruby kept repeating it to herself as she took in the sights before her, sweaty, smoky tears stinging her eyes. She stumbled out of the truck, scarcely remembering to put it in park before her body spilled out onto the driveway. Her home was very different—it was not the home she'd held in her heart the past eighteen years—but it was still standing.

That's what mattered, right?

The house itself looked the same, tinted gray from the smoke, but otherwise familiar. The trees were gone. Only fragments of the picket fence remained. The air was still; the only audible sound was the *pfft-pfft* of the sprinklers, which spun about incessantly, spraying their entire yard in a constant mist. Though she couldn't see the horse corrals from the front yard, she could usually hear the horses whinnying and snorting from the driveway. The unfamiliar silence told her they were not there.

Was *anyone* there?

Her mother's Jaguar was parked in the driveway, covered in so much soot it no longer looked pearly white, but her father's Range Rover was missing from its usual spot right beside it.

She found herself paradoxically frozen with dread, unable to move her feet, as she knew the answers she'd driven all this way for were just on the other side of her front door. Her pulse was thudding so loudly behind her eyes, she only distantly registered Millie's presence beside her. They exchanged a look, and Ruby noticed a faint layer of ash darkening Millie's hairline, after just moments outside in the smoke-filled air.

Without a word, they nodded at each other, almost in unison. In a haze of both smoke and heart-wrenching fear, Ruby moved numbly up her front steps with Millie a step behind her.

She placed her hand on the doorknob, and the front door swung open with ease. It wasn't locked. It hadn't even been shut all the way.

They only left the door unlocked if they were home, she thought with the briefest spark of relief. Unless they'd left in such a hurry that they'd forgotten to lock it.

As she stepped inside, she immediately sensed the lifelessness in the house. The lights were off. The air felt trapped and unmoving. There wasn't a sound, not a single indication of anyone inside their home at all.

At least, no one alive.

No. If they were still here in the house, they'd be okay. The house was still standing, after all.

But if they weren't here, then where were they?

There was only one way to find out if anyone was home.

"Hello?" Millie called out, almost reading her mind. Her voice was clear and sharp, and echoed throughout the cavernous entryway.

They stood together, straining to hear any sign of life, but the silence did not falter.

Ruby clenched her jaw. A huge part of her was tempted to remain in that moment in the foyer, to live in the uncertain possibility where maybe her family was hurt, but maybe they were safe inside the house—asleep, perhaps. But she knew that was ridiculous. She needed answers. She'd come all this way for answers.

Her legs unfroze, and she bolted up the stairs toward the bedrooms, shouting their names as loud as she could. As she pushed each bedroom door open, she found each room dark and empty. And untidy.

Like they'd been rifled through hastily. Like things had been flung about in an emergency.

They'd evacuated, and it looked to be in a hurry.

Ruby heard Millie's footsteps as she made her way upstairs; she appeared in the hallway, slightly out of breath. The intent crease in her forehead told Ruby she was piecing things together, too.

"Maybe they went to your grandmother's house? You said she lives an hour or so away, right?" Millie offered, her eyes drifting across the family portraits mounted on the wall. Rows of beaming Ortegas, joyful and together safely behind the glass of their picture frames.

Ruby thought of the worried voicemail she'd received from her grandmother the day before and nervously pulled out her phone to call her before she remembered the whole reason she'd set out to come home. No service.

Should she venture all the way to Chula Vista when she didn't know where her family was? Were the roads even passable at this point? What if they were still in Buena Valley? What if they were in danger?

She sat down on the top stair of the staircase, her breath shaky and uneasy. "I—I don't know what to do. I don't know where they are." Each word she uttered was a struggle.

Millie sat down beside her and gently patted her shoulder. "Hospitals usually have backup generators and servers and all that stuff," she said. "If we go there, you can try to get in touch with your grandmother."

This was probably true, but Ruby suspected Millie's logic wasn't entirely altruistic; she'd come all this way to see her dad, too, after all.

But she didn't have any better ideas. She got to her feet. "And I guess if they're hurt they'll probably—"

Millie stood, too, again reaching out to touch her. "No. Don't let yourself think that way. We'll go to the hospital, and you can call someone. That's it." There was a brightness in her amber eyes, the subtlest kind of bravery. It was the same expression Ruby'd detected the night Ashton had told her he'd dropped out of school. Then, it had seemed foolish to her, a naive kind of optimism that had aggravated her.

And perhaps it still was naive, but Ruby found herself nodding anyway, succumbing to Millie's hopeful determination as she followed her back to Remy's truck.

17

Ruby's nerves were so frazzled with unmitigated terror, she had a difficult time processing what was happening around her as they made their way to the hospital. She experienced everything in snippets, bursts of sound and color that were disjointed and jarring.

Consequently, Millie insisted on driving, against Ruby's futile protests that she didn't know where they were going. The bleak roadside whizzed past them as Millie drove, parks and storefronts and homes and entire lives reduced to blackened rubble, tragic and somehow monotonous.

The brilliance of the fluorescent lighting of the crowded hospital waiting room stunned Ruby's senses when they finally arrived. It was noisy, filled with the urgent intercom and anxious chattering, but no sounds fully penetrated Ruby's brain as she watched Millie check in with a weary nurse.

Ruby stared at the bright screen of her cell phone, watching the bars in the corner flicker as it sought out a signal. She didn't even notice she was walking, following Millie down a hall lined with stretchers and open doors. Millie was saying something, looking over her shoulder and gesturing toward a room ahead of them, but her words never reached Ruby.

Her eyes were locked on her phone with such concentration, willing it to connect to enough service to provide some sort of link to her family, that she hadn't even registered her sisters' presence in the family waiting area Millie had led her to until Carla was flinging herself into Ruby's arms.

She wrapped her arms around both her sisters, burying her face in their hair, entire body heaving with tearless sobs of disbelief and gratitude. Their heads pressed against her chest; their thin arms wrapped around her middle. They were here. Alive. Safe. They were okay.

She lifted her head briefly at the sound of rapid, heavy foot-steps behind her. Two doctors sprinted down the hallway. Ruby watched their white coats disappear around the corner with a de-tached sense of confusion, her cheek still pressed against Carla's nut-brown hair, the smell of smoke mixed in with her lavender shampoo.

She met Millie's eyes; she was standing closest to the doorway. Ruby was surprised she was still there. She would've thought she'd have rushed to see her father by then. Her stiffness was strange. Her tense frown should've been a hint of what was to come, of what Millie had overheard the nurses saying.

But in her uncomprehending relief to see her sisters, she failed to interpret what was about to happen. Even as it unfolded, very little made sense. Her mind just couldn't piece it together, couldn't even begin to consider why her sisters were here in the first place, why their arms were covered in small scratches, or where her parents were.

When the sound of her father's voice echoed down the hall, roaring with agony, it took her several beats to recognize it.

Dressed in a hospital gown, he was pounding on a closed door, two nurses at his side trying unsuccessfully to pull him away.

All three Ortega girls gaped from a distance. Ruby didn't understand what he was doing, or why he was doing it. Or what *she* should do.

It wasn't until Ruby finally grasped what he was screaming that reality began to pierce through the fog of shock she'd been floundering in. That she finally began to register that something bad had happened, something that had harmed her sisters a little, but had done something far worse to her parents.

Her mother.

Finally, she rushed to her father, moving as quickly as she could but still experiencing the world in slow motion. By then, his strength was spent and he was slumped against the door, calling out one word, over and over.

"Eleanor!"

RUBY COULD ONLY HANDLE THE INFORMATION IN SMALL doses, mulling over one horrible piece of information at a time. If she took it in all at once, the throbbing, terrible tragedy of it all, she'd never be able to hold it together. And now, more than ever, she needed to be strong. For her sisters. For her father. And, in a way, for her mother.

There had been an accident, Carla and Elena told her through their tears. They'd finally made the decision to evacuate, but it had been too late. The roads were a mess of debris and closures, clouded by thick, blinding smoke. Their father's SUV had crashed into a fallen tree about ten miles from their house. Concealed by smoke, the tree had been hidden from view until it was too late, and though he had swerved as quickly as he could, it just hadn't been fast enough.

Ruby had to get the rest of the story from the nurses, because beyond the ghastly crunch of metal against wood, the girls couldn't remember any more.

The truck had collided with the tree on the passenger side.

Carla and Elena had escaped with just some cuts and bruises.

Their father likely had a concussion but would make a full recovery.

Their mother had been unconscious when the paramedics arrived and had been unresponsive since they'd gotten to the hospital.

Until the scene Ruby had witnessed.

She didn't understand exactly what the doctors meant when they said, "She coded," and no matter how many times they tried to break it down into bits she could comprehend, it never fully made sense, and she wondered if it ever would.

Her mother was . . . dead.

It didn't seem possible, not as she held her crying sisters, not as she watched her stunned father sign a stack of baffling papers, not even as she said goodbye to the lifeless body that had once been the woman who had guided and loved her her entire life.

Her mother was dead.

She'd come all this way, and now her greatest fear had been realized.

Her mother was dead.

What was she supposed to do now?

18

Ruby knocked quietly on the closed door to her father's study but didn't wait for a response. "Daddy?" she called softly, easing it open.

His back was toward her, hunched over his computer. His head hung so low between his shoulders, for a moment Ruby wondered if he was asleep. She started to call him again, but he turned to face her before she'd finished the word.

"Ruby Catherine, what are you doing here?" His words were soft and unsteady, as if he didn't know the end of his question even as he spoke it.

It had been a week since her mother's death—though the pain of her loss remained so raw and fresh, every second felt like she was learning the news for the first time.

She had been doing everything in her power to restore some semblance of normalcy to their lives. She sensed they needed it, and it brought her some solace to focus her energy on tasks like washing all the smoke-filled linens in their house or taking out her anger on the internet company arguing about when their service would be restored.

But in between these chores, every now and then, she'd stumble into a quiet moment like this that made her mother's heart-wrenching absence overwhelming.

She took a deep breath, forcing a passive expression onto her face. "Dinner's ready, Daddy," she said.

He gave her an exasperated look, peering up from haphazard stacks of paper. "I have work to do here." He held up a manila folder, which appeared to be empty from where Ruby stood in the doorway.

Ever since the doctor had broken the news to them, her father had fluctuated between two different versions of himself that Ruby found equally distressing. One moment, he was frozen by the misery of having lost his beloved wife, painfully aware of her death and broken from the certainty that he was responsible for it. And the next, he seemed to be operating in another world, preoccupied with menial, nonsensical tasks, in complete denial of her mother's passing.

Ruby honestly wasn't sure which was worse.

He looked utterly defeated, and it was all she could do to suppress the stinging of tears at the back of her throat.

Stacks and stacks of papers had accumulated on his desk over the past few days, surrounded by half-empty coffee mugs. Every single file cabinet drawer was left ajar, some drawers completely empty, some looking like a bear had rummaged through them. About a dozen Post-it notes clung to his computer monitor with phone numbers and other indecipherable messages scrawled on them.

As children, they were *never* allowed in this room, so Ruby's memory of it was mostly just distant glances from the hallway. But in these brief glimpses lived a glossy desk with never more than one folder on it, bookshelves alphabetized with binders of financial records, a blueprint or business flyer tacked to one wall for consideration. Nothing like the room she stood in now.

She took another deep breath before she was able to formulate a response, scrambling for some scrap of composure. "I just . . . Let me know if I can do anything to help."

Her father wasn't wrong. There was an unfathomable amount of work for them to do. Between her mother's funeral arrangements and cleaning up after the fire, there was a never-ending list of loss and recovery.

And though she didn't know where to begin with the logistics of her family's next chapter, she had a hard time believing whatever it was her father was doing in here would make any kind of difference in the daunting decisions that awaited them.

"Okay, mija," he said with an impatience that surprised her. "Tell your mother I'll be down in a little bit."

His words tore through her as she nodded and shut the door behind herself.

ALMOST IN A TRANCE, RUBY FOUND HERSELF ON THE BACK porch after dinner without really considering how the charred air would be anything but fresh. She coughed bitterly.

"¿Estás bien, mija?"

Ruby jumped at Mama Ortega's voice and found her sitting in her father's favorite chair in the semidarkness of dusk, a fatigued expression of concern on her deeply lined face.

Ruby nodded, despite the fact that she did not feel okay at all. Mama Ortega gestured to the chair next to her, and Ruby sank into it without hesitation.

"Every time I think there's no way I could possibly feel any worse, I remember how much is destroyed out here," Ruby admitted softly, her heartbeat heavy inside her chest as she let her eyes linger on the gray ruins spread out before them.

In hindsight, she wondered how she could've been so foolish not to have checked the surrounding property the day she and Millie arrived, but she also knew that small oversight, in her frenzied state to find her family, might have been her saving grace. Losing her mother was already inconceivably horrific in and of itself; if she had realized then how much more she had lost, how would she have ever survived that day?

It hadn't been until the next day, after they'd made arrangements for her mother's body and signed all her father's discharge paperwork, that Ruby finally understood the full weight of their current situation. After an eerie car ride home—in which Millie anxiously fiddled with the air conditioner and radio dials, offering any modifications to make them more comfortable, as if something as stupid as music could ease their pain—Ruby had finally found the courage to make her way to the back porch. To the exact spot where they sat now, where she'd sat so many evenings with her father.

The sight of the devastated land shocked her. Even now, she couldn't believe how much destruction the fires had caused.

"Mm, there is a lot of work to be done, yes," Mama Ortega said sympathetically. Ruby thought that was a serious understatement, but her grandmother continued before she could cut in. "The bed-and-breakfast is still standing, at least."

Ruby snorted dejectedly. True, it hadn't burned down. The silhouette was still more or less familiar, but even from a distance, it was clear it had suffered serious damage. The white walls of the barnyard exterior were coated black and gray.

"The beautiful thing about trees and plants is they grow back, mi amor," Mama Ortega said, gesturing at the masses of skeletal tree branches and dark stumps.

"I need to go down there and figure out what exactly can be salvaged, what needs to be done," Ruby responded heavily. "I just . . . haven't been able to make myself do it yet."

Mama Ortega made another noise of agreement and patted her hand. "We've been dealing with a lot, mija. It's okay. Things like this, they take time."

The sun had almost sunk beyond the distant hills, and even though Ruby knew the fires in the visible distance had all been extinguished, the orange glow of the sky against the dark terrain made it look like her world was still very much ablaze. It turned her stomach.

She thought of the distinct feeling of love and connection she'd felt for this place the night she'd stood here just before she'd left for college. This may not have been the place she remembered, but it was at least something. Something unfamiliar and ugly, yes, but *something*.

"I know it seems impossible now, but Ortegas have a long history of overcoming hardship." Ruby's grandmother took her hand and held it in her lap. "Though I wish it never would've come to this, I know we'll get through it together."

Ruby's eyes swept over the yard once more, the last bit of sunlight now gone, rendering the land before them a shadowy mosaic of blacks and grays.

"We'll be okay," Mama Ortega said. "It'll be hard and it will probably be different than before, but it'll be okay."

19

Ruby gazed at her reflection in the full-length mirror that had hung on the back of her bedroom door since middle school and tried to smooth the ill-fitting fabric of her dress. Yesterday, she'd driven to the mall in San Diego to buy black dresses for herself and her sisters because most of the stores in Buena Valley were closed due to lack of staff or fire damage. Picking out clothing for her mother's funeral was a hard enough task, but the hassle of the long drive through her destroyed community plus the blissful ignorance of shoppers who had been unaffected by the disaster were overwhelming in their unpleasantness. Ruby had torn through the department store and slung three dark dresses over her arm with little regard for size or fit. She had just needed to get out of there.

Now, of course, she was paying for her apathy as she realized glumly that her dress was about two sizes too big and hung off her frame in frumpy folds.

It was the kind of oversight Eleanor would never have allowed.

She hadn't once imagined what she was supposed to look like for her mother's funeral, but she knew this wasn't it. As she glared at her reflection, like it was the mirror's fault Ruby looked so unpolished, there was a soft knock at her bedroom door.

"How are you doing?" Millie asked as she peeked in.

Ruby bit her lip. How was she doing? How did Millie *think* she was doing? What a pointless, inane, *ridiculous* question. She was minutes away from her mother's funeral, a ceremony that was mostly a weird formality since it would only be attended by her immediate family given that travel was still nonexistent in their area. Eleanor had been an only child, and her parents had passed away before Ruby was born, but their kitchen was filled with decadent bouquets and condolence cards from cousins and friends of her parents as if they were expecting hundreds of attendees. These tokens of sympathy now struck Ruby as unbelievably frivolous, and the overpowering fragrance of lilies whenever she went downstairs made her want to throw up.

The one small glimmer of hope that Ruby had been clinging to with a viselike grip had been the fact that Ashton was due back today. His parents had, of course, called and sent a particularly opulent floral arrangement, but it was the prospect of Ashton's physical presence that kept her going. However, he'd unexpectedly gotten a late start getting on the road due to some mandatory overtime, and with the road closures from the fires, it looked like he wouldn't make it in time for the funeral. She tried to remind herself that he would be there eventually—afterward—but the idea of saying goodbye to her mother without the comfort of her best friend put Ruby on edge.

Millie stepped through the doorway into Ruby's room, still waiting for her response. She was wearing a navy blue shift dress with a Peter Pan collar. Though Ruby thought the dress was far too juvenile for a twenty-one-year-old, she noted with envy that at least it fit. She resisted the urge to snap at Millie for barging in—what was the point of knocking if she didn't wait for a response?—and instead responded with just a sigh.

"The pastor arrived a few minutes ago. Your grandmother is helping him get set up downstairs," Millie told her with the apologetic tone she'd adopted recently, which sounded like her words themselves were tiptoeing. "I checked with your sisters, and they're all dressed. But . . . I thought you'd want to make sure your father is ready?"

Ruby grimaced but nodded. As much as Millie's excessively cosseting demeanor drove Ruby nuts, somewhere deep inside her—deep, *deep* inside—she found scraps of appreciation for the sense of caring consistency she brought in this terrifying period of transition. She was staying at the Ortega household while her father recovered, and in between visiting him at the hospital, she helped with the kinds of things Ruby was sure would've fallen through the cracks without her. Though Mama Ortega was there, too, and did the big chores like cooking meals and washing their clothes, Millie was there to hug Carla when she cried or meet up with Remy to return his truck. Things Ruby knew needed to happen but was unable to summon the effort to execute herself.

The exception, of course, was Ruby's father. Ruby was in no way equipped to deal with him, but that was one area in which Millie dared not meddle. Ruby and Mama Ortega had been tag-teaming, making sure he was bathed and fed and had at least one foot in some semblance of reality, but even between the two of them, it was an impossible ordeal.

He was a man unmoored, drifting and flailing. She had begun to suspect her mother had been the sole grounding force to keep this wild man under control, and now, perhaps, that responsibility had fallen to her. But Ruby was nothing like her mother, as much as she wanted to be, and Eleanor was who he needed right now.

THE SUN HAD FINALLY SET, AND RUBY FELT A GLINT OF relief as she watched her sisters clearing the patio table through the kitchen window. Mama Ortega had made chiles rellenos, which she had lovingly proclaimed was their mother's favorite dish. Eleanor had actually hated those stuffed peppers but had known how happy it made Mama Ortega to believe she enjoyed them. Eleanor Ortega, tactful to the end.

Ruby turned on the sink to begin washing the dishes the girls had already brought in. Carla had wanted to hold the ceremony outside since it was their mother's favorite place. Eleanor was so often found admiring her garden or feeding the horses a handful of carrots or even just running through a checklist while sipping a cup of coffee in one of the patio chairs. But the place that her mother had loved was very different than what they saw now. Ruby personally had found it even more depressing to grieve surrounded by such a graphic reminder of their loss, but Carla had been insistent. At least Ruby had been able to persuade her sisters to hold off on scattering her ashes on the property until after the land had recovered. Ashes on ashes would have just been too morbid.

A flash of light suddenly illuminated the room—the headlights of a car pulling into the driveway.

"Now, who could that be?" Mama Ortega asked with a perplexed scowl, clutching a water pitcher to her body.

Suddenly, Millie gasped and plopped a small box of tea lights onto the table before dashing down the hall, toward the front door.

Then it struck Ruby, like an electric shock igniting every inch of her body.

Ashton!

She turned the faucet off forcefully and chased after Millie. She could hear her sisters' steps behind her, their inquisitive whispers.

"Oh my God!" Ruby cried from the front door as she finally took in the sight of his familiar Prius at the curb. He stood next to the driver's side door, arms outstretched as Millie flung herself at him.

As Ruby stepped forward, ready to race down the steps toward him, she felt a small hand on her elbow, and glanced over to see Carla eyeing her questioningly. "Maybe you should let them have a moment together first?"

Ruby scoffed. "I—"

Elena appeared on her other side, an eyebrow cocked suspiciously. "He's *her* boyfriend, isn't he?" she said, her voice dry and critical.

Ruby rolled her eyes but didn't respond. The brief feeling of reprieve she'd felt at the sight of Ashton's sinewy frame and dusty-blond hair coiled into a tight knot in her stomach. Carla patted her arm tenderly, and her younger sister's pity was more than she could take.

All the white-knuckled restraint she'd been exerting over the past several days—at the hospital, at home with her family, at the damn funeral where she'd clutched the porcelain urn of her mother's ashes—began to crack.

She'd endured so much, and now *this*. He'd come all this way to be with her, hadn't he? Then why did he still feel so out of reach?

Something snapped inside her, and for the first time since she'd been home, she burst into tears.

20

The day after the funeral, Ruby awoke just after sunrise, the sky still dusky and purple, and pulled on a pair of jeans and a sweatshirt before dashing downstairs. The house was completely silent. As she made herself a quick cup of coffee, she surveyed the darkened property out the back window, all shadows and cinders in the wintry morning light.

The time for grieving was done. She had to get a handle on what needed to happen next. She couldn't let the fact that she didn't know what to do stop her from getting to work.

She splashed water on her face in the kitchen sink and tied her hair into a ponytail as the coffee pot gurgled to life. She took her cup to go and bolted out of the house.

She'd been putting it off, but she needed to see the bed-and-breakfast and the construction site for the half-built reception hall. She had to walk through and understand exactly how much had been damaged. She might not have known what exactly to do with that knowledge, but she figured that was the first step in recovering from a natural disaster. It was anyone's guess what was next. Insurance? Repairs? Didn't the government have something to do with it all?

She'd figure it out. If she didn't, it wasn't clear who would. Her father was certainly in no condition to make any decisions, and she had no idea when he would be. Her mother had always been the backbone of the family, holding them together no matter what. Ruby didn't have the grace or poise Eleanor Ortega had possessed, but she hoped she could attempt to fill her mother's shoes with sheer stubbornness; she'd work on the grace part later.

She'd heard on a news segment a few years ago that houses with pools often stood a better chance of surviving a wildfire, with the water serving as a kind of moat to prevent the flames from reaching the home. It was eerie to see that scenario played out in real life, but the house and backyard were virtually untouched, aside from a layer of gray soot, while the land at the base of the hill was more drastically affected.

Ruby crunched through the dead grass as she made her way down the hill, a journey she'd made countless times throughout her life.

She'd start with the bed-and-breakfast. Not only was it closer, but there appeared to be more to salvage. Then she'd make her way to the ruins of what was supposed to be the next phase of the Ortega empire.

Her eyes coasted across the scorched remains of the horse corrals and pasture, and her heart gave an icy lurch as the reality of the horses' absence sank in with the unavoidable visual. She knew animals were often set free to make last-minute escapes from the fires, and though she'd registered their absence from the beginning, the fact that they were either roaming the wild or gone from this world suddenly set in.

Her mother had loved those horses.

It must've killed her to leave them behind like that, Ruby thought, before she could catch the cruel irony in her word choice.

She swallowed, her throat sticky and dry, and dragged her gaze instead to the sullied barn that loomed before her. Its chic white exterior was now black and gray. The rustic chandelier that normally hung above the entry lay in a heap on the ground, the metal frame warped and the bulbs shattered. Many of the windows had exploded in the heat of the blaze, leaving only jagged glass barely hanging from their frames. The ones that had survived were so dark with soot that they may as well have been painted black. Everything around the bed-and-breakfast was crisp and dead—the leafy shrubs that lined the walkway, the flower boxes that sat beneath each window, the towering trees whose branches once draped overhead—but the building itself still stood. Tarnished, but resilient.

She tried to drum up some gratitude for that win, but it felt so small in light of everything else.

She stepped through the shards of broken glass and clumps of indistinguishable black debris, and gave the heavy wood door a good tug, its large iron doorknob cool and gritty to the touch. It jerked open with a cloud of dust that hung in the air as Ruby stepped through the murky entryway.

As she took in the room around her, she drew in a sharp breath that instantly turned into a sputtering cough.

It was . . . *okay*, she realized as she tried to catch her breath.

She left footprints on the unswept wood floors as she explored, running her fingers along the chalky banister or flipping a nonfunctioning light switch.

It would take a good deal of work before they were ready for guests again, but Ruby reminded herself that the important thing was that they would be ready at some point. These were things they could fix—somehow. The exact steps remained a little less clear, but Ruby could see an end goal underneath all the ash and dirt.

The back doors that opened off the small dining area led to the patio, where Elena's quinceañera had taken place over the summer. Usually, you could see the lush hills of their property stretching out past the flagstone courtyard, the surrounding avocado and citrus trees, and the vacant land that had been set aside for a vineyard. Now she peered out the clouded windowpanes of the double doors at the blackened decimation, taking in every sweep of ruin.

So much of what had lived on this land had perished. They could rebuild and repair, but they could never resuscitate the living things that had been lost.

She made her way through what remained of the orchard—what was once a grove of blossoming orange, lemon, and avocado trees and was now a graveyard of charred stumps mixed in with a few singed survivors. As the construction site came into view, she realized despondently it was much easier to assess it according to what had persevered rather than what had been destroyed.

The cement foundation, which outlined the plans and dreams for the building more than anything else, seemed to be intact, though it was blackened in the few patches that were visible underneath the thick layer of rubble. The towering wood framework was gone. A few seared beams stretched upward, but for the most part, it had burned down.

She ran her hand along a soot-coated beam of wood meant to frame the exterior wall, desperately trying to conjure the place this was supposed to be, the glamour and elegance her family had envisioned. Even the handful of beams that still stood would probably have to be replaced anyway. There was no inch of this site that had been unscathed.

It was heartbreaking to take in this amount of ruin, but it made her insides seize up to think of the logistics of the repairs. Not just the money and progress they'd lost, but the costs to rebuild.

And what about the future plans? Would they be able to fix this place up in time for Governor Cortez's event in July? Would she even want to have her event here anymore?

It was supposed to be the beginning of a new era for Ortega Properties, a gateway to new ventures, but Ruby could feel it slipping through her fingers like the ash that surrounded her.

She knew she needed to take pictures; the insurance companies would need documentation. Hands shaking, she pulled out her phone and silently began snapping photos. She drifted around the ruined site, carefully stepping over fallen beams and hunks of indistinguishable wreckage, the computerized shutter sound of her phone camera clicking away. She avoided looking at the actual pictures as she took them.

Behind her, she heard the crunch of a footstep and perhaps if her senses weren't so overwhelmed, it might've startled her. Or perhaps she had been expecting him, hoping beneath her sorrow that he'd find her. She turned to see Ashton a few steps away from her, his hands in the pockets of his Phoenix Fire Department sweatpants. His eyes glided across the destruction in a disbelieving, dreamlike kind of way before they met Ruby's gaze.

"Do you remember when we used to play hide-and-seek in the orange grove?" he asked, his voice tight. He took a step closer to her, gesturing toward the remaining trees as if she'd need a reminder.

She sighed, her grief heavy in her chest. "Yeah, until that big spider landed on you and you refused to go back."

The half smile that found its way to his face was sad and nostalgic in a way that ripped Ruby apart. "Things were a lot simpler back then," he mused.

"How are you handling all of this?" she asked. The familiarity of him—his rosy cheeks in the cold morning air and his mussed bed head—in this unsettlingly broken environment was torture.

They'd barely had a moment alone together since he'd arrived yesterday, a hug or two and a handful of glances across the room. It had all been so fast and overwhelming, she hadn't even begun to wonder how he was feeling—what it was like to not have a home to come back to but having both parents safe. They had both endured life-altering losses, but their situations couldn't have been more different.

Ashton shrugged, keeping his eyes on the gray hills in the distance, freshly illuminated by the hazy glow of sunrise. "It's . . ." He shook his head, casting aside whatever the end of that sentence was in the process.

When he finally did look at her again, Ruby found herself also struggling for what to say.

"I'm so glad you're here, though," she said softly, knowing how desperate and disjointed the words sounded as they spilled from her mouth, but not entirely caring. She needed him—needed to feel connected to him—even if it made her sound like a complete fool.

He sighed, nodding.

She stared at him openly, his handsome profile framed by both the dawn half light and the darkness of the destroyed orchard. Her mouth opened several times, summoning words she simply did not have for this agonizingly beautiful boy in the wake of the worst disaster of their lives.

After a few minutes, she resigned herself to the profound and stifling silence, and turned her gaze to the ruins around them, too. She'd hoped that they'd come together in their losses. They'd be able to grieve together, to understand the darkness and heartache they were both experiencing. But in that moment, their sadnesses felt somehow separate and isolating, an insurmountable wall of anguish between them.

She inhaled deeply; the air that rushed in tasted filthy and lifeless.

"This was a beautiful place," was what he said finally, chewing on his lip thoughtfully.

A reactionary bristle rose inside Ruby at Ashton's use of the past tense, but before she could be fully bothered by it, he reached out and draped his arm around her shoulders. He rested his head against hers, softly rubbing her left shoulder as they stood there, taking in the devastated land around them.

21

Wildfires were a seasonal occurrence in California, almost as expected as a heat wave or Halloween. But even though they were expected to occur *somewhere*, Ruby never once expected they'd occur in Buena Valley. It was a safe, beautiful place. It was hers. It was not the type of place where these things happened.

She realized now that her unshakable belief that she was somehow exempt from the harshness the rest of the world endured left her wildly unprepared for dealing with the aftermath of the disaster. Before all this, she had never done so much as make her own dentist appointment or pay her own cell phone bill. She didn't even understand what a mortgage was or what utilities included, so taking on the day-to-day management of her household and business felt like way more than she could handle.

But her sisters had to eat. Her father needed a bed. They had to keep their home. So Ruby began to work.

She'd thought she'd already endured the worst of it when her mother died, learning that a whole part of her life had vanished and could never fully be restored. And while nothing would ever compare to that pain and shock, the hours of phone calls and dozens of emails about property damage quickly taught her that the uncertainty of what would happen next held its own unpleasant challenges as well.

They had fire insurance, yes, but that was about the only definitive answer she seemed able to get from anyone. How much would it cover? When would the insurance money get here? How could they start rebuilding without that money? How were they expected to get their lives back in order if no one knew the answers to any of these questions? How could they even manage their basic needs—food and supplies and whatever other expenses her parents usually took care of—without answers to any of these questions?

Not to mention that it was impossible to get an insurance claims adjuster or construction crew out to the property. With a whole region gone up in flames and scrambling to put together the pieces, there simply weren't enough workers to go around.

She couldn't even begin to think about the fact that she couldn't get ahold of any of their employees—or former employees—it seemed. Not even Paola and Jorge, whom she'd always thought of as more family than staff. It appeared that pretty much everyone who had ever worked for Ortega Properties had jumped ship and had no plans of swimming back.

Perhaps most disconcerting of all was how few answers her father had to any of these questions. All her life, he'd lived and breathed for the business, but now he was so lost Ruby wondered if he even recognized himself.

"Ruby Catherine, it's been a long time since I've had to deal with this level of decisions," he'd snapped wearily one night after hours poring over old order forms.

Her father had aged ten years in the past few weeks. His thick black hair appeared grayer and stood on end, giving him a perpetually shocked appearance. Dark circles framed his eyes, and his feeble, uncertain tone of voice made him seem like a bewildered old man.

And, of course, the weight of her mother's absence was omnipresent, penetrating—something they could neither escape nor address. Still, even though Ruby felt like she was in way over her head, it was much easier to focus on the business than her father's heartbreak.

Ruby sensed that her sisters, in their own unique ways, were trying to help—or at least trying not to be unhelpful. Elena had made herself generally scarce, which, for her, was a charitable effort. Carla appeared from time to time with vaguely optimistic pieces of information or to offer Ruby a snack.

"Millie says Mr. Hamilton will be discharged this week," she said one night, nestled on the couch in her plaid pajamas and a fuzzy fleece blanket.

Ruby nodded but couldn't manage a more focused response.

"Are—are you all right?"

Ruby's eyes quickly met her sister's and noticed them glistening with tears. Of course she wasn't "all right." Nothing had been "all right" in weeks, and dark corners of her mind worried nothing would ever be all right again.

Nevertheless, she forced a swift nod—for Carla's sake. "Yes, yes.

It's just a lot," she muttered. "It doesn't help that Jorge and Paola and anyone on our staff who knows anything about anything have completely abandoned us. I can't reach anyone useful. Not even a phone call back. It's like they've completely forgotten about us."

Carla shifted awkwardly, her gaze heavy on Ruby.

"What?" Ruby barked, sensing her sister's reluctance.

"Well . . . maybe they're having just as hard of a time as us," she suggested softly, smoothing out the folds of her blanket. "Maybe they lost someone, too. Maybe they want to come back but can't. I've been seeing on the news that a lot of the areas with the most casualties were places where mostly immigrants lived." She spoke slowly, choosing her words carefully. "They're saying it's because of language barriers. Most of the evacuation notices were only available in English. And then, of course, not everyone could afford to evacuate—transportation and hotels and missing work and stuff. All I'm saying is, a lot of homes were ruined. And, I mean, you know firsthand how hard it is to get stuff fixed right now. There's so much to deal with. Who knows what they've got going on?"

Ruby frowned, flipping through the same stack of bank statements for what felt like the hundredth time. Kind and empathetic Carla was usually prone to more tender insights than Ruby could ever string together, but still, her sister's remarks gave her pause. She hadn't thought of it that way.

I don't have time *to think about it that way,* she corrected herself. *We've got enough to deal with ourselves without worrying about everyone else's sob stories.* She had to be pragmatic and realistic and maybe even a little bit ruthless if she wanted to make any real progress.

Ruby's cell phone vibrated a few feet away, and she nodded at

Carla to retrieve it for her. Somberly, Carla read the message aloud. "It's Patty. Isn't that your roommate? She wants to know when you're coming back."

Ruby exhaled, rubbing her temples. She'd been officially gone for nearly a month now. Patty tended toward worry in far more normal circumstances; she was probably beside herself at this point. "Um, tell her probably not till after winter break." That should buy her some time, at least, though things were such a mess, it was hard to imagine what could possibly be different in a month.

Carla typed silently, then relayed her next message after a few minutes. "She wants to know if you want her to send you any of your things? Textbooks? Clothes?"

Ruby shook her head. She had enough clothes here to make things work, and with the semester wrapping up, she didn't see any point in mailing something as heavy as textbooks. Especially when the idea of making time for homework seemed laughable.

"No textbooks?" Carla repeated, eyes wide.

"No, Carla."

"Well, what are you doing about school?"

Ruby shrugged. Truthfully, she'd contacted her advisor a few days ago about a leave of absence for the upcoming semester. Though the money spent on her dorm was already gone forever, she could still get a partial refund on her classes, and that was money they needed, she was beginning to realize. Her father's budget for the reception hall had been based largely on profits from the bed-and-breakfast. She was able to manage their daily expenses, but getting their property up and running again was going to take some creative problem-solving.

Carla was still staring with saucerlike eyes.

"Don't worry about it, Carla. I've . . . got it all under control." It was a feeble lie, and though she knew Carla saw right through it, she was nice enough not to press any further.

WHEN RUBY FINALLY MADE HER WAY UPSTAIRS LATE THAT night, she was relieved to see the light under Carla's bedroom door was off. Her poor younger sister was so desperate for reassurance and familiarity, and though Ruby wanted to be able to provide what she needed, she also felt completely incapable. She could take care of the practical things like buying Carla's favorite cereal or reminding her to brush her teeth before bed. But what about when she caught Carla lingering in her parents' bedroom, running her fingers over their mother's dresses, as she had the past four mornings?

The first time, Ruby simply asked what she was doing.

"I just wanted to feel close to her," Carla had whispered, and Ruby instantly wished she hadn't asked, wished she hadn't stumbled upon this heartbreaking ritual at all. What did she know about raising a young girl, especially when this gentle, sensitive child was nothing like the headstrong one Ruby had been years ago? And besides, even if she did have any clue what she was doing, she had so much on her plate. Where did Carla's feelings fall on her list of her priorities when their family business lay in ruins just outside?

She was on her way to her bedroom, eager to put yet another bleak and frustrating day behind her, when she heard footsteps coming up the stairs.

"Elena, if that's you coming in just now after we talked about your curfew, I swear to *God*—" she called, folding her arms across her chest irritably. The girls were due to return to school tomorrow—or some semblance of school. The building itself had burned down, so the classes were divvied up among a variety of community buildings for the time being. She needed to drop Elena off at the recreation center, and Carla's class was in a conference room at the mayor's office. Ruby had been adamant with Elena, however, that just because their father was taking a hiatus from parenting and the school situation was unusual, didn't mean she could do whatever the hell she wanted. The thought of her slinking upstairs at this hour made Ruby's blood boil.

"Whoa, easy there! It's just me," Ashton said breezily as he appeared at the top of the stairs.

"Oh." A warmth immediately spread over her as she realized he was alone. "Sorry. Where's Millie?"

"She's spending the night at the hospital tonight. Mr. Hamilton is supposed to get discharged first thing in the morning, and she thinks if she's there to badger the doctors, he'll get sent home faster. He's pretty anxious to get out of there." He ran his fingers through his hair, his eyes glassy with fatigue. "But seeing as I head out soon, Millie thought I should take advantage of sleeping in an actual bed while I can, so she insisted I come home—er, here, I mean." He smiled sadly at his slipup, though it made Ruby's heart swell to hear him refer to her house as his home.

"When do you have to go back to the fire line?" she asked.

"Day after tomorrow. I'll have to get on the road pretty early. Our camp's a three-hour drive from here." He gazed at her seriously, and

Ruby couldn't help but wonder if he could sense her disappointment. After two weeks away, he was only granted a week at home before being sent out again. The fire was no longer a risk around here, but it was still raging farther north, and he didn't know how many more tours it would take to get it extinguished. "Listen, I know it's kind of late and you're probably exhausted, but do you want to have a beer with me? I could use a drink."

Without hesitation, Ruby nodded. The chance of catching him on his own was all that kept Ruby going some days, and her entire body ached for this moment alone with him—especially before he left again.

As she rummaged through the fridge to find two lone Coronas tucked in the back behind a jar of mayo, Ruby desperately tried to conjure a feeling of familiarity for this moment. She'd coerced Ashton into busting into their parents' alcohol cabinets a handful of times in high school, but she felt distinctly aware of how different things felt now.

Was it because of the kiss they'd shared back in Arizona? With everything that had happened over the past few weeks, she hadn't had much time to mull it over, but she thought of it every now and then. Though it had been so abrupt, it was a small respite for her in her grief.

She wished that kiss had changed everything for them, but she knew deep down that wasn't it. At least, that wasn't all of it. After all, he hadn't acknowledged it in any way since that night—and the longer it went unspoken, the more nervous Ruby got about bringing it up.

Maybe it was just that he *looked* different. His hair was a little shaggier than normal, not quite as long as that summer he'd hiked the Appalachian Trail with his dad, but longer than he normally kept it. He was lean, too. He'd always been slim, but Ruby suspected days spent on his feet doing manual labor had contributed to his taut frame.

Or maybe it was his eyes. There was something dark and drowsy underneath their hazel surface.

She just couldn't put her finger on it.

"Do you like firefighting?" she blurted in a sudden urge to hear his voice, then felt her cheeks grow hot. "I'm sorry. That's a silly question. I know it's hard and probably really sad."

Ashton half smiled and nodded. "It's both those things, yes. But it's nice to feel like I'm doing something that matters."

Ruby sighed. "I think I know what you mean."

"I talked to my parents for a while this afternoon." He took a big gulp of beer, and Ruby watched his Adam's apple bob. "They said they're not planning on coming back."

"What?"

Ashton nodded again, spinning the beer bottle idly on the arm of his chair. "They said they're going to take the insurance money and buy a house in Bakersfield, near my aunt."

Ruby's jaw hung open in shock. "But this is their *home*. This is *our home!*"

Ashton's eyes searched her face, and he hesitated, as if not sure how to proceed. He was sad, and Ruby couldn't tell if it was because of his parents' decision or her reaction. "I guess some people would rather start over fresh."

"That sounds a lot like giving up," she muttered.

Ashton sat in silence for a moment, fixated on his beer. "Not everyone is as tough as you, Ruby. I know it's hard for you to imagine, but some people can't face everything that's been destroyed and try to make sense of it. Sometimes it's easier to start over new."

Ruby tried to wrap her mind around what he was saying, but he might as well have been speaking another language. All she heard was that they were abandoning their community and their memories because it seemed too *hard*. "Well, what do you think you'll do? Are you going back to Arizona? Or do you think you'll move up to Bakersfield?" Her words came out sharp and accusatory, but secretly she was praying he'd stay with her, that he loved and believed in their home as much as she did and he was willing to face the hardships with her rather than run away. She bit her lip, waiting for his response.

Slowly, he shrugged. "Millie and I haven't really talked about it yet. Just need to make it through the fire season first."

Her heart sank at his noncommittal answer, and she took a long swig of her beer to hide her disappointment.

His weighty, undecipherable gaze lingered on her, and for a moment she hoped he'd ask what her plan was or what she thought he should do. But instead he said, "I hope Millie asked you about Mr. Hamilton staying here until her aunt is able to come pick him up this weekend?"

She hadn't so much asked as talked around the issue, annoying Ruby until she interrupted her rambling to say it would be fine. It wasn't ideal, but what else could she say? At this point, what was one more person? "It's not a big deal," she mumbled.

He leaned forward, his elbows resting on his knees. "We both know it is. You're doing a lot."

Ruby's heart surged in a thick mix of sadness and love for him. It killed her to see Ashton, who she'd always thought of as idealistic and cheerful, regard her in this serious way. She had always gotten the impression that Ashton viewed the world as his for the taking, with every opportunity and path open to him. It was an attitude she'd admired and related to.

But the darkness in his eyes, the careless slouch in his shoulders, made her think that attitude was wearing away within him, that these recent weeks were taking a toll on the way he saw himself and the world. And maybe the way he saw her, too.

She could face a lot of the destruction the fires had caused. Mostly because she had to, but also because buildings could be repaired. But could people? Where was she even supposed to begin with her father and Ashton and everyone else who had been completely undone by all this?

"To be perfectly honest, Ashton, I feel like I'm not doing anything. I don't know if I can do it." She fought to conceal a tremor in her voice, an unsteadiness that threatened to give way to a flood of tears she'd been holding in longer than she cared to admit. It would feel so good to finally let go of some of these feelings—to confide in someone she trusted and loved—but something she couldn't exactly explain stopped her, and she clenched her jaw to force down her fear and anxiety.

Sighing, she leaned her body against the armrest of the couch. There was only about a foot between them. If he wanted, he could reach out across the space between them and touch her.

"Isn't there anyone who can help you?" he asked half-heartedly.

Inside, Ruby ached. She wanted *him* to help her! She needed *him*. Even if he couldn't help with all the stupid business stuff, just having him by her side as they rebuilt would be enough! She could bear it all so much better with him. She knew it, even if she couldn't explain it. She would be stronger and smarter and more patient, just like she needed to be.

She sat silently with her eyes fixed on him, trying to make him see that, urging him to read the message in her face.

"Your dad? Any employees or business partners?" he continued weakly.

She shook her head. "Not yet, anyway. No one's been much help so far."

At last, Ashton reached between them and set his hand on top of hers. Ruby was surprised by the feeling of new calluses on his palm. Ashton's gentle, book-reading hands were so rough now! Eyes wide, she waited breathlessly for what would happen next.

He seemed to be mulling over his words, something heavy and difficult running through his mind. Finally, he said, "You're doing a good job, Ruby. You're strong and smart, and that's what it takes to make it through something like this. I'm sorry I don't have anything more helpful to say. I know you miss your mom—I miss her, too. I wish I could tell you how to fix your B&B or get your insurance money, but I don't have any of those practical skills. I don't know anything about the real world."

Ruby shook her head, placing her other hand on top of his. "That's not true. You're doing so much! You're out there fighting fires! You're strong and smart, too, Ashton!"

He withdrew his hand and finished his beer with one long swig. "What no one actually tells you is that wildland firefighting is basically just extreme gardening. I'm out there clearing brush most of the day. I don't even really see the fire," he muttered. "I mean, I'm glad I'm doing it. It needs to be done, and I'm happy to be doing *something* meaningful for once." Again, he paused, and Ruby wondered if his eyes were so shiny because it was late and he was tired, or if he had tears in them. "Do you know what I'm worried is going to be even harder than firefighting, though?" His voice trembled.

Ruby nodded, though she had absolutely no idea what he was about to say. The intimacy with which he was speaking thrilled her. Had he ever been so open with her? Certainly not since Millie!

"Coming back here," he croaked. "Facing this place and figuring out what to do now that everything I've ever known is gone or different. Doing what *you're* doing now. I don't know if I can do that."

She opened her mouth to insist that of course he could, that he was Ashton Willis and he could do whatever he wanted! But nothing came out. She didn't know what to say to that kind of self-doubt, so instead she let her eyes rest on his hand, the hand that had been touching her just a moment ago.

He grimaced, his gaze leaving her face and focusing on something distant, something Ruby sensed she wouldn't be able to understand. Something only in Ashton's mind. "But there's no going back, I guess. Just figuring out a way forward."

That's life, Ruby thought in puzzlement. *What other choice do we have?* She didn't understand Ashton's desolate astonishment at the changes the fire had brought, and she wondered despairingly if Millie would.

He rose to his feet, seeming to shake off the temporary trance of raw reflection they'd shared. "I'm sorry for babbling. It probably doesn't make much sense to you because you've never been afraid of figuring out what comes next. You're a brave person, Ruby." He smiled tenderly.

Her heart fluttered in her chest as she stared up at him longingly. Again, the words caught in her throat as she thought wildly, *You're brave, too.*

A tense silence passed between them, filled with so much expectation Ruby felt the noiselessness practically bursting.

"I love ya, pal. You've got this," he said gruffly, snapping the moment in half and tossing it away with the same finality that he tossed his bottle in the bin before disappearing upstairs.

AS RUBY WENT TO BED THAT NIGHT, DAZED AND THROBBING from all the confusing things Ashton had said, something gloomy and irritating in the back of her mind reminded her there was someone she could call. Someone who was in the area. Someone who had helped her in the past. Someone who knew something about the hospitality business.

Someone who abandoned me in the middle of a crisis.

She physically shuddered at the idea of asking Remy for help ever again. Though there was no way he could've known that he was sending her off to face her mother's death, she still resented him deeply for the abandonment.

Perhaps if they hadn't had to make his heroic pit stop, she would've made it to her mom's hospital room in time to see her alive one last time. She knew that was highly unlikely—they hadn't even let her father in, she had been in such critical condition, and he'd been there the whole time—but impossible, unresolvable notions like that fueled her anger in a way that was dimly satisfying.

Things would have to get a hell of a lot worse for me to even consider calling Remy Bustillos was her final thought before drifting off to sleep.

22

The next few days were marked by comings and goings. Mr. Hamilton was discharged from the hospital and spent two nights sleeping on the couch and easing about the first floor in a wheelchair until Millie's aunt arrived to transport him back to Arizona. Ruby had expected Millie to leave with her father, but she'd shyly expressed her interest in staying when Ruby had questioned her.

"Why? Don't you want to go home?" Ruby had asked.

"Yes and no. I love Arizona and I love seeing my dad, but I just feel like there's more important stuff going on here," she'd said. "My dad has a big support system there with my aunt and her family, and his fire crew. And I can always visit." Something unspoken glinted in Millie's expression, something almost pitying. Perhaps someone else would've been touched by her decision, but Ruby was mostly annoyed by her sympathy.

Even though it was a little awkward living alongside a girl whose boyfriend she actively pined for—and had recently kissed—Ruby had to admit she was a help to have around.

Ashton left the morning after Mr. Hamilton was released, as he'd said. Ruby watched sleepily from her bedroom window as Millie sent him off at three a.m. She'd planned on waking up with them, but Ashton had cornered her after dinner and said he thought they should do their goodbyes then, before bestowing a loose, casual hug on her and continuing to clear the dinner table.

He'd be gone for another two weeks. He'd miss Christmas, but judging by the way things were going, Ruby suspected no one would be doing much celebrating anyway. Millie seemed optimistic the fire would be out before a third tour was necessary, and Ruby hoped she was right for once. That would be enough of a Christmas present for her.

Recently, Ruby had taken to coaxing her dad down the hill to the bed-and-breakfast with her in the mornings after she dropped her sisters off at their makeshift school sites. She'd broached the topic of therapy with him on a handful of these trips, gently and tentatively, feeling like she was the parent instead of the child. But he'd met each of these conversations with bewilderment that verged on outrage, which wasn't terribly surprising to Ruby. She supposed it didn't matter too much anyway. All the doctors she'd reached out to had either not yet reopened or were not taking new patients at this time.

One small win, however, was finally getting an insurance claims agent out to the property. He wasn't able to provide many answers, but he took all the notes and pictures he needed to get the process rolling and issue her a claim number. So while they waited for a check, Ruby thought they might as well start fixing up the B&B. Each day, she and her family set about the various grimy tasks required to clean up the wrecked place: Shop-Vaccing dust out of every nook and cranny, scrubbing soot from the walls, and cleaning the air ducts. Her dad was slow moving and easily distracted, but she told herself he needed the purpose in order to find himself again. It was one menial, arduous task after another, but Ruby felt like she was not only restoring the B&B but also ridding their collective history of the fire itself.

And now that her father was gone and Ashton was back at work, Millie often joined them, too. Carla constantly gushed about how nice it was of her to volunteer to help, though Ruby thought it was the least she could do given that she was living with them for free.

At some point in all this, Mama Ortega had returned home to Chula Vista. The air quality was better down there, and she seemed to sense some semblance of normalcy returning to their lives. Ruby was sad to see her go, but she figured it was a good sign if Mama Ortega, who never sugarcoated anything, thought they were getting back on their feet.

It certainly wasn't easy, but she was beginning to feel like they were at least doing *something*.

MILLIE WAS WRINGING OUT A SOAPY RAG OVER A BUCKET OF bubbly water when Ruby joined her in the B&B's dining room with her own cleaning bucket. She gave Ruby a tired but uncomplaining smile as she resumed scrubbing the faux-antique floral wallpaper, which had once been a robin's-egg blue but was now the hazy color of smog over a freeway.

Ruby sighed as she set her bucket down with a slosh. "I think we might need to repaint. Or re-wallpaper, or whatever," she confessed with a scowl.

Millie didn't stop cleaning. "Maybe. But we'll need the walls to be clean either way."

That was probably true. Painting or wallpapering weren't chores she'd ever undertaken, but it sounded right, even if the idea of adding another task—and expense—to her to-do list made Ruby's head throb.

She just knew that they needed to get this place running again. Last week, she'd received an email from Governor Cortez's assistant checking in on the property in light of the disaster and requesting updates. She hadn't been able to bring herself to respond to it quite yet. She couldn't lie to the woman—that was just bad business—but she also knew the truth wasn't particularly promising either.

Her eyes drifted out the window, where she could see the vaguest outline of the burned remains of the reception hall construction site, looking shadowlike and eerie against the cloudless afternoon sky. She hadn't even begun to work over there, hadn't even visited since that first morning of exploration—except for in her nightmares, where she often found herself hammering and sawing pieces of wood that would spontaneously burst into flame.

"We also need to deal with all that," Ruby muttered, gesturing irritably toward the site. She wondered quickly why she'd said *we* when it was truly her responsibility, but fortunately Millie didn't point it out.

"Once we get the B&B open again, there will be enough income to get back on track with the construction," Millie said matter-of-factly.

Ruby sighed, only slightly convinced. "I mean, I guess the insurance money might be enough to get started, but I still haven't found any contractors with a full crew." She retrieved her rag from her bucket and began rubbing a tarnished doorknob with nowhere near enough force to do anything other than dribble water onto the floor.

Many of the construction crews were short on workers, as she'd heard reiterated to her countless times throughout her desperate phone calls to get *someone* to come out and help them.

The day laborers who hadn't been driven out by the fire were driven out by the police, who were cracking down on what they thought were transient people and looters, with pretty much no leniency, given the level of displacement everyone was experiencing. Ruby's memory jolted to the horrifying scene they'd witnessed with Remy as they'd entered town, and she got the sense that that was only the tip of the iceberg of what was really going on throughout her community.

The distant sound of her father's voice drew her out of her thoughts for a minute, and she spotted him outside the window, where he was supposed to be scrubbing the exterior walls. Instead, he was standing with his back to the building, waving his arms as he delivered an impassioned speech—to no one. He'd been doing this a lot lately, talking to himself. Ruby suspected in his mind he was talking to her mother, which was even more disturbing.

"One step at a time! Have you gotten any updates on when the insurance check should get here?" Millie asked, an urgent hitch to her voice. As Ruby turned to her, she caught Millie glancing at her father's silhouette, too, and recognized her frantic attempt at distraction.

"The agent said the money for the initial damages should be on its way, but I guess we have a policy for money we've lost because of the disrepair, too. Like, the income we're losing because we can't open. Which is good news, but it sounds like that one's a little harder to track and prove. We've got to submit a lot of receipts and evidence of what we normally made and what we are spending now. And even then, it's a mess." She dipped her rag into her water bucket and began scrubbing at the beveled texture of the chair rail, this time with a little more vigor than was necessary. "He said I could apply for some of the FEMA grants, but there's so many people doing that, he didn't think our odds were good. They don't have enough money for everyone, and apparently we aren't in as bad of shape as most people." She could hear a hint of resentment in her tone with that last piece of information, and though it wasn't intentional, she hoped Millie didn't hear it.

"Well, I guess that's one thing to be thankful for," she said. Her eyes searched Ruby's face thoughtfully, and Ruby couldn't help but feel a pit of dread form as she wondered what was about to come out of Millie's mouth next. "You're not . . . worried, are you? About money, I mean? It's not my business, of course, but if you're worried, I could always get a job or get my own place or . . ."

The rag squished within Ruby's viselike grip; she hated revealing her vulnerability to Millie, but she figured there was no point lying now. "I mean, we have some savings. And the insurance money will help, whenever it gets here." The property insurance wasn't going to solve all their problems, though. It pained Ruby to even think about, but her mother's life insurance payout would be a god-send, even though that could also take a while. "I either need to get this place open and full of guests, or I need to find a contractor who will help us out on good faith that the money will get here eventually."

"Your dad doesn't have any old contacts who might be able to help?" Millie's eyes darted, almost imperceptibly, to the window through which Mr. Ortega's voice could still be heard.

Ruby had asked herself and her father that several times and had rummaged through every file and business card she could find in his study, but to no avail. "I don't think so. I'm going to go into the back office and see if the old property manager left anything useful. I haven't checked all those files yet. Did you bring a charger down here?" She withdrew her cell phone from her back pocket. The service was still spotty, and her phone was constantly searching for a signal and dying quickly. She'd left about a hundred voicemails with construction companies and was paranoid about missing a returned call.

Millie nodded and held up a small black brick with a couple of charging cords hanging from it. "I can plug yours in, too. I'm charging mine. Would you mind if I kept it up here with me while I work? I've been listening to this DIY home-improvement podcast. They're discussing how to replace the rubber seals on doors and windows. Did you notice some of them have melted? I think we'll need to fix that soon, too."

Ruby nodded, only half listening while she handed Millie her phone. "Sure. Just let me know if anyone calls."

AFTER OVER AN HOUR OF FRUITLESSLY CLICKING AND SKIMming through the manager's computer with nothing more to show for it than a few thousand reservation confirmations and a series of employee evaluations, Ruby was interrupted by Millie calling her name from the front desk.

Ruby sprang up anxiously and bumped into her—wide eyed and clutching Ruby's ringing phone—in the doorway.

"What is it? Is it a contractor?" she snapped, snatching the phone from Millie's hands.

No sooner had Millie shaken her head than Ruby's eyes landed on the incoming caller's name.

Remy Bustillos. What could *he* want?

Ruby frowned and shot Millie a confounded look.

"Aren't you going to answer it?" she asked uncertainly.

"After what he did to us?" Ruby snorted, glaring at the name on her phone screen but neither accepting nor rejecting the call. "Why would I? Why would I care what he has to say?"

Millie shrugged. "I don't know. But doesn't he work in hospitality, too? What if he has some connections that could help you out?"

Ruby had been wondering the same thing the past few days, but her pride had kept her from speaking the words out loud. But hearing them, even from Millie, whose judgment Ruby frequently found questionable—well, it was hard to argue with the logic behind them. She was desperate. And it wasn't a terrible idea, even if asking him for another favor repulsed her.

In her hesitation, the call ended, and the room fell silent once more.

"He's called twice already. I missed the first one, but he called back right away. That's why I thought it might be important," Millie explained, clearly fighting to conceal the disappointment in her bright eyes.

Instantly the phone began ringing again. With a bleak inhale, as if she were about to plunge into shark-infested waters, Ruby accepted the call and placed the phone to her ear. "Hello, Remy."

SHE WAS OUT THE DOOR MOMENTS AFTER HANGING UP, BE-fore she could give herself a chance to talk herself out of helping him.

It's not helping him *really*, she reminded herself as she slung her purse over her shoulder and charged up the hill. *It's helping us. My family. I just have to do something small for him to get what I need.*

"Ruby! Wait!"

Millie burst out of the B&B's entrance and quickly began making her way up the hill to join her. Her steps were clumsy and uneven as she clutched a small bundle to her chest.

When she reached Ruby, heaving slightly from the exertion, she extended a fistful of the B&B's travel-size cosmetics toward her: a bottle of lotion, a small comb, and a wet wipe. "We both know he likes you. It couldn't hurt to freshen up a little before you ask him for help," she suggested with a bashful smile. "You've got some dirt on your nose."

With a decisive nod to Millie, like a soldier bidding adieu to her unit before heading off on a dangerous mission, she raced through the back gate, where her red Jeep was parked in the driveway, just on the other side. She settled into the driver's seat, clutching the beauty products Millie had given her, and glanced at herself in the rearview mirror. Her ponytail was lopsided, with chunks of her thick, dark hair matted to her scalp with sweat. Dust frosted the bridge of her nose and temples. Dark circles under her eyes and a few splotchy blemishes stood out to her as clear indicators of how little sleep she'd been getting and how hard she was working.

It would take a lot more than a mini lotion and a comb to remedy this, but she'd have to make it work.

HE'D CALLED FROM THE POLICE DEPARTMENT, MAKING IT clear he wasn't asking for bail money; he'd already been released, but his car had been impounded, and he needed a ride to pick it up. Ubers and taxis were still hard to come by, and he said he didn't know who else to call.

"I figured you owe me one since I let you make off with my truck for a few days," he'd teased in his irritating sultry voice.

Though Ruby thought he was the one who owed her for abandoning them, she bit her tongue. "Why were you arrested?" she'd snapped.

"I'll explain everything when you get here," he'd promised. "What do you say?"

The station was on the opposite side of town, and she had no idea where the impound lot was, but she didn't see what choice she had. She was running out of options for people who might be able to help her get their property fixed up, and if she didn't help Remy, he wouldn't be able to help her.

When she pulled up, he was leaning against the brick wall of the police station, looking annoyingly cavalier and almost *bored*. She was disappointed to note that aside from mussed hair and a wrinkled shirt, he appeared very alert and energized. Who looked so pert after a night spent in jail?

He popped the passenger door open as her Jeep rolled to a stop, calling over his shoulder, "Until next time, muchachos!" with an exaggerated wave at a couple of officers sipping coffee by their cruisers. Finally, he turned his sparkling dark eyes on her, smiling wolfishly. "Ruby Ortega, thank you for the ride. I didn't know if I'd see you ever again." He eased his large frame into the passenger seat and clicked the seat belt into place with strange enthusiasm.

She pursed her lips, refusing to return his cheerful energy, and backed out of the parking space. "Yeah, well, that's what tends to happen when you ditch people on the side of the road."

He cocked a thick eyebrow at her in pretend shock. "You're not still mad about that, are you?" He typed in the address of the impound lot and turned on the directions app. "I'd hardly say I 'abandoned' you. I gave you my truck!"

He obviously had no idea what she'd been through, the kind of hardships she had faced since they'd last seen one another. She bit back her incredulous anger, keeping her eyes locked on the road in front of her so as not to reveal how raw her resentment still was. She hadn't come all this way to hash out the betrayal of their last encounter; she'd come to solicit his help. There was no point in getting riled up or unleashing her true feelings about what had happened.

She forced a wry smile onto her face. "No, of course not. I'm only teasing."

He nodded, and while Ruby thought she saw a brief wave of relief pass over him, a more curious, suspicious expression lingered on his face. She was going to have to try a lot harder to conceal her true feelings if she was going to get what she needed. "Good. Turn left here," he said. "I thought you'd understand. *Eventually*."

The condescension in his tone—and the notion that her anger was just a product of her lack of understanding—made her insides boil.

"So, what's new with you?" he asked, breezy and infuriatingly oblivious.

She clenched her jaw and chanced one more scrutinizing glance at him out of the corner of her eye. How to answer that question?

So much had changed since they had last seen each other. *Everything* was different for her. But how much did she actually want to share with him, this arrogant, flippant person who popped in and out of her life on a whim?

The pragmatic part of her wondered if he'd be more likely to help her if he knew she was mourning the loss of her mother. With Remy, it was hard to know exactly how he'd react. But the idea of sharing something as personal as her own grief made her entire body stiffen in dread. She couldn't bear to gamble with her mother's memory like that.

She'd save that as a last resort.

"I've been very busy," she said vaguely. "I've been helping my father with the business. There's been a lot of stuff to do now that the fires have passed. I'm sure you know."

He nodded, his gaze flicking down at his phone in a mildly disinterested way. He flashed the phone screen at her to show she needed to merge onto the freeway. The estimated travel time was twelve minutes. She had twelve minutes to make her case and get him on her team. She also had twelve minutes to suppress the urge to push him right out of the moving car.

She could do this. She *had* to do this.

His expression was one of comprehension, if not sympathy. "The property's okay, though? Your house is okay?"

"The house is fine. There was some damage to the rest of the property that we are dealing with." She paused to gauge his reaction.

Again, he nodded, his face stern but unreadable. "I'm sure. Those fires did a number down here. It's unbelievable that they're still going up north, too. Speaking of that, how's your boy Ashton doing? Is he keeping himself out of trouble?"

She jerked toward him in surprise, unthinkingly swerving the car with her. A truck passed with a loud honk as she returned to her lane. Remy was goading her, testing her. She exhaled deeply. "Yes, he's fine," she said as nonchalantly as possible. "So, *why* were you arrested? You said you'd explain." She prayed a subject change would distract both of them from the topic of Ashton, which was sure to derail her plans.

"Well, it's safe to say you remember *why* we parted ways a few weeks ago?" His voice was soft and gentle, a sharp distinction from the teasing jabs he'd fired at her about Ashton.

She nodded. "The police, and all those people?" Though she wasn't willing to admit she still didn't quite understand all of it—the situation or his motives—she felt she had a clear enough recollection.

"Well, they've been doing that all over the place," he explained somberly, and she felt his eyes searching her face for a reaction.

Doing what? she wondered. She tried to return his grave expression, hoping that was the correct response.

He grimaced, running his hand along the sharp line of his jaw as he spoke. "A lot of people have been displaced by these fires, not just immigrants. But of course, *they're* the ones who are being targeted in what's already a terrible situation for everyone." He shook his head. "They set up these checkpoints throughout town, and they say it's to cut down on looting. And maybe that's true. But you know what they're also doing at these checkpoints? Checking people's ID's. And if you don't have an ID? Well, they're not just turning people away from town. They're detaining them. Trying to *deport* them." He was flushed, his eyes lit up with passion and urgency.

"Detaining them?" she repeated. "Why bother with that? There's more than enough to do around here without rounding people up and holding them in some detention facility." That just seemed more trouble than necessary.

Remy nodded. "Well, they're not doing this to everyone. Just the brown ones." He drummed his fingers along his forearm as if using his own skin tone as an example. "*That's* why they bother with it."

It was hard for Ruby to imagine this was happening all throughout town and she hadn't heard anything about it. But then again, she'd been pretty absorbed in her own business. There wasn't time for much else. Still, she couldn't fend off the slimy feeling that what Remy was saying was probably true. "But what does that have to do with you? Did you get arrested for not having an ID?"

"In a way," he acquiesced, head bobbing back and forth in a

manner that indicated there was much more to his story. "That's what the police say, anyway. I don't live here, I don't have any business being here right now, I might be a looter. I've been spending time at these checkpoints to help out some of the families who are trying to come home. Some don't speak English, so I translate. Sometimes I take videos. I record badge numbers. I take down any contact information for people I can call to let them know their family members have been detained, if it comes to that. Whatever they need, really. But the cops don't like it. They can't hold me on much; I have proof of citizenship even if I'm not a California resident, so they keep me a night and then I'm free. I must've really pissed them off this time, though. They'd never towed my car before." He chuckled bitterly, shaking his head in amusement.

"How many times have you been arrested?" She was intrigued, despite herself.

"This is my third time. Take this next exit."

"Wow," she choked in what she hoped sounded like astonishment. She was running out of time. They'd be at the impound lot in a few minutes. "I just—I just can't believe any of that." She reached across the console and placed her hand on top of his.

There was the faintest glimmer of apprehension on his face before he squeezed her fingers in return. "I'd hoped you'd understand. It doesn't feel like enough, and these little 'rendezvous' with the police are getting a little out of hand, but it just felt like something I had to do. These people live here, too, and it's not fair what's happening." He tilted his head toward his window. "That's the impound lot, just up there."

She turned right, her pulse loud in her ears. This was it. This was her last chance.

He released her hand as he unbuckled his seat belt. "Thank you again, Ruby. Maybe I'll see you sometime soon." His black eyes were somehow warm and affectionate, and even with his disheveled hair and a thick dust of stubble—even after everything that had happened between the two of them—she was struck by him, his warm bronze skin, his thick lips, his full lashes. He opened his car door and stepped out.

She flung her own door open, her words sticking in her throat like she'd just swallowed a spoonful of peanut butter. "Wait!" Clumsily, she hurried around the front of the car to stand face-to-face with him. He frowned curiously, but he didn't move.

She took his hand in hers again, hoping he wouldn't notice the grimy blisters that had formed on her palms from hours of clearing dead plants and sweeping broken glass, hoping that even in her hastiness she could suppress her violently conflicted feelings about this frustrating and fascinating person. "I just want to know you'll take care of yourself," she murmured softly. She lifted her gaze up to meet him at a slow, tantalizing pace.

His brows furrowed as he nodded. "You don't need to worry about me, Ruby." A small smile crept onto his face, and he tilted his head down toward her ever so slightly.

"This has all just been so hard. For everyone," she crooned, leaning into him. If he were inclined to kiss her in her desperate plea for help, she'd let him. It was a small price to pay for his assistance, she figured, and he did look so rugged and handsome, even if it vexed her to admit it. "For these people you've been helping and for everyone else. It's been unfair. I know with all the work our property needs, I've been really struggling. There's only so much I can do, and I'm at a point where I need help." The loss of her mother hovered on her tongue, but she couldn't bring herself to say it, to share that small, terrible piece of her life with someone so volatile. "Remy, I . . ." She paused, gazing at him with all the intensity she could muster. "I need a construction crew, and I don't have much money yet, and they're so hard to find since the whole city is rebuilding. I need help. Do you . . . have any contacts? Anything at all?" She whispered the last few words as if it were a romantic proposition, as if she could fool him with just the sound of her voice and the batting of her eyelashes.

"Oh." He withdrew his hand from hers as he took a sudden step backward, away from her.

Shit. "I know it's not the right time to ask, and I wouldn't if I weren't *desperate*. But I don't know what else to do. I don't know who else to turn to!"

"No, no. I should've known," he mumbled sadly, cutting short anything else Ruby might've had to say with a slow shake of his head. The charming sparkle in his eyes had disappeared, like a door had slammed shut somewhere inside him. "Ruby, I'm planning on re-signing as CEO. I'm meeting with the board next week. I'm stepping back from my private business to focus on things that really matter, on people who actually need my help. I'm sorry, but I can't help you." He turned toward the small stucco office of the impound lot, shoulders slumped.

Couldn't help her? Or *wouldn't* help her? "What do you mean? *I* really need you!" she called frantically. "I—"

He paused, his back still toward her, and she wondered briefly, desperately, if he'd had a change of heart. However, when he turned, expression darker than she had ever seen before, she braced in icy terror for what he had to say. "Ruby, I know you truly believe that. And I really admire how cutthroat and sincere you are. Someday, I think those traits will serve you well. But right now, I can't help you. I can't help you see that *you* are not in need. *You* have all the privilege in the world to help yourself, even when things are unpleasant or challenging like they are now. I know because I'm in the same boat. However, I am going to use my privilege and power to help others who do not have the same advantages, and you could, too. I thought you might." He bit his lip and shook that idea away. "But I know how to admit when I'm wrong. Good luck with the B&B. I don't think you'll need it. You're the kind of person who always lands on her feet. Thank you again for the ride."

She stood there, long after he'd disappeared, with a thousand interjections rising up in her chest and fizzling into wordless, incoherent bursts of anger. How *dare* he? How dare he lecture her about privilege and challenges when he had no idea what she'd been through?

But no matter how angry, how self-righteous, how *wronged* she felt, she couldn't ignore the fact that it didn't make any difference in the end.

She was on her own.

It was up to her to find her way forward.

23

As Ruby toiled away at the B&B over the next few days, she couldn't help but dwell on the words Remy had called to her across that parking lot. It wasn't just the tart sting of rejection that lingered, though that certainly was part of it. Whether she liked it or not, she rolled what he'd said about power and privilege around in her brain; the more she sat with it, the more uncomfortable she felt. Was he right? Was there more she could be doing? Was she supposed to be doing something else? Something bigger?

It wasn't as if she were relaxing in an ivory tower, unaffected by everything that had happened. They'd had hardships—hardships he couldn't even imagine—and she was doing her best to cope with them.

But she did have a home and the support of loved ones to come back to, as well as resources to start over, even if she had endured significant losses.

She shook her head. She had enough on her mind without wondering if her problems were philosophically fair. It was exhausting. So she took out her fatigue and frustration in the most efficient way she could think of: by bullying those around her.

"I can't believe we have to go to school *all week* and when we finally get a break, you're forcing us to come here and do manual labor! How is that fair? We have homework! Don't we deserve a break?" Elena shrieked as they entered the B&B, the smell of lemon-scented cleaning products finally starting to overwhelm the musty, smoky scent they'd been battling. "I don't know why you suddenly think you're in charge around here, anyway!"

Ruby's sisters hadn't had to help clean quite as much since they'd started school again, but Ruby was in a frantic hustle to reopen; it was all-hands-on-deck. "Elena, we are so close to being ready for guests again. Quit your whining," she said, nodding a quick greeting to Millie, who had been working her way through each of the guest rooms with rolls of painter's tape for hours.

Elena's lip curled at Ruby's curt tone. "Who in their right mind would want to even stay here?"

Ruby herself had been fixated on that exact question every time her eyes swept over the apocalyptic property, but Elena's attitude infuriated her nevertheless. Thankfully, Millie cut in before Ruby could give in to the temptation to smack her spoiled sister upside the head.

"It's really not as bad as you're making it out to be," Millie assured them patiently, passing them paint rollers. " 'Many hands make light work' is what my dad always says."

Elena responded with a resigned scowl and stalked upstairs.

Remy's words about privilege echoed once more through Ruby's thoughts. Elena's shrill outrage at being subjected to even a few hours of labor left Ruby with the suspicion that he hadn't been entirely off base.

That sneaking suspicion became unavoidable when, a few hours later, Ruby went to tell her sisters she'd make them lunch and let them go home early to reward them for their hard work, only to discover Carla painting alone.

"Where's Elena?" Ruby barked from the open doorway.

Carla froze, a few globs of paint dripping from her roller onto the tarp. "Um," she peeped, looking down. "I don't know. She left."

"She *left*?" Ruby folded her arms across her chest and fixed her youngest sister with a scrutinizing stare. "Where did she go?"

Carla sighed and shook her head, caving in to Ruby's glower without much resistance. "I'm not sure. Really. She was texting someone, and then she left. She didn't tell me. I promise."

With a huff of exasperation, Ruby stormed up to the house and tore through the rooms, throwing the doors open to find each one empty, save for her father's study, where he'd apparently snuck off to take a nap and now was slumped in his desk chair, snoring. With every door Ruby flung open, her annoyance grew. *Is it simply too much to ask for her help for one damn morning?*

She burst into the front yard, searching the street for a clue as to where the hell Elena could've disappeared to. She was only fifteen; she couldn't have gone far.

The houses to her left had mostly suffered the fate of the Willises' and were now either blackened lots or some grotesque assortment of uninhabitable remains. Ruby doubted Elena, or anyone for that matter, would have much to do in that area. But further up her street, there were a few other surviving houses that had also escaped with relatively minor damage. Though Ruby hadn't had much time for neighborly socializing, she had noticed many of the families had moved back in and were piecing their lives back together just like Ruby's family was: Shop-Vaccing dust, replanting destroyed shrubs, clearing debris from downed trees or melted patio furniture.

She tented her hand over her eyes as her gaze raked over each home, searching for some sign of her sister's whereabouts.

At last, she spotted a white work truck parked outside the Borowskys' house two doors down, and on the other side of the cab bobbed a mousy brown ponytail.

She marched up the street to find Elena leaning against the truck. As Ruby closed in, she could see a gawky teenage boy standing next to Elena, shoulder pressed against the passenger door and eyes locked on her sister in an awkward but unmistakably flirtatious stare.

Elena's back was toward her as she coquettishly twirled her curly ponytail, her paint-speckled maintenance uniform shirt tied around her waist, leaving her in a thin white tank top despite the wintry breeze. The boy stroked her bare arm with a goofy, crooked grin on his face.

Ruby felt her blood boil. If Elena had time for romance, she certainly had time to take on some more responsibility. And if she had the gall to sneak away while everyone else was working, then Ruby could see no problem with causing a big embarrassing scene. Of course, the fact that Ruby had spent most of her high school years doing this exact same thing was completely irrelevant; things were different now.

She approached them, still unbeknownst to Elena, who was immersed in the dreamy brown eyes of her beau, when another figure caught her attention. A stout guy—maybe a year or two older than Ruby—wearing a construction hat and wielding a toolbox exited the Borowskys' back gate and strolled purposefully toward the two teenagers, ignoring the walkway and cutting straight across the lawn.

The boy saw him, too, and squawked, "Ugh, is it really time already?" just as Ruby rounded the tailgate of the truck and placed a firm hand on Elena's shoulder.

Elena paled at the sight of Ruby, then quickly turned bright pink. "Uh, h-hi, Ruby. I was just taking a quick break to say hello to a f-friend. I was just about to head back over," she sputtered, eyes flicking between Ruby and the boy nervously.

"No need," Ruby said with a fake grin. "Carla filled me in, so I thought I'd join you two lovebirds! Who do I have the pleasure of meeting here?" She aggressively thrust her hand out to shake the boy's hand, and he acquiesced apprehensively.

"E-Eli," he squeaked.

The older guy standing next to him lowered his sunglasses and squinted at Ruby with noticeable interest. "We didn't mean to step on any toes here. We just stopped by to check out the workers' progress. My crew's doing some work on the Borowskys' outdoor kitchen, and Eli asked if he could see his little girlfriend real quick since she was just down the road. I was right over there the whole time. Swear." He shrugged in a what-are-you-going-to-do kind of way before flashing Ruby a smirk that was hardly apologetic at all. "I'm Frank, Eli's brother." He held out his hand to shake hers, and

Ruby noticed a gaudy platinum watch gleaming in the sunlight that seemed very at odds with his work clothes.

"Ruby Ortega," she replied, not half as charmed by his little monologue as he was clearly hoping but taking note of his tool belt and the logo on the side of the truck, nevertheless. KENNEDY AND SONS CONSTRUCTION. She placed her hand in his, feeling a mix of trepidation and curiosity. "I'm Elena's sister. Maybe I overreacted a bit. This is all just brand-new information to me, and to learn it when Elena is *supposed to be* working . . ."

Frank elbowed Eli in the ribs conspiratorially, which annoyed Ruby—but she was suddenly struck with an idea that dulled some of her irritation. She forced a smile onto her face and mimicked his careless shrug. "Young love, I guess," she murmured tepidly.

Frank laughed as Eli and Elena erupted into groans. Though he had returned his knockoff Ray-Bans to his sun-worn face, Ruby could still feel his eyes raking over her. "Can't stop it, you know."

"You said you're checking in on your . . . crew? You work in construction?" Ruby patted the bed of the truck and saw Elena roll her eyes in mortification.

"Yeah, it's a family business. But I just got my contracting license, so I'm starting to take on some jobs of my own." He puffed out his chest ever so slightly as he hooked his thumbs in his belt. "We had to hop on over here to help out the Borowskys. The fire took out their shed and built-in barbecue, made a real mess out of their backyard. Things have been real busy for us with all the damage and rebuilding that's happened lately." He put his hand on the back of Eli's neck and gave the scrawny kid a shake that toed the line between embracing and roughhousing. Ruby couldn't help but notice his excited confidence as he spoke, the kind of sentiment that came from new, unexpected success, she thought.

She nodded and began twirling her own ponytail, just like Elena had moments before. "I definitely know what you mean. Elena and I were just doing some work at our bed-and-breakfast right over there." She gestured over her shoulder with a sultry flick of her eyelashes.

"Nice," he said in a low voice that Ruby had to assume referred to more than just the B&B. "Well, listen. I'm sorry about this mix-up. Is there, uh, any way I can make it up to you?" He ran his hand along his coppery goatee.

Bingo. "Maybe we should exchange contact information to prevent any future misunderstandings like this," Ruby offered.

Frank's face lit up as he quickly fumbled through his pockets to retrieve a business card. "*Absolutely.* That's me."

Ruby accepted the crisp white card, letting her fingers graze his a moment longer than necessary. "Perfect, thank you. And, you know, maybe we can sit down for dinner sometime, too. Talk about these two, and whatever else is on your mind."

Ruby was filled with vicious glee as Elena succumbed to a full-body eye roll at the same instant that Frank's ruddy cheeks flushed bright pink.

Part Three

"You burn like hell,
*   pure red and stormy,*
*   and I fly like smoke,*
*   pure black and gloomy."*

—Mirza Sharafat Hussain Beigh

24

Kissing Frank, Ruby often found herself thinking of childhood games like Whac-a-Mole or Hungry Hungry Hippos. It was the rapid, erratic way he kissed her, his tongue thrusting into her mouth unexpectedly and withdrawing just as abruptly, as if it wasn't sure it belonged there. In fact, all his mannerisms generally felt a bit forced and uncoordinated, from the way he often spoke a little louder than necessary to the way he made sure to leave the receipt somewhere Ruby could see it whenever he paid for her.

Frank was a guy who was still finding his place in the world, like most people in their twenties, but who was also desperate to conceal it with all the bravado and swagger he could gather.

They were certainly a strange pairing, and while she didn't exactly dislike the time they spent together, she knew the main incentives for their romance were, in fact, not romantic.

She didn't probe too much into the unsettling feeling she got when she thought about the origins of their relationship, but she told herself it wasn't entirely self-serving. She was able to get an in with a construction crew, and Frank—well, he got to spend time with her. She knew it was too egotistical to ever admit aloud to anyone, but she saw the way his dull eyes went fiery with lust and validation when she entered a room, and if that was enough for him, who was Ruby to question it?

Elena, who had been promptly dumped by Eli following Ruby and Frank's first date, had accused her of whoring herself out, but Ruby chalked it up to the bitter words of a broken heart. It wasn't her fault Eli had said he was too weirded out by their siblings dating each other. And even more importantly, she was *not* whoring herself out for his business services. Sure, her womanly wiles may have convinced Frank to prioritize the work she needed done, but she was paying him just like any other customer. If he sometimes felt inclined to tinker with the random broken odds and ends around the bed-and-breakfast when he picked her up for dates, well, that was just standard boyfriend behavior—even if she hesitated to call a white guy with a tribal neck tattoo her boyfriend.

Spring approached, and wildfire season drew to a close, which meant Ashton was finally able to come home. Just like camp counselors or ski lift operators, apparently wildland firefighting was a temporary job, and once the threat of fires subsided, firefighters resumed their daily lives in other occupations. Considering his former life had been at school in Arizona, Ruby was surprised but also overjoyed to learn that his off-season ambitions included returning to California and trying to make sense of life there. In January, he and Millie had driven back to Phoenix to pack up their old apartment (and collect the boxes of Ruby's stuff from her dorm room that her old roommate Patty had kindly packed, now that Ruby had officially withdrawn from the university), and they moved into an even smaller apartment a few miles away from Ruby's house. Now that they finally had a few guests, Millie continued to help out at the bed-and-breakfast while taking online classes, and Ruby, upon seeing the outrageous rent they were paying for their apartment, insisted that Ashton help her out as assistant manager—despite the fact that she hardly needed one. Even though none of their previous employees had returned, a fact that still needled and perplexed her, they'd been able to scrounge up a meager handful of guests over the past few months. A few families displaced by extensive home repairs, a church group volunteering with debris cleanup, and one bridal-party-to-be trying to ascertain whether the area would be suitable for a small outdoor wedding in a couple months. Ruby had watched that final group with hawklike intensity and had been a little heartsick when she'd heard them ultimately decide against a Buena Valley wedding.

She'd corresponded with the governor's assistant on and off as Frank's crew broke ground and thought she was able to deliver enough vaguely optimistic updates to ensure they were still proceeding with the event as planned. They'd hinted at visiting the property over the summer, and though that was still months away, it made Ruby anxious, nevertheless. They were making progress, but Ruby was endlessly impatient; the return to normalcy was underway, but it was agonizingly slow.

Mama Ortega visited for a few days around New Year's as well, and as they sat around the kitchen table folding shredded beef into tamales, Ruby thought, for just a moment, their life felt like what it had been before the fire. Her mother's absence around the holidays had been particularly raw and visceral, but she felt a small flickering of hope deep down that these kinds of familiar moments would become more regular.

Even her father was starting to be somewhat recognizable, a detail that was no doubt related to Mama Ortega finally convincing him to talk to a therapist. He was no longer dazed and helpless, and his weekly appointments were clearly helping him make sense of everything, but he still hadn't resumed his position as head of Ortega Properties. Ruby was increasingly concerned that he never would. However, his therapist suggested he build some new routines, so in addition to his morning walks and washing the dishes after dinner, Ruby issued him to-do lists every few days with tasks like calling vendors or interviewing handymen. Most of the time he completed them, but he did not seem to have the desire or capacity to take on any more responsibility.

Ruby felt, somehow, it was her duty to restore him to the man he'd been before tragedy struck. He'd taught her everything she knew about hard work and resilience, and she should be able to return that favor. But the way everything had played out these past few weeks—with Frank, with dropping out of school—she just wasn't sure how to broach things with him.

Not to mention, there was the whole fiasco at the nursery.

It had all started with something Ruby had been thinking about for a while. Something she hated the idea of—that she knew would break her father's heart—but something she couldn't see any way around. She had decided they desperately needed to sell some of their land. They needed to expedite the construction to get it done by summer, and Frank had been clear that wouldn't happen without some additional manpower and probably some overtime.

The vineyard they'd dreamed of adding was no longer in their budget, and she knew the land would fetch some much-needed capital. On the surface, it seemed like a logical solution, but she knew it would drive a stake right through her father's already broken heart.

Their land was part of his identity, and it had become even more important as a remaining link to her mother. Ruby often caught him gazing out the window, muttering about memories the two of them had shared in their home. And the vineyard had been her idea, her dream.

She'd been procrastinating telling him, but she knew it had to be done—if only because his signature would be necessary on all the paperwork.

One morning, she talked him into going into town with her to purchase some new trees and shrubs to plant around the B&B. He'd always loved gardening, and even this listless version of himself perked up at the errand. It wasn't perfect, but she figured this was as good of an opportunity as any. Hit him with the bad news while he was doing something he enjoyed—in public, so he wouldn't be tempted to take off his shoe and hit her with it.

He was admiring the fronds of a small palm tree when she forced the words out of her mouth.

"I think we should sell the land we'd marked for the vineyard and a couple more acres," she began, then spewed out the reasons and rationale she'd rehearsed in her head the entire drive over.

He remained slightly stooped, the pointy leaves of the palm tree still in his fingers, as he glanced up at her. He inhaled deeply, looking physically pained by the effort. "And what about your mother, Ruby Catherine?" His voice was soft and low, a snarl almost.

"Daddy, I—"

Abruptly, he stood without looking at her and disappeared down an aisle lined with fertilizer and wheelbarrows.

She decided to give him a few minutes to cool off. She'd gather what she came for—some sod, an assortment of flowers, maybe even a citrus tree if they were on sale—and she'd try to raise the subject again. Maybe he'd be more receptive if he had time to think it over on his own.

However, as she pushed her overloaded cart down rows and rows of plants, her father was nowhere to be found. She peered out the gates of the outdoor nursery; she had the car keys so he couldn't have left her there, but he was clearly no longer on the premises.

She parked her cart by the entry, calling to an employee that she'd be back in a moment to check out, and stepped into the parking lot.

And that was when she saw the flashing red and blue lights of a police car parked on the side of the lot.

At first, the colors caught her attention, but she didn't think anything of it. It wasn't a terribly uncommon sight around town these days.

But then she heard her father's voice.

And he was . . . *screaming.*

She hadn't heard him howl like that since the day her mother died.

She didn't remember racing over there, to where her father

stood clutched between two uniformed police officers, but her body had transported her there in a primal, instinctive way that hadn't involved her brain, apparently. "Get your hands off of him! What are you doing?" Her pulse raced, heart thudding as she watched her father try to jerk free from their grip, his face flushed with exertion and mortification.

"That's my *father*!" Ruby bellowed. "What's going on here?"

Finally, one of the officers glanced up at Ruby and seemed to experience a beat of indecision. He was a relatively young man, probably in his thirties. His dark hair was cropped to a buzz cut, and when he turned to face her, she saw the name on his badge read DELGADO. "Ma'am, stand back," he barked, a hardness in his voice that sounded unnatural.

"You need to take your hands off of my father!"

The officers exchanged a look over her father's writhing body, and they loosened their grip on his forearms but didn't fully release him. "Is he armed?" Delgado asked flatly.

Ruby scoffed. "What? No. Of course not. We're shopping for flowers, for Christ's sake."

"Do you have any reason to believe he is a danger to himself or others?" Delgado's tone was monotone and robotic, like he was reading from a script.

"*No!*"

"Is he a legal resident of the United States?"

Everyone froze. Delgado and his partner went rigid. Her father even stopped struggling. Ruby inhaled sharply.

"Are you fucking kidding me?" she growled through gritted teeth.

"Ma'am, answer the question," the other officer, a freckled man with glossy red hair, said. He refused to look at Ruby as he spoke, and instead fixed his eyes on the asphalt.

"He's a citizen! We live down the road. Now take your hands off him!"

At last, the two officers straightened and slowly released her father. Ruby reached out to him as he staggered toward her.

"What happened?" she pleaded. She was speaking to her father, but it was Delgado who answered.

He was fidgeting with his belt. "We got a call that there was a man in the parking lot causing a bit of a . . . disturbance. Talking to himself. Shouting. Appeared to be in an altered state." He gestured to her father, who was breathing deeply with his eyes closed, a frown of pure humiliation creasing his face. "When we arrived, he was noncompliant with requests to see identification."

Ruby's jaw dropped. "Oh yeah, so a Mexican man walking around without his wallet must be up to no good," she said indignantly. "Jesus, are you even listening to yourself? You assumed he was here illegally because he didn't enthusiastically comply with your racial profiling? Don't you hear how fucked up that is?"

"Now, wait a minute," the red-haired cop said in a huff, with an admonishing tone that made Ruby want to knee him right in the groin.

She glared at Delgado, ignoring his partner. "Is that right? Did it occur to you that his skin is the exact same color as yours, Officer Delgado?" She rolled the vowels of his name around in her mouth, in an exaggerated Spanish accent. "Of course not. You didn't think twice about how absurd and *racist* it is to accost him like that until the nice white girl showed up, did you?" Her lip curled involuntarily, disgust creeping up on her as she recounted the events.

Delgado opened his mouth to interject, but no words came out.

"You should be ashamed of yourselves. Haven't we been through enough? This place has enough issues without pigs like you behaving like this," Ruby said, grabbing her father's arm. It broke her heart to note he was trembling.

She glared at the badges of Delgado and his partner, Vickers, before tugging her phone out of her pocket and snapping a quick picture of their badge numbers, just like Remy had mentioned doing. "I'll be reporting this bullshit," was the last thing she said before she led her father across the lot to her Jeep.

Though he no longer appeared to be angry, her father was too stunned to even get into the car by himself. Ruby helped him in and even fastened his seat belt for him once she was in the car herself. As she put her key in the ignition, she watched the police cruiser hastily tear out of the parking lot as a couple of the nursery employees peered over the fence.

She sighed, jaw clenched, as her father broke into silent sobs beside her.

THAT NIGHT, HE SIGNED THE PAPERWORK TO SELL A THIRD OF the land they'd earmarked for the vineyard, and by the end of the week, they'd accepted an offer several thousand dollars more than what they'd asked. People were eager to cash in on the fragile state of Buena Valley, and though it repulsed Ruby a little bit, she was relieved to reap some of the benefits.

Her father hadn't said much about it, not when he'd numbly moved his pen across a fat stack of paperwork or when she'd shown him the check. In fact, all he'd said was, "I don't recognize this place anymore."

And Ruby thought that was quite an understatement.

25

Sometimes after a day at the B&B, Ruby would stop by Frank's parents' house, cutting straight through the backyard to the pool house where he lived. She would never stay the night, though. It just seemed like a hassle for them to explain. After all, Ruby's father only had a vague, unspecified inkling that there was someone in her life—and probably preferred to keep it that way. He'd had enough trauma this year. And Frank's parents, who could see into the pool house from their kitchen window, often popped by unannounced to pepper them with random questions, making them seem much more like babysitters than landlords, no matter what Frank said.

Most nights, Frank would reheat whatever his parents had made for dinner and they'd curl up on the couch, where he would watch news or play video games and Ruby would review the upcoming tasks for the week.

One evening, as she was settling down next to him to ask for an update on the ductwork at the reception hall, he handed her a dubious-looking plate of food he called "Frito pie" as a jarring image flashed across the television screen. Frank was mumbling a complaint about his mom buying the generic brand of corn chips, but Ruby quickly shushed him and lunged for the remote to turn up the volume.

The newscast featured a crowd of people, not unlike the one Remy had stopped to help that day so long ago, huddled among tents and suitcases in an open field. The scrolling text at the bottom of the screen read LOCAL GROUP SEEKS TO HELP MIGRANT AND IMMIGRANT WORKERS DISPLACED BY WILDFIRE.

The scene depicted was upsettingly familiar. Ever since that whole debacle at the gardening center, Ruby had been thinking a lot about what was going on in her community. There were the obvious signs of some deeper injustice, like headlines about mass deportations or an increased police presence in the neighborhoods where Hispanic families usually lived, where cops often stopped people demanding proof of citizenship. But then there were the subtler ones that made Ruby just as concerned because not everyone seemed to realize they were related. The HELP WANTED signs at pretty much every restaurant in town or the fact that Ruby herself still wasn't able to hire any housekeepers or landscapers. Or the open way people now talked about "us" and "them," whose country this really was, who deserved access to aid and resources as they rebuilt. She found it all very unsettling and took note of the way it was dividing Buena Valley as it gradually recovered.

But that wasn't what had drawn Ruby's eyes to the television, at least not initially.

As the camera panned over clusters of worried-looking families, a curly-haired reporter in a blue dress appeared in the corner of the screen, describing the situation that was unfolding behind her. And to her left, answering questions about the needs of displaced people and the challenges they faced, stood Remy Bustillos.

Frank snorted loudly. "Can you believe all this?" he grumbled, helping himself to a forkful of the watery chili that sat untouched on Ruby's plate.

She quickly glanced at him before returning her eyes to the television, where Remy was describing efforts to collect toiletries and household items for people in need.

"Everyone's had a hard time getting back on their feet after those fires," Frank growled. "*No one* had it easy, but that's life. We play the cards we were dealt. We work hard and we figure it out. That's what we do in this country. We don't wait around asking for a handout like this." He used the fork to gesture to the huge TV she was fairly certain had been purchased by his parents when they'd redecorated the pool house a few weeks ago. He glanced at her, seemingly surprised by her silence, and raised his bushy eyebrows. "Like your dad. From what you said, he's a self-made man! No handouts."

Ruby stiffened at the mention of her father. She'd never introduced them, and Frank only had the vaguest idea of who he was and absolutely no understanding of his current troubles. He certainly didn't have enough information about her family to make those kinds of sweeping generalizations.

"I guess," she said mildly. "But everyone's experience is different. Don't you think some people have more challenges than others, through no fault of their own?"

He scoffed. "Life isn't fair, babe. Shit happens."

"But were you stopped and detained when you returned to town? Did you lose your job and your home and everything you owned?" She stopped herself before she asked if he even paid rent to live here, but she was pretty sure he could read the question on her face anyway.

Frank's chocolate-brown eyes darkened, and he set the plate down on the coffee table, as if the conversation had made him lose his appetite. "Well, no. But I'm a citizen. I'm a contributing member of society. Those people are illegal; *that's* why they're 'displaced.' Most of them don't even speak English! They don't pay taxes, but they expect a handout? Fucking ridiculous."

She'd suspected Frank harbored feelings like this, feelings that demonstrated how out of touch he was with the experiences of people who were different from him, but this was the first time he'd admitted them so explicitly, and it made her stomach tighten.

Her first instinct was to tell him off, to rant and rave about his race and privilege, but she worried all that would do was piss him off and lead him to pump the brakes at the reception hall, a gamble she wasn't willing to take at this point. They still had several weeks of work left until they could officially open its doors, and though it didn't please her to do it, Ruby felt she could bite her tongue until then. If shattering Frank's delicate worldview led to a breakup, she could deal with that, but if it halted work on her event venue this late in the game, then she'd basically be back where she started.

She inched away from him on the couch and returned her eyes to the television screen, desperate to look at anything but Frank's smug face with clumps of chili in his stupid goatee. She averted her attention just in time to hear Remy's closing statement.

"What we really need is lodging, though," he told the reporter soberly. "We are working on helping people get jobs and legal assistance, but that takes time. We can't keep sleeping in tents, like what you see behind me. We are working to secure temporary shelter right now, but if anyone at home has any resources or donations to help us out, please contact me. Everyone deserves aid and compassion as we rebuild." The reporter thanked him and flashed Remy's contact information on the screen before transitioning to a segment about exploding cell phones.

She may not have been able to speak her piece to Frank just yet, but suddenly she knew what she *could* do.

26

Remy had seemed pleased, but not altogether surprised, to hear from her, and he good-naturedly agreed to meet her at a coffee shop the next day.

"I'd like to offer you a few rooms at our bed-and-breakfast," she said matter-of-factly after a perfunctory handshake and greeting. She had no desire to dwell on small talk or the awkward intimacies of their past few meetings. She knew what she wanted to do, and she sensed he would be receptive. It didn't have to be more complicated than that.

His dark eyes sparkled with amusement as he brought a cup of black coffee to his lips for a meditative slurp. "I'm assuming not for personal use? I've heard you've got a new boyfriend, so that would be an especially inappropriate proposal."

She rolled her eyes, refusing to even wonder how he knew about Frank. This didn't *have* to be a complicated matter, but of course Remy would want to make it so. "Don't be gross. I saw you on the news last night, and you said you need lodging for the people you're working with. We have vacancies, so I thought we might be able to house some people temporarily."

He nodded with a bright smile. "That would be excellent, actually. How many rooms do you think you're able to spare?"

"It's a small place, as you know, but I think I could commit to six rooms until the summer. When busy season comes around, we may need to reassess," she explained, looking down at a paper napkin she was twisting between her fingers. "They'd need to tend to their own rooms since we don't have cleaners, but we've got a couple suites that are spacious enough for families. I think it'll work out well."

She waited for a response, and when she finally looked up at him again, he was staring at her with clear enchantment, his eyes crinkled in a warm smile. Puzzled by the flush it brought to her cheeks, she snapped, "What?"

"That's an amazing offer, Ruby. Thank you. I'm just waiting to hear what you need."

Again, she rolled her eyes. "I don't need a thing from you. I want to help."

"That's certainly a change." He laughed tauntingly.

"You'd think you'd want to be nicer to someone who just offered up something you need," she spat in irritation. "I thought about what you said last time, and while I don't agree with everything you said—and let's be honest, I'll probably *never* agree with everything that comes out of your mouth—maybe there was *some* truth to it. I'm in a position to help now, so I wanted to do something." Exasperated by his startled expression, she added, "Oh, don't give me that look. Just because I've never been nice to you doesn't mean I'm not a caring person! You don't know me very well; you just *think* you do. Besides, I find you so irritating most of the time, I doubt you'd ever see the nice parts of me even if we spent every waking moment together!"

Remy's eyes lit up jokingly at the mention of her "nice parts," and she instantly regretted her choice of words. All he said, however, was, "Understood." He extended his hand out toward her and said, "Well, I'd like to accept your offer, in that case. And even though I do love to see you all riled up, I'll make every effort not to irritate you so much so as not to jeopardize our arrangement."

She placed her cool hand in his smooth, warm one, and they shook. However, as she moved to withdraw her hand, his grip tightened slightly. Not enough to be aggressive, but enough to make her pause and keep her hand resting in his.

"Listen, I heard about your mom," he said, his voice surprisingly tender, barely audible among the surrounding noises of clanking coffee cups and polite chatter.

She froze, watching him warily. "You . . . you did? How?"

He nodded, and she noticed he was stroking her fingers softly, almost absent-mindedly. "When I signed all of the paperwork to re-sign from Capitán, a colleague mentioned it. I am so sorry, Ruby. I know that must be really hard."

Instinctively, she shifted away from him, avoiding his deep, earnest gaze and trying again to pull her hand away. But he held both, apparently determined to say his piece.

"We parted on weird terms the last time we saw each other," he said. "And while I meant what I said, I would've phrased it a little differently if I'd known. I know you're just doing the best you can for your family under hard circumstances."

Finally, quickly, she pulled out of his reach and forced a shaky but breezy half smile. "Really, Remy. It's okay. I don't want your pity."

"It's not—"

She waved his words away with probably too much flourish, but she was desperate to move on from this conversation. The only way she had been able to cope with everything was to push all the difficult things down while she tackled the immediate issues. She absolutely could not wallow here, *now*—with *him*. "If you hadn't said what you said, then we wouldn't be here at all. So let's not split hairs about what we could've done differently. Let's just focus on where we go from here."

A flash of resistance crossed his face, but it quickly melted into a smile. "Fair enough, Ruby Ortega. I'm looking forward to doing business with you." As they gazed at one another across the round bistro table, Ruby swore she felt the tension between the two of them gradually subsiding into a moment of partnership and . . . what was shockingly close to friendship.

THOUGH SOME OF THE UNEASINESS ABOUT INVITING REMY and his judgmental jokes back into her life certainly remained, the general excitement when she shared her plans at the dinner table that night made it feel a little less foreboding.

"Oh! I just think that's amazing, Ruby," Millie said, heaping some fried rice out of one of the takeout boxes in front of her and onto Carla's plate. "That all has been on my mind ever since—well, you know. Since we got here! How wonderful that we can help out."

Carla said a quick thanks to Millie as she added a few dumplings to her plate, too. "Do you think ... do you think some of our old employees might be there? What about Jorge and Paola?"

Ruby could only shrug, her hopefulness sputtering at the mention of them. "I—I'm not sure," she admitted, watching the brightness in her sister's eyes dim as she spoke.

"That would be a pretty weird coincidence," Elena cut in harshly. "It's not like all Mexican people know each other."

"That's not what I meant," Carla insisted, her voice taking on a high-pitched note of panic. "I just . . . I don't know. I miss them! I thought maybe ..."

"Maybe we'll be able to find someone who knows something about what happened to them," Ruby said, shooting Elena a warning look that barred any further comments from her end of the table. She could handle Elena's bad attitude, but she would not allow Carla to be the target.

Carla nodded, looking down at her plate.

"Either way, we'll be helping people who need it—whoever they might be," Millie said, giving Carla's hand a quick pat. "Don't you think this is amazing, Ash?"

Ashton jolted at the sound of his name, clearly not expecting to be drawn into this conversation. He cleared his throat. "Yeah, it sounds really great." He shifted in his chair before looking up at Ruby. The expression on his face was one of mild concern, protectiveness almost. Perhaps it was a little residual jealousy from his previous encounters with Remy. But still, he seemed to understand what they were trying to do, and even if he didn't like the source of this arrangement, Ashton was the kind of person who wanted to help others. That's just the way he was. That's what she loved about him.

"Are you going to mention it to Frank?" Millie asked, busying herself with twirling some lo mein noodles onto her fork in an effort to appear nonchalant. However, when she peered up at Ruby, the sharp curiosity on her face was clear as day.

She'd mulled over this question herself and had ultimately decided that no, she wouldn't tell Frank. The construction site was about two acres from the bed-and-breakfast and separated by what had once been the orchard. It was an arduous walk between the two sites, and he only made the trip occasionally. And after his rant last night, she had a sick suspicion he wouldn't have kind things to say about this new undertaking. It was better to just keep those parts of her life separate until she was able to remove the parts that no longer made sense.

She also decided not to tell her father. Would he even be able to make sense of it? Would the added turmoil baffle him further? Or would he see the good she was trying to do in these difficult circumstances? He was doing better; his routines helped, but any minor deviation could throw him completely off course. Earlier today, for example, he stumbled upon her mother's wedding ring in a drawer and had been locked in his bedroom ever since.

In her heart, she saw how proximal her family was to the communities suffering most, not just physically but culturally, too. Ruby and her sisters had been spared the hardships of being penniless immigrants, but that was just because her father and grandmother had borne those challenges for them. She had faith that someday her father would see and appreciate that the good she was trying to do was largely inspired by him, but she worried he wasn't quite ready to wrap his head around it just yet.

MOVE-IN DAY SAW A RAGTAG CARAVAN OF TRUCKS AND MINI-vans clustered in the dusty parking lot, with what felt like an endless flow of families buzzing back and forth, carrying garbage bags and tote bags full of belongings. Ruby had almost forgotten what this place looked like with a crowd, she realized, standing in the lobby, mesmerized by the sound of rapid, excited Spanish and the bustle of young children racing up and down the stairs. Through the window, she watched Remy help an elderly man carry a bulging duffel bag up the newly swept walkway to the side entrance. As she craned her neck to watch them make their way inside, she caught sight of Ashton standing behind the check-in desk, staring at her. When Ruby met his gaze, he quickly pretended to occupy himself with something behind the desk.

A few moments later, she heard heavy, purposeful footsteps echoing down the hall, and Remy's booming voice.

"Ashton, I didn't realize you were a concierge now," he said with a slow grin, taking in the sight of Ashton in his light blue Ortega Properties polo. "Is that a typical career path for a firefighter?" He extended his hand toward Ashton for a handshake as he crossed the room, and Ashton reluctantly accepted.

"It's the off-season," he grunted. He shot Remy a petulant look before continuing to slam drawers and riffle through papers.

"Ashton's been *indispensable* in getting this place back to normal," Ruby interjected defensively, as Ashton rearranged a stack of brochures. "Really, he's been such a huge help. I don't know how we got along without him when he was away."

Truth be told, Millie was far more helpful, but she'd be damned if she'd admit that under Remy's derisive stare. Ashton lacked the organizational skills necessary for managing a B&B; he often day-dreamed in the back office, forgot to charge for extra nights, or misplaced important forms, but Ruby would've endured far more cumbersome challenges if it meant having him here with her every day. Now that Millie had her online classes to tend to, there were many days when it was just Ashton and Ruby working together, and Ruby truly did not care how much of that precious alone time she spent fixing his mistakes. It was magical to be able to do so in a room where it was just the two of them.

"I'm sure he's very *indispensable*," Remy growled as they both observed Ashton fumbling to collect a cup of pens he'd just knocked over. Remy strode toward her, the beguiling sparkle that had been in his eyes just moments ago turning devilish the closer he drew. "The more things change, the more they stay the same, I guess?" She didn't fully understand the dark tone in his voice, but she didn't like it all the same.

Her jaw clenched. What did he know about her love for Ashton? Remy bobbed in and out of her life depending on which one of them was in a state of crisis, and that was fine for him. Ashton was a constant. Ashton was reliable and trustworthy and kind. Ashton was more than Remy would ever be able to understand.

27

In an effort to avoid both Frank and her father, Ruby found herself spending even more time holed up in the office of the B&B, something she hadn't thought was possible. Ashton and Millie gently encouraged her to take a day off, but she wouldn't hear of it. In a way, the hill that separated her home from her workplace had become like an emotional barrier, closing her off from the pain and loss that haunted the house so she could focus on the much more manageable chores of the business.

And though Ruby knew deep down Remy was more than the galling know-it-all that he enjoyed being, she was nevertheless surprised to see glimpses of his caring, nurturing side as he spent more time at the bed-and-breakfast, too. He kept himself busy helping their clients, as he called them, track down family members or search for jobs. He was always so warm and helpful as he switched fluidly between English and Spanish, darting about to tackle any task with urgency and careful detail. She couldn't help but feel proud and hopeful about the partnership they'd created, even if she was still unclear about what all it might entail.

"You're not staying here, too, are you?" she asked Remy sharply one afternoon as the two of them, seated on opposite couches in the front room, clicked away on their laptops.

"I might ask you the same question." He chuckled. "I have a place here now, an apartment on the outskirts of town. I just like to be around in case anyone needs anything. What's your excuse? Don't you ever take a break?"

"There's a lot of work to be done—and the internet is so much faster down here than at the house now that Emanuel installed all those booster things," Ruby told him. A Mexican American college student who had moved in just a week ago, Emanuel begged Ruby to let him tinker around with the Wi-Fi so he could access his online coursework at UCLA. The connection Ruby had set up in the midst of all the other renovations was just not cutting it for his computer science classes; she had been so impressed with his work, she'd paid him a small fee to set up the digital cash registers and security cameras at the reception hall, too.

"That guy does good work," Remy agreed, sprawling backward on his couch cozily. "What are you working on?"

"A little bit of everything. Picking out appliances, reviewing our budget, price checking the tile I want to use in the bathroom. Frank says we'll finish up next door by early summer, so there are a lot of decisions I have to make before then."

"Frank," he repeated, making an exaggerated *k* sound as he let the name roll off his tongue. "That's the boyfriend." He didn't say it like a question, but his eyes were gleaming over the top of his computer as he waited for her response, nevertheless. "You don't talk about him much."

"I wouldn't call him my boyfriend," she said with a shrug as she avoided his piercing gaze.

"Why not? Millie said you've been seeing him since January. That's a couple months."

Of course Millie found time to gossip with him. "Yes, that's true. But it's just not . . . like that."

"Oh," he said with a knowing nod. "It's because of the other man in your life, isn't it?"

Ruby felt her cheeks instantly heat up as she sputtered to find the words to reply.

"Not me, of course," he teased, pressing a palm to his chest in mock flattery. "You know, Asht—"

"*Sssh!* Shut up, will you?" she hissed, glancing around to make sure that they were alone. Ashton had the day off, but Millie was around somewhere.

He pretended to zip his lips, but he continued talking anyway. "Sorry, don't want to blow your cover. But I'm right, aren't I? Can't pledge your heart to anyone else while he lives and breathes? And so near, too! How can you stand having him right under your nose but still not yours to claim?"

"Why do you care?" she huffed. "You wouldn't understand anyway."

"I wouldn't understand that he loves you?"

Her heart leaped up in her chest, and she stared at him in disbelief. She told herself all the time that Ashton loved her, but to hear someone else say it out loud . . .

"That you believe he secretly pines for you, he just hasn't figured out how to tell you yet?" he continued. "Why wouldn't I understand what it's like to love someone like that?"

She gasped, her lips trembling wordlessly. Was he being sincere, for once? Or was this just another opportunity for him to poke fun at her feelings?

"Are you why he and Millie are still here?" he asked, closing his laptop and crossing his legs as if he were settling in for a serious conversation.

"Buena Valley is his home, too," she said with a guarded frown.

"Well, it *was*, right? His house was destroyed, and his parents decided not to come back," he said, and again, Ruby cursed Millie's big mouth. Didn't she have better things to do? "Why didn't he and Millie go back to Arizona? To school? To Millie's family? Why is he here?"

"Millie is in school still; she's just taking her classes online. And she said she wanted to be part of the work that's happening here. Perhaps that's something you can understand a little more easily."

Remy nodded earnestly. "I do understand that. I admire that. But what about Ashton? Did he just wake up and realize it was his dream to work in hospitality?"

He's just taunting me again, she thought with a sour mix of embarrassment and disappointment.

"He's a *firefighter*," she reminded him defensively.

"Yes, of course. A few months a year, he is a firefighter. But the rest of the time—*now*—he's what, Ruby? Basking in your presence until he can build up the courage to ditch his live-in girlfriend and profess his undying love for you? Or just coasting off the ambitions of the strong women around him until he can figure out what the hell he's doing with his life?"

At these words, Ruby's heart stung, like Remy had stripped open something raw and bare inside her. Maybe he had a point.

He must've sensed the hurt he'd just caused, because he solemnly rose from his couch and took a seat beside her, so close their thighs and shoulders brushed up against one another. She refused to meet his eyes, but she could feel his dark, heavy gaze on her, could see his head tilted toward her out of the corner of her eye. "I've told you before how much I like your resilience." His voice was soft and silky. "You're unstoppable. But sometimes I wonder if those traits do you more harm than good." When she finally brought herself to look at him, his lips were slightly parted, and she waited for him to continue speaking, to utter whatever was so clearly on the tip of his tongue.

They were so near to each other, Ruby couldn't help but feel a little stunned by the tingling fascination she felt for him. This unpredictable, daring person who said things that lit her on fire. She couldn't take her eyes off him, and just as she wondered whether he was actually beginning to lean closer to her or if she was just hoping he was, Frank entered the office balancing a pizza box in his hands.

"I'm not interrupting anything, am I, babe?"

28

"I got pizza," Frank said frostily, raising the box in his hands.

Ruby sprang up from the chair, bumping her knee against Remy's in the process. *"Frank!* Pizza! Great!" she exclaimed, her brain frantically scrambling for words that were not just loud observations. She took a deep breath and smiled. "Frank, this is Remy Bustillos."

Remy rose, a lot more gracefully than Ruby had a moment before, and issued both of them a bemused grin. He extended his hand to Frank, who shifted the pizza box to meet him in a handshake.

"Nice to meet you," Remy said.

Frank grunted something that was a garbled greeting of some sort. He turned his distrustful gaze toward Ruby. "Thought we could eat outside."

Ruby nodded. Embarrassed by both his brusqueness and her compliance with it, she smiled apologetically at Remy before following Frank out the door toward the front courtyard.

The door had barely shut behind them before he began chiding her for the cozy moment he had just walked in on.

"I know we haven't had the talk about whether we're 'exclusive' or not, but come on, Ruby! Right in front of my freaking face?" he huffed. "Have you been hooking up with other people?"

"*Frank*, come on. When would I have had the time for that, even if I wanted to? I'm at work or I'm with you!" She groaned in frustration. "Remy is a ... colleague."

"He works in hotels?" Frank muttered, his brows shooting upward in clear-cut suspicion.

"Well, he used to. That's how I met him a while ago."

"Used to? So the cuddling that I interrupted wasn't exactly 'business,' was it?" He paused by the worn picnic table that sat beneath the spindly branches of a recovering oak tree. He threw the pizza box onto the table and stood with his hands on his hips, squared off in a way that he seemed to think made him appear taller than he was.

"Don't take it out on the pizza!" Ruby joked with what she hoped was a charming smile, but Frank's sullen expression was unaffected. As much as she wanted to avoid the specifics of Remy's presence at the property, she could see Frank wasn't going to drop the issue without an explanation. She flung open the pizza box and grabbed a slice; it was cold, but she wasn't going to launch into this doomed endeavor without sustenance.

She hadn't expected him to approve, but she hadn't expected to be lectured either. After Ruby explained the partnership she had arranged with Remy, Frank had taken it upon himself to enumerate, in haughty detail, why he thought it was a waste of time for her and an altogether misguided decision.

"Okay, well, it's my B&B," she said tersely. She had managed to eat three slices of pizza throughout the course of his spiel, both as an effort to pass the time and to keep herself from angrily interjecting about how biased and judgmental his unsolicited rationale was.

"Actually, it's your dad's," he pointed out with a sneer. "I, of all people, understand what that's like, babe."

"Whatever." She bristled at the implication that she was nothing more than "daddy's little helper." She had been running the show for months, and for him to imply she didn't have the insight to make an important decision sparked a flame of fury inside her. "Besides, I don't know if you remember, but my dad's family also immigrated here not that long ago, so I really don't think he'd take issue with me helping out people who aren't so different from us."

"You don't *think*? So you haven't told him?" Again, Frank's raised eyebrows were clear markers of his disapproval.

Ruby bit her lip. If her father were in any other state, he might've noticed the changes going on around the property, but now that the bed-and-breakfast was cleaned up and operational, he rarely ventured past their backyard. And anyway, his grasp on reality was so fleeting and shifting, it was impossible to know what would actually register with him as unusual. "Things are busy, and he's not as interested in the day-to-day operations. He trusts me." *And of course, I'm terrified he'll completely lose his mind if I tell him.*

"I think you know this isn't a day-to-day thing. You just turned your upscale boutique B&B into a glorified homeless shelter," Frank said. "All I know is my dad would definitely want to know if I were using our business as some sort of half-baked charity behind his back."

The phrases *half-baked* and *behind his back* needled her, but before she could protest, his attention returned to Remy.

"Fuck it, it's your business. It's your choice if you want to hand out stuff for free to whoever wants it," he grumbled dismissively. "As long as you can pay my guys, I guess it doesn't affect me, does it? All I need to know is that there's nothing going on with you and that Remy guy."

"No, Frank," she said tiredly. "Honestly, we can't even stand each other most of the time."

Though he didn't say anything more about the matter, she caught a shadow in his narrowed eyes that told her he wasn't exactly convinced.

IT WAS NEARLY DARK WHEN RUBY CLIMBED THE HILL THAT evening to find her father sitting on the back porch with a wistful expression on his face. Although the view was still a far cry from the yard he had once surveyed, the image of him in his favorite spot, holding his crystal cocktail glass against the arm of his chair, was soothingly familiar.

"Ruby Catherine," he greeted her warmly. "You're home early."

Ruby smiled. "I wanted to tell you something." Frank's words had been echoing around in her head all day, and she felt like if she didn't let them out, she'd explode. She steadied herself against one of the large wooden posts that formed the perimeter of their porch. "Daddy, I'm working with Remy Bustillos and housing some displaced people at the bed-and-breakfast—people who are being targeted by all of these immigration raids and regulations. They needed lodging. It's not profitable, and honestly, I'm not sure it's a wise business decision, but they need help and we're in a position to provide it." She paused, then took a deep breath. "I'm sorry if you don't approve; I know you've been having a hard time with a lot of the changes around here, and I hate disappointing you. I just don't want you to think I've forgotten where we came from, because when I think of these people, I think of everything you and Mama Ortega went through, and maybe I don't understand it completely because my life has been made so much easier because of everything you've done, but I wouldn't want you treated the way people are treating them. And this seems like the right thing to do. And . . . I just wanted you to know."

Her father took a sip of his tequila, maintaining eye contact with her as he tilted the glass back and smacked his lips. For the first time in so long, she recognized something clear and understanding in his eyes. "Okay, mija," he said softly, a smile playing at the corner of his lips.

29

March turned to April, and with the warmer weather came many changes. The reception hall drew closer to completion, though Frank's casual and unnecessary strolls across the property became more frequent. Remy's clients flowed in and out of the bed-and-breakfast every day as new challenges and new opportunities arose. And finally, for some reason that completely confounded Ruby, Ashton's typically easygoing demeanor began to change into something noticeably more sour.

She wasn't exactly sure what had done it; there were, in fact, many developments and unusual aspects of life that could've set him off, she supposed. She liked to think it was perhaps his jealousy, over Frank or Remy, though she didn't really see the likelihood of anyone being jealous about Frank. Whatever it was, Ashton never talked about it with her. No matter how many hours they spent at the B&B alone together, Ruby checking and redoing the inventory he'd completed earlier or explaining to him for the dozenth time how to reset a deactivated key card, he remained obstinately silent about what was troubling him.

This was especially bewildering for Ruby, who had never been sad about anything for more than a day before launching into immediate action or at least a temper tantrum, whichever was most likely to bring about the results she desired. What was the point of wallowing?

But Ashton was infinitely more sensitive and thoughtful, she reminded herself. If he felt the need to linger in his sadness, she was sure he had a good reason. She just wanted him to share it with her, to let her help him.

However, it also seemed the more remote Ashton was, the warmer and more open Remy became. She was far too smart to assume this was a coincidence, and while she would've gladly traded Remy's companionship for Ashton's, she was actually enjoying the glimpses of friendliness that peeked through Remy's generally snarky demeanor. These days, she felt like she could talk to him about almost anything, things she wouldn't bother trying to explain to Frank or lay on Ashton's plate. Remy approached her with a level of understanding that used to make her feel vulnerable and bare, but now Ruby realized allowed her to be honest and uncalculated. She could tell him what she was really thinking. Whether that was because they were finally in a place where she no longer needed to manipulate him to get what she wanted or because they were genuinely friends, well, she wasn't exactly sure.

"I had this idea about the work you're doing," she told him one night as they both sat in the lobby of the B&B, eating taquitos and upholding the pretense of working.

"The work *we're* doing," he corrected her affectionately.

Ruby nodded. Frank had plans to see a movie with some friends, Millie had been blathering on all day about a date night with Ashton, and Ruby was pleased to find herself with an evening that felt unscheduled and free. It probably should've alarmed her that her first instinct was to enjoy that freedom at work with Remy, but when he sprang for takeout and started giving her positive updates on some of the families who had transitioned out of the B&B, it had shaped up to be kind of an appealing night. "Right. The work *we're* doing." The nervousness that fluttered in her chest as she waited for his response surprised her.

He took a sip from one of the two strawberry Fantas he'd brought for them, his lips making a popping sound against the rim of the glass bottle. "Do go on." His eyes twinkled.

"I know you're not running Capitán anymore, but you're still involved, right? Like, you own the idea and the technology for the app?" she ventured.

He paused before speaking, a strange, pensive frown crossing his face for just a moment. "I'm still the founder, and I have a seat on the board of directors, though I haven't been the best board member as of late. Why?"

"Well, I was thinking that other businesses might be interested in doing what I'm doing here," she said, grabbing a rolled taco from the Styrofoam box that sat between them and using it to gesticulate around to the surrounding property. "You know, a lot of local businesses are interested in helping out in times of crisis, but they don't always know how. I think big companies have corporate giving programs, but sometimes smaller businesses lack the resources to conduct outreach or really understand what needs the community has. I was thinking you might be able to use your app as a platform to connect businesses to people in need after a natural disaster, or really any kind of emergency, I guess. It could be especially helpful for people who are nervous about using the services run by the government, people who might feel more comfortable interacting with the private sector." Nervously, she took a large bite out of the end of her taco and waited for his response. "Businesses can upload what they are able to offer, and users can enter what they need: shelter, clothes, work. Like . . . Tinder for disaster relief."

He issued her an unreadable stare, lasting several beats, before he stood and crossed the room without a word.

She twisted her body in the armchair, watching him as he bent over and rummaged around in his work bag behind the front desk.

"I know it's not profitable, exactly, but I think people generally want to help each other . . . and maybe we could find a way to make it profitable someday? Sponsorships or ads or something after we get it going," she added anxiously. Still, not a word from Remy. "What are you doing? Tell me what you think!"

After another moment of silence passed, he finally turned to face her. "Sorry, I was grabbing my laptop." He leaned over and snatched a taquito from the box nearest her, popping the end in his mouth like a cigar. "And stealing one of these," he mumbled, words slurred by the taquito hanging from his lips. He settled back into his chair and removed the taco, licking the excess guacamole from his mouth playfully. "I think that's an amazing idea. I love it. I want to get started on the proposal right now. I'll call the board tomorrow, and we'll get moving." He opened his laptop, eyes still gleaming at her from across the room. "You're brilliant, Ruby. I love—I love this idea."

She was unable to stop a warmth from spreading to her cheeks down to her chest and finally settling deep in the pit of her stomach. She was immediately thankful the room was too dim for him to notice her blushing. Their eyes locked in a moment brimming with excitement, mutual understanding, and . . . something else. Something deeper. She waited for him to say more, but suddenly his laptop powered on, illuminating his face in a bluish light, and they got to work.

THE NEXT DAY, REMY SEQUESTERED HIMSELF IN THE BACK OFfice for a conference call to pitch the plan they'd stayed up until midnight putting together. She'd asked if she should join the call, too, but he insisted they would be more receptive to the project if they could talk privately as a board. She was a little disappointed by that, but she also knew she was way too nervous to sit through a meeting anyway. She needed to occupy her mind with something else until they made their decision.

Ashton was picking up a pair of AirPods he'd left at the front desk as Ruby was getting ready to head out to the reception hall in an effort to distract herself. She greeted him brightly, buzzing with frenetic energy despite not having slept much last night. Ashton remained impassive as he pocketed the earbuds without putting them in a case.

"Hey, what are you doing right now?" she asked as he started to trudge out the front door.

"Same as usual. Nothing. Heading back to the apartment until Millie gets off work," he mumbled.

"Come with me," she said, an enthusiastic plea rather than a question, unwilling to give him the chance to turn her down. "I'm going to check out the construction progress. I haven't been over there in a couple of days. I'd love a second opinion."

"Isn't Frank's opinion a second opinion?" he said with a dubious scowl.

She rolled her eyes. "From someone unbiased, I mean. Someone I trust."

Unconvinced, he sighed and let his gaze drift out the front windows, where his Prius, sorely in need of a wash, was parked crookedly in the gravel lot.

"Please, Ashton."

He half nodded, half shrugged. "Sure. Sorry. Of course."

"I really appreciate it," she purred, patting his knobby shoulder affectionately.

As they silently made their way over the sloping earth of the meager avocado grove, Ruby couldn't help but take stock of his skinny, pallid appearance. The bronze he had acquired from weeks on the fire line, running drills and being exposed to the elements, had faded, and his skin had the sort of ashen, see-through paleness of someone who spent too much time indoors. His hair, which was usually longer and worn swept to the side, was shaggy and untrimmed, hanging in his eyelashes and past his earlobes. His lips remained pursed into a thin line as he shuffled along mutely with a serious crease fixed across his forehead just above his eyebrows, barely visible beneath his unkempt bangs.

"Ashton, what's going on? What's wrong?" she asked suddenly.

He glanced at her, his hazel eyes revealing a mixture of fatigue and surprise. "Nothing," he grunted unconvincingly.

With a defiant shake of her head, she stopped walking, squaring her body so she was directly in his path. "No, not nothing. You've been sulky and quiet for a while now. Something's up. Is it something I did?" Her heart pinched in her throat as she waited for his response.

He groaned. "No, Ruby. It's not you. How could it be you?" He inhaled deeply, and she watched his chest rise and fall slowly. The midmorning sunlight through newly sprouted leaves dappled his face, casting small round shadows. "After everything you've done for me and Millie, it could never be you. I owe everything to you."

She felt relief wash over her for a brief, warm moment, until she realized he hadn't answered her initial question. If it wasn't her that was bothering him, what was it?

"*Ashton*," she nudged gently. "Is it your parents? Do you miss them?"

"Yes, of course. But it's more than that, too. It's . . . I miss everything." The words fell from his lips as if they were a strain for him to conjure, sharp and heavy as they hung in the air. "I feel so lost."

She frowned, uncomprehending. "What do you mean?"

"My whole world is gone, is different," he admitted shakily. "My home is gone. My parents are gone, and they've completely resettled without looking back. Did I tell you they bought a house? Nothing's the way it used to be, and I feel like . . . like I'll never be able to get used to how it is now. I feel like being here only makes me miss the life I had before."

"Have you told Millie this?"

Ashton shook his head, his shaggy locks swaying across his forehead. "No. You and Millie both have just *adapted*, you know? You picked up right where you left off and started something new, and it's amazing." He gestured around him to the flourishing greenery that surrounded them, a world that was literally coming back to life right before their eyes. "I can't tell Millie how sad it all makes me when she hasn't been beaten for a moment. She dropped everything to support me when I was in the field, and then to be here for her dad and you and the community. If anything, she's dealing with more changes than me. I can't tell her it's too much. She'd never be able to look at me the same."

Ruby sighed grimly. "Well, we both know that's not true. Millie would love you and understand no matter what." It gnawed at her to admit it, but it was undeniable. Millie was a natural caregiver, her commitment to Ashton unfaltering and almost overwhelming. Caring for him was one of the few areas where Ruby thought Millie measured up to her.

"But do you see what I'm saying?" Ashton asked, eyes round with an unbridled pleading.

Ruby wished with everything in her that she did, but she was only able to grasp the thinnest understanding of what he meant. He was sad because the fire had changed their hometown, sure. It *was* very sad. But why now? They'd endured the worst of it already, hadn't they? Things were finally starting to recover and make sense again. It was sad, but the hope and possibility of their circumstances were finally coming to fruition. How could he be sad about that part?

"When the fires broke out and I joined the wildland crew, it just felt *right*. It felt good to drop everything and do something that served others. It was the *right* thing to do. It was hard, but I'm glad I did it. It was important. Every day, I felt like I was working to return our lives to normal. That was my goal. It just never crossed my mind that things would never be back to how they were." The muscles in his jaw tightened, and the last bit came out hoarse and choked. "I knew it'd be hard, but not *this* hard."

She felt like he was talking in circles, trying to convince himself more than anything. He'd said many of these same things to her before, but the sense of hopelessness in his voice was new. Darker.

"I don't have school, I don't have a home, I don't know what's next for me. Another season of firefighting? But then what? What do I do in between? Do I just continue to let you allow me to fuck up your B&B?" His voice had started to tremble as he spoke. Ruby opened her mouth to interject, but he continued, "Don't even try. I'm terrible at managing. I know you spend half your time fixing my mistakes. It's okay. I appreciate you giving me chance after chance, but I know it's not the right job for me. I just don't know what is. My entire plan for my life went up in flames, too, and I didn't even realize it. And I know this makes me an enormous asshole for saying all of this to you of all people, with how much you've lost and how far you've come, but I just don't know what I'm supposed to do now." He looked at her once more and laughed bitterly. "You don't know what I mean at all, do you?"

Her heart ached, briefly but piercingly, at the mention of her losses, as it always did when she thought of her mother. "I *think* I do. Ashton, of course all this is hard. It was hard for me, too. It's still hard. Nothing about how things are is how I pictured they'd be a year ago, but I just don't see the sense in dwelling on what could've been when there's so much going on now. Maybe this isn't what you planned for yourself, and that's hard, but come up with a new plan!"

She meant it to sound hopeful and inspiring, but she feared her irritation at not comprehending his sense of helplessness peeked through in a kind of shrill, frantic tone. Did he think this had been easy for her? She'd lost her mother. She'd dropped out of school to take on a business by herself. Everyone else had gotten to grieve and wallow, but it had been up to her to keep things afloat and put food on the table. What would've happened to her—to her family, to Ashton and Millie, for goodness' sake—if she'd just sat around crying about how difficult it was? She'd had to face it! She hadn't had any other choice. And now things were definitely different than she'd planned, but she was able to find fulfillment in the problems she'd conquered and create a plan for herself as she navigated this new reality. How could he not see that? There were new opportunities; you just had to search for them!

As he looked at her once more, she realized they'd both shared something very important, but neither of them were equipped to decipher the other's message. The air hung heavy between them; the only sound was the rustle of leaves overhead. The sight of him standing there, exhausted and closing in on himself while the world around him was bursting with color and new life, was tragic in a way she couldn't put into words. They each nodded slowly, for lack of any other gesture, and continued walking without saying anything more.

She didn't see Frank's truck as they left the cover of the trees, but she didn't spare a thought to wonder where he was. Her heart and mind wanted to focus on Ashton.

However, Ruby found herself immediately distracted by the scene before her. Frank had been saying for the past few weeks that the project was nearly complete, but Ruby had interpreted that as his normal tendency toward exaggeration. He was constantly trying to make things out to be better than they were; Ruby thought it stemmed from a sense of insecurity more than anything else. She'd been so caught up with other matters that she hadn't actually made it over to the site to verify Frank's claims for over a week. But as Ruby nabbed two hard hats for herself and Ashton so they could make their way through the construction site, she was astonished to see that Frank had been honest after all!

There was drywall and flooring and a ceiling, details that she once would've found mundane but now made her ecstatic. It looked more like a building than a construction site, which was more than she could say about her last visit. The cavernous rooms, the gleaming arched windows, the immense arched doorways, and neat cement pavers—it was all *stunning*.

She couldn't believe it!

"It looks really great, Ruby," Ashton told her, running his hand over the white stucco that coated the outer walls. "It's even better than I ever could've imagined."

As they floated through the entryway, she noted the remaining tasks: some walls needed to be painted, light fixtures needed to be mounted, doors and signage needed to be installed, and of course the furniture was yet to be delivered. But these were all manageable details, almost minor tasks when she considered where they'd started. They'd definitely be ready by the Cortez event; there was no doubt. She could open this beautiful place, this next step in the Ortega empire, and it would be like a whole new chapter!

She felt a pinch of guilt about her excitement, especially after Ashton's emotional disclosure, but she could barely contain her delight. After all her hard work—clearing the debris, fighting for the insurance money, hell, even enduring Frank's company—it was finally paying off. She flung her arms around Ashton's neck, burying her irrepressible smile in the collar of his T-shirt with a squeal of glee.

"Excuse me, señorita Ruby?"

She lifted her head from Ashton's embrace to find a stout man in a hard hat and yellow vest surveying them apprehensively.

Her joy petered out as she took in the man's expression. "Yes?"

"You're Gerardo's daughter? You work with señor Remy, ¿sí?"

"Yes." He was vaguely familiar, but she was unable to place him.

"My wife and son just moved into your bed-and-breakfast yesterday," he said, his voice barely above a whisper.

"Yesterday?" Ruby pursed her lips in thought. "Alma and Mateo?"

He smiled and nodded. "Yes, that's them. It's a nice place. It's a good thing you are doing. I'm very glad to have them somewhere safe." He paused, tilting his head to gesture in the direction from which Ruby and Ashton had just come.

"Your family is staying at the bed-and-breakfast, but not you?" Her eyebrows dipped in confusion. She wondered why he wouldn't be staying there with his wife and son, but her mind caught on other questions first. "And you work here? For Frank?" *What a weird coincidence.*

"Sí." He glanced around, his eyes clouded by an anxious message she didn't understand. "You probably don't remember me, but I'm Jorge's brother. He used to work for your father? We lived with them before the fires. We visited them here sometimes, very nice place."

Her heart surged at the mention of Jorge and his wife. "Oh! How are they? *Where* are they? We've really missed them."

The man shifted uncomfortably. "We lost the house to the fires," he confessed sadly. "Jorge . . . it was just easier for them to go back to Mexico, I think." His somber eyes said there was much more to the story, but Ruby dared not ask.

Had they not been legal citizens? She had never once imagined that was the case. She realized guiltily she had never really considered who they were beyond favorite employees, two people who always paused what they were doing to reward Ruby and her sisters with a Chupa Chups or some other treat as they darted about the property.

Ruby sighed. "I am so sorry to hear that. They . . . they meant so much to us. Will you tell them that, next time you talk to them?" She smiled feebly as he nodded once more. She wasn't sure what else there was to say in regards to such tragic, unfair circumstances, but he didn't move. "What's your name?"

"Benito," he told her. "I wanted to thank you, but . . ." He cast an uneasy glance at Ashton before adding, "También quería hablarte en privado sobre un asunto serio. Se trata de señor Frank." Ruby's rudimentary Spanish had been getting some more practice since she and Remy had begun working together, but with Benito's quiet, rushed voice, the only words she caught were *private* and *serious* and, of course, *Frank*. It was enough for her to pick up on Benito's clear distress.

"Come with me," Ruby said, knowing what she was about to hear would add yet another weight to her already heavy burden.

30

"There's a reason the Kennedys are the only ones with work crews," Benito told Ruby in an ominous tone as soon as they retreated into a freshly painted room.

"What do you mean?"

Benito took a bracing breath before continuing. "Frank Senior, he's rounding up workers—people who lost their homes in the fires, immigrants mostly—and setting up camps at some of his job sites." He paused, his expression a complex mix of apprehension and anger. "But it's not like here—not like what you and señor Remy are doing. We are sleeping on the ground, under tarps, separated from our families or anyone who is unable to work at his sites. Hundreds of us. He says if we stay there, he protects us from being deported."

Ruby frowned, her pulse beginning to race. Frank didn't seem to care too much about the people being forced out of Buena Valley, but Ruby wasn't sure how much of that sentiment was shared among the rest of the Kennedy family. How much did Frank actually know about what his father was up to?

"Why would he do that?" she asked, a flush of outrage heating her cheeks.

"So he can pay us less. He takes out money from our paychecks and says it's for room and board. We make less than half of what we should even though he has us all working sixty or seventy hours a week," Benito told her. "He says he'll call ICE or the police if we quit. A few people have tried to leave, to join their families wherever they might be. I don't know if they found somewhere safe or if señor Frank did what he said." He cast his eyes downward. "We don't have many options. We lost our homes. We lost our jobs. Some of us don't have the right papers. We don't have anyone here we can turn to. No tenemos nada. So when señor Frank comes along and says he has somewhere for us to stay and a job, it sounds good. But when we get there, we realize what it is, and now there's no way out. We're trapped."

"I had no idea," Ruby breathed painfully, guilt jabbing at her throat and ribs as she spoke. How could she have involved herself so intimately with Frank and Kennedy and Sons Construction without seeing what they were truly up to? It made her sick. Even if Frank had been kept in the dark, too, Ruby couldn't help but feel it didn't excuse her ignorance. "I am so sorry, Benito. I—I just . . . tell me what I can do to help."

RUBY HAD NEVER ACTUALLY HAD A PARTICULARLY BAD breakup before, which she figured was because she had never truly cared about anyone other than Ashton. It was hard to be heartbroken about people whose presence she inevitably found inconsequential compared to him. However, with Frank, she learned it was possible to both not have deep feelings for someone and also be sent skyrocketing into a fit of screaming rage as they parted ways.

Timing was everything, so while Ruby's initial gut reaction was to take a sledgehammer to Frank's work truck, she also knew a few things needed to happen before she became the unhinged ex-girlfriend her gut told her to be.

Remy was pacing in front of the B&B with his cell phone clasped in his hands when Ashton and Ruby emerged from the orchard, sweating and winded. The excited glimmer in his eyes dimmed as he took in the sight of the two of them alone together. "What's wrong?"

Despite his clear dismay to have discovered Ashton with her, he listened attentively as she filled him in on everything Benito had said. He didn't ask questions. His expression remained passive, as if he were working out a math problem rather than listening to a shocking story of racist exploitation. When she'd finished, he nodded affirmatively and shoved his hands in his pockets. "Well, I guess that means we'll have to beta test Buena a little sooner than expected."

Ruby frowned. "Buena?"

"Yeah, I was waiting out here to share the good news with you. The board loved the idea, and they're already planning out and developing the functionality from the existing app features. I came up with the name while we were talking; it just kind of hit me. I hope you don't mind. *Buena* like *good*, *welcome*. But also like Buena Valley, where we got it started."

Their gaze met for a brief intimate moment in shared excitement, and Ruby was struck with the sudden impulse to leap into his arms. Sure, things were ugly and bad and problems were appearing left and right, but they were able to make something incredible out of all these challenges, and in spite of everything, she loved it.

Out of the corner of her eye, she saw Ashton shuffle awkwardly. She tore her eyes away from Remy. "So we need to get everyone out of the Kennedys' 'camps,' and we need to help them get jobs—normal jobs, not this medieval serfdom shit. How do we do that? Where do we start?" She knew Remy was likely the one with the answers, but she deliberately looked between the two of them to include Ashton, who was looking increasingly withdrawn and out of place.

"Well, obviously the app will do that *eventually*, but right now it's nothing more than requirements and wireframes; Emanuel is going to help with a mock-up, but we need to get moving on this ASAP," Remy said firmly, like a quarterback issuing instructions in a huddle. "So we do it the old-fashioned way for now. We call everyone we can think of and see what they're willing to spare."

RUBY HAD ALWAYS ASSUMED HER FIRST YEAR AT COLLEGE would be filled with all-nighters: studying, watching Netflix with her roommate, or slinking into the wee hours of the morning at a party. She did not imagine that those all-nighters would include teaming up in the B&B office with Remy, Ashton, Millie, and whichever of the guests were able to help find temporary housing, transportation, and leads on work and legal assistance for the hundred or so undocumented workers her boyfriend and his family had coerced into indentured servitude.

Life was wild and unexpected (and exhausting, if she was completely honest), but she did not have a moment to spare to ponder that. There was far too much to do.

It was just before noon the following day when their work had finally started to reach a lull. Millie had had the genius idea to keep Frank busy—and far away—by claiming there was an emergency at one of his other job sites. Ruby had a pretty good idea of his biggest projects and selected the condominiums near Oceanside, which she knew would take him a while to drive to. Millie adeptly downloaded a shady app to not only conceal her real phone number but make it look as if she were calling from somewhere else entirely. Ruby was pretty sure it was designed by and for scammers but figured they could excuse that small detail given their extenuating circumstances. Once she heard Millie adopting a formal tone and pretending to be a police officer reporting serious vandalism at his construction site, Ruby was too overcome with a newfound respect for Millie to worry about much else.

While Frank raced out to Oceanside—a fact that was confirmed by a succinct text from him to Ruby saying he wouldn't be around until late this afternoon—all the workers had been picked up from the Kennedys' bleak camps and transported to places that were safer and more humane: other hotels Ruby's dad and Remy had convinced to help, churches, even people's houses; Ruby had a family staying in Mama Ortega's guest suite above the garage right now. A lot of the hotels and local businesses they'd called were in the same predicament Ruby's B&B was in, unable to find cooks, receptionists, handymen, maids, and landscapers—jobs that were traditionally filled by Buena Valley's immigrant population—and were eager to offer up some work. They weren't all dream jobs or perfect fits, Ruby realized, but she figured they were all stepping stones to something more ideal—not unlike her own journey.

After hours of urgent, tense scrambling, it appeared only one task remained.

Dumping Frank on his racist ass.

IT MIGHT HAVE BEEN EASIER TO CALL HIM, BUT RUBY WAS barely keeping her fury under control, and she didn't want to risk getting into it with Frank over the phone. She yearned in a deep, smoldering way for this to be face-to-face.

She marched across the property, the silhouette of the new building peeking over the tops of scraggly trees in the blaring late-afternoon sun. Her phone had been vibrating for hours with increasingly panicked texts from him as he tried to piece together what was going on with his crews. She knew he'd be headed over to her soon to debrief after what was assuredly a troubling day for him.

As her boots crunched into the freshly paved parking lot, she spotted Frank pacing in front of his truck, directly below the newly installed sign that bore the name *Tierra Ortega Reception Hall* in trendy cursive script. A distressed scowl was plastered on his face, visible even at a distance. He paused at the sight of her and began shouting as soon as she was within earshot.

"I don't know what the hell is going on!" he bellowed, kicking his work boots around against the asphalt. His ruddy face was redder than usual, and as he tugged his sunglasses off, she noticed something wild—scared even—aglow in his brown eyes.

"What do you mean?" Ruby asked as she approached him warily.

"The whole fucking crew is *missing*! And not just here, at all my other sites!" His voice peaked into a shrill, panicked tone as he flapped his arms, gesturing to the emptiness and silence. "I got all the way to Oceanside after this prank call, and there wasn't a single person there. I've been running around to every single job site all day, and *everyone* is gone! I don't know what's happened!"

This was . . . unexpected. She'd anticipated his dismay. In fact, she'd been looking forward to it. But he didn't seem to have put two and two together, to have understood Ruby's role in his current predicament.

Which, in hindsight, seemed silly for Ruby to have overlooked. She had bitten her tongue many times when it came to the tenuous social and political climate of Southern California, so perhaps Frank hadn't given much thought to the possibility that Ruby's views did not align with his own. Also, who was Ruby kidding? If she was dating him primarily for the perk of his professional services, he was dating her for her physical appeal. Her political leanings probably never even crossed his mind.

"I mean, all of them! A hundred workers, *missing*! Just gone!" he shouted, rubbing the back of his neck and shaking his head incredulously.

"Frank."

"I've worked with some flaky losers, but for a whole crew to just not show up—that's unheard of. This shit's going to put us behind! And we're so close here. Well, *you* know!"

"Frank."

He wasn't looking at her. His eyes darted across the building before him, and he continued shaking his head. "My dad's gonna fucking kill me!"

"*Frank.*" She said his name a little more sternly this time.

At last, he cocked an unruly eyebrow at her, his thin lips pursed.

"I know where your crews are," she said flatly. "And I know where your crews have been staying."

Suddenly, his flushed cheeks paled and his eyes narrowed. "*What?*" he hissed between gritted teeth. "What did you do?"

The hot rage that had been simmering in her chest since yesterday suddenly ignited her entire body, and she felt the sharpest prickle of sweat form at the back of her neck. "What did *I* do? Frank, don't you know that your father has been exploiting these people?"

There was a fractious pause for a moment when Frank just stared at her, jaw clenched, and Ruby clung to the faint hope that maybe he was unaware of what Frank Sr. had been up to, too. Somehow. It wouldn't absolve him of course—just like it wouldn't absolve her—but it would be slightly easier to bear.

He clicked his tongue at her, his lip curled in disdain. "Not just my father. You have been exploiting them right there with us. Who do we work for, babe?"

"I didn't know about any of this!"

He let out a bark of bitter laughter. "Ignorance is bliss, right? We only see what we want to. You would've done just about anything to get someone to fix this place up. You're telling me if I had told you exactly why we are the only construction company with fully staffed crews, you would've turned me down?" He glared maliciously as Ruby tried to sputter out a response, tried to deny his ugly accusation. "Please. We were both trying to make the best of a shit situation. You got your property remodeled. We got a lot of business. And hell, the workers got some money in their pockets and a safe place to sleep away from the police. You can make us out to be the bad guys all you want, but this is just how the world works."

"*Worked*," she spat out hotly. "Past tense. People like you and your dad with power and privilege take advantage of others every chance they get, and you rationalize it by saying at least you threw them some scraps in the process. And you're right, people like me were bystanders to all your bullshit because we were afraid to lose our privileges, too, because we didn't want to make any sacrifices or face anything too difficult. But if there's one good thing that's come from these fires, it's that they've exposed these ugly truths. And personally, I'm not going to stand for it."

Frank rolled his eyes. "You're being naive."

She crossed her arms, squaring up with him defiantly. "Well, you're a self-interested bigot who's just been fired. And dumped. And if I hear anything about you and your dad trying to pull this shit again, I will call, tweet, and email every news outlet I can think of until your narrow-minded, prejudiced ass is so well-known there won't be a single person who would hire or work for you." She pulled out a crumpled check from her back pocket, squeezing it into a little ball in her hand before tossing it at him. "There's your final payment. Now get the hell off my property."

31

As Ruby watched Frank's truck peel out of her parking lot, she felt a fierce sense of pride for standing up to him, even if it had presented unexpected challenges. Her mother would probably have managed the issue with a little more tact—hell, she probably would've been sensible enough to not get mixed up in all that in the first place—but Ruby liked to think she would've been proud of her, too.

She'd be lying if she said it didn't pain her just a little bit to call things off when they were so close to finishing construction. Not enough to have changed her mind, of course, but enough to spark just the faintest hint of remorse when she thought of how much she'd been banking on opening with time to spare for the Cortez event.

That's not what's important, she reminded herself. Though a voice at the back of her mind quipped, *Paying bills is important, too*.

Ruby sent a quick text to her friends and family letting them know Frank had hit the road and that she was okay. As her phone buzzed with celebratory words and emojis, her gaze drifted up to the beautiful new building, gleaming white in the sunlight. It was incomplete, sure, but it was still incredible. It had taken a lot of work, and still needed a lot of work, but Ruby felt hopeful despite everything that had happened.

She wondered if she owed Elena an apology for having unabashedly steamrolled her relationship in order to get to Frank. And maybe she should explain her motives for pursuing him, though she wasn't sure her self-centered business mindedness was any more flattering than her willingness to canoodle with someone whom she had no interest in and nothing in common with. She just hoped her family—and Ashton, Millie, and Remy, for that matter—could see some faint hint of her good intentions without judging her too harshly for the passive role she'd unknowingly, but perhaps not entirely innocently, played in the Kennedys' scheme. Hopefully it counted for something that she'd tried to make it all right in the end. That she'd learned something and would carry that lesson with her in the future.

SHE DIDN'T RETURN TO THE B&B AFTER DEALING WITH Frank. She wasn't quite ready to rehash it all with Remy, Millie, and Ashton. She could only think of a shower to wash herself of him—their relationship, his business, their breakup, *everything*. She was relieved to find the house empty when she arrived; she couldn't remember the last time she'd actually been alone. Even her sleep was peppered with interruptions from her sisters or text messages and phone calls from work. And as she fought back the chest-tightening urge to crumple into sobs, she was very much grateful for the solitude.

She heard her father and sisters enter the house as she was drying off from her shower, but no one sought her out, thankfully. She still didn't know what to say to any of them. Head aching, she lay down for a quick nap before she had to begin the arduous task of finding a new contractor.

She awoke the next morning with sunlight streaming in through her bedroom directly onto her face. She jolted upright, realizing that she'd forgotten to set an alarm and had apparently slept straight through the night and into the next day. She fumbled for her phone in the tangled mass of sheets and blankets covering her bed. It was just past nine a.m.; she hadn't slept that late since she'd left college. But even more surprising, there were no messages or missed calls waiting for her. She'd been dead to the world for fifteen hours, and no one had needed her? No crises had developed? No questions had arisen that only she could answer? No one had *worried* about how she was doing?

She eased herself out of bed and glanced in the mirror. Her hair was matted in every imaginable direction from falling asleep while it was still damp, and she could see the seam of her pillowcase indented into her right cheek, along with a charming crust of drool extending down her chin. However, the dark circles that had taken up permanent residence under her eyes seemed a little lighter, and she couldn't help but notice a brightness in her green eyes she hadn't seen in weeks. She felt guilty for sleeping in so late, but there was no doubt that her body needed it.

She tamed her wild hair into a loose bun and splashed water on her face. Pulling on the tennis shoes, leggings, and sweatshirt that had become her uniform in the days of cleaning the B&B, she began running through the tasks that remained at the reception hall. What had seemed like manageable details a couple of days ago with a full construction crew at her disposal now felt deeply daunting as she tried to wrap her head around working on them on her own. But she had to at least try.

As she hurried downstairs, she noted again with curiosity that the house was still empty. She glanced at her phone again. It was Monday, so the girls were at school, but it was unusual for her father to be gone—especially after the long hours they'd pulled over the weekend. Though he had been noticeably more active lately, attending his weekly therapy sessions, tinkering in the garden, or whipping up chorizo and eggs for dinner—his go-to meal—he was almost always home.

She peered out the back window one more time. She was normally far too rushed to take in the big picture of their immense property, but now she was struck by the shades of green that painted the land. What had once been black and dead and desolate now had patches of grass and a few budding sprouts of shrubbery and flowers. The bed-and-breakfast was so bright and cozy, with its fresh white paint and blossoming flower boxes. Simple signs of life, like guest cars in the small lot, evoked a sense of giddiness inside her. And across the increasingly less sparse orchard, where the trees were regrowing at astonishing rates, was the reception hall, a small Spanish mission–style castle on the perimeter of their property. White walls and dark shutters, palm trees and flagstone pavers. It was gorgeous.

It certainly was not the place she had known as a child, and that still tugged at her heart, but she was nevertheless taken aback by how far it had come from the charred hellscape it had been just a few months ago.

She lingered a few minutes more, admiring their handiwork, before finally collecting her things and heading down the hill toward the reception hall, desperately hoping that just being there would help her figure out some sort of plan.

Crossing the threshold into the spacious entryway, the same place where Benito had unraveled Frank's secret just two days ago, she found Remy crouching in the open doorway of one of the smaller rooms; once the velvet chaise and floor-length mirror were delivered, it would be used for brides to get dressed in or take pictures. He knelt beside a small child Ruby recognized from the property, Lupe. He was handing her screws as she turned a screwdriver against the brass doorknob.

"What are you doing?" Ruby called by way of a greeting, flashing Lupe a quick smile.

He patted Lupe on the shoulder before getting to his feet, removing the spare screw from where he'd had it clasped between his teeth. He grinned. "I'd think that's pretty obvious. We're installing doorknobs."

She started to roll her eyes but caught herself as Lupe peered up at her. "Well, yes. But *why*?" She glanced down the hall to see all the doors featured gleaming new knobs.

His grin twisted into a cheeky smirk. "Again. I thought that would be obvious to you of all people." He laughed. "You fired and dumped your contractor, so I didn't think *he* was going to be inclined to do it."

"I'm helping!" Lupe chirped, giving the knob a hearty jiggle to test out her craftsmanship. "Mr. Remy taught me righty tighty, lefty loosey!"

She smiled at Lupe again before returning her gaze to Remy. Though he was clearly trying to do something kind—and the image of him working side by side with this curly-haired child did things to her heart she wasn't ready to investigate—she was still frustrated by his deliberate elusiveness. Why was nothing ever a straightforward answer with this guy?

"This place is so close to done, and I know that must've been a hard decision for you yesterday," he finally conceded, his snarky sneer softening into something warm and genuine. "I rounded up a few people to help with those finishing touches so hopefully you won't be too far behind schedule."

"Oh. That's really . . . nice." She couldn't conceal the tone of surprise in her voice.

"Yes, well, I've been known to do a nice thing here and there. But don't tell anyone." He winked at her as he took the screwdriver from Lupe's tiny hands. "It's not just me, though. Lupe has been fantastic. Your dad got here bright and early; he's working on the kitchen appliances. Benito and some of the guys from Frank's old crew wanted to say thank you, so they volunteered a couple of hours as well. Last I heard, they were finishing up the toilet installations." He turned to Lupe. "Speaking of which, you should run off and play before they rope you into the dirty work. Thank you for your help, chiquita." Lupe beamed at him before darting happily down the hallway. "And of course, your buddy *Ashton* stopped by, too. I think he's caulking baseboards." His eyes gleamed mischievously.

Ruby nodded, shifting her weight back and forth on her feet uncertainly. "Wow. Okay. Well—what should I do, then?" It felt strange to ask Remy for instructions at her own property, and she chuckled uneasily.

The awkward swap of roles did not escape Remy, whose full lips curled into a bright but playful smile. "Well, the cabinets need hardware. Do you know how to install knobs and handles?" Despite the condescending phrasing, his eyes appeared unusually earnest.

Ruby rolled her eyes at him, though for once, it was without a trace of irritation. "*Please*. Who do you think did all the work around here before Frank showed up?"

Remy laughed. "Of course. What was I thinking? Come on, then."

AFTER A WEEK AND A HALF OF LABOR, DURING WHICH SHE repeatedly found herself working in the same room as Remy but rarely catching a glimpse of anyone else working on the site—most noticeably, of course, Ashton—Ruby began to grow suspicious that Remy had something to do with it. However, she was elated by the progress they were making, so she resisted the urge to point out the strange coincidence that out of the entire complex—which included three ballrooms of various sizes, a full kitchen, two sets of bathrooms, and a myriad of other nooks and crannies that needed attention—the room in which she was working always had a random task for Remy to do, too.

Besides, though she'd never say it to him, his presence often made the time go by more quickly. There was a comforting ease about him these days. His taunting edge still lurked around the corners of his personality; she'd catch a glimmer of it every now and then when he'd make a snide comment or ask a loaded question. But for the most part, he was helpful and open in a way she hadn't expected.

"Where'd you learn to do all this stuff, anyway?" Ruby asked one afternoon. Their backs were to each other as they crouched near opposite walls, screwing in faceplates on the outlets.

"You know that you tend to figure these things out when you have to," he replied. He glanced over his shoulder at her to see she was staring at him, waiting for an actual answer. "When I was little, my mom sent me to live with my tía in Texas. She had a lot of small kids in this tiny little house, and we didn't have much money. So when things broke, which happened a lot, someone had to fix them or else we'd just be living without running water or a door that locked. So I learned."

Ruby nodded, scooting along the carpet to the next outlet. "Why did you go live with your aunt?" Images of a wild and reckless adolescent Remy flashed through her mind. Had he been too out of control for his mother? Was he sent to do manual labor as a punishment to calm him down and instill some values?

"My mom didn't think it was safe where we were living, this tiny little town outside of Mexico City. The schools were bad. A lot of boys got caught up in gangs. She thought it'd be different if I lived in the US." He glanced up at her thoughtfully but refocused on the faceplate in front of him before continuing to speak. "I, uh . . . was getting into some trouble. I've always had an 'innovative' streak. Always finding new ways to give her gray hairs, she'd say."

She paused from turning the screwdriver as she considered his words. "But she just sent you? She didn't come with you?"

Remy shook his head even though they weren't looking at each other. "No. She planned to get her citizenship stuff figured out and meet me, but she wanted me out of there as soon as possible. Besides, my tía's husband wasn't very good to her, and with all those kids, my mom thought I might be able to help her out."

They both stood as they finished their last outlets in the room, and Remy stooped to collect the box of faceplates so they could move to the ballroom next door. As he stepped toward the door, however, Ruby remained where she was, surveying him with a solemn, curious gaze. She was so surprised by this information about him, she could feel the confusion as a tightness in her chest. Remy's life was so glamorous and well ordered, it had never once occurred to her that he hadn't grown up with the same comforts and securities she had.

"Well, did your mom make it here?" she asked quietly.

He shook his head. "No. She filed the papers, but after a few years of waiting, a lawyer said it would just be easier if my tía adopted me. Easier for me, that is. She stayed in Mexico. Remarried. Had a few more kids. I used to go down and see them a lot."

"Used to?"

He averted his eyes and opened the door, standing halfway in the room and half in the hallway. "Yeah. She died a few years back. Cancer."

Ruby clasped a hand to her mouth with a soft gasp. Just the mention of losing a mother evoked immediate waves of pain throughout her body. "Oh, Remy. I'm so sorry."

His expression was soft and sad as he finally brought his eyes back to her. He shrugged. "I wish she'd had an easier life, and I wish I'd gotten to spend more time with her, but I hope she's proud of where my life has ended up."

Ruby nodded. "I'm sure she would be. You've accomplished so much."

His eyes brightened slightly at her uncharacteristic praise, and he managed a thin smile, but something distraught lingered in his expression just below the surface. "Come on," he said, clearing his throat suddenly. "I bet I can install more faceplates than you in the ballroom. If you win, I'll buy you an ice cream."

32

It had been just over a month since Ruby had dismissed Frank from both her business and her life, and as June approached, it finally seemed as if they were nearing the end of the lengthy list of "little things" that needed to be finished. Kitchen appliances had been installed, tables and chairs were scheduled to be delivered later that afternoon, and the fire inspector had approved all their safety precautions and commended her on the defensible space she'd included around the perimeter of the property in preparation for next fire season.

Ashton had returned to his normal shifts at the bed-and-breakfast, which Ruby knew was necessary, but disappointing, nonetheless. She invented errands to stop by and see him most days, but their interactions were always abrupt. He hadn't said much about how he was feeling since that day he'd opened up about how lost he was, and Ruby had been too nervous to pry. His attitude didn't seem to have changed much, if at all, but she tried to convince herself that maybe that was just because they were spending far less time together. Was she even around enough to notice a change?

She wanted so desperately to be there for him, for him to confide in her about something she knew how to fix. But even if she'd been available, she hadn't the faintest idea of how to help him find purpose in his new life. She saw that as something someone had to do on their own, something that no amount of moping could resolve. But she figured that wasn't what Ashton would want to hear, and since she didn't know what else to say, she often let their moments together pass with aimless small talk and friendly glances at each other.

Like it or not, her focus was on getting the reception hall ready for the Cortez event. Rumors had begun swirling around the governor and her interest in running for Congress; recent details from her staff had led Ruby to believe this event was in fact a fundraiser for this highly speculated-upon campaign. And while the idea of having a Latina represent her beloved state filled her with a distinct sense of promise and pride, the prospect of hosting such a high-profile, VIP event was even more exhilarating. All sorts of important figures would be in attendance. Pictures of the venue would be everywhere.

It was going to be a hell of a grand opening, and Ruby was determined to get it right.

REMY SAT IN THE ENTRYWAY OF THE EVENT HALL, RECLINING comfortably on the new cream-colored chesterfield sofa he'd helped her pick out weeks ago. It had been pricier than the set of love seats she'd bookmarked, but she realized he'd been right. With the rustic chandelier and earth-toned Turkish rug, it really did look much better.

"We should celebrate tonight, after the furniture's here," he said suddenly from behind his laptop screen.

"Well, it'll take a while to unpack and get organized. I don't know if *that* will be done tonight." Her father and sisters were supposed to come down after dinner to help remove plastic wrapping and begin assembling the various pieces the furniture would likely come in.

"Okay, tomorrow, then. Or whenever we're finished getting organized," he countered brightly, undeterred.

She shook her head, preoccupied with thoughts about the linens and artwork. When were those supposed to arrive? *This week, for sure, but is it tomorrow or the day after? I should find the order form.* "Maybe it would be better to wait until after the governor comes by, or even after the fundraiser? Or maybe until—"

He snapped his laptop shut firmly. "Ruby, I would like to take you to a nice dinner. What we are celebrating is irrelevant to me." She opened her mouth to point out that they ate dinner together all the time. In fact, she was more often found eating takeout in some corner of this place with him than dining with her own family. However, he clearly anticipated this, because he rose from his seat with a playful smirk and moved to where Ruby was distractedly scribbling away at her to-do list. "I want to take you on a date. Celebrating the furniture, or whatever you want to celebrate, was just a pretext. All I care about is that you're there."

She blushed. Any interest she'd suspected he'd had in her had always been veiled by his coy sense of humor. Hearing him speak so candidly left her nearly speechless.

He leaned against the counter nearest her, looming over her

with his dark, glittering eyes. "You know I like you, Ruby—that I've liked you for a while. And I realize you just ended things with Frank, but who knows when the next crisis will happen? I won't keep waiting around, hoping to catch you between convenience boyfriends."

A bark of incredulous laughter escaped her lips. She knew deep down that her involvement with both Charlie, which seemed like a lifetime ago, and Frank had really just been a means to an end, stepping stones to her goals. But to hear someone else—Remy, of all people—acknowledge it so matter-of-factly was something else.

"Come on. When was the last time you did something just for fun? Don't you think you deserve it?"

She bit back the urge to ask him what made him so sure an evening with him would be fun. He had been so open and warm lately, sharing details about himself and responding to her in a caring, guileless way she'd never seen from him. Besides, Remy was a lot of things, but he was not boring. She thought back to the night at the gala and couldn't help but feel a little excited and curious about what another night out with him would entail.

When exactly had she become this person who so readily denied herself a good time?

"Okay," she said, not without a bit of hesitation. "Tomorrow night. Let's . . . go on a date."

A satisfied grin spread across his face as he stood upright. "Not that you don't look beautiful in leggings and a paint-covered sweatshirt," he said, gesturing to the dirty outfit she'd been wearing for the past three days of chores, "but maybe let's do something a little more formal for Friday." He winked and sauntered back to his chair as she rolled her eyes, wondering if she'd regret saying yes.

✦ ✦ ✦

SHE'D SUGGESTED THEY MEET AT THE RESTAURANT, BUT Remy had dismissed that idea right away and refused to disclose where he was taking her, as if to prove a point. It was a date, he'd insisted, and he intended to pick her up from her house.

Ruby had mixed feelings about this. Normally, she would've accepted this kind of courtly gesture as the proper protocol for wooing her; in the past, any boy too lazy or shy to pick her up was unworthy of her time.

But things were different now. She'd kept her father separate from so much of her life throughout the past year, due to both the complicated nature of her relationships and the fragile dynamics of their family. It felt uncomfortable to revert back to old customs after so much had happened.

"I'm glad to hear you're going out," her father said, pausing in front of the open bathroom door as Ruby ran her fingers through freshly curled hair. His tone was affectionate, but a little mournful, and Ruby wondered if he, too, was missing her mother in this moment. How many times before a date had she helped Ruby comb her hair or fasten necklaces in the hall bathroom the three Ortega sisters shared?

Ruby smiled hopefully, meeting his gaze in the mirror.

She was beginning to feel pangs of guilt about this outing, but her father's words were reassuring. She couldn't exactly put her finger on what was making her feel so conflicted. She wondered vaguely if it was the prospect of taking a night off when there was still plenty of work to do, but she suspected her remorse was more likely related to Ashton. Was she ashamed to entertain the idea of dating Remy when she knew her heart still belonged to Ashton? She hadn't felt that way about Charlie or Frank, of course, but Remy was . . . different, to say the least, and she suspected Ashton knew that, too. Would he care if he knew they were going out? And what would Remy say if he knew her thoughts were still preoccupied by Ashton moments before he was due to pick her up?

"I found the dress you were looking for," Carla called, popping her head in the doorway next to their father. "I laid it out on your bed."

Most of Ruby's clothes were still packed away in the boxes Patty had sent, since she hadn't had any need for anything other than work clothes and a hotel polo in so long. Even when she'd met up with Frank, she had never felt the need to throw on anything more formal than a sweater and a pair of jeans, though they had never done anything Ruby would've considered an actual date. Finding an outfit worthy of this occasion had been a mission that required assistance.

She glanced at the bathroom clock. As she remembered from the last two times Remy had picked her up for something, he tended to be early. With one final tousle of her brown, wavy hair, she hurried into her bedroom to get dressed.

June had brought evening warmth to Southern California, so she was finally able to don a breezy sundress and the platform sandals she'd wanted to wear the night she met Millie for the first time all those months ago. It had taken her a while to successfully scrub all the paint from her hands, but now she couldn't help but admire how much she looked like her old self, the version of herself whose biggest concern was making it home before curfew.

Almost as if on cue, Ruby heard the doorbell ring. Outside her bedroom window, she spotted Remy's black truck parked along the street. As she collected her purse and gave herself one last spritz of perfume, she could hear her family's footsteps racing down the stairs to meet him.

Her father was topping off his glass of tequila as she descended the stairs and rounded the corner to where Remy stood at the center of the room, her two sisters gaping at him from the couch. "Now, normally, I'd offer you a drink, too," her father was saying, "but since tonight you are taking my daughter out, I've only got water for you. No drinking and driving, of course."

Remy nodded with a courteous smile. "Of course." He wore a navy-blue suit with a crisp white shirt unbuttoned at his neck, just enough to give him an air of casualness.

"Oh, Ruby! You look so pretty!" Carla gushed with girlish glee.

Elena tore her eyes away from Remy, who she had been staring at as if she'd never even met him. They had all worked together at the hotel countless times, but the new circumstances appeared to have thrown her sister for a loop.

Remy's eyes also followed, and she was pleased to find a warm grin on his face as he took in the sight of her. "Wow," he said by way of a greeting, and he visibly lit up at the blush Ruby felt heating her cheeks.

Her father cleared his throat. "We'll expect you home around midnight. Yes, Ruby Catherine?" he interjected assertively, interrupting the smoldering gaze Remy had locked on her.

Ruby smiled at her father. She was eighteen and definitely responsible enough to decide what a reasonable time to be home was, but she didn't dare question his authority, not when he seemed so like his old self. Ruby's last date with Remy had turned into an all-night adventure—though her family didn't know that, nor did they know it hadn't been the kind of overnight experience her father was concerned about—but Ruby had absolutely no intention of staying out all night with Remy. An evening of fun and frivolity, sure. That was one thing. Spending the night with him was something entirely different, something she assured herself she was not interested in at all.

"Shall we?" Remy motioned toward the front door, and Ruby nodded in response.

THEY ARRIVED AT AN UPSCALE RESTAURANT DOWNTOWN, IN sight of the twinkling lights of boats and yachts in the harbor. The kind of place where the waiter assumed no one underage could afford it and poured her a generous glass of champagne at her request.

"Well, this is nice," she commented happily, pressing her glass to her lips and scanning the menu—lobster, foie gras, filet mignon.

"I'm glad you think so. I wanted to go somewhere special."

"Oh, yeah? Why is that?" Her eyes darted up from the menu to find him watching her across the candlelit table. The shadow of the flame danced magically along his broad face, highlighting his sharp jawline and full lips in a way that made her squirm excitedly.

He reached across the table and placed his large warm hand on top of hers. Goose bumps immediately erupted down her body at the unexpected contact. "I'd like to be honest with you, Ruby. Ever since the first time I saw you—angrily smashing beer bottles in a cocktail dress—I knew there was *something* about you that I loved." Ruby's pulse raced, both at the infuriating memory of their first meeting as well as at the frighteningly exhilarating use of the word *love*. "I've tried to keep it to myself." He laughed before adding, "Well, maybe I haven't tried very hard. But I know we've both had other things going on, other things to worry about. It just wasn't the right time. I see that now. But now it seems like . . ." He paused, his dark eyes intently searching her face. For what? She wasn't sure, but she held her breath as she waited for him to continue. "We've become good friends—and, hell, even good business partners—these past few months. But I feel something more than friendship for you, and I think—I hope, at least—that you do, too."

Dizzy with excitement, her mind raced for the words to respond. She did care for him. It was true. He could be irritating and confusing, without a doubt, but most of the time she found him smart and intriguing. She loved working with him and valued his opinion. But did that amount to more than friendship?

Inevitably, her thoughts fell to Ashton. Was it possible for her to care about Remy in the way he described while Ashton still occupied such a prominent place in her heart?

"I'll just say it. I want to be with you. I want us to be together." His words did not carry a hint of impatience or nervousness. He said it as directly as he'd asked her out, as if he were ordering the wood-grilled salmon from the waiter rather than spilling his heart to her.

"Oh," was all she could muster, a breathless sound that barely escaped her mouth.

His eyes narrowed, decisive and analytical beneath his thick lashes. "I thought you might hesitate, but Ruby, when was the last time you were with someone because you *wanted* to be? Don't you think you deserve to care about someone, to enjoy your relationship, after all that you've been through? We could be good together if you're willing to take that chance." He withdrew his hand and took a swig from his whiskey, apparently satisfied with having said his piece and willing to wait for her to formulate her response.

The waiter arrived, and Remy inquired about the fish of the day before amicably ordering the surf and turf and asking Ruby if she'd decided. His eyes flashed at the double meaning of his question, and she managed to stammer that she'd have the lobster ravioli.

The date resumed as if his emotional interlude had never taken place. Remy chatted away about the neighborhood, recent trips, updates on Buena, and though it took Ruby a few minutes to recover, she soon found herself caught up in his upbeat energy. He had completely flipped a switch, and not even the faintest remnant of his earlier seriousness remained. It was like it had been an entirely different person who had sat across from her, confessing his true feelings. Either way, whether it was the champagne, the rich food, or his intoxicating conversation, by the end of dinner, Ruby had nearly forgotten about the weighty revelation he'd laid on her before the first course, just as he'd appeared to.

Maybe it was just the nerves talking, she thought as they left the restaurant, though he hadn't seemed nervous at all.

As he pulled up to her house, he offered to walk Ruby to the front door, but she insisted he'd better not. "Carla and Elena are definitely spying from somewhere in there," she told him, casting a suspicious glance at the darkened windows of her home as she unbuckled her seat belt.

He ignored this, nevertheless, and exited the truck with her. As she rounded the hood of the truck, he said huskily, "I guess I'd better do this here, then."

His hands found their way to her waist and drew her body close to his with such speed and intuition Ruby wondered if he'd been thinking of doing this all night. She turned her face up to his wonderingly, her throat tight with anticipation. His lips hovered just above hers, so close she could feel his warm breath.

"Say you want to be with me, too," he murmured, inching his face slightly closer to hers so the tips of their noses brushed softly.

Of course, he had not forgotten. How could he have?

She was awash with a sense of tingling alertness, awake to every inch of him, every movement he made as they stood together in the summer darkness, steps away from the glow of the newly repaired streetlights.

"Yes," she whispered, the word spilling forward before she even knew she'd thought it. A wave of warmth—equal parts desire and curiosity—fell over her, and it peaked deliciously as Remy's lips met hers, at first soft and tender but increasing in intensity. He stepped toward her, pressing his body against hers and pinning her gently to the front of his truck. She felt one of his hands move thrillingly from the small of her back to her hair, and she responded by draping her arms around his neck, giddy at the feeling of his taut skin and coarse hair under her fingertips. As her mouth opened in response to his, she couldn't believe the *yearning* coursing through her, like some unknown dam giving way inside her. How long had she wanted this? She'd had no idea kissing him, kissing anyone, could feel like this. So freeing, so mesmerizing, so—

Is there even a word for what kissing Remy Bustillos is like?

At last, they broke apart, and he sighed happily, rubbing his stubbled cheek against hers in a playful nuzzle.

"Wow, I . . ." Words eluded her; it was hard to even catch her breath. She toyed with the crisp collar of his shirt, her fingers brushing against the small bit of flesh exposed at his neckline. She could feel his pulse beneath her opposite hand, and she was delighted to find it just as quick as her own.

His eyes gleamed as he pulled away just far enough to rest his forehead on hers. "You should be kissed often," he said. Despite their close proximity, mere centimeters from one another, she saw him wink before adding, "And by someone who actually knows what they're doing—preferably me, of course." He claimed her lips once more, and she was struck by a fleeting urge to giggle at this infuriating, self-assured, gorgeous, intoxicating person. Remy Bustillos—he was so many mind-boggling things, she could hardly wrap her head around it. So instead, she wrapped her arms around him and melted into his kiss once more.

Part Four

*"From a little spark
may burst a flame."*

—Dante Alighieri

33

Ruby hated to admit it, but dating Remy was . . . *fun*.

His company made even the most mundane task enchanting—and not just because he was likely to sweep her up in his arms at a moment's notice, though that certainly added an element of excitement. But she found, to her surprise, that she enjoyed the times when they weren't making out just as much. He was perpetually buzzing with eager energy as they toiled away at the reception hall and the app, and in between work, he always seemed to find some new joke or story to tell her. Ruby found the more she uncovered about Remy Bustillos, the more fascinating she found him.

And of course, being pinned in a supply closet while he tugged at her work polo to trail kisses down her collarbone didn't hurt, either.

He was the smooth-talking, refined entrepreneur she'd imagined him to be—but he was also so much more. Every time she thought she'd figured him out, she'd unravel some new, intriguing detail about him. He was like some decadent dessert: each layer she sank her teeth into was richer and more intricate than the last.

Most of the time when she spoke to guys, she was left with the unsavory impression that she was being talked *at* rather than talked to, and though Remy certainly was never short on words, he never made her feel that way. He completely immersed her in conversations about their childhoods, sharing his own memories of working in the lettuce fields in rural Texas with his aunt while asking about her experiences at horseback riding camp, as if they shared the same cultural richness or character-building complexity. He'd ask her about her goals and school in between sharing his vision for the Buena app and for the country, because his ambitions extended so much further than himself. When he thought about the future, his plans spanned across the globe. He had opinions and ideas about everything from climate change to the federal government to bike lanes—things Ruby often found either too insignificant or overwhelming to think about were playgrounds for Remy's imagination.

Ruby had never dreamed that a person as vibrant and unexpected as Remy existed beyond books and movies. All her life, she'd assumed she understood the world around her and the people who filled it for the most part. But the more time she spent with Remy, the more she wondered at how much she'd been missing by failing to look beneath the surface.

Was Ashton this full of history and aspirations, too? Millie? Her sisters?

Hell, she even began to wonder if there were some deep, lingering details about herself she'd never given herself time to explore.

She could feel herself growing and learning and opening up to a world that felt brand new to her—which was something she'd never experienced before, and definitely not something she'd ever had with a boy.

It was uncomfortable and confusing but also enthralling.

One evening, Remy invited her over to his apartment for pozole; after weeks of trying to charm a group of elderly women staying at the B&B into sharing their recipe with him, he'd finally been successful. This had become one of Ruby's favorite routines with him: dinner, wine, and conversation that fluctuated between strategic business planning and flirty banter, switching back and forth at lightning speed. Each of these topics made Remy's inky eyes sparkle in a way that Ruby couldn't get enough of.

It really was unbelievable how Buena had taken off over the past few weeks. She'd been worried about managing it along with the venue, but she was stunned by how seamlessly it was all coming together. Sure, the days were long and tiring, but she felt like there was nothing that could stop them. And it wasn't even just her and Remy anymore. Many of the Buena clients had stepped up, offering support with anything from graphic design to business outreach, and Ruby was increasingly hopeful they'd be able to offer them paid roles within the organization soon. Along with the occasional expertise and manpower of her family, Millie, and even Ashton, it felt like every problem had a solution and every solution turned into some exciting new opportunity.

They'd also been able to transition several families out of their hotels and partner facilities and into new apartments of their own, securing jobs using the app. A few other nonprofits around

the country had reached out for information on how to repli-
cate their model in their own communities, and Remy's eyes had
brightened at the opportunity to provide consulting to other organizations. They'd held an impromptu press conference in one of
the new ballrooms just the other day after a blog had gotten wind of
their temporary housing partnerships. After their recent meeting
with Governor Cortez and her staff, the governor had even mentioned setting up a meeting about how she could support the work
Buena was doing. It was truly incredible. Ideas about lobbying local
politicians—and maybe even running for office themselves—now
dominated their plans as they looked at the progress they'd made
and dreamed their way forward.

"No, you know the guy," Remy told her with a chuckle, taking a
hearty swig of his wine after a particularly spicy spoonful of pozole. "He has all the commercials. The goofy jingle?" He waved his
utensil in the air as he hummed an upbeat melody. Ruby shook
her head with a perplexed shrug. "Well, anyway. He's corny, but
his parents immigrated here from Bolivia forty years ago, and he
was really excited about what we're doing. He wants to donate five
hours of legal aid a week, pro bono. He even thinks he can talk a
couple colleagues into doing the same." He grinned, pushing his
nearly empty bowl away from him in surrender and reclining backward into the couch.

"That's amazing." She set her own bowl down next to his and
rose to reach for the bottle of wine they'd opened. As she leaned
across Remy's extended legs to top off his glass, his feet resting
on the edge of the coffee table, she felt his thick arms wind themselves around her waist and pull her toward him. A few drops of

wine sloshed out of the open bottle as she was tugged off balance and onto his warm body. He settled her across his lap, her legs straddling him, and Ruby relished the sharp breath he drew as she lowered her weight onto him.

"*You're* amazing."

She felt the words vibrate through his chest, more of a guttural growl than speech. He brushed her thick brown hair away from her neck and pressed his lips against the newly exposed skin, sending goose bumps racing down her body. She took a drink of wine straight from the bottle she was still holding before placing it on the table as Remy's kisses traveled from her throat to her collarbone to her shoulder, where he was gently tugging at the fabric of her tank top to reveal more flesh.

His dark eyes flicked up at her for a moment, and she was briefly taken aback by the deep, unguarded longing that smoldered in them. She couldn't help but delight in how powerful it made her feel, though she wondered distantly if she'd ever be able to return such passion to anyone other than Ashton. Her affection for Remy, though sincere, would always be muted by her love for Ashton, and the way Remy was looking at her with such raw emotion made her more than a little uneasy. Would she ever be able to match that? Would Remy know if she couldn't? Would he know why?

With a faint smile dancing on his lips, he swept her into his arms, standing so she was slung over his shoulder like he was an evil villain stealing away a damsel in distress. She laughed, her guilt dissipating, as he carried her into his bedroom. He placed her tenderly on the bed and sprawled out next to her, his head propped up with one hand. His other hand rested on her waist, underneath her shirt so the warmth of his palm was flush against her skin. "I want you, Ruby," he whispered to her, though not with the lust she'd expect from him in this situation. He regarded her so solemnly, so preciously; she had a tingling suspicion that he meant so much more than "want."

Does he really mean . . . ? No, he couldn't possibly, Ruby told herself. It was just her imagination.

As she always did in these increasingly frequent moments of intimacy, she thought of Ashton once more. She couldn't shake the feeling that her relationship with Remy was disloyal to Ashton, even though she remained well aware that he had his own relationship that was likely far more intimate with Millie. Each time she felt her heart opening toward Remy, she worried that meant she was giving up on Ashton, which was probably warranted but still felt so . . . *wrong*. Remy was wonderful: handsome, funny, driven, caring.

But he wasn't Ashton.

She stroked the warm, firm skin of his forearm, letting her hands drift up toward his shoulder, finally resting on the hard muscles of his chest. He tightened his hold on her, drawing her even closer. She felt herself melting into the solidity of his body with each breath he drew. Maybe it was the wine or the satisfying feeling of a belly full of home-cooked soup—or perhaps it was the irrepressible anxiety that Ashton and Millie were currently locked in a similar embrace without even the most remote concern about Ruby's feelings—but she heard herself murmur, "I want you, too, right now." And she did. She longed to know what it would feel like to be wrapped up in one another, to be so close to someone that the world around them fell away for the night.

She saw the quickest flash of something indescribable in Remy's eyes as she tilted her head upward and pressed her lips against his. Shock? Fear? Disappointment? She couldn't be sure. She was afraid to find out.

Whatever it was, it didn't stop him from pulling her on top of himself again in one swift and urgent motion and meeting her kiss.

RUBY REACHED ACROSS REMY'S EXPOSED CHEST TO RE-trieve her cell phone from the nightstand. She tapped the screen: 2:57 a.m. She watched his chest rise and fall in slow, rhythmic breaths. Even in the darkness of his bedroom, he looked so differ-ent without his glimmering eyes on her—so vulnerable, so much simpler.

Slowly, so as not to disturb him, she eased herself out of bed. He groaned and rolled over, his arm flopping across the sheet almost like he was reaching out for her in his sleep, but his eyes remained closed. She quietly began collecting her clothes from the floor.

She tugged her tank top over her head and allowed her eyes to fall on the handsome half-naked boy in the bed one last time be-fore she made her escape. Goose bumps trailed down her body as her mind flitted back to the events of the evening—to the way he'd looked, the way he'd felt, the way he'd made her feel.

She couldn't help but smile at him. She knew Remy cared for her, and though she might not have been able to return his feelings in the same way, she cared for him in her own way.

She glanced at her phone again: 3:04. She needed to go.

She was unlocking the front door when she heard Remy's voice behind her.

"You make a guy feel cheap sneaking out like this," he called sleepily from his bedroom doorway.

She smiled bashfully at him as he crossed the room. "Sorry. I didn't want to wake you."

His hair, normally perfectly in place, had a few rogue tufts splayed across his forehead, giving him a more playful, boyish look as he reached for her hand, clad in nothing but his boxers. "One easy way not to wake me is to not get out of bed in the first place," he murmured with a smirk.

She kept her other hand on the doorknob. "I know," she conceded, avoiding eye contact. "But I should get home before anyone notices I'm gone."

His brow furrowed, and Ruby noticed his posture stiffen. "So secretive," he said, a biting edge to his tone that Ruby hadn't anticipated.

"I live with my father and little sisters, Remy. You understand." She took her hand off the doorknob and placed both of them in his, finally meeting his eyes.

The look on his face remained undecided, but he didn't push any further. He nodded and briskly kissed her cheek. "Of course." He reached behind her to open the door, his bare chest brushing up against her. "Do you want me to drive you? It's late."

Ruby shook her head. "No, it's okay." It kind of defeated the point of discreetly sneaking in to have Remy's truck barreling down her street and her car remaining here. "I'll be fine."

A trace of skepticism lingered on his face, but once more, he bit his tongue. "All right. Drive safe. I'll see you at work tomorrow? Text me when you get home."

Remy's unsaid words, whatever they were, hung ominously in the air. Ruby nodded, perplexed as to what could be troubling him after the night they'd shared. Surely he wasn't this irritated that she had cut short their cuddling by a couple of hours when they'd spent the past several hours intertwined?

She forced a thin smile, attempting to hide her confusion, when she heard a door pop open in the hallway. Remy's eyes followed the sound, and his familiar taunting sneer fell over his face. He had complained a few times about his neighbor, an elderly woman who drove aggressively through their parking lot with a bumper sticker slapped on the back of her car that obnoxiously urged everyone to PROTECT OUR BORDERS, PROTECT OUR CHILDREN. Before she even turned to look, Ruby knew by his derisive glower that it had to be her.

"Buenos días, señora Williams," he greeted the gray-haired woman peering at them in her bathrobe and slippers from the doorway across the hall.

Wide-eyed, her jaw fell open at either Remy's near nakedness or his mocking demeanor. Or the heady combination of both.

The woman pursed her lips, clutching her pink bathrobe close to her body. "I—I heard a commotion out here. It's the middle of the night," she stammered uncomfortably. Her eyes flitted between Ruby and Remy in judgment. "You know, Mr. Bustillos, this is a *family* building." She cleared her throat with a high-pitched, wheezing cough that somehow communicated her condemnation of the situation.

Remy grinned. "Of course, señora. I'm so sorry we woke you. I'll just say goodbye, and my sister here will be on her way." His eyes glimmered deviously as he placed a dramatic open-mouthed kiss on Ruby's lips and a hand squarely on her right butt cheek.

Ruby couldn't see Mrs. Williams's face, but she heard the horrified squawk that escaped her mouth before she slammed her door shut.

Whatever momentary feelings of irritation that had fallen over him seemed to have been chased away by his performance. As she finally said goodbye, she noticed that Remy's wolfish good cheer had returned.

34

"About last night," Remy greeted her in the lobby of the bed-and-breakfast the next morning, offering her a paper cup of coffee. She'd expected him to look changed somehow after the night they'd shared, though she couldn't explain how exactly. But here he stood, in a familiar blue button-down with the sleeves rolled up over his muscular forearms, hair combed into the same swoop as always. The same Remy Bustillos she'd always known.

Ruby bristled slightly. Ashton was due any moment, and she definitely did not want to be rehashing any of their late-night escapades when he walked in. Her eyes darted to the clock. Actually, his shift started three minutes ago. She had been dreading addressing his frequent tardiness with him, but for once she prayed he'd be late enough to miss whatever Remy had to say about the night they'd shared.

He leaned against the counter, waiting for her to stop riffling through the receipts she was sorting before he continued. "I was thinking about last night. About you leaving and what you said about your family."

Ruby frowned. *That was the most memorable aspect of our night to him?*

"What if you moved in with me?"

If she thought Mrs. Williams had been shocked last night, the heavy wave of befuddlement that fell over Ruby now certainly trumped that. Her lips quivered wordlessly as she struggled to formulate a response.

Remy took a sip from his own coffee cup, apparently entertained by her speechlessness. "Don't hurt yourself. You don't have to answer right now. Think about it."

She sighed. "Remy, we've only been seeing each other for like—"

"Just two months, I know," he interrupted. "It's soon, I know. But who cares?" He shrugged, the corners of his eyes crinkling into a smile that lit up his whole face.

Ruby couldn't bring herself to even attempt a smile. Move in together? It was so settled, so *serious*. Remy was fun, and she was enjoying the time they spent together; she even cared for him much more than she had ever anticipated. He was the perfect thing for *right now*, but she was not planning on committing to him in the kind of way living together would mean. Besides, if he thought her father would be any happier about them living together than he would be about her slinking into the house at all hours of the night—well, he clearly didn't know much about Gerardo Ortega.

Who cares? was not a compelling argument either. He might not give much thought to the opinion of others, as was evidenced by his performance in the hallway last night, but Ruby's actions were often driven by the opinions of one person in particular, who she imagined—or at least hoped—would have some thoughts about them moving in together. Ashton lived with his significant other, so he knew exactly how serious it was. What would he have to say about her living with Remy?

He must've sensed her shock spiraling into apprehension because he dropped the silly grin and adopted a more soothing tone. "I didn't mean to upset you. I just thought, we are always working together on the hotel and the app, and it might save some time to be in the same place more often. Wouldn't it be nice not to have to race back over here late at night, when you're already exhausted, and try and sneak back into the house?" He gave a slight shrug, holding her gaze. "And maybe that time we save can be time put toward going back to school or something more important than sitting in traffic." He attempted a casual, neutral expression, as if all along this suggestion was nothing more than a practical solution to commuting.

She eyed him, unconvinced. Despite his cool demeanor, she knew there was more to it than that. They wouldn't simply be roommates and co-workers. Living together said something important about their relationship. It said they were going somewhere, and Ruby wasn't ready to consider where exactly that was.

"Remy, I don't think now's the right time," she whispered nervously.

He put his hand up to stop her. "Just . . . give it a couple days. Mull it over. Please?"

Ruby gave a slight nod before she turned her attention back to sorting the receipts, or at least pretending to so this conversation would end.

Remy either enjoyed her discomfort or didn't notice it; it was often hard to tell with him. He lingered idly at the counter, sipping his coffee as if he were taking in a picturesque view rather than languishing in what Ruby thought was a suffocating silence.

"Um, anything else?" She tried not to sound as curt and impatient as she felt, but she was desperate for him to give her some space. Not only did she not want Ashton to catch them in the throes of this major relationship decision, but she also needed a moment to herself to process what had just happened. Not to mull it over exactly, like Remy had suggested, but to try to understand how they had wound up here in the first place. When had her exciting, distracting fling turned into a committed relationship with a future?

Remy chuckled, enjoying some joke Ruby wasn't sure she understood. "Have you looked into transferring your credits?"

She frowned. "What?"

"School. It'd be a shame to let all your hard work at the beginning of the year go to waste. I know you didn't finish the semester, but maybe some credits will transfer. Especially since you're still so early on in your degree. Most of them were general education classes, right? Have you looked into transferring to a school out here yet?"

Ruby was taken aback by his swift transition. He had just introduced a pretty serious issue for the two of them, which she couldn't imagine had gone the way he had hoped. And now, almost without skipping a beat, he seemed to be performing the function of a university registrar. Maybe asking her to move in really *was* a matter of location to him, not the romantic gesture she'd feared it was. Maybe it was no big deal, just one of many creative ideas that popped into his mind at any given moment.

"Um, no," she answered cagily.

His thick eyebrows shot up. "No? Why not?"

It was her turn to laugh. She rolled her eyes and gestured to the lobby around them. "Gee, I don't know, Remy. It's not like I've been *busy* or anything."

His jaw clenched into a dismissive scowl as he shook his head. "Okay, but what about now? The Cortez event is just around the corner, and most of the big things have been taken care of. After that, it'll be smooth sailing! You can cut back your hours; even with Ashton's 'help,' you've got a nice rhythm at the B&B with the new hires from Buena. We've got a good balance with everything. It seems like the perfect time. You might even be able to start in the fall."

Ruby sighed. "I mean, yeah, maybe."

Remy set his cup down on the counter a little more forcefully than necessary, and Ruby watched a few drops of coffee splash out of the plastic lid. "You *are* planning on going back to school?" His eyes were inquisitive, but his stern tone made it sound like more than a question.

She started to nod but shrugged instead. "Eventually. *Probably*."

Remy exhaled loudly, his eyes fixed on her with an exasperated hardness. "What the hell does that mean?"

She nudged the stack of receipts aside and returned the same unyielding expression. "It means what it means," she snarled, throwing her hands in the air. "It's not a priority right now. I need to focus on the business. Maybe when things calm down I can think about it, but I'm not worried about it right now. And you shouldn't be either."

Remy's dark glower told her he was unsatisfied with that response, but she reminded herself it wasn't his business. It didn't matter what he thought about her education; it was, after all, *her* education. *Her* decision. And, sure, she had promised her parents that she would graduate, and that unfulfilled agreement weighed on her, especially when she thought of what her late mother would really want for her life. And it might be easier to run the properties with a few more classes under her belt. Google could only get her so far when it came to long-term financial goals. And she missed it, of course. Not only had she worked her entire life for that opportunity, but generations of Ortegas had striven so one day she could earn a college degree. She found herself pushing that thought aside from time to time. But the fact of the matter was she was *needed* here, right?

Well, she needed to be here, at least. She wasn't ready to let go.

She glanced at the clock once more. Ashton was now a full fifteen minutes late. If it were anyone else, she would've called them five minutes ago.

So what if Remy made a good point about being able to delegate some of her responsibilities to others? She knew it would never work out as he described. Right now, Ashton was too unreliable, too distant to be trusted with more responsibility. He needed her, her support and direction. And, perhaps even more so, she needed the rare time when it was just the two of them. It was one of the few places where they had moments alone, and Ruby wasn't willing to throw those away to go back to school, especially since he'd recently started talking about the next wildfire season. Their time was already so limited. She didn't need one more thing pulling her away from him.

As she watched Remy consider her sharp dismissal with a stony, unreadable expression, she found herself wondering if Remy realized these exact concerns dwelled in the back of her mind. Perhaps that was precisely why he'd brought it up. "It sounds like you've got your reasons then, Ruby. I'm sure you know what's best," he said dryly, an uncharacteristic slump in his shoulders as he turned away from her and walked out of the room.

DAYS PASSED, AND WHILE REMY DID NOT BRING UP MOVING in or going back to school again, Ruby could feel the weight of these topics festering between them. The ease and comfort that she'd felt with him were now tainted by her refusal to entertain even the notion of a future with Remy, and the realization that they had considered their relationship so differently was inescapable. Remy was as lively and driven and energetic as ever, but every now and then, especially in moments of stillness when it was just the two of them, driving in Remy's truck or lying side by side in his bed, she sensed something different. Discontent. Distance. Something dark and lonely. The sparkling sense of hope and possibility he had once been full of when he pulled her close had completely vanished.

Perhaps this big change stemmed from her indecision, but how could he possibly know everything that was coursing through her mind? She couldn't put into words all her fears about Ashton's place in this next chapter of her life. And even if she could, she wouldn't have brought it up with Remy. Perhaps it was just the novelty of their relationship wearing off. Perhaps she was just imagining it.

After all, Remy never mentioned anything bothering him, and

Ruby reminded herself often that Remy was not the type to keep his opinions to himself, especially when something was not to his liking. As Buena grew and their impact increased, she'd heard him tell off more than one local politician with the kind of venomous vigor that was hard to believe came from a man as suave and refined as Remy.

The Cortez fundraiser was just one day away, and each time Ruby double-checked a schedule or glanced over a seating chart, she was struck with how much this event could mean for her. Not only could it usher in a slew of other large-scale, high-class events, it could also be the beginning of a professional relationship and more support for Buena from both the governor and any other powerful individuals who might be in attendance.

The governor and her staff had arrived from Sacramento that morning and were eager to finally see the venue. And though Ruby was a bundle of nerves about the possibilities that awaited her, after months of planning, she knew she was ready. Since returning home, she'd felt like every major step she took had been scrambled and chaotic. But not this. It was almost unnerving to watch their plans unfold in peace for once.

This is what he was talking about when he asked about school, she thought uneasily. Things were settling. Her hard work was paying off. It *was* time for her to return to her own goals—a sentiment that was reaffirmed as she led the governor and her entourage of three fastidious staff members through the pristine halls of the event center.

"And this is where the podium will be," said the governor's personal assistant, an Amazon-like woman named Inez Warren with whom Ruby had exchanged countless emails. She gestured to an area near the freshly cleaned bay windows with an elegant flourish.

"You'll have a step stool, right? The attorney general is introducing me, and he's very short," Governor Cortez said matter-of-factly.

Inez glanced at Ruby, who responded, "Definitely. I'll make sure it's tucked underneath the lectern." She typed *step stool* into the notes app of her phone.

The governor nodded approvingly and exchanged satisfied glances with Inez. "Well, I just think it's perfect. It's the perfect place to make this announcement. A local, family-owned business, in an area that's recovered from such hardship. I really think what you've done here epitomizes what we hope to accomplish when I'm in office."

Ruby felt as if she were floating as she took in the praise. She nodded in her most restrained manner and gave the governor a polite smile. "That . . . that really means a lot, ma'am. Thank you."

As they made their way to the exit, Inez peppered Ruby with a few more details from her hefty binder—reminders about tablecloths, inquiries about hors d'oeuvres distribution, updates on the bar budget—and Ruby's heart swelled as she fired back responses that Inez marked down with quick check marks.

"It's a very remarkable thing you've done here. I really can't say it enough," Governor Cortez said meditatively as they walked across the parking lot toward the governor's car. "I'll admit, we were a little worried given the reports of all the destruction in the area, but the progress you've made is truly incredible. And on top of your community work?" She exhaled in a thoughtful way as she gazed around the vibrant property, with its fresh paint and lush soil and blooming flowers. "You're someone to watch out for, Ruby."

Ruby couldn't fight the proud grin spreading across her face. "Thank you," she stammered once more. She reached forward to shake the governor's hand, and just as she opened her mouth to launch into the pitch for Buena that she'd been carefully practicing in the mirror every night, both women found themselves distracted by a strange snorting sound coming from the side of the building. Alarmed, Ruby turned to find Millie pacing in front of the staff entrance, her hand clasped to her mouth and a rigid tenseness to her gait.

"Um, I'm so sorry, you'll have to excuse me," Ruby said distractedly, turning back to the governor with a forced smile. "I'll see you tomorrow evening. Please call me if you need anything before then."

What on earth was Millie thinking? She knew how important it was they make a good impression; they'd been working toward this moment for a year! What could possibly be so urgent and distressing that she'd choose now of all times to have a meltdown?

She watched the governor's black sedan disappear around the corner before turning to where Millie was still trudging near the dumpsters. Millie looked up at her as she approached, and the hardness in her expression stopped Ruby in her tracks.

She swallowed, her throat tight. "What—what's going on?"

Millie stiffened, her shoulders squared and her jaw clenched. The warm optimism that usually glowed within her was noticeably dimmed; in its place was something hurt and confused. "I just spoke to Ashton," she said slowly, her words wobbly and unsteady.

Well, that was nothing unusual. Ruby waited uneasily.

"He . . ." Her voice cracked, and she took a deep breath, her eyes closed. "He told me you two kissed." Her eyes shot back open as she said that final word, and the furious intensity in them made Ruby's stomach drop.

"*Oh.*"

She couldn't begin to fathom why Ashton had told her this *now* or why he wouldn't have given Ruby a heads-up—but she still couldn't say she was totally surprised. He had been so withdrawn and unreliable lately; something had clearly been on his mind. She couldn't have guessed their kiss all those months ago was what was weighing on him, and she certainly didn't know what exactly it meant for them—or for him and Millie.

"Yeah, 'oh,'" Millie snapped, folding her arms across her chest. "Were you ever going to tell me, Ruby?" She shook her head as if predicting the answer to her own question. "I knew you liked Ashton. And I even knew you didn't like me." She laughed joylessly. "It's not like you made it hard to figure out. But Ashton cares about you, and you needed someone through all of this, so I put those things aside because that's what I do. I help people when they need it— when they don't even know they need it." Her words were gradually becoming clearer and firmer, the sad shakiness falling away as she spoke. "I thought eventually you'd *grow up* enough to see that."

Ruby stepped toward her, unsure of what to say, but the fierce glower Millie shot her stopped her again.

"I know it's not *just* your fault. He told me he kissed you."

Ruby's eyebrows shot upward. "He did?" Despite herself, she couldn't keep a perverse curiosity out of her voice. Why would he have bothered specifying his own guilt? Was he finally breaking up with her?

"I bet you're wondering why." The coolness to her tone gave Ruby chills. "I want you to know that when he told me, I didn't believe him at first," she said, walking toward Ruby with purposeful, measured steps. "I was sure that neither of you would ever do this to me. I know you both have your flaws—*believe me*, I know that—but I've never been anything but caring to you—to both of you."

"It was a long time ago," Ruby added feebly, unsure of whether that mattered at all.

Millie was within an arm's length of Ruby now. "It *was* a long time ago. It was before he left for the fire service. All sorts of things have happened since that kiss, but nothing's changed between the two of you. He didn't run to you. He kissed you, but he stayed with me." She let a weighted pause settle between them. *"Because kissing you was a mistake."*

Ruby opened her mouth, but words eluded her.

"It was a mistake for him to kiss you, Ruby." Her eyes narrowed, not so much looking for Ruby's reaction but driving home her point. "He was scared, and he made a mistake."

They stood squared off in a writhing silence, and Ruby felt almost as if Millie were daring her to speak. Finally, she managed, "So what now?" And though she was wound up with curiosity, she knew there was a fearful edge to her words as well.

Millie nodded like she'd anticipated that question. "I forgave him." Though her words were even and unhesitating, they hit Ruby like a punch to the gut. "And I forgive you."

"You . . . *what*?"

"You probably think that's stupid of me, right? One more dumb thing sweet, naive Millie has done to foil your plans," she continued, and Ruby blushed at the accuracy. "But we are different, Ruby. This is who I am. I love and support people through things—even their own mistakes, even when it's hard. I'm hurt and disappointed, but

I can't help but see the bigger picture: how scared he was then and what his honesty now means about how he's changed. I can't help it; I believe people can be better. I know he can, and I know you can. We're different." She sighed. "And that's why he loves me, and not you."

RUBY COULDN'T BREATHE. SHE WAS CHOKING ON HER OWN thoughts, sputtering as if caught in a cloud of smoke, as she watched Millie calmly walk to her car and leave.

What the *fuck* was that?

She had to talk to Ashton.

He must be here, right? Why else would Millie have shown up at the reception hall so upset?

Though as she burst back inside the building, she remembered that Ashton had the day off. In fact, Ruby knew she had deliberately scheduled Daniella, one of the new hires from Buena, to run the front desk because she couldn't risk any of Ashton's careless mishaps on this particular day.

Which meant Millie had come over with the sole purpose of confronting Ruby.

Damn.

Standing in the entryway, she could hear the sounds of their new staff members setting up tables and chairs in the ballroom down the hall, but she shut all that out. She needed to talk to Ashton.

To hear his voice.

The first call went to voicemail, but she was undeterred. She tried again immediately.

He answered on the third ring, and even his *Hello* sounded full of dread.

"Ashton!" she all but cried. "What's going on? I just—I just talked to Millie and—"

"Then you know what's going on," he snapped.

"Ashton."

"Listen, I'm not mad at you. I'm mad at myself for . . . for all of this. For everything." She opened her mouth to protest, but even though he couldn't see her, he sensed her opposition and cut her off. "I kept waiting for everything to feel like normal again, but I'm realizing there's no going back to that. There's just forward. I can't keep living my life swept up in the circumstances, not taking responsibility for what's happening. I'm going to ask Millie to marry me before I go back out in the field. I couldn't do that without being honest with her about what happened. That kiss was a mistake. I shouldn't have done that to you. I hope you can forgive me. I hope both of you can forgive me."

Was this really what he wanted? Was Millie truly who he wanted?

"I'm sorry I've gotten you all caught up in this, really, Ruby. I've got to go." Before she could say anything at all, he hung up.

Ruby stood with the phone pressed to her ear, bristling with countless feelings—most of all, her powerlessness in all this. The fact that Ashton had refused to see her role, her own feelings and decisions, and just assumed he'd "caught" her up in his actions. What about what she wanted? He hadn't even given her a chance to speak.

But in the end, she couldn't escape the fact that it didn't really matter.

He was gone.

THAT NIGHT, SHE RESTED HER HEAD ON REMY'S CHEST, LIStening to the rhythmic *thump* of his heart as her conversations with Millie and Ashton ran an agonizing loop in her mind. He had his arm wrapped around her and was lightly brushing his fingertips along her shoulder and upper arm, but she couldn't focus on the tenderness of his embrace. She could only think about Ashton.

He was going to propose to Millie.

After everything that had happened, he was going to *marry Millie.*

She sighed, exhaustion creeping in on her. Never before had she been faced with a problem that was truly outside her control, not like this. Even with the fires, she'd found her way forward against all odds. Surely there was something she could do now.

Abruptly, Remy jerked his arm out from underneath her and jolted her from her thoughts as she was tossed away from him.

"Hey—ow!" she yelped.

"We should get some rest. Tomorrow's going to be a long day," he said gruffly, rolling over so his wide back was toward her.

She stared at his rigid, hunched figure outlined in the dark, unsure of what had just happened. Although she could tell by his breathing that he was still awake, he pretended to sleep and did not utter another word, even when she left.

35

The morning of the fundraiser, Ruby rose around dawn and drove her Jeep down from the main house, its back seat packed full of vases, votive candles, and other spare pieces of decor she thought they might need for the event. She stopped at the B&B to grab some extra napkins and business cards just in case and was surprised to see Remy's truck in the parking lot as she pulled in. Most of the windows were still dark, the handful of guests and Buena clients likely still asleep. But as she approached the front door, she could see the faint glow of a light where she knew the welcome desk to be. She swung open the door to find Remy standing next to the computer with a concentrated scowl on his face. He flinched as she entered the room, and though his expression remained the same, something subtle in his demeanor changed as she approached.

"What are you doing here?" she asked, trying to sound pleasant amid her confusion.

Remy snorted but kept his gaze on the computer, clicking the mouse a few times before looking at her. "Were you expecting someone else?" he asked, and Ruby wondered if he realized he was echoing himself the night of the gala, so long ago. Though then his voice had been light and joking; now there was something mean and harsh in the way he spoke to her.

She shook her head. "That's not what I meant. It's just . . . it's early, is all. I didn't know you'd be here." She inhaled, walking toward him. "What are you working on?" She angled her head to try to see the screen, but he stepped away from both the computer and her almost instantly.

"I couldn't sleep, so I came over here to do some work. Jesus, Ruby, what's with the interrogation?"

Ruby felt her eyes widen at his brusqueness. They'd fought before, and they'd exchanged impassioned words, of course, but he'd never addressed her like this. His words burned and crackled with anger. He wouldn't even look at her as he spoke.

With a rising sense of panic, she watched him collect his car keys and phone from the desk. "Remy, what's *wrong*?"

He paused, and slowly brought his gaze to meet hers. "What gives you the impression that anything's wrong, mi querida?" he snarled, referring to her as his *darling* for an extra jab, Ruby thought.

Again, she stepped toward him, but the reflexive curl of his lip as she did so halted her. "Is it because I haven't answered you about moving in together?" she asked.

The corner of his mouth twisted into a smile that was wholly mirthless. It was the expression of a bloodthirsty hunter whose unwitting prey was about to stumble right into his grasp.

"Because you said I could have time to think about it," she continued. "And, well, I have thought about it."

He was unmoving, except for one dark eyebrow that rose expectantly.

"And . . . I'm just not sure it's the right time. My family still needs me. My sisters. My father. There's still work to be done around here." Her voice trailed off as she spoke.

Remy let out a disbelieving puff of air. " 'The right time.' Right. Your *family* is the reason." He rolled his eyes, shoving his keys into his pocket and moving toward the front door.

"What's that supposed to mean?" she called out, unmindful of the rooms of sleeping guests just upstairs, but the door slammed shut before she could even be certain the words had reached him.

THEY HAD A FULL TEAM HELPING SET UP, BETWEEN RUBY'S friends and family, the event center staff, Buena clients she'd hired, and the governor's team, but Ruby still felt like the day dragged on endlessly. Of course, the fraught, forced greeting she, Remy, Ashton, and Millie had shared at the morning meeting probably set the tone for everything that followed. She hadn't told anyone what had transpired between the four of them over the past day, but she figured the awkward stiffness told its own story. No one would even look at her, let alone speak to her, except for employees with logistical questions—and even then, her frustrated tone rendered those few and far between.

She fought to push this tense silence aside as she watched the ballroom transform. They'd been organizing this event for nearly a year. It was a crucial part of her goals for both Buena and Ortega

Properties, and she couldn't afford to let her roiling emotions interfere with its success.

She and Remy were supposed to deliver a short welcome just before dinner, introducing themselves, the progress she'd made at Ortega Properties since the fires, and a little bit about the work Buena was doing. The governor had framed it as a kind of "community spotlight," and though her personal assistant had been very firm that it was not to exceed three minutes, Ruby knew it was critical she use that limited time to make an impact on the guests. They'd rehearsed countless times, and she'd felt great about it, until now. Remy was a wild card, and he was probably capable of choking down his irritation with her long enough to give a dazzling performance, but *would* he? She had seen his temper flare up before, but never the kind of slow-burning fuse she was witnessing now.

At four o'clock, her family returned to their house to get ready. Ruby and Remy had brought their changes of clothes to the reception hall's office to save themselves a trip. She'd also stashed a bottle of champagne in there so they could toast to their success—which now struck her as absurdly optimistic.

Ashton congratulated them on a job well done, surveying the fruits of their labor wistfully. There were at least twenty tables, decked with crisp white tablecloths, sparkling tea lights, and large vases overflowing with flowers native to Southern California: an elegant mix of succulents and warm wildflowers. On easels scattered throughout the room were CORTEZ FOR CONGRESS posters bearing various campaign slogans and promises in bold blue letters. At the very front of the room, above the podium where she and Remy would speak, hung a large banner that read CLAUDIA CORTEZ FOR ALL CALIFORNIANS.

It *did* look good. As she admired the neatly curated decorations, she was reminded of the charred wasteland this place had been when she'd first arrived. She had not only willed into existence this night but this building. Everything she laid her eyes on was a direct result of her hard work and commitment to her family's dream. It filled her with a dizzying combination of both pride and terror.

As her eyes took in all the spectacular details, she noticed Remy glancing at his ringing cell phone with clear distress. His eyes darted upward shiftily, noting her gaze on him, and he turned his back. Even from across the room, the low, discreet voice he used to answer the call before slipping out one of the doors leading to the patio sent prickles of suspicion throughout Ruby's body.

What was that about? she wondered, unconsciously taking a step toward the door as if being a few more inches closer to him would clarify things.

"Is this where you want the brochures?" Ashton approached her, holding a large cardboard box full of the glossy pamphlets and business cards she and Remy had ordered a few weeks ago.

"Uh." Ruby tried to drag her thoughts away from Remy to focus on the question.

Without waiting for an answer, he dumped the contents onto the table and began haphazardly scattering them in every direction.

"*Uh,*" she said, a little more firmly, holding her hand out to stop him. "Ashton, maybe . . ."

He paused briefly, but when he looked up, his gaze was focused on something behind Ruby. She turned her head to see Remy closing in on them, the same unhappy expression on his face. He was shoving his phone in his pocket as he sneered at the brochure table.

"Are you fucking kidding me? That looks terrible. God, Ashton, I know you don't give two shits about this event or Buena, but come *on*. At least a little effort for once would be nice," he snapped.

"Remy!" Ruby hissed, eyes wide with shock. She reached out to him, as if she could shove his harsh anger back toward him, but he jerked out of her reach before she'd even made contact. "It's a few stacks of paper. It's not a big deal—"

He was visibly fuming. "Oh, of course not! Whatever he does, it doesn't matter! He can ignore you—run your life into the ground—it doesn't fucking matter! He's the good guy here. You'll defend him no matter what!" His chest heaved, his fury simmering along every inch of him.

Ruby was speechless as Ashton began collecting the brochures, clearly desperate for some sort of distraction.

What had gotten into Remy? Obviously, he'd been irritated all day, but what on earth could've set him off like this?

Remy shook his head, his jaw clenched. "Forget it. Awesome job, as always." He rolled his eyes and began trudging toward the exit, rubbing the back of his neck.

36

One thing Ruby had learned about Remy over the past year was that he was not the type of person who got dressed quickly. Normally he spent nearly as much time as she did selecting an outfit, combing his hair, and preening over his reflection. Ruby had never known a guy to do that, but she also didn't know any who were as finely dressed and neatly manicured. She had often wondered if his meticulous grooming came from a childhood without such luxuries or even from a desire to overcompensate and impress in situations where he thought he might be judged by his background, though she'd never felt emboldened enough to ask. It was just one of those mystifying things she accepted about Remy.

However, despite the importance of tonight, he got dressed in record speed. When she'd finally followed him to the office after his tantrum, she eased the door open to find him pulling his shirt over his taut torso, forcing the buttons with clumsy, furious fingers. He glared as she entered and turned to face the wall as he finished buttoning and tucking in his shirt.

She was surprised to find him there at all, alone in this confined space in a state of relative undress. It felt so intimate compared to the brutal distance that had been simmering between them. Every few minutes, she thought she saw him, out of the corner of her eye, start to turn to her. His breathing pattern, gruff and rushed, would change for a moment, and she'd think he was about to say something. Perhaps he was finally going to talk to her? Or perhaps she was just imagining it. He was so hard to understand sometimes.

Whichever it was, she would never really know, because he fled their makeshift dressing room without a word, his tie looped around his neck and his gleaming leather shoes in hand, apparently unwilling to spend even another instant in her presence.

Alone in the quiet office that she had designed, with its built-in bookshelves and plush armchairs, she gazed at her reflection in the small antique mirror that rested on the meticulously styled shelves between leather-bound books on Californian history and horticulture.

She thought again of the gala she and Remy had attended last year and the way she'd primped herself to shamelessly flirt with him, without consideration of his feelings or even poor Charlie's feelings. All she'd cared about then was feeling pretty and enjoying herself, no matter what.

She smoothed the emerald-green skirt she'd found at the back of her mother's closet a few weeks ago, a knee-length pleated number that was shimmery but sensible. The tags had still been on, so Ruby suspected Eleanor had bought it for an event before finding something she liked even more, a frivolous habit her mother had been famous for. She missed her so fiercely in that moment, her perfectionism, her drive, her intuition. She'd surely know what Ruby should do—about Remy, about Ashton, about the rest of her life.

With a quick glance at the clock, she stuffed her work uniform into her duffel bag and began collecting her things. The governor would be arriving soon, with the rest of the guests surely not far behind, and she hoped to run through her speech one final time before things got underway. Easing the tension with Remy was highly unlikely at this point, so the least she could do was make sure she wouldn't fumble over her words.

She swung open the door to find Ashton hovering awkwardly on the other side, light from behind falling on him to give him an ethereal appearance, like Ruby had summoned him here with her imagination alone.

He smiled wryly. "You look nice."

She stroked her hair absent-mindedly as she stepped out of the doorway and into the entry area, bright and empty and sparkling clean. "Thank you. Why aren't you at the welcome table?" Her heart raced. She wasn't sure if she was worried or pleased to find him here. They hadn't had a moment alone since the whole issue with Millie and their kiss, but he had agreed to collect tickets, after all.

His dark suit hung a little loosely on his frame, a clear reminder of how skinny he'd grown over the past few weeks. "Your sisters are covering for me. I wanted to talk to you before . . . before all of that out there."

"Oh geez, you didn't knock over one of the centerpieces, did you?" she joked, but his eyes were somber. She was anxious to get to the event, but just as Remy had said, she was unable to deny him anything. Even with everything else going on, her mind quieted to him and her heart opened up to whatever he had come to say to her.

He reached out and took both her hands in his as he struggled to find his words. At the feeling of his cool skin against hers, Ruby was stunned at how his touch, which she had once longed for day and night, felt markedly different in this strange moment. Usually, it sent an electric shock down Ruby's body, in which every fiber of her being sounded alarm bells, the exhilarating sensation of his physical proximity. However, as Ashton gently stroked her fingers, she felt a sense of calm instead. Comfort and peace rather than trembling anticipation. His tender golden eyes and quiet seriousness were still the same qualities she'd fallen in love with. But, in this moment, her heart regarded him differently, almost detachedly.

She pushed this thought from her mind. There was too much for her to think about this evening for her to fixate on this change of heart now.

"You deserve to have an amazing night," he said. "You've worked really hard—on this and everything else—and you deserve to enjoy yourself and enjoy your success." His bright eyes were glassy beneath his long lashes. "You know, I think we've both changed a lot through all this. You, of course, hit the ground running and seized every opportunity you could find, no matter how hard things were. I wish I had been smart or strong enough to do that. I've fought it every step of the way, hoping to feel like my old self or find my way back to what our home had been. But all that's done is make me feel sad and lost. I've been hiding from what our world really looks like. And I—I just wanted to thank you. I don't know if I've been very fair to you, but you've always stood by my side, even when I didn't deserve it. Even when I was . . . cruel to you."

Normally, he lost Ruby pretty early in these introspective monologues, but for the first time ever, she felt like she not only understood what he was talking about but understood *him*. Perhaps her feverish love for him had always clouded her ability to see him clearly, but now—at last—she saw him like she never had before.

"Oh, that's not true," she assured him feebly, with a sympathetic squeeze of his hand. But even as she said it, she knew deep down that he was right.

"I've never known what I wanted from life. I've been fortunate enough that I've had a lot of opportunities presented to me and I could try things out and change my mind without much consequence, so it didn't matter that I didn't know," he continued.

Ruby felt a strange kind of remorse as she listened to him— because she finally understood Ashton's own sadness and because even though she knew he was laying himself bare for her in such an honest, intimate way, she couldn't help but wish he'd hurry it up so she could get downstairs. She smiled nervously. She'd spent so long pining for his praise, and now that he was finally bestowing it on her, it only made her feel pity. "I miss our old life, too, sometimes. Parts of it. But there's a lot of good in what we have and what we can do now, too," she pointed out quietly with an uncomfortable shrug.

Ashton nodded, the expression on his face a complicated mix of fear and hope.

Ruby dropped her gaze; she felt torn in two. The gentle way he was still holding her hands and the open, if heartbreaking, way he was confiding in her touched parts of her heart that she had saved for him for years. But she realized, perhaps for the first time, that those parts of her belonged to a past version of herself, a girl who didn't exist anymore. A girl who had rarely looked outside her own little bubble and her own desires. She had been a happy kid, but with everything that had happened, Ruby couldn't pretend that she could be that girl anymore. Her love for Ashton belonged to that girl from the past.

She felt a sudden, heart-wrenching pang of sadness just then, as it occurred to her that perhaps the reason she and Ashton would never be together, never be happy, was not the differences that he seemed to be stuck on. Perhaps it was because they were too similar. He was clinging to a past that he had glamorized in his memories, despite the complexities and problems this season of strife had revealed. Though Ruby had reacted differently, she saw now that she treated Ashton the same way he treated his feelings for Buena Valley. She obsessed over her love for him, which she now saw was only a girlish crush, something she had amplified and intensified beyond reality as time went on. She'd glossed over the flaws, their incompatibilities, almost as a way to comfort herself as she plunged into an unfamiliar world. But at last, as she stood before this unsure, uneasy person whom she cared for immensely, she knew she couldn't spend her life trying to sustain their love and coaxing Ashton to embrace this changed world they occupied—one that she felt inspired and excited by, and that he wanted to hide from.

Sure, the future was scary and challenging, but wouldn't it be boring if it weren't? What was the alternative? How would she learn and grow if the world were always the way it had been? She could love Buena Valley for all it had been and all it would be because love was supposed to push you and inspire you.

Just like my relationship with Remy, she thought with a jolt.

Finally, she looked up at Ashton, and in the silent moment they shared, she knew he understood, too. Her hopes for a romance between the two of them were extinguished at last. They were part of a world and childhood they'd once shared and loved, but a world that only existed in their memories now.

He pulled her into a hug, their moist cheeks pressed against one another's. It was not a passionate embrace, but an easy gesture shared between two people with a common history. Two people who were in vastly different places in the present but had shared a lifetime's worth of memories.

She wasn't sure how long she stood there, so near to him that she could hear the steady beat of his heart. It wasn't until she heard the front door slam behind her that she was pulled from this moment and reminded that she needed to go.

THERE WERE SEVERAL CLUSTERS OF PEOPLE IN COCKTAIL ATtire milling around the courtyard when Ruby finally managed to disentangle herself from Ashton.

She entered the ballroom to find it sparkling in the ambient lighting—and despite her eagerness to get everything going, she forced herself to stop there in the double doorway. To take it all in. All her hard work. All her struggle. All her sacrifice. Her eyes swept over every magical detail, the chandelier glimmering overhead and the tea lights on each table twinkling like starlight. There were a few people inside already, dawdling near the bar and chatting at their tables. Benito's wife, Alma, adjusted a floral centerpiece on the table marked for the governor's staff, and she shot Ruby an excited smile as she plucked a brown leaf out of the arrangement. Ruby's father's steady voice could be heard above the din of conversation, and she noticed him not far from herself, pointing out an unlit Sterno burner to one of the catering staff.

Ruby's heart throbbed with a thousand feelings mixed together in a dizzying swirl of emotion. She was nervous, yes, but she was so hopeful and proud, too. And though she was often still surprised when life turned out different than she'd expected—even after everything that had happened—she was learning to find the beauty and promise in the outcome, nevertheless.

Even when it was hard.

Her eyes landed on Remy up front standing beneath the banner, flipping through a stack of note cards, looking striking but stoic. Though they had been together not too long ago, she felt like she was seeing him for the first time in ages.

As she crossed the room to join him, hoping he could set his temper aside long enough to practice their speech together one last time, she was stopped yet again.

She turned to find her old roommate, Patty, standing before her in a knee-length, ruffled dress that vaguely resembled a nightgown. A step behind her was her girlfriend, Hannah. She was sporting a chic black shift dress and now wore her hair in a pixie cut, a look Ruby thought was hard to pull off but made Hannah look like a supermodel.

"What are you two doing here?" Ruby laughed, pulling them both into a hug.

Patty beamed, cheeks rosy with delight. "My stepdad went to

college with the governor, and when I saw on the news that her fundraiser was being held at your venue, he bought tickets for our whole family." She gestured behind her to a table filled with stout and jolly people who had to be related to Patty.

"Claudia Cortez is so amazing," Hannah added brightly. "We're excited to be here."

"This place looks *incredible*!" Patty gushed, her round eyes floating across the room. "I can't believe you did all this! We've missed you *so* much, but look how busy you've been! I just can't believe it."

Ruby thanked them and was surprised to feel herself blushing at their praise. "I really am so happy to see you, and I promise I'll come visit later tonight, but I do need to get going right now." Her eyes sought out Remy once more. He was now pacing as he flipped through his cards, but he hadn't moved from the front of the room.

Patty's eyes followed Ruby's gaze, and she nodded knowingly with a playful scrunch of her nose. "Oh, of course! We'll talk soon."

She was grateful so many people she cared about were here to support her, but she couldn't help but feel slightly harried by these disparate lives she'd led and the people here to remind her of exactly how much had changed. It seemed as if the universe were determined that her past and present should collide tonight.

"You ready?" She greeted Remy with a shaky smile.

The eyes that met hers were cold and murky. He nodded stiffly.

"Do you want to practice one last time?"

His glacial silence made her want to disappear inside herself. How was she supposed to feign cheerful optimism in front of all these people when she knew something so dark and furious brewed inside him, between them?

"Why? Ashton didn't want to practice with you?" he growled at last.

The slamming door, she thought with dread. He'd seen her hugging Ashton, and though Ruby knew there had been nothing romantic about that moment, she also knew how it must have appeared to Remy.

This had all started that night when she'd been thinking about Ashton in bed, and though she couldn't imagine how he'd known her thoughts had been on Ashton, he had. She was certain of it.

But why did he come back to the office in the first place?

"Oh, Remy, I can explain," she assured him desperately. If only he knew what had just transpired between her and Ashton, that she was finally putting her old feelings for him aside, there was no way he could still be hurt and jealous.

"Don't bother. Let's just get through this thing." He reached into the inside pocket of his suit jacket and held out a stack of note cards. She reached out for his arm instead, to beg him to listen, but he just thrust the cards at her, careful not to let their hands touch at all, and turned away.

Puzzled, she trailed after him to the podium. As they made their way through the tables, her eyes swept over the crowd of nearly three hundred smartly dressed people, smiling and laughing excitedly. At a table near the front of the room were her family, Ashton, Millie, and Millie's father, whom Ruby hadn't seen since he left Buena Valley. His cane rested against the side of his chair. Millie looked luminous in an off-white gown, her hair pinned into a neat bun. She shot them a tranquil smile and lifted both her hands into two thumbs-up. Despite the distance, Ruby noticed with this happy gesture that Millie now wore a gleaming diamond ring on her left ring finger. Modest and dainty, but beautiful, just like Millie.

A wave of understanding hit her, heavy but not altogether unpleasant.

Ashton had proposed. That's why he'd come to see her. She'd never know for certain why he hadn't been able to get the words out, but she felt again, with resounding certainty, that her love for him was impossible, that it always had been. Not just because he was marrying Millie, but because they were two different people caught in two different realities. She had loved him as an idea of a person he could never be, and he had only seen her as a person she no longer was.

Ruby smiled back at Millie, perhaps for the first time without a trace of envy or bitterness, and was heartened when Millie nodded, her amber eyes locked on Ruby.

Ruby took a deep, steadying breath and let her gaze fall to her father this time, who was watching her with a reverent, knowing look on his face. A look she hadn't seen in so long.

"Proud of you, mija," he mouthed, and though Ruby's lip began to quiver slightly, she felt bolstered by his silent words, nonetheless.

Remy held out his hand to help her up the three steps leading to the podium, and Ruby confidently placed her hand in his. They stood side by side as the room fell to an eager hush. Hundreds of eyes landed on them, glittering expectantly. Governor Cortez stood to the left of the podium with an excited but focused expression on her face. Ruby took a deep breath, sneaking one last glance at Remy out of the corner of her eye. He was still glowering, but he met her gaze. This was it.

♦ ♦ ♦

THE NIGHT PASSED IN A BLUR. AS SOON AS THEY HANDED over the microphone to the governor, Remy bolted from the podium as quickly as he could without breaking into a full-on run. Though the seating chart she had devised with the governor's staff had Remy seated next to her, he never once made an appearance at their table and was instead found casually chatting and laughing with guests at every other corner of the room. Avoiding her seemed to be no trouble at all for him.

Well, I don't have time to worry about that now, she repeatedly reminded herself every time she heard his voice booming across the room or bristled at the mention of his name. *I'll have to think about all that later.* She was determined not to let Remy or her recent epiphany about Ashton distract her from the task at hand: using her charm to network and build connections to benefit her work, a task she felt born to accomplish.

She thought of all the daunting things she'd been forced to learn out of necessity in the aftermath of the fires. She had feverishly wanted to disappear inside her grief, scared and frustrated and lonely, but she'd figured it out because she'd had no choice, no matter how ill-equipped she'd felt. She'd had to do it all, and though it had transformed her into a different person, she was proud of herself for the way she'd faced those challenges.

But tonight was a small beckoning to the girl Ashton had been talking about, the girl Ruby felt like she'd lost in the fires, the girl who'd had a mother to guide—and occasionally chastise—her: the party-loving, reckless, passionate girl who felt most herself in a beautiful dress flirting with a crowd of adoring boys. Ruby thought of tonight as her last hurrah with that young girl, one last turn on the dance floor with her before she relinquished her to the past.

The event ended at eleven, but it was past midnight when the final guests staggered out of the ballroom. The governor sat at her table still, surrounded by several manila folders as two of her staff members rattled off updates and insights from the night. Ruby's father had taken her sisters up to the house hours ago, the exhaustion of the past few weeks evident on their faces. After being nestled in a corner in a world all their own for the final hour of the event, Ashton and Millie had finally snuck out to enjoy their newly engaged bliss alone.

"I'm going to go," Remy told her flatly. His fitted black suit was somehow still crisp and neat. He had removed the black tie he'd been wearing, however, and Ruby noted its tail hanging out of his pocket. The top button of his shirt was undone, exposing a small patch of bronze skin.

"Oh?" She was clutching an armful of tablecloths to her body, and she repositioned them against her chest anxiously as she waited for more information. They still had to clean up and take down decor, and though it wasn't technically Remy's responsibility, it was unlike him to leave without helping. And what if the governor wanted to speak to them? Wouldn't he want to stay for that?

"I'm going to catch an early flight to New York. I need to speak to my lawyers."

Ruby's heart was struck cold. "About what?" she croaked.

"Buena. Us. This." His expression was unreadable.

Her mind raced to try to understand what he meant. They were not just dating; they were partners in this venture. If he was meeting with his lawyers, did that mean they were breaking up in every sense of their relationship? She physically ached to think about it.

"Remy, I wish you would just talk to me about this. Earlier—"

He put his hands in his pockets, shaking his head. "I'm not who you want, Ruby. I'm sick of pretending. It just . . . I'll talk to you when I get back." He inhaled deeply, staring at her with bottomless dark eyes, and for a moment, it looked like he was going to say something more. But instead, he just shook his head one last time and walked away.

Ruby was immobile, with either pain or shock, she wasn't sure. It felt like Governor Cortez was talking to an entirely different person when she called Ruby's name, as a dozen tablecloths spilled from her grasp in unfurling white waves.

Part Five

"Love, they said,
burns you
and builds you."

—Kamand Kojouri

37

"You haven't heard from him *at all*?" Carla gaped at her as she kneaded a ball of masa flat onto the table.

Ruby shrugged, feigning nonchalance. Carla's shocked tone had drawn the attention of both Elena and Mama Ortega. Ruby was met with a row of arched eyebrows.

"So, are you broken up, then?" Elena asked, with a pointed curiosity Ruby found rude.

However, that was a question she had been wondering herself. Remy had been gone for almost a week, and though their last exchange certainly suggested she shouldn't expect much contact, his silence still stung. They hadn't ended their relationship explicitly, but Ruby had to assume his disappearance wasn't exactly a positive development.

"I-I'm not sure," she admitted, numbly flattening her own ball of the corn dough into the open corn husk in front of her. She plucked a single olive from the bowl on the table and pressed it into the center of the meat filling. It was an Ortega family tradition to tuck one surprise olive into each tamale. Mama Ortega said it was for luck, something Ruby knew she needed a little extra of these days.

Carla stared at her sympathetically from across the table. "I'm sure he'll call soon. Sometimes people just need space."

Ruby hadn't been able to bring herself to confide in anyone the full details about what had transpired between herself and Remy. The unpleasantness of it all was so overwhelming, she'd hardly even been able to celebrate Governor Cortez's offer of an internship in her office. She was too distracted by her heartache.

Though her sisters and grandmother were certainly well intentioned, Ruby especially yearned for her mother's sage advice. She had never fully appreciated her mother's all-knowing wisdom growing up, and it was one of many things Ruby bitterly regretted taking for granted all those years. For all Ruby had been able to conquer without her mother's guidance, matters of the heart still felt unmanageable.

"Ten paciencia, mija," Mama Ortega said sweetly, stacking an assembled pile of tamales inside a large silver pot. "There are a lot of things you can control, but other people's hearts aren't one of them."

"You could call him," Carla offered.

Ruby nodded. She could. And she'd thought about it many times. However, something always stopped her. Her own pride or fear or something else altogether. She just . . . didn't know what to say. She wanted to explain to Remy that she was no longer in love with Ashton, that she probably hadn't been for some time, if at all, and that she was so sorry for not seeing it sooner. But she wasn't sure he'd believe her. And, even worse, she wasn't sure he'd care.

♦ ♦ ♦

REMY HAD BEEN GONE TEN DAYS—NOT THAT RUBY WAS counting with agonizing anxiety or anything.

She had tried to busy herself with things that she could control, like Mama Ortega had advised her, though she also found herself scrolling through endless amounts of news coverage about the governor. Praise for her support of local California businesses like Ortega Properties, a sense of hopefulness about a woman of color in a leadership position, and of course, a smattering of more critical pieces that focused on her pro-immigration agenda, the conservative incumbent whose seat she was after, and even her unmarried status.

Ruby could've spent days poring over all the search results; they included countless candid photos of Remy's irksome, handsome figure in his tailored suit as well as a myriad of social media posts not just about the governor but about Buena, too. Some forums applauded them for forward-thinking, community-based service of others, while others accused them of circumventing government aid organizations or even white saviorism, a claim Ruby found particularly fascinating. She supposed she did have a good deal of privilege, some of which was tied to her fair complexion, but she was also working in partnership with many other Latinx people—Remy and their clients and people with a wide variety of experiences. There were also a few obscure blogs and posts about Remy, alluding to a sordid past and impending lawsuits. Had they gotten wind of his meetings with lawyers? How had they figured it out before she had?

She was beginning to think the more she learned, the more

questions she'd have—and she wondered if it was that way for everyone.

She also focused on checking in with their clients, spending hours of her time visiting with them over cups of cafecito in their new homes, listening to their stories. She exchanged several emails with the governor's campaign manager, accepting the internship and proposing setting up an advisory board of Buena clients to provide guidance on her work supporting marginalized communities. She hired two managers and scaled back the time she spent at the B&B. She requested her college transcript and began the applications to a couple of universities closer to home.

These were all things she needed to do and things that brought her peace and a sense of accomplishment—and also things that, for the most part, kept her from obsessively checking her phone for calls from Remy.

On the eleventh day since his departure, her phone rang at two in the morning. She hadn't been sleeping restfully ever since he left, so her eyes sprang open on the second ring.

It was him.

"Can you come pick m'up?" His voice was rough, lazy. His words melted together sloppily.

"What?" she asked eagerly, bolting upright in bed.

"'M at the airport. Can you pick me up?"

"Of course." She was out of bed before the words even left her mouth. It took a few more minutes to coax his exact location out of him—he seemed unusually confused and distracted—but then she was on her way to him.

🔥 🔥 🔥

HE WAS SLUMPED AGAINST A WALL IN BAGGAGE CLAIM WHEN she found him. She'd called twice to pick him up at the curb, but he'd been unable to understand her directions both times, so she gave up and parked instead. When she took in his disheveled appearance, she finally understood why.

He was drunk. *Really* drunk.

His checkered button-down shirt was half-untucked from his jeans, and several splotches stained its hem. He had his legs folded against himself, with his head resting on his knees. Thick black stubble coated his cheeks, and his mouth hung ajar, lips moist with spit.

"Remy? What are you doing?" was all she could manage to say. It was clear he was trying to pass out on the floor of the second terminal, but she couldn't begin to fathom why or how he'd gotten so drunk here of all places.

His dark eyes flitted to meet hers under heavy, tired lids. "You came," he groaned, a strange helplessness to the way he peered at her.

She nodded and crouched next to him. "What's going on?"

He tried to shake his head, rolling it along his kneecaps in an uncoordinated wobble. "Tried to call an Uber but couldn't find 'em. Tried four diff'rent ones. Jackasses." He sighed. "You're th' only one who could find me. You don't work for Uber, d'you?"

"No, but that's okay. I don't mind. Let's get you home." She had never seen him like this before. They'd enjoyed drinks together, but Remy was a person who was always in control of himself, polished and deliberate no matter the circumstances. Ruby reached out for his arm.

He withdrew from her touch, nearly tipping over in the process. "I didn't want to call you," he assured her with a sharp, unmistakable tone of suspicion. Even in his drunken stupor, he clung to his anger.

"I know. Come on. The sooner I get you home, the sooner I'll leave you alone." She reached out her hand once more to help him up, but again he recoiled.

He clumsily hoisted himself to his feet, pressing both arms against the wall as he inched himself upward. He swayed defiantly, jaw clenched in focus. Ruby took his suitcase but did not offer to help him again, even when he stumbled across the parking lot as they made their way to her Jeep.

He dozed half-asleep the entire drive to his apartment, wheezing and snoring loudly with his cheek smashed against the window. He awoke when she arrived at his complex, but she still had to nearly drag him up the steps to his door. He hunched over the stair rail as she unlocked his front door and staggered inside as if he had tripped over something and was being propelled forward by gravity. He kicked off his shoes and threw himself at his fridge, tugging it open vigorously.

He withdrew two beers and slammed them on the counter. "Want a drink?"

Ruby hovered in the doorway, confusion, fear, and concern bubbling inside her like a frothy poison.

For the briefest of moments, the hard cruelty in his eyes gave way to a flash of vulnerability. Desperation. He popped the caps off the beers, holding one out to her. "C'mon. Don't make me drink alone."

Ruby let the front door swing closed behind her. "I think you've had enough to drink, Remy," she murmured, but she accepted the cool bottle, nevertheless.

He smirked, took a loud swig of his own beer, and tossed himself onto his couch with his feet hanging over the arm, the rest of his body concealed from view from where Ruby stood in the kitchen.

Tentatively, she crossed the room and perched on the armchair across from him. He was watching her under lowered lids, reminding Ruby of a stealthy predator waiting patiently to make his move. Her skin prickled with anxiety, but she couldn't bring herself to leave.

"So, are you going to tell me what you and your lawyers discussed?" After over a week of silence from him, she was worried if she didn't ask now, she might not have another opportunity to get some answers from him.

He took another long drink, a few drops spilling onto the couch. "You're not the only one with a secret, Ruby Ortega. There's something I never told you." His words were steady and measured as if he were exerting a lot of concentration on enunciating clearly. "The intellectual property for the app. Well, apps. Capitán and Buena, both, I guess. It's not technically . . . mine." His brown face took on a pallid hue, and Ruby wondered if he was going to be sick. He winced, took a deep breath, and continued. "There's a guy I knew in college who's claiming I stole the idea from him."

Ruby's entire body stiffened. "Did you?"

His gaze hardened. "Does seem like something I'd do, doesn't it?" he growled flatly, deliberately avoiding the question. "Anyway, this guy, Chad Waters, he's gone to the media. He's filing a lawsuit. He's going after everything."

She inhaled, but the breath entering her lungs was uneven and riotous. She felt like she couldn't breathe. The phone call he'd taken the night of the fundraiser. That had to be it. "And you just found out about this? Why now?"

Remy chewed on his lip, focusing his attention on picking the corner of the beer-bottle label with his fingernail. "He contacted me a long time ago. Before I met you." She sensed he was being purposefully indirect in the details, and she wasn't sure if that was alcohol or shame, but she let him keep talking for now. She'd press for the specifics, either from him or his lawyers, later. "We were going to settle it out of court, pay him what he thought he deserved. Keep it private, off the record. It was going well."

His dark eyes flicked up, so bloodshot and glassy it startled her for a moment.

"But when he heard about what we were doing with Buena, saw that we were attached to Cortez, he asked for more money. A *lot* more money." He cleared his throat, his gaze returning to the beer bottle in his hands. "He figured if we had the funds to run a charity, we could pay a lot more than we were letting on. But, well, you know. The opposite was true. I've been covering a lot of Buena's expenses with my own money. He made some vague threats about reporting our clients to ICE if we didn't play ball, and I don't know if he could—if he *would*—do that, but I'm not really willing to gamble with people's lives like that. Either way, he's suing for the ownership of both apps."

"Oh, *Remy*." Her voice was tight with heartbreak, with disappointment, with powerlessness.

"I made sure you're kept out of it. My name's on everything. You can tell that to the governor, too—that it was all me, not you. You and your business and everything are safe. But everything I have—everything we built with Buena—will go to Chad. We can make recommendations about how he should use the funds, but at the end of the day, Buena and the technology will be his. And, based on our conversations, I think it's safe to say he's not interested in the charity aspect. He'll probably shut Buena down."

"Shut Buena down?" Hearing the words escape her own lips felt surreal.

Remy nodded, and for a moment they sat in silence, grieving together. The sadness was so profound, Ruby wondered if they were mourning the death of Buena or their relationship, too.

"Maybe we would've been better off if I'd been more like your precious Ashton after all," he muttered so softly, Ruby wasn't entirely sure she'd heard him correctly. He shifted in his seat, as if trying to hide from Ruby's gaze. "This whole time, you wished I was him, anyway." She was so caught off guard by the abrupt subject change—and the vulnerability in his words.

Her breath caught in her throat as she searched for the right words. "I'd loved Ashton for a long time, or at least I thought I did, and I held on to it longer than I should have. But it's done now."

He rolled his eyes, his guard back up with that simple gesture. "Obviously it's done. He's marrying Millie." He gritted his teeth. "But that's not what I said. Our whole relationship, Ruby, you've wanted him over me. Would've rather been in his arms than mine." The words seemed to turn sour in his mouth as he spoke them, and the corners of his lips turned downward in a grimace.

She didn't understand what he was doing—sifting through more painful details when he was already clearly in so much agony—but she forced herself to nod anyway, only able to manage two stiff jerks of her chin. "I guess that's true. But Remy—"

He nodded, a strange, sad smile on his face that seemed to be the only thing keeping him from unraveling completely. "I know I've fucked up, but I thought . . . I thought together we could be better people, you know? We could grow together. Isn't that what love's supposed to be like?" He shook his head, as if hearing for the first time how these words sounded and deciding they were nonsensical. He got to his feet, tottering slightly but clearly determined to be on the move. "But instead you kept yourself locked away from me in the same way Ashton kept you out. You just gave your heart to him without ever seeing that he'd never be able to understand you or be interested in even trying to understand you. *I* wanted you. I wanted everything about you, just as you were. I thought we could've been happy if you'd ever stopped thinking about him long enough to give us a chance. You threw away something that could've made you happy, hoping for something that would *never* make you happy. Just threw it away!" He was pacing now, and he paused, his back to her.

He turned his head ever so slightly, his profile heartbreaking to her in its sad handsomeness. He watched her out of the corner of his eye. "I wanted to be a team with you. I wanted to make the world a better place with you. And now, I guess, we've got nothing. I ruined Buena and you ruined us." The words caught in his throat, and he shook his head, slower this time. "Even at the bitter end, we're quite the pair, huh?"

Her chest throbbed as the anguish that had been building up inside her gave way to hot tears. "*Remy*, I—"

He held up his hand to cut her off, his movement so rapid and forceful that it made her flinch. She wanted to explain, to tell him that she knew he was right and she'd realized it days ago, but she also knew it didn't matter. Remy had had enough. That much was obvious.

Wordlessly, she stood, wiped her face, and collected her car keys from the counter. She cast one last glance toward Remy, who still stood facing his back door. She noticed an almost imperceptible tremble in his shoulders and wondered if he, too, was crying, but she didn't dare go to him now.

She swung open his front door, let it slam behind her, and ran down the stairs.

She'd lingered at her Jeep for a few minutes, trying to catch her breath and distantly hoping he'd come after her.

He didn't.

THE SUN WAS CREEPING OVER THE HILLTOPS AS SHE DROVE, the sky a muted purplish blue with singed hints of orange peeking up along the horizon. It took her about half the drive to convince herself that if he'd kept that secret from her about the apps, he never could have loved her at all. Her notions of love, though perhaps misguided, demanded more loyalty than that. If he had loved her, he would've been honest. And if she had truly loved him, she would've been more open about her conflicted feelings about Ashton rather than stowing them away inside herself. Her love for Ashton may have been misplaced, but it seemed her feelings for

Remy had been based on lies. People who loved each other didn't keep secrets like that. She felt sure of it.

She was so certain, so fixated on this idea, that she didn't notice her car drifting across the winding yellow lines that divided the road in the hills that led to Buena Valley. So focused on Remy and every moment that led up to tonight, she didn't see the truck rounding the corner, headed directly toward her.

Just like with Ashton, she didn't see what was happening until it was too late to do anything about it.

38

Ever since the wildfires, time had ceased to have much meaning for Ruby. The minutes either crept by at a painfully glacial pace, or the days flew out of her grasp without any warning. There was no in-between, no consistency. The passing of time was not something she could rely on. So it wasn't too difficult for her in the hospital when time stretched and oozed in every imaginable direction, rendering night and day, yesterday and now, hours and seconds indistinguishable.

Though the time wasn't difficult, there was no shortage of things that *were* difficult. There was the relentless throbbing in her ribs, the hazy dredging of her brain, the dryness of her mouth, the blurry parade of faces at her bedside, the constant beeping and chirping and poking of the machines and nurses. And the confusion.

What had happened? Why was she in the hospital? Was she okay?

And perhaps, most persistently of all, was Remy here?

THE DIM, FUZZY EDGE FINALLY WORE OFF TO REVEAL HER FATHER at her bedside. He sat hunched in an armchair with a worn paperback clutched in his hands, though his gaze had wandered from the pages. He sprang to his feet when he spotted her open eyes.

"Ruby, you're awake!" he exclaimed breathlessly, hurling his body across the room and crouching by her bedside.

As she took in her surroundings, her memory immediately lurched to the last time she had been in a hospital, looking for her family and discovering that her mother had died. How awful this must've been for her father to be here with her, reliving the pain and fear of that terrible day.

"What happened?" Ruby croaked.

He took her hand, careful not to touch the IV protruding from it, and stroked her fingers. "You were in a car accident, mija."

Ruby frowned. She remembered being at Remy's apartment; perhaps she remembered that *too* well. His words still stung her in a sharp, piercing way that was unaffected by the painkillers that had the rest of her body feeling numb. She remembered leaving his house, though less clearly. The need to flee overshadowed the details in her mind about how . . . She must've driven, but she couldn't recall even getting in her car, let alone the drive or the crash itself.

"A car accident," she repeated.

Her father nodded. "You were probably way too tired to be driving."

"It was . . . my fault?"

He hesitated a moment, but he nodded again.

With everything that had happened this year, how could she have been so careless?

Dread unfolded in her stomach. "The other person? The other driver? I hit someone else, didn't I? How are they?"

"You hit a semitruck. He's fine. You and your Jeep took all the damage." Her father tsked his tongue in mock scolding, though his eyes revealed his true concern. "When you do something, Ruby, you really do it big. I am just so thankful you're okay. It could've been so much worse. The paramedics who brought you in said you're lucky to be alive." His voice cracked tearfully as he spoke, no doubt reliving the pain and guilt of his own car accident. "They couldn't believe you made it out with just a banged head and some cuts and scrapes. They kept you overnight to monitor you for a concussion, but the doctor just came to say you're ready to go home later today." He sighed, a look of apprehension crossing his face. "Your sisters and I . . . we tried to reach Remy, so he'd know what happened. I left a voicemail, mija, but we haven't heard from him."

Ruby clenched her eyes shut, a sharp pain coursing through her body as he spoke.

"It's still early, though," he added, gesturing to the clock that showed it was nearly ten in the morning. Hardly early, but Ruby didn't have the energy to point that out. "Maybe he hasn't checked his phone."

Ruby nodded, unconvinced. At least she hadn't hurt anyone else, though. She was tired of hurting others with her thoughtlessness. At least this time she'd managed only to hurt herself.

39

Ruby had hoped to return to work immediately. She was desperate for *something* to distract herself from her heartbreak, but her father wouldn't hear of it.

"You've done a lot, but you don't need to keep running yourself into the ground anymore, Ruby. We are in a good place now, thanks to you," he told her as she tried to go into the office for just a few hours. "Enjoy it. Take care of yourself. ¡Relájate!"

His words were disturbingly similar to Remy's all those weeks ago, and just the thought of his name, let alone the reiteration of such frustrating advice, made her stomach tighten.

"But I don't *want* to relax—"

"Fine." He held up his hand, silencing her. "If you insist on being busy, do something for the next chapter of your life. Finish working on your college applications. On the couch. In your pajamas." He patted her shoulder and bustled out the front door before she could say anything else.

She knew he had a point, though she wouldn't have admitted it even if he had stuck around long enough for her to respond. Like it or not, the B&B didn't need her anymore. Though it had certainly been the most challenging year of her life, it filled her with an inexplicable dread to feel it come to a close. How many times had she wished those brutal days away? Those days of unfathomable grief and loss, of abandoning her life as a normal college student and throwing herself into a new world, of rebuilding their business, of pushing aside her feelings about Ashton and Millie, of watching her family struggle, of seeing her community in ways she'd never seen it before. It had been indescribably hard, and often the only thing that could get her to the next day was fantasizing about what it would be like when it was all over.

Maybe that's why I'm so sad, she thought, idly flipping her laptop open. This new reality, this next chapter was nothing like she'd envisioned it would be throughout all those months of hardship. She'd dreamed of so much more for Buena, and it was incredibly disappointing to feel like it had fizzled into nothingness. If she hadn't been so distracted by her infatuation with Ashton, would Remy have trusted her with his secret and let her problem-solve with him? Would it have mattered? Could she have saved it from ruin? Hell, could she have saved her relationship with Remy if she had taken a moment to look beyond her childhood crush?

She knew her determination had saved their business and done a lot of good things for her family and community, but she couldn't ignore how much it had sabotaged as well. How much better would life be if she hadn't been so fixated on Ashton? If she had seen Remy as he truly was, the good and the bad? So many people, including she, faced challenges because of factors that were out of their control. It was so distressing to know that she had made things so much harder for herself.

The regret gnawed at her insides.

I guess life doesn't come with an instruction manual, she thought glumly, staring at her computer's home screen. *I should just be thankful things aren't worse than they are.* Slowly, she opened an internet browser and chicken-pecked the URL for the application she'd started before the accident. *I'll think of all that later, I suppose. Daddy's right. It's time to focus on what's next.*

DUSK HAD CREPT UP ALONG THE HORIZON BY THE TIME RUBY had clicked submit on the last of her transfer applications. Though she had been reluctant to start the task, she found herself filled with purpose and even a little excitement as she entered the required information and began to imagine herself at each of the campuses. She'd pushed it from her mind out of necessity over the past few months, but as she typed, she reveled in how much she'd missed school. She'd always liked fixing her mind on problems and achieving solutions, and while she'd had no shortage of problem-solving lately, she was looking forward to considering new problems, perhaps more theoretical ones, without the high stakes that had come with saving her family's livelihood.

She scrolled through the submission confirmation emails neatly stacked upon each other in her inbox. Just over a year ago, she'd been doing the same thing—applying to colleges—but she couldn't believe how much was different this time around. Last year, she'd been itching with eagerness to leave her home, leave California, and strike out on her own. But now her relationship to this place was so different, so much more complex and meaningful; she was more inextricably bound to her home than she could explain.

As she finally closed her laptop and set it aside, she heard a soft knock at the front door and the sound of her father crossing the hallway to answer it.

Ruby could hear two sets of footsteps making their way down the hallway to the family room, where she was sprawled out on the couch.

Immediately, her heart began thumping in anticipation of seeing Remy round the corner. Had she summoned him here in her contemplation? She hoped so deeply that it was him, she didn't even bother to worry about the fact that she was braless in a pair of sweatpants and hadn't brushed her hair since she left the hospital. She didn't even notice that she was holding her breath.

"Ruby?" her father called softly. "Someone's here to see you, honey." He entered the living room with a tentative smile.

A step behind him was Millie.

"H-hi," Ruby stammered uncertainly.

"How are you feeling?" Instantly, her soothing tone put to rest any lingering worries Ruby had that Millie was there to continue their confrontation. They'd arrived at the understanding they needed to in order to sustain this friendship, unraveling their distinct roles in Ashton's life as well as each other's—and, of course, there was nothing like a near-death experience to reveal what was truly important.

"Oh, you know. I've been better." She laughed uneasily. "I mean, not recently, of course."

Millie nodded sympathetically, sitting down on the couch next to Ruby. "It certainly has been a hard year. Especially for you." Her round eyes swam with emotions Ruby couldn't quite make sense of. Affection and pity, perhaps, but also nervousness. "Did your sisters tell you Ashton and I came by to see you in the hospital? You were asleep."

"Carla told me. Thank you." Ruby gestured to a stack of get-well cards on the coffee table, signed by several Buena clients. She had no idea when Millie would've had the time to gather them. On the top of the pile was one from Millie and Ashton, wishing her a speedy recovery in Millie's neat cursive.

"Good," she said, tucking her hair behind her ears in what Ruby thought was an oddly anxious way. "We, um . . we also ran into Remy as we were leaving the hospital, Ruby." Her words came out clunky and unsure, like she couldn't decide if it was bad news or good news.

How come no one had told her this earlier?

"Well, I guess . . . I guess I should clarify. I think the details are important here." She was speaking slowly, and normally this would've irritated Ruby, but she was too caught up in unsettled anticipation to be bothered. "He and Ashton crossed paths in the parking lot. I was still inside. I had to use the restroom, and Ashton went to get the car—which is when he and Remy saw one another."

Though it seemed like such a minor detail, Ruby instantly knew what Remy would've seen the moment he laid eyes on Ashton. Another instance where Ashton rose in Ruby's estimation, while Remy lagged behind.

"He was pretty upset, even by the time I got there," Millie continued.

Ruby gulped loudly, her throat suddenly dry. "We got in a big fight that night," she confessed.

Millie nodded. "He said something like that when I finally caught up to him."

"We broke up," she said, feeling the strangeness of the words on her tongue. She'd been thinking them for so long, but she hadn't actually said them out loud. "We may have already been broken up, actually. I'm not sure. But we *really* ended things that night."

"He said that, too."

Ruby felt a painful tightening in her chest. "What else did he say?"

Millie reached across and placed her hand on Ruby's, a gesture that Ruby was shocked to find comforting. "When I came outside, he was halfway to his truck, trying to leave. I tried to persuade him to go inside and see you—I really did. But . . . I don't know, Ruby. He was in a lot of pain, too, I think. He said he'd told himself he couldn't lose something he'd never had."

Ruby's eyes stung as tears threatened to spill out.

"I told him you were going to be fine, and that's when he told me everything. He was crying and—"

"Remy was crying?" It was hard for her to imagine, not because Remy was necessarily a stoic person, but because she couldn't believe he cared that much. He had been emotional that night, sure, but he'd also been out-of-his-mind drunk. It was difficult for her to reconcile his anger right before the crash with what Millie was describing.

Millie nodded, a sad smile playing on her lips. "Oh, of course,

Ruby. It took him a long time to calm down enough to talk." Millie searched Ruby's face for a moment before continuing. "He told me what's going on with the apps. The intellectual property issues."

"Yeah, that came up the other night, too."

"I know he's made his share of mistakes, but I really think he's scared, Ruby, and he doesn't know how to let himself be scared. He thinks . . . he thinks this is all his fault." She gestured toward the bandage on Ruby's forehead. "He said he did this to you. That he'd been so mad at you and wanted you to hurt as much as he did—and because of that, this awful thing had happened to you."

Tears trickled out of Ruby's eyes without reserve, and she shook her head, as if denying it would make it untrue.

"He loves you, Ruby."

The word *love* electrified everything in Ruby, and she nodded shakily. Her mind was in a thousand places, thinking about every moment she'd shared with Remy throughout the past year—all the meals they'd shared, all the laughs, all the nights in bed when they were so close physically but still separated emotionally because of Ruby's damn stubbornness. Each flash of his dark, handsome face in her mind made her ache.

She knew she'd hurt him, but a small portion of her had believed it was mostly his pride. He was a guy who'd gotten what he'd demanded from the world one way or another, and it had upset him that Ruby was the exception. She hadn't really believed he'd cared for her so deeply. Or maybe she had, but she'd been unwilling to acknowledge it because of her feelings for Ashton. Had he really cared for her this much all along? And had she really been so selfish and inconsiderate toward his heart? How could she have done this?

"Thank you for telling me, Millie. Thank you for everything. I know I've been awful to you, but I really don't think I would've made it through this year without you. I'm sorry for everything. Ashton's so lucky to have you. We both are."

Millie waved it all away with a bashfulness that was so distinctly her, and they sat in amiable silence for a moment before Ruby suddenly sprang to her feet. Millie shot her a perplexed look as Ruby toed her sandals out from underneath the table with clumsy, urgent movements.

"What are you doing?" she asked.

Ruby froze, cell phone in hand, head racing from the combination of painkillers and a surplus of information. "I—I don't know. I just feel like I should do . . . something. I feel like I need to see him." She stared at the front door anxiously. There was no way she could drive. She'd already made too many mistakes being thoughtless.

Before she even had a moment to contemplate asking Millie for yet another favor, Carla and Elena spilled out from behind the kitchen counter, where they'd clearly been crouching to eavesdrop.

"I can take you!" Elena exclaimed. Ruby didn't have a chance to ponder this uncharacteristically generous offer before Elena added, "Daddy took me to get my learners' permit a few days ago. I haven't hardly gotten to drive *at all* because you were in the hospital."

That made more sense. Ruby nodded eagerly.

Carla and Elena exchanged hesitant glances.

"What is it?" Ruby snapped.

"Ruby, I know you're in a hurry—" Carla ventured in a neutral tone.

"—but we can't let you go over there looking like . . . *that*," Elena finished with an exasperated wave of her hand toward Ruby.

She didn't dare waste a moment feeling irritated by her sister's bluntness. She nodded once more.

Again, her sisters exchanged glances, but this one Ruby was able to wordlessly interpret. The three of them bolted in opposite directions: Ruby into the bathroom to comb her hair and brush her teeth, Carla upstairs to retrieve a sundress, and Elena to her own room to grab some perfume to spritz Ruby with.

Ruby tugged the dress—green, coincidentally—over her head, barely taking a moment to make sure the light, airy fabric covered all the necessary parts, and smoothed her hair. Carla gave her an encouraging smile, while Elena expressed her approval by barking, "All right, let's go already! We haven't got all day!"

For the third time, Ruby could do nothing more than succumb to her sisters' orders.

As she dashed to the door, she paused and glanced over her shoulder to where Millie still stood in the doorway. A thousand thoughts of nervousness and gratitude bubbled up inside her, but she couldn't put them into words. Millie had been there for her through so many hardships this year—sacrificing so much to support her without Ruby even asking. She hadn't fully appreciated it until now, until she was ready to face this unthinkable thing without her.

Millie smiled, as if reading her mind. "You can do this, Ruby. Go get him."

40

It was dark by the time they arrived at Remy's apartment complex, and Ruby was struck by how eerily similar it looked to the last time she had been here. It almost felt as if she had turned back time to before their fight, before her accident.

If only.

"We'll wait here?" Carla offered curiously, almost as if she hoped Ruby would invite them in with her.

Ruby appreciated their rally in sisterhood, but she knew this was something she had to do on her own. She stared at her sisters' faces uneasily. "Thank you for this," she said softly. "For all of this. I know I've been really hard on you both this past year, and I'm sorry. I've needed and appreciated your help, even if I haven't always been the best at showing it." She forced a feeble smile, staring at Elena's stony face in the driver's seat and Carla's sweet expression poking in between them from the back seat.

Carla nodded, placing her small hand on Ruby's shoulder. "We know that. We're family." From anyone else, it would've sounded sickeningly cheesy, but from her kind, earnest little sister, it made Ruby's thumping, anxious heart warm for just an instant.

Elena offered a good-natured roll of her eyes. Ruby knew that she had been particularly tough on her, though at times she had certainly deserved even harsher treatment.

Elena inhaled deeply. "It obviously hasn't been easy," she admitted with a smirk. "To be honest, you've *never* been easy to live with. But this past year, you've been kind of like the fires, I guess."

Ruby frowned. *Destructive? Devastating?*

Elena shrugged, glancing at Ruby uncomfortably in the way teenagers did when being vulnerable. "What I mean is, things have been hard, and a lot of times it seemed like you made things harder than they needed to be, but in the end, we're better for it. You brought out a lot of good stuff. In all of us." She flushed. "Now stop stalling and get the hell out of this car. We didn't come all this way for nothing!" She leaned across Ruby's body and flung the passenger door open.

Ruby nodded swiftly, bolstered by Elena's brusque and unexpected pep talk, and exited the car before her resolve could fizzle away.

The window of Remy's apartment glowed, and behind the curtains, Ruby could see a shadowy figure moving back and forth across the room. She hadn't thought about what she would have done if he hadn't been home, but now that she saw he was there, she was even more convinced this was meant to be. Their path to each other had been long and crooked and painful, but it was what they had needed. It was right. This was right. This was how it was supposed to be.

Still, she trembled with nerves as she made her way upstairs.

She extended her arm to knock on his door; it wasn't until her knuckles made contact with the wood that she realized it was slightly ajar. It swung open as soon as she touched it to reveal Remy standing in his hallway with a suitcase in his hands.

Warmth rushed over her body at the sight of his face, his sleek dark hair and thick brows, the stern line of his jaw and his full lips. She was so overcome with relief to see him that she ignored his stiff, closed-off posture.

"Remy," she breathed, entering his apartment without waiting for an invitation.

He clutched the suitcase closer, like a barrier between them, his broad shoulders squared defensively. Though he did not seem at ease, there was no sense of surprise in his eyes. In fact, they looked weary as he took in the sight of her, heaving breathlessly in her thin sundress, her wild hair spilling over her shoulders, and the thick, gauzy bandages that covered the cuts on her arms and forehead.

Instead of rushing to her the way she'd hoped he would or asking her what she was doing here or even *how* she was doing, he sighed, set his bag down, and said, "Sit."

She took a step toward him, but he automatically moved out of her reach and sank into his own kitchen chair. He gestured with one of his large hands toward the chair across from him, and numbly, Ruby sat.

"Why didn't you come see me in the hospital?" The words were not the profession of love longing to burst from her heart, but she had to start somewhere.

His fingertips scratched at the unkempt layer of stubble that still dusted his cheeks and neck, his expression inscrutable. "It seemed to me you had who you wanted there."

"I hope you know that isn't true." She held out her hand to touch his forearm, but he leaned back, just out of her reach once more.

Remy snorted, his anguished gaze drifting around the room, landing everywhere but on her.

Ruby continued despite his dismissiveness. "Millie told me what you said, and I came to tell you—"

He shook his head, finally looking at her, his black eyes fierce and unyielding. "I know what you've come to say, and I . . . don't want to hear it." The last few words came out raw and raspy, like they hurt him to utter.

Her jaw fell open. "But—"

"You're disappointed and sad and hurt, and all of these terrible things make me seem pretty good in comparison. But that doesn't *mean* anything, Ruby." The muscles in his jaw clenched tight.

"Remy, I don't care about the lawsuit," she sputtered, frantically trying to both understand what he was saying and refute it at the same time.

His eyes glowed angrily. "Well, then you're an even bigger fool than I would've thought."

Ruby shook her head, undeterred by his hurtfulness. "No, what I mean is, I trust you, Remy. I want to face this—to deal with it—together! Like you said."

Remy sighed, visibly frustrated. "I'm the kind of guy who does bad things for good reasons. You're used to ones who do good things for bad reasons. I'm not sure what's worse. Or if it matters." He was fidgeting, uncomfortable in this suffocating moment, running his fingers through his hair. "They're saying I stole the idea, and I guess that's not entirely wrong, but it was *my* idea." His wandering gaze flitted to meet hers quickly, eyes stormy with something Ruby didn't fully recognize—something that made her desperately want to take his hands in hers. "I didn't have much money in college, so I tended to get creative with how I made ends meet. I worked a couple jobs, but I did other people's homework, too." He shook his head, gnawing on his lower lip in the kind of stark distress she'd never seen from him. "It sounds so ridiculous now, like something out of a TV show, but it is what it is. Anyway, Chad was a 'repeat customer.' He asked me to do this project for him where they had to design a lifestyle app. He paid me for the ideas behind what would eventually become Capitán—he called it Chadventure, of course." He gritted his teeth, disgust all over his face. "He wasn't even going to *use* it. It was a homework assignment. He was interning for his dad's magazine. He was never going to start a business." The anger behind his words seemed so weary and practiced, she knew it wasn't the first time he'd had this thought. "See? You had it right all along. I'm a cheat, a liar. An asshole."

"No, that's not it at all!" she insisted gently. "I know you're not perfect, but neither am I. Who is? That's not what matters. What matters is . . . I love you. I have *loved* you. I'm not interested in perfection. I want what's real. I want to keep growing into a better person, with you. Just like you said." She leaned forward, resting her palms flat on the table.

He shook his head again but didn't respond.

"My feelings for Ashton were something I should've let go a long time ago. A crush, but I made it into something more," she thought aloud. "The more I saw how different my home was and how much I had to change, the more I clung to this idea that I loved him because . . . maybe because it was familiar. I was so fixated on it that I didn't stop to notice that it wasn't real or right."

He was silent for a while, his furrowed brow and deep breathing unreadable. At last, he muttered, "It doesn't matter."

"It doesn't matter?" she repeated incredulously. "How could it not matter? Of course it matters! *Everything matters!*"

He shrugged. "Maybe, but everything has its end, Ruby. The fires ended. Buena ended. We ended. I loved you, sure. That might be true. But that's over, too. Everything runs its course sooner or later."

"No!" she insisted. "Things change, but they don't have to end, Remy. We move forward; we decide what to do next. It doesn't have to *end*—not if we work at it."

Remy's eyes floated slowly back to her, and in this movement, Ruby could see tears collecting on his thick eyelashes. "For the last year, I've tried to push through all of this bullshit, telling myself that eventually it would all be okay. Everything with the app and everything with us. I really thought together we could face any hardship. We've had some tough times, but you're so strong and fearless, and I just wanted to be with you. I thought life would be so much better if we were just together through it all. That we could make life better, the world better. I mean, we had Buena and that was *so good*. We were so good at it." A tired calmness washed over his face as he brushed the tears from his eyes. "But look at everything that's gone wrong, Ruby. How can we ignore it? It's just too much. It shouldn't be this hard." Remy shrugged, his whole body seeming to crumple just a little bit. "We've been in lockstep ever since the beginning. One of us takes a step forward, the other takes a step backward. No matter what, we can't seem to get to each other. I can't do it anymore." He shook his head, staring at his hands in his lap. "Oh well. It doesn't matter now."

"I love you." She said it forcefully, like a command.

"Maybe you do. But some things can't be put back together. Not everything can be rebuilt."

"So that's it?"

He took a deep breath. "I'm leaving, Ruby." He jerked his head toward where he'd set the suitcase he'd been carrying down against the wall. It wasn't until then that Ruby noticed there were several other bags piled next to it.

"Leaving?" she repeated. *Again?* "Where? When?"

"Mexico. First thing tomorrow morning."

"Mexico."

"I just . . . I don't know what to think anymore. I've got nothing left here. I'm going to visit where my mom and I used to live, and start there. Maybe we were going about it all wrong. Maybe the way to make a big difference is . . . I don't know. Like I said, everything ends. I need something new. I can't be here anymore."

She of all people could understand the importance of going home, though it pained her to admit it. "How long will you be gone?" she asked weakly.

Again, he shrugged.

"I could come with you!" she blurted out suddenly. "Although, I just finished applying to go back to school and there's the internship with Claudia Cortez, so I'd need to be back by the fall—"

Finally, Remy reached forward and placed his warm hand on

hers. She met his gaze eagerly, leaning in toward him. She seized her opportunity—this small movement toward her, this pause—and kissed him. She propelled herself forward so forcefully, the table wobbled under her weight. She felt his body relax as soon as her lips met his, felt him soften and open up to her, felt the warm tenderness of his mouth responding to her need.

But then he caught himself. He pulled away rapidly, like he'd been burned. His lips were pressed firmly shut into a thin line as he scooted his chair back from the table. "Ruby, I don't care what you do, but you can't come with me."

"But I love you," she pleaded once more, inching toward him, not caring how desperate she seemed.

He opened his mouth ever so slightly, drawing in a quiet breath. "No me importa," he said finally in a tone much firmer than Ruby had anticipated. *I don't care.* He gestured toward the door, his arm sweeping through the air dejectedly. "It's too late, Ruby. I just—I don't give a damn."

THE CAR RIDE BACK WAS A SILENT ONE. IN THE SAME wordless way Ruby and her sisters had been communicating all evening, Carla and Elena seemed to understand without Ruby saying anything that it hadn't gone as they'd all hoped, though she supposed it probably hadn't been hard to figure that out.

She peered into the dark roadside beyond her window, her chest heavy and tight with longing.

How many times in the past year had she felt like all was lost? And how many times had she triumphed?

Remy was wrong. Not everything had to end. At least, not for good. Things could end to be reborn into something better.

Besides, just because something was unfinished didn't mean it was over. Life's most important tasks were complex and flawed and required ongoing love and effort. She thought of the affection she'd had for Ashton or even Buena Valley itself, and how she'd adored their simplicity and perfection. She knew now how ignorant she'd been. They were only simple because she'd failed to see them clearly. How could you truly love someone or something without seeing their flaws, too? And what was true love if it wasn't working together—overcoming obstacles and looking hardship in the face—to be the best possible version you could be? Love wasn't forcing things to be the way you wanted or idealizing them. Love was the fine balance between letting go and staying true to what was important. Love was work, but it was worth it.

They pulled into the driveway of their house, and though Carla and Elena hesitated, unsure if Ruby would need more time before going inside, Ruby burst from the car and immediately ran to the backyard, leaping over the waist-high side gate. She broke out into a full sprint and only stopped when she'd reached the bottom of the sloping hill that separated their patio area from where the horse corrals and vegetable garden had once stood. Now, on this patch of land, stood one rebuilt corral and a small new flower bed with bright green sprouts of leaves bursting from the dark soil. A few thin saplings bordered the area, spindly branches stretching wide and wavering in the evening breeze.

She inhaled deeply, the smell of rich, fresh soil thick in the air. Her home was certainly not what it had once been, but it was beautiful all the same. This was the place her story, her family's story, had begun years ago, and it was the place they'd begin again, now and for years to come. Her mother's physical absence was still excruciating and inescapable, but her spirit lived on—in the home she'd made for them, in the hopes and dreams she'd had for their land, in each flower bud that emerged against all odds from the charred dirt. Though Ruby still felt sad for what they'd lost, she loved her home so much more for all the care and hard work they had poured into it this past year.

The wind stirred around her, the soft fabric of her dress fluttering against her legs and her hair whipping across her face. The thin strap of her dress fell down over her shoulder, a shoulder that was now taut and lean after months of manual labor. She heard footsteps behind her and wearily gazed into the fresh darkness of the night to see Millie's figure approaching. Her glistening eyes and sagging shoulders were visible even at a distance, and Ruby knew instantly she understood what had happened. After a year of being the closest, truest friend Ruby had ever had, of course she understood.

"Oh, Ruby," she said softly, her voice barely audible above the coursing wind.

Ruby nodded, noticing the shapes of her family gathered behind Millie on the back porch near her father's grill. She now detected the familiar scent of carne asada, one of her favorites, hanging in the air. She turned her gaze outward, toward the rolling hills of their land, toward the twinkling city lights of Buena Valley beyond.

She'd let Remy go to Mexico. And she would remain here. If he needed a fresh start, then he could get it, but she knew her place was here. She'd go to school; she'd work; she'd be home. There was so much to do with the business and the community—more than even Buena had offered—and underneath her heartbreak, she was still brimming with possibility. He'd go back to where his story had started, and he'd do what he needed, whatever filled him with purpose.

She understood that some things required more than sheer will-power. Some things—the important things, the hard things, the things that defined you as a person—required patience and trust and listening, too.

They'd let each other go. For now, at least.

But not because what they'd had was over or ruined. It, like so many other things, was unfinished. Unfinished, yes, but Ruby had to believe it was still filled with so much promise.

Their love had been tested—there was no doubt about that—but with time and hard work, it could rise again into something bigger and better. She was certain of it.

I still have time. I'll figure it all out later.

She nodded to herself. She was young, and still had so much life and love left in her. She was aching but hopeful—and hungry.

Epilogue

Ruby adjusted her seat belt for the dozenth time. She just couldn't get it comfortable. *She* couldn't get comfortable.

Her entire body pulsated with an anxious jitteriness that hadn't subsided at all throughout the five-hour flight. She'd traveled enough with her family to know she wasn't a nervous flyer, even if it would be easier to tell herself that. This—this was something else.

It was her first international trip on her own, yes. It was also an entire semester in another country, fulfilling a dream that had lived somewhere inside her ever since Ashton had set off for Spain.

It was a brand-new chapter, one of bigger goals and foreign lands and . . .

She could dance around it all she wanted—in fact, she'd spent the better part of this past year doing just that—but as she watched the plane's wing slice through fluffy white clouds, she knew the time for denial was behind her.

She unfolded the paper in her lap once more. It was soft and heavily creased, as she'd been carrying it around and rereading it almost nonstop since it had mysteriously arrived in the mail a few months ago, postmarked with a Mexico City address.

Her eyes raked over the picture of blocky buildings and vibrant murals that took up the top half of the flyer. Underneath the logo of the Universidad Nacional Autónoma de México, bold text read PROGRAMA DE TURISMO Y GESTIÓN HOTELERA INNOVADOR. Innovative Hotel Management and Tourism Program. She knew the rest by heart, owing to a combination of Google Translate, her gradually improving Spanish, and the powers of memorization. *Emphasis on sustainability. Highlighting local cultures through resort experiences. Engaging guests in critical consumerism. Serving communities through tourism.*

It was a competitive course, her advisor had warned when Ruby laid the piece of paper on her desk at one of her frequent check-ins since she'd transferred to San Diego State University. There weren't many slots, and with the previous interruption in her studies, her advisor didn't want to get Ruby's hopes up.

But Ruby had already made up her mind. She may have changed a lot over the past couple of years, but she still wasn't the type of person to take no for an answer.

She could learn how to grow Ortega Properties. She'd delegate more responsibilities and release some of her iron control over the business, something she and her new therapist both agreed was necessary.

And . . .

Her heart fluttered in her chest as the thought began to materialize. She closed her eyes and took a deep breath before letting her eyes settle on the single line of text handwritten at the bottom of the paper in the choppy, even script she'd instantly recognized.

One more adventure?

Equally elusive and enchanting, just like him.

She rubbed her thumb along the words, the faint indents the pen had made in the paper almost worn smooth from her frequent touch. It was the only contact they'd had since that night—though Ruby had thought of him every single day with a longing and anticipation that had grown so familiar, it almost felt like an essential part of her.

The pilot's voice over the intercom interrupted her thoughts. "Flight attendants, please prepare for landing as we begin our descent into Mexico City."

In spite of everything that had happened—or, perhaps, *because* of everything that had happened—one thing was for certain: Ruby Ortega was always up for one more adventure.

Acknowledgments

No book is written alone, and I am so deeply appreciative of everyone who has touched these pages in one way or another.

First and foremost, this book wouldn't exist without my husband, Mitch. From the moment he caught me covertly typing into an unnamed Word document, he has been nothing but supportive. He held crying babies so I could jot down ideas. He arranged interviews with firefighters for my research. He commiserated with me over the many pitfalls of the publishing roller coaster. He proofread. He brainstormed. He cheered me on. He believed in me when I needed it most. I am forever grateful for his partnership, in this and all things.

My agent, Amy, was one of the first champions of this book. Her vision and advocacy for this story has helped it grow into what it is now, and I feel so lucky that I get to benefit from her insight and wisdom.

Thank you to my editor, Jenny, who made my wildest dream

come true. We crossed paths years ago at a writers' conference where she gave me some valued feedback and encouragement for the rough pages that would eventually be this book. I've always felt we were meant to work together on this; her expertise and love for these characters has truly made this story shine. The whole team at Penguin Random House has been wonderful; Jeff Ostberg gave me the book cover I'd imagined since the very first drafts of this story.

I am appreciative of my entire family for their support—for celebrating with me, for telling their friends about this book, and for babysitting my children so I could work. I am especially thankful for my parents, who have always made me feel like I could achieve anything. Everything I've accomplished in life is because they told me I could.

And thank you to my girls: my two daughters, Helen and Marian. I started drafting this book shortly after I became a mother, and I know that's not a coincidence. You both are the reason for everything I do.

A big thank-you also goes to the many early readers who helped shape each draft, especially Kirsten, Katie, Taylor, and my mom, Erin. Thank you to the crew at Scottsdale Fire Department's Station 613 for all your help understanding the details of wild land firefighting. Thank you to Jonah and Nick for the emails about immigration law (you wouldn't believe how many legal questions come up when you're writing a young adult book!). And of course, thank you to any and all readers. Your support means the world to me!

Finally, the idea for this book started when my grandmother

gave me my first copy of *Gone with the Wind* about ten years ago. Though she passed away shortly before this book was published, I hope she knows how much she changed my life—both by introducing me to Scarlett and Rhett and in countless other ways.